Shiny Adidas Tracksuits and the Death of Camp

and other essays from *Might* magazine

Shiny Adidas Tracksuits and the Death of Camp

and other essays from *Might* magazine

BERKLEY BOULEVARD BOOKS, NEW YORK

SHINY ADIDAS TRACKSUITS AND THE DEATH OF CAMP
AND OTHER ESSAYS
A Berkley Boulevard Book / published by arrangement with *Might* magazine
PRINTING HISTORY
Berkley Boulevard trade paperback edition / August 1998

Book design by Nigel French
Cover design by K. McSweeney
Cover photograph: FPG International
Interior illustration and photography credits: Phil Campbell, p.1: Phillip Campbell;
Tiresomeness of Flight, p.10: Marc Herman; Hail the Returning Dragon, p. 14: Joel
Elrod; Shiny Adidas Tracksuits, p. 35: Bart Nagel; Design Intervention, p.41: Chris
Harris; Cool Like Me, p. 46: Marcus Hanschen; On the Bus, p.59: Marc Herman; Jews
in Rock, p.74: David Moodie; Paradigm for Sale, p.77: David Ball; Green Bay, p. 81:
Mark Todd; Wake Up, p.94: Stephanie Rausser; Babylon, p. 113: Katherine Streeter;
Adam Rich, p. 137: Robbie Caponetto; T-shirt, p. 147: Bart Nagel; Pardon Me, p. 153:
Rick Barnes; Arpies, p. 158: Bart Nagel; Listener Appreciation, p.179: Aaron Mecham;
Quit Your Job, p.188: Ches Wajda; Slow Boat, p.202: Brian Clarke; Falling Down,
p.220: L.W. Schermerhorn; Virtual Enlightenment, p.225: Bart Nagel, who is a saint.

The Penguin Putnam Inc. World Wide Web site address is
http://www.penguinputnam.com

ISBN: 0-425-16477-2

BERKLEY BOULEVARD
Berkley Boulevard Books are published by The Berkley Publishing Group, a member of
Penguin Putnam Inc., 200 Madison Avenue, New York, New York 10016.
BERKLEY BOULEVARD and its logo
are trademarks belonging to Berkley Publishing Corporation.
PRINTED IN THE UNITED STATES OF AMERICA

10 9 8 7 6 5 4 3

Contents

We Tried.

We thought briefly that something would come out of it. Then, slowly but unmistakably, we realized that relatively little would. Little, of course, in the way of job stability, return on investment, the ability to meaningfully affect change in this society we share, or at least parlay the experience into a career writing postmortem quips in blockbuster action movies. We did get some great mail. And a few of us appeared on cable TV. We even met Puck, who starred on *The Real World*'s second season, and is completely nuts. That—that and all the correspondence from convicted murderers—well, that somehow makes it all worthwhile.

A history, briefly: *Might* was a magazine, started in 1993 in San Francisco by four friends who had grown up together outside of Chicago: David Eggers, David Moodie, Marny Requa and Flagg Taylor. Mr. Taylor, who realized early on that the whole thing was never going to have anything to do with his ability to pay the rent, or for lunch, cut out before the first issue. Then he went into nonprofits.

Might called itself a bimonthly, but at its best published five issues a year until mid-1997, when we quit. Along the way, we picked up other hopeless stragglers, most often through San Francisco's juvenile furlough program. Paul Tullis was cranky, paranoid and had a number of unsettling personal habits. He fit right in at *Might* and, because he had a lot of time on his hands and didn't mind talking for hours to lonely record company publicists, soon became senior editor. Zev Borow was our first non-WASP, and he had a goatee, so in the interest of diversity, we took him too. We had some help along the way from an actual former Merchant Marine, Miles Hurwitz, who was "older," who had "been around," and who told us he knew "something" about "running" a "business." We trusted him, mostly because he had been to Eddie Money's 1984 wedding, and had the cut-off pink T-shirt to prove it. Finally, Lance Crapo, at first our ad director and finally our publisher, came to us through one of those programs where you adopt kids who lived near Chernobyl. Despite his many grotesque physical deformities, he did fine, chiefly because one doesn't have to be physically appealing to run a failing magazine.

So for a while, during the occasional hours when we weren't working waiting tables and doing mind-numbing work for other publications to earn actual money, we would all sit in a small office in San Francisco, think of things to publish, and then publish them. It was relatively easy, and often fun. Yes, yes, there was frivolity, and many fabulous parties, and a good deal of sex in the office, but make no mistake, there were also rules. One rule was that every issue of *Might* had to have a lot of swearing in it, ideally in the headlines. Another rule was that, even though we had about a month or two to put each issue together, the magazine had to go to press with somewhere between thirty and forty egregious spelling and grammatical errors. But the one rule that really got us into trouble, the one that basically doomed us from the start, was this one: We would not publish anything we didn't care about. We once published a piece about whether one could or could not safely drink one's urine because we honestly wanted to know whether one could or could not safely drink one's urine. Similarly, we published a piece featuring eleven pictures of one of our writers, Amy Krouse Rosenthal, letting strangers touch her pregnant stomach, because we thought it was interesting that one of our writers, Amy Krouse Rosenthal, was letting strangers touch her pregnant stomach.

The big problem, though, was that in observing this rule, the rule that said we had to like the things we printed, we were precluded from publishing the sorts of the things that might have kept the magazine afloat: namely, articles about celebrities, clothes, electronics, makeup, cars, video games, beer, nightlife generally, and shoes.

This book contains what we consider to be the some of the best essays we published during our brief stint. A few pieces which could have made the cut quality-wise were left out because of their time-sensitivity, or if they had been published in other collections.

Things to know that will help in your enjoyment of this book:

1) Every once in a while we published something that we pretended was real, but actually wasn't real. For example, we might publish a sentence such as: "Ladybird Johnson liked Lyndon to wear his Haggar leisure slacks high and tight." Now, we would publish this under the respectable auspices of *Might* magazine, which was of course recognized as a premier journal of news and commentary, even though we knew the statement "Ladybird Johnson liked Lyndon to wear his Haggar leisure slacks high and tight" to be false. We do not know why we did this sort of thing in the first place, but in the interest of historical accuracy, we have in this book let stand the magazine's many falsehoods.

2) Some of the titles have been changed because the original titles were not good.

3) Some of the pieces have illustrations, and some do not. There is no good reason why this is the case.

4) Some of these essays are have funny parts in them, some do not.

5) A few of the essays included herein never actually made it to print in *Might.* The thing about the word "fuck" and the thing about nail polish were both scheduled to run in *Might* #17, but then we folded and they were left homeless. The "fuck" thing did end up being published in the *New York Press*, while the nail polish thing appears for the first time here.

6) We never paid any of our writers, so that will explain a lot.

––––––––––––––––––––

People often ask us if we have advice for aspiring magazine publishers. Many of those posing this question are themselves aspiring magazine publishers. Many of them are, incredibly enough, from foreign lands where their languages and customs are very different from our own. They all want to know the same things: Should they do it? Is it worth it? Is there any way at all to start from scratch—we started with under $10,000 and two small computers—and become something more than a freakish mid-'90s fringe-culture artifact, to grow into a viable commercial entity, surviving in the sprawling free market of consumer magazines, and in doing so make a living for you and your friends?

The answers are simple: Yes, yes, and of course not, never, never, no way, dummy.

— *Might, April, 1998*

Phil Campbell? Phil Campbell. Welcome to Phil Campbell.

T he second Phil Campbell, a real estate broker from Idaho, arrived Thursday evening after flying into the Huntsville International Airport and renting a car.

I get up early to meet him for breakfast. A short, balding man, he wears a brown collared shirt riddled with geometric designs, and from a distance I can see his chest heaving from the strain of climbing the hill along Highway 43. For the first few moments I wave to him frantically to make sure he doesn't miss me.

"Are you Phil Campbell?" I say, grinning as he approaches.

"Well, you must be Phil Campbell," he says, extending his hand and wheezing slightly. He pauses for a moment, then says, "I just had a pacemaker put in last week."

Phil Campbell from Idaho and I head into Scarlet's Restaurant in Russellville, just a few miles north of the town of Phil Campbell, Alabama. By tomorrow, twenty-two Phil Campbells—and one Phyllis Campbell—from all over the country will converge on Phil Campbell for the First Annual Phil Campbell Convention, organized by me, Phil

Campbell. In just thirty minutes, however, Idaho Phil and I have to meet the mayor of Phil Campbell to make the final preparations. We decided it would be important to have breakfast first.

Before I have a chance to contemplate how I feel to be sitting next to another person named Phil Campbell, Phil starts to tell a series of unrelated stories. He tells me everything he knows about the Campbell clan, material quoted from a book he had read on the subject. He launches into an anecdote about the Speer brothers, who became one of the richest families in the United States when they developed a bullet shell that allowed for greater accuracy. He talks about how the salmon die every year traveling through the turbines of the dams near his home because the ventilation system creates too much oxygen for their respiratory systems.

"Lewiston was actually supposed to be the capital of Idaho," he says, warming up to another anecdote, "but the people from Boise came up and stole the charter."

"Is your wife going to make it?" I ask. It is ten minutes after ten, and we are making the mayor wait.

"She takes her time getting ready, and you can't rush her," he says. "You want to know how you can tell when my wife is really ready to go? The last thing she'll do is throw two Tic Tacs in her mouth."

Just then Barbara, Mrs. Phil B. Campbell, enters the restaurant. She moves slowly because two weeks ago she received a bunyonectomy and a hammertoe correction. About five feet tall, she has high, curly brown hair and rose-tinted glasses. One of the best Mary Kay saleswomen in Lewiston, her plentiful blush makes her a convincing advertisement for the company. While Barbara eats, Phil expands upon another story, this one about the Potlatch mill in Lewiston, the city's largest employer. After Barbara finishes her eggs and pops a couple of Tic Tacs, we pay the bill and leave to meet the mayor.

I discovered the town of Phil Campbell two years earlier, when my college roommate and I were bored, half drunk and watching some guy on a "Hee Haw" rerun give a big howdy to the folks of Phil Campbell. Several months after that, I visited the town myself, and learned that there are only three cities in the entire country with the full name of a person: Phil Campbell, Alabama, Carol Stream, Illinois, and Jim Thorpe, Pennsylvania. Chevy Chase, Maryland was named after an old English ballad about a border raid in Scotland, and is, therefore, immaterial.

The original Philip Campbell was a train engineer in Alabama during the 1880s. A local merchant convinced Phil to put a side track through his land and build a depot there. In exchange, the town that grew around the depot would be named after him. Phil agreed, delivered the goods and moved on. He never actually lived in Phil Campbell, but the town was his, even if by name only.

There is a computer database that contains the published phone numbers and addresses of 234 Phil, Philip and Phillip Campbells living in the United States, from Roseville, California, to Seekonk, Massachusetts. Determined to assemble Phil Campbells from all over America, I went through $125 in postage and two sets of form letters before definite responses began to come in. Phyl Campbell Matteson of Schoolcraft, Michigan, wrote an eight-page letter that included blown-up photos of her deceased father, Phil. Some called me to ask how we would deal with the fact that Phil Campbell is in a dry county. Others didn't seem to mind. "We gonna get together," Phil Campbell from Limestone, Tennessee, told my answering machine, "and we gonna hang out in the big house!" His cousin, the other Phil Campbell of Limestone, could be heard guffawing in the background.

While the mayor is giving me a tour of the area, a seemingly endless wave of Phil Campbells begins to arrive in Russellville at the Windwood Inn. Unfortunately, sorting out the room assignments becomes an exasperating chore. The general manager of the Windwood hadn't bothered to tell her front desk clerks that two dozen people with reservations under the name Phil Campbell would be checking in on the exact same day.

Later that afternoon, Phil from New Hampshire stirs up some trouble with his son-in-law, Joe Graham. The two sit outside their motel room on the second floor and begin drinking, at first unaware and then indifferent to the county's dry laws. They try to persuade a Windwood Inn employee to change the motel marquee to read, "Welcome Phil Campbell." The worker can't because he doesn't have enough letters, so he uses our initials instead. "Welcome P.C." Afterward, Phil and Joe go to the Speedy Pig restaurant, and Phil eats so much barbecued pork that he has to take a nap.

Phil and Dorothy from Los Osos, California, arrive in the afternoon, but few people actually see them. When they get into town, they can't find a place to hook up the motor home's electricity. Frustrated, Phil tries to get a hotel room, but the Windwood Inn is booked. They end up discreetly parking the RV in a corner of the motel parking lot, where I later find them baking in the Alabama sun.

Phil from Stuart, Florida, brings his wife and a box of T-shirts she had designed that read, "Hello, we've come to take our town back" on the front with the town's name, the convention's name and the date on the back. They sit in their hotel for a while watching CNN and are shocked to see a reporter in Bosnia interview a U.S. Air Force captain named Phil Campbell. I figure my form letters didn't get forwarded overseas.

After having dinner with these Phils and the Phils from Thornton, Colorado, Paxinos, Pennsylvania, and Raleigh, North Carolina, we return to the Windwood Inn for a 9 p.m. meeting. All I really need to do is pass out the itinerary I had hastily printed out before dinner, but the Phils stick around to meet each other. Alexis Campbell diligently stands near the T-shirts, even though Phils are only coming in every twenty minutes. These include Phil Campbells from Anderson, South Carolina, and Baltimore, Maryland. My sister Veronica, her husband, Chris, and her two children are also present. After learning the significance of the gathering, my five-year-old nephew Ben starts laughing. He runs up and down the room saying, "Hi, Phil. Hi, Phil. Hi, Phil."

Phil Campbell from Auburn, New York, has been in town all afternoon, but he doesn't come down to get an itinerary or to meet the other Phil Campbells. I call his room upstairs from the front desk. Our conversation is brief. "Just tell me where and when we're meeting tomorrow," he says. "I'll see you then."

On my way back from the phone, Phil Campbell from Viola, Wisconsin, grabs me. "You ain't no long-haired weirdo with an earring," he says joyfully. "I was worried you would be. You're all right," he beams, slapping me on the back with a giant paw. This Phil is heavyset; his suspenders strain mightily to reach his pants over his belly. He sports a hat he bought at the Cracker Barrel which is covered with pre-arranged buttons that have little sayings on them. He is so happy to be here at this convention of newly found brethren that he grins from ear to ear regardless of whether anybody is talking to him or not.

Phil Campbell, Alabama, is so isolated from the rest of the world that it takes an hour and a half to get to Huntsville—population 151,000—the closest large city. When the federal government was pouring money into interstate highways, northwestern Alabama was ignored. It's about fifty miles in any direction to reach a major expressway.

The tiny burg of Phil Campbell has no real economy to speak of, unless you count the Chat n' Chew diner, the florist, the Piggly Wiggly grocery store, and the small storefront studio dedicated to teaching the art of tae kwan do. Most of Phil Campbell's 1,500 residents earn their living in the factories of neighboring cities, making pants, furniture, or mobile homes. Others work on the outskirts of Phil Campbell farming the cotton and corn fields.

Phil Campbell Mayor Ted Murray knows all this and thinks the Phil Campbell convention can help the town's situation. The assumption is that we will bring reporters, photographers and TV cameras, and, hopefully, a few column-inches or a little air time devoted to the beauty of the region. Tourists—both Phil Campbells and non-Phil Campbells—would then visit and give a leg up to the local economy.

That's why Murray doesn't mind waiting for me. That's why he orders Phil Campbell Police Chief Larry Swindle to drive me around in the city's brand-new unmarked police car. That's why, when I ask him about the nearby William B. Bankhead Forest, he calls another mayor in a town closer to the forest to arrange for a tour. That's why he gives me his home phone number and tells me to call if I have any problems whatsoever.

He also tells Swindle to get some minimum security prisoners at Hamilton Work-Release to rip the city limits sign out of the ground along Highway 43 and put it anywhere I want. "If we don't give them something to do, they just sit around and drink their Cokes," Chief Swindle says. I have them put it in a grassy area near the public pool so I can organize the group photo shoot. The prisoners also clean up after us, Murray tells me later.

Saturday morning rolls around. There is nothing planned until 11:30 a.m., and the Phil Campbells are restless. They scatter themselves across the four-square-mile town, shooting photos of themselves in front of anything they can find that has their name on it—water towers, churches, the high school, police cars, the city limits sign. The post office is an especially popular place, because anybody who has a letter can get the town name postmarked on it.

That's where Phil from California and his wife, Dorothy, run into Phil from New York and his parents. Eddie and Victoria Campbell are outside of the car, but Phil from New York is still in the driver's seat. In the spirit of things, Dorothy walks over to Phil from New York and asks if she can get a picture of him and her husband in front of the Phil Campbell post office.

"Won't you come out here?" she asks.

"No. I don't want to get out," he replies. Later, instead of coming to the day's planned activities—the primary functions of the entire convention—Phil from New York opts for a drive down Highway 24, heading west. He stops and turns around only when he realizes that he's crossed the Mississippi state line.

By noon, city hall, a natural gathering place in the center of town, is packed with people. Our numbers reach into the sixties because most Phils have come with family members. Teresa, the assistant city clerk, herds everyone into a meeting room, and they wait for directions on how to get to the convention site. There is a general, uncomfortable silence while they wait, broken only by the occasional joke Florida Phil tells. This is the first time all the Phils have been gathered, but introductions are, of course, unnecessary.

After we all get in our cars, Mayor Murray leads us by caravan to the convention site at the Phil Campbell public pool and pavilion, which is about a minute-and-a-half away. By now we have eighteen Phil Campbells, including two father-son Phils from Tennessee, one of whom is just six years old. The Associated Press reporter who has dropped by is satisfied with a count of seventeen, but throughout the day more Phils pull in. The two Rev. Phil Campbells arrive in the afternoon. Rev. Phil from Denver didn't think he'd even be able to come, but at the last moment he stumbled onto a standby ticket to Atlanta and rented a car. Rev. Phil from Iowa drives up just as the three o'clock group photo session is ending.

The convention itself goes smoothly. Phil from Baltimore joins my sister at the barbecue to help prepare the food, and Phil Jr. from Hermitage, Tennessee, and Phil from Etowah, Tennessee, and his wife, Kathy, get into the beach volleyball games that have formed. Most Phils and their wives, however, are content to sit underneath the pavilion and talk. Several people have brought camcorders and they sometimes get in each other's way scanning the picnic benches, the frolicking kids and the little pods of Phils eating barbecued chicken and corn on the cob by the pool. Phil from Thornton, Colorado, and New Hampshire Phil share the JR cigars New Hampshire Phil had ordered from North Carolina.

In fact, New Hampshire Phil has formed a small clique of sorts. He organizes small parties on the second-floor balcony of the motel. His son-in-law Joe, Florida couple Phil and Alexis, California couple Phil and Dorothy, and my sister and her husband, Chris, gather there to drink beer until the wee hours. New Hampshire Phil and Joe enforce the one strict rule at the parties: No one goes to bed until all the Miller Lite is gone from their Styrofoam cooler.

No one knows where Phil from New York is, but the rumors about him have been circulating since the morning. Needless to say, he misses the group photo session.

"I saw Phil from New York outside the motel," Alexis Campbell of Florida tells me in a hushed tone later that evening. "He's kind of strange." She theorizes that he is a fugitive running from the law.

Her husband looks at her strangely. "Why then," he asks, "would he come to this convention?"

I drop by his motel room before going to the dinner the mayor is throwing for us. I find him in his parent's room. I had seen him briefly before, but this time I take a good look at him. He is about five feet nine inches tall and has wavy, dirty blond hair. His eyes continually move back and forth. He starts to apologize for missing the barbecue, but then his parents see us.

"Come in, come in," Victoria urges me. She turns to her son. "He's kind of weird. We're a little off our rockers." She sits on the far bed, constantly adjusting her weight to get comfortable.

"Sit down. Come in." Phil's father Eddie is lying on the bed.

"He's in, Dad."

"Phil's a lawyer. So watch out," Victoria says.

After a little small talk, Phil excuses himself from his parents and walks me to my car. "I'll get them straightened out for dinner," he reassures me.

True to his word, Phil does show up for the dinner, but he and his parents leave abruptly after eating, without saying anything. I decide later to meet him privately that night.

It's cooling down outside, but Phil has the air conditioner on full blast. He wears jeans and a blue-collared shirt with a white T-shirt underneath. He has been reading a book, but when I enter he turns it on its spine and offers me a beer. I sit close to the window in the corner of the room and he retreats with his Budweiser to sit by the pillow of the far bed.

There are several awkward silences.

"Tell you about myself? I don't know. I'm a child of the '60s. I went to Woodstock," he says. "My wife died a year and a half ago, and I've been at loose ends ever since."

Phil is forty-five years old, and his parents dragged him to Alabama for this. "When I first saw your letter, I thought it was cute. I didn't intend to do anything. But then my dad said, 'Well, we're going to go, goddamnit.'" He pauses. "I don't know why the people here are so grateful to us. I mean, I didn't contribute anything to the local economy.

"I didn't come down for the photos because, a) I think I'm kind of shy by nature, and b) I think it's kind of stupid. The town will always be here, and I will always have the same name. But if you ask my dad that, he'll say, 'I'm coming back next year.'"

He then turns to what's on his mind, what is, apparently, always on his mind: Christine Campbell, his wife of twenty years. He gets up once to show me her picture, a black and white photo taken years ago. She has very white skin and blond hair tied up in a bun. After I give the photo back he returns to his side of the room. "She was an angel," he says.

On a late September morning she started to complain about not feeling well, so she stayed inside and rested. Around 8:30 p.m., she grabbed her chest and said, "Oh, my God!"

"I looked at her and she wasn't breathing," Phil says. "I did CPR, called the hospital, all that fun stuff." She died on Oct. 3, 1993 from brain damage, after being in a coma for sixteen days.

Worried about his ability to cope, Phil's parents made him move from Florida to their home in Auburn, New York. Living so close to his parents at age forty-five has been a trying experience, though. They have a few idiosyncrasies that took time to adjust to. For example, when they are traveling, Victoria sometimes wakes up around midnight, showers, dresses and insists that they continue on their way. She is adamant, and Eddie and Phil have no choice but to leave while most people are still sound asleep.

When I finally leave Phil's room an hour later, I see that Florida Phil has joined New Hampshire Phil, his son-in-law Joe Graham, my sister and her husband on the second floor of the motel. They had been joking and carrying on about what we were doing inside New York Phil's room. I sit down with them, but I am unable and unwilling to answer their jocular questions.

At the Mayor's dinner that evening—a buffet banquet back at City Hall—the other Phils are considerably more festive than Phil from New York. Phil and Kathy Campbell from Douds, Iowa, have their picture taken with Phil and Kathy Campbell of Etowah, Tennessee. Phil from North Carolina and his wife, Bonnie, have changed out of the convention T-shirts and into matching shirts of their own. Bonnie's shirt says, "Who the heck is Phil Campbell?" Phil's shirt pronounces, "I am." A loyal customer of his auto repair shop made them for him.

Teresa, the assistant to the city clerk, passes out Phil Campbell Police hats along with key chains and other souvenirs, compliments of the two banks in town. The mayor picks names out of a hat (our addresses are included) to choose which Phil Campbell will be the honorary mayor, police chief, and so on. Everyone stands to applaud six-year-old Phil Campbell Jr. from Tennessee when he is named honorary fire chief.

The mayor supplies everyone with a mailing list with all our addresses on it. He wants to host the convention again next year and the year after that, with more Phil Campbells and more media coming each time. Some of the wives of Phils decide they want to go further. They want to assign each attending Phil Campbell some Phil Campbells from the original mailing list I used. They want to include photos from this convention and a personal letter to each—perhaps that will persuade the 211 Phil Campbells that didn't make it here to come in 1996.

"We should have a convention based on middle names," Rev. Phil from Denver suggests. "My middle name's Elston."

"Mine's Gerard," I say.

"Kendle," says Phil Sr. from Tennessee. The idea doesn't go very far.

I approach Chief Swindle as the other Phils finish eating. "Hey, Larry, do you think we can get a police escort to the Dismals?" Dismals Canyon is a series of gullies and rock formations that boast the presence of the dismalites: small, rare glow worms that locals boast can only be found in Phil Campbell, Alabama. It's also the place where Aaron Burr reportedly hid out for three days after killing Alexander Hamilton in a duel.

"Sure. John Cheek will take you out," Swindle says immediately.

Sixteen cars line up behind Officer Cheek as he turns on the flashing blue lights of his squad car and leads us slowly through town. People who have houses along the road come out to their porches to see the spectacle. Other residents watch the parade from the beds of their trucks along the road. Phil from North Carolina admonishes his wife. "Put your Coke down, sit up and stop laughing. They think we're in a funeral procession."

As the caravan advances in the evening half-light through the stops signs of Phil Campbell, the cars are full of noisy chatter. Tomorrow, the conference attendees will disperse to their own personal corners of the country. But tonight, as the procession rolls out of town onto Route 43, one thing is undeniably true: It's good to be Phil Campbell. ■

December, 1995

MARC HERMAN

Notes on the Growing Tiresomeness of Flight

I am going to explain how to get free cars for easy frequent travel, but first I would like to outline some personal aspects.

In Missoula, Montana, where I lived briefly two years ago, the woman next door made her own apple butter. She used Granny Smiths from Wenatchee, Washington, vinegar from a witch's wineglass, sugar left to her in Josephine Baker's will, and cinnamon ground by a jeweler, it seemed. I received a fresh jar every two weeks. It tasted like lust must feel to an octogenarian. I ate it blissfully every morning with my own homemade bread, slowly, with tea, because I did not have to work until ten. I enjoyed the cat's meow of breakfast set-ups in Missoula.

After I had left Missoula for Washington, D.C., I was foolish enough to be surprised that recalling the apple butter did not bring me ghostly tastes of it. Garrison Keillor and other characters of his warm milk ilk had claimed it would, and I had believed them. Not the case, though. Instead, coldly, it became unignorably clear that I could not be in two places at once.

Trying also brings unkind beatnik associations to mind. Romantic as that is, it's false and wrong. When I moved back to the District, as an example, I met a friend who walked like Sinatra. He could take a sack suit off the rack and make it swing like a sail. He played the saxophone and only drove American cars; he danced like a Pip, quoted poetry like it was liturgy, and moved through a room in paragraphs. Now he's at Harvard Business School. He knew that any adult who rides around in a school bus but isn't a school bus driver is probably a fool, and an example of what not to become.

So I'm looking at highways more objectively now, less romantically. I now admit that road food is generally unappealing. Truck stop apple pie is atrocious. Moreover, Pennsylvania state troopers have permission to shoot out your tires at whim.* The last North Carolina cop who pulled me over reminded me of Duvall in *The Great Santini* and carried surgical gloves in his utility belt. A sagging mattress in an I-40 motel is about as romantic as a wet spot. There is no Zen in roadside maintenance. Finally, the truckers have to get to Bangor before 40,000 pounds of tomatoes spoil, and they don't need you in their way.

I now feel that if you have to hit the road, do it early and often, but at least try to have a destination.

Moving a lot in the United States, while preventing one from buying many houseplants, does instill a certain logistical savvy. One ace in the hole I find worth being familiar with is driveaway agencies.

Auto driveaway agencies are companies that pair people who want to travel with cars that need shipping. There is no fee to the driver. Many driveaway clients are corporate. Occasionally, even often, drivers take advantage of the agencies. They do not travel just from point A to point B, but rather from A to B via, say, point R. Which is illegal.

Like much lawbreaking, it has its advantages, though. Is there any real harm in fudging? Well, the people to whom you are falsifying your intentions might get fired if you are caught, and you may be subject to a fine and criminal prosecution. Still, with driveaway, you can get more or less anywhere in the U.S. for the price of gasoline, and if you do not mind altering some paperwork, you can also travel interesting side roads where the food and scenery are compelling and the fuel is cheaper.

Over ten days, a friend and I drove a nearly new $50,000 sports car from Syosset, Long Island, to Orange County, California. We rode the

* *Not actually true.*

car like a Pony Express horse, went several hundred miles off our prescribed route more than once, faked the odometer reading and got away with it. All told, it was a lot of bang for our buck.

My co-conspirator was my pal Jennifer. Jen is an easy traveling companion, and had the right two weeks off work, but she drives worse sober than most do drunk and we needed to return the car unscathed. So aside from a four hour section from Floyd, Tennessee, to somewhere near the Georgia line, she mostly navigated.

As for the car: Why the company let this machine out of its sight is something I will never understand. That vehicle was a cherry bomb, an emerald green hot rod Lincoln V-8 with low-profile tires and computerized brakes, tan leather interior, a six-CD changer, Bose Speakers, a sunroof, and a digital compass built into the dash. The company that owns it makes car alarms. Apparently it's the vice president of the outfit's office ride. Greased lightning.

I wouldn't say that any grander fairness was served between New York and L.A., or that one can construct a general cultural commentary out of our misbehavior. It is not clear to me that these companies—the owner of the car, the driveaway agency, and their respective policy carriers—deserved such abuse of their trust. Certainly pranks have an allure, and if one wants, for example, to go to Birmingham to have an uncomfortable reunion with an old flame, then out to the Rockies to soak in mountain hot spring after long months in the city, then joy riding in other people's cars can even be rationalized as necessary and deserved.

And problems were few. In the Shenandoah mountains, in fog like cotton, we tried to see how fast we could take blind curves and nearly wasted Bambi. Per cliché, the beast stood there staring on the double yellow line for a good thirty seconds while we waited to get rear-ended. Jen shrugged and cued Merle Haggard's "White Line Fever."

There was also the gum thing. The CD player was actually in the trunk; we operated it with a remote control that Jen aimed at a small plastic receiver on the dash, which displayed the CD numbers and little LED arrows and sent the signal to the player astern. This box came unglued our first day out, so Jen and I chewed up fifteen cents-worth of Bazooka bubble gum each and mashed the thing back into place. That lasted about a day, then became a real mess.

Generic cleanser from the Wal-Mart in Winslow, Arizona, took the finish off the dash, so we had to cover the carnage with double-sided tape moments before returning the car. It probably fell off half an hour later.

Smokey Bear, for his part, was apparently hibernating. Our closest call was in Arkansas. Jen had a friend in Little Rock who worked in the office of the Special Prosecutor for Whitewater Bullshit, so we got a tour. We ended up surrounded by twenty-eight-year-old G-men with artillery on their hips, but it all worked out and we ended up going out to an El Torito for drinks with the office staff. I think amongst themselves they though the whole Madison Guaranty thing was a bunch of hooey. The prosecutor resigned a few weeks later, of course.

Other than that, we did not encounter the law.

There are a few other cautionary tales, though: In Flagstaff, Arizona, Jen wrote a mutual friend, Lilya, a terribly boring postcard, so I added a postscript to the effect that we had gotten hitched at a roadside chapel. Lilya took this seriously and started pumping out e-mail, so by the time we got to L.A., everyone in the country was counseling us not to rush into anything. Three months later I saw a woman at a party whom I had not talked to in a while, and she congratulated me on my new wife.

Besides that, we saw *Mighty Ducks 2* in Shawnee, Oklahoma, but failed to find a country bar in Nashville.

Lastly, no one in the IHOP in Amarillo seemed to care a whit about Kurt Cobain eating his gun. Jen seemed initially bothered, but she forgot about it once we saw the plastic cow in front of the Big Texas Steak Ranch.

When we got to L.A., I jumped in the ocean. It was night and the water was black and warm.

I occasionally wonder, following these trips, about Kuwait. I opposed the Persian Gulf War. In all fairness, gas should probably cost three or four bucks a gallon. It costs a dollar and a half in the United States at most, though more like a dollar away from the coasts.

So the bug is still there. Where I live now, New York City, I often consider walking into the driveaway office two blocks away from Madison Square Garden and taking the first car they have—driving away from Kate Moss's fifty foot ass, hung over Times Square but still looking too small, and on the wherever it is the car is going. Sometimes I call just to see what is available. ■

April, 1995

DAVID FOSTER WALLACE

Hail the Returning Dragon, Clothed in New Fire

You know this love story. A gallant knight espies a fair maiden in the distant window of a forbidding-type castle. Their eyes meet—smokily—across the withered heath. Instant chemistry. And so good Sir Knight comes tear-assing toward the castle, brandishing his lance. Can he just gallop up and carry the fair maiden off? Not quite. First he's got to get past the dragon, right? There's always a particularly nasty dragon guarding the castle, and the knight's always got to face and slay the dragon if there's to be any carrying off. But and so, like any loyal knight in the service of passion, the knight battles the dragon, all for the sake of the fair maiden. "Fair maiden" means "good-looking virgin," by the way. And so let's not be naive about what the knight's really fighting for. You can bet he's going to expect more than a breathy "My hero" from the maiden once that dragon's slain. In fact, the way the story always goes, good Sir Knight risks life and lance against the dragon not to "rescue" the good-looking virgin, but to "win" her. And any knight, from any era, can tell you what "win" means here.

Some of my own knightly friends see the specter of heterosexual AIDS as nothing less than a sexual Armageddon—a violent end to the casual carnalcopia of the last three decades. Some others, grim but more upbeat, regard HIV as a sort of test of our generation's sexual mettle; these guys now applaud their own casual sport-fucking as a kind of medical dare-devilry that affirms the indomitability of the erotic spirit. I cite, e.g., an upbeat friend's recent letter on AIDS: "...So now nature had invented another impediment to human relations, and yet the romantic urge lives. It defies all efforts—human, moral, and viral—to extinguish it. And that's a wonderful thing. It is, in fact, possible to be encouraged by the human will to fuck, which persists despite all sorts of impediments. We shall overcome, so to speak."

Cavalier sentiments, etc. But I can't help thinking some of today's knights still underestimate both AIDS's dangers and its advantages. They fail to see that HIV could well be the salvation of sexuality in the 1990s. They don't see it, I think, because they tend to misread the eternal story of what erotic passion's all about.

The erotic will exists "despite impediments"? Let's go back to that knight and fair maiden exchanging lascivious looks. And here comes the knight, galloping castleward, mammoth lance at the ready. Except imag-ine this time that there is no danger, no dragon to fear, face, fight, slay. Imagine the knight's pursuit of the maiden is wholly unimpeded—there's no dragon; the castle's unlocked; the drawbridge even lowers auto-matically, like a suburban garage door. And here's the maiden inside, wearing a Victoria's Secret teddy and crooking her finger. Does anyone else here detect a shadow of disappointment in Sir Knight's face, a slight anticlimactic droop to his lance? Does this version of the story have any-thing like the other's passionate, erotic edge?

"The human will to fuck"? Any animal can fuck. But only humans can experience sexual passion, something wholly different from the biologi-cal urge to mate. And sexual passion's endured for millennia as a vital psy-chic force in human life—not despite impediments but because of them. Plain old coitus becomes erotically charged and spiritually potent at just those moments where impediments, conflicts, taboos and consequences lend it a double-edged character—meaningful sex is both an overcom-ing and a succumbing, a transcendence and a transgression, triumphant and terrible and ecstatic and sad. Turtles and gnats can mate, but only the human will can defy, transgress, overcome, love: Choose.

History-wise, both nature and culture have been ingenious at erecting impediments that give the choice of passion its price and value; religious proscriptions; penalty for adultery and divorce; chivalric chastity and courtly decorum; the stigma of illegitimate birth; chaperonage; madonna/whore complexes; syphilis; back-alley abortions; a set of "moral" codes that put sensuality on a taboo-level with defecation and apostasy... from the Victorians' dread of the body to early TV's one-foot-on-the-floor-at-all-times rule; from the automatic ruin of "fallen" women to back-seat tussles in which girlfriends struggled to deny boyfriends what they begged for in order to preserve their respect. Granted, from 1996's perspective, most of the old sexual dragons look stupid and cruel. But we need to realize that they had something big in their favor: as long as the dragons reigned, sex wasn't casual, not ever. Historically, human sexuality has been a deadly serious business—and the fiercer its dragons, the seriouser sex got; and the higher the price of choice, the higher the erotic voltage surrounding what people chose.

And then, what must have seemed suddenly, the dragons all keeled over and died. This was just around when I was born, the '60s "Revolution" in sexuality. Sci-fi type advances in prophylactics and anti-venereals, feminism as a political force, TV as institution, the rise of a culture of youth and its gland-intensive art and music, Civil Rights, rebellion as fashion, inhibition-killing drugs, the moral castration of churches and censors. Bikinis, miniskirts. "Free Love." The castle's doors weren't so much unlocked as blown off their hinges. Sex could finally be unconstrained, "Hang-Up"-free, just another appetite: casual. I was toothless and incontinent through most of the Revolution, but it must have seemed like instant paradise. For a while.

I was pre-conscious for the Revolution's big party, but I got to experience fully the hangover that followed—the erotic malaise of the '70s, as sex, divorced from most price and consequence, reached a kind of saturation-point in the culture—swinging couples and meat-market bars, hot tubs and EST, Hustler's gynecological spreads, *Charlie's Angels*, herpes, kiddie-porn, mood rings, teenage pregnancy, Plato's Retreat, disco. I remember *Looking for Mr. Goodbar* all too well, its grim account of the emptiness and self-loathing that a decade of rampant casual fucking had brought on. Looking back, I realize that I came of sexual age in a culture that was starting to miss the very dragons whose deaths had supposedly freed it.

If I've got this right, then the casual knights of my own bland generation might well come to regard AIDS as a blessing, a gift perhaps bestowed by nature to restore some critical balance, maybe summoned unconsciously out of the collective erotic despair of the post-'60s glut. Because the dragon is back, and clothed in a fire that can't be ignored.

I mean no offense. Nobody would claim that a lethal epidemic is a good thing. Nothing from nature is good or bad. Natural things just are; the only good and bad are people's various choices in the face of what is. But our own history shows that—for whatever reasons—an erotically charged human existence requires impediments to passion, prices for choices. That hundreds of thousands of people are dying horribly of AIDS seems like a cruel and unfair price to pay for a new erotic impediment. But it's not obviously more unfair than the millions who have died of syphilis, incompetent abortions, and "crimes of passion," nor obviously more cruel than that people used routinely to have their lives wrecked by "falling," "fornicating," sinning, having "illegitimate" children, or getting trapped by inane religious codes in loveless and abusive marriages. At least it's not obvious to me.

There's a new dragon to face. But facing a dragon doesn't mean swaggering up to it unarmed and insulting its mom. And the erotic charge of hazard surrounding sex and HIV doesn't mean we can continue to engage in sport-fucking in the name of "courage" or romantic "will." In fact, AIDS's gift to us lies in its loud reminder that there's nothing casual about sex at all. This is a gift because human sexuality's power and meaning increase with our recognition of its seriousness. This has been what's "bad" about casual sex from the beginning: sex is never bad, but it's also never casual.

Our sexual recognition of what is can start with the conscientious use of protection as a gesture of love toward ourselves and our partners. But a deeper, far braver recognition of just what kind of dragon we're facing is now starting to take hold, and—far from Armageddon—is doing much to increase the erotic voltage of contemporary life. Thanks to AIDS, we're expanding our imaginations with respect to what is "sexual." Deep down, we all know that the real allure of sexuality has about as much to do with copulation as the appeal of food does with metabolic combustion. Trite though it (used to) sound, real sexuality is about our struggles to connect with one another, to erect bridges across the chasms that separate selves. Sexuality is, finally, about imagination. Thanks to brave people's recognition of AIDS as a fact of life, we are beginning to realize that highly charged sex can take place in all sorts of ways we'd forgotten or neglected—through non-genital touching, or over the phone, or via the mail; in a conversational nuance; in a body's posture, a certain pressure in a held hand. Sex can be everywhere we are, all the time. All we need to do is really face this dragon, yielding neither to hysterical terror nor to childish denial. In return, the dragon can help us relearn what it means to be truly sexual. This is not a small thing, or optional. Fire is lethal, but we need it. The key is how we come to fire. It's not just other people you have to respect. ■

November, 1996

TED RALL

College Is for Suckers

In Stephen King's novella *The Long Walk*, the biggest event in post-apocalyptic America is an annual race-walk featuring a hundred boys. To ensure a lively pace, flatbed trucks carrying soldiers shadow them along the side of the road. Whenever their speed falls below three miles an hour, the soldiers bark out a warning. The fourth time, they get shot. The contestants hike down I-95 until they're killed or drop dead of exhaustion. The last survivor receives The Prize. The Prize is anything the winner desires. The Prize is all anyone ever talks about. In the end, of course, there is no prize. After the crowds go home, the winner is quietly executed.

In pre-apocalyptic America, parents force their kids to run an eighteen-year-long marathon for a similarly futile remnant of the American Dream called The Promise. Graduate from the right college, The Promise goes, and you'll learn all you need to know, land a good job, have a great life. The catch is that you have to survive countless filters—grades, tests, demographics, luck—to get into a good school. For the lucky few, being admitted is merely a prelude to the ultimate challenge: finding the cash to pay insanely high tuition bills. For most, the only answer is to take out huge student loans, setting up yet another financial gauntlet to survive long after graduation. In no time at all, The Promise says, you'll pay back the loans, earn more money than the losers who didn't make it and leave your kids an obscenely huge inheritance.

The Promise is based upon several faulty premises:

• College makes you more marketable, especially during difficult economic times. Although there are a few advantages to being a college graduate when you're looking for work, the difference is slight compared to the cost of tuition and fees.

• Highly competitive admissions processes select for the best and the brightest. Given the way our society selects who will go to college, there is little evidence of this. Having worked in an admissions office at a highly competitive university, I can assure you that the process is arbitrary as hell. Often the best and brightest don't stand a chance.

• Without a college degree, you will shrivel up and die like a desiccated bug. Actually, you might be better off both financially and professionally.

• Although the best way to ensure a high-paying job is to major in something "practical," a liberal-arts degree is better than none at all. Wrong. There's no financial advantage to going to college as a liberal-arts major.

• College is a worthwhile learning experience, vital to shaping the leaders of tomorrow. College students mainly learn how to fuck, snooze and get soused.

I understand The Promise well. My mother, like many immigrants, was obsessed with the importance of education. Because she was a high school teacher, by age ten I knew all about sucking up to teachers to set up letters of recommendation, entering essay contests to get scholarships and volunteering to work for my local Congressman to get sponsored for one of the military academies. My entire life from then on was devoted to the single goal of gaining admittance to and financing attendance at a prestigious eastern university—ideally an Ivy League school. In eighth grade, I planned out all fifty-six of my high school classes through senior year, and I stuck to my plan. I worked three jobs to save money for school, but kept the money in cash in my safety deposit box (so the financial aid office wouldn't take it into consideration). I joined countless inane extracurricular activities because I thought they'd help me get into a good school (I can still feel the polyester outfit I wore in marching band while playing the clarinet part to "Don't Cry Out Loud [Just Keep It Inside]"). Like most teens, I wanted to go to parties and have girlfriends, but I worked on extra-credit assignments instead. I couldn't let anything stand in the way of escaping my Ohio suburb.

In the end, I got into Columbia. Because I'd done well in math and science in high school, my mom insisted that I pursue an engineering degree. (Parents often confuse academic ability for interest.) "Look at your dad," she said. "He makes good money." I knew she was right. But courses like Nuclear Engineering E3001 and Partial Differential Analysis G4305 didn't hold my interest for long. I slept through almost every lecture, either in bed or in class. Three years later, I'd racked up an impressive string of Ds and Fs, particularly in physics. When my dean called me to tell me I'd been expelled, he told me they couldn't decide whether it was for academic or disciplinary reasons. I had twenty-four hours to vacate my dorm.

By early 1990, I was working at a bank. (I'd told my employers that I had a degree to get the job.) The phone hadn't rung much since the '87 stock market crash, and a lot of my friends had already gotten laid off. Motivated by fear and boredom I reapplied to Columbia, but as a history major (I'd been reading a lot of Vichy France books). I was shocked that they admitted me; maybe my old discipline records got lost. I still wasn't convinced that blowing $25,000 in savings on one year of school was a wise move—my $36,000 salary disqualified me for financial aid—but I was worn down from listening to my mom and future in-laws hassle me about it. I wanted to finish what I'd begun ten years earlier and looked forward to being an undergraduate at age 28.

I graduated in 1991. Since then, the central premise of The Promise has evaporated. Measured by traditional indicators like the Dow Jones average and the unemployment rate, the American economy has boomed, but the average employee hasn't noticed. Not only are corporations not hiring, but they've laid people off 43 million times since 1979. From 1990 to 1994, the top 5 percent of wage-earners saw their paychecks rise 17 percent. The rest of us lost ground.

Most Americans go to college in order to land on the first rung of the comfy, safe corporate ladder. Now that those corporate jobs are either low-paying or non-existent, we should ask ourselves:

Why Go to College?

Nazi physician Josef Mengele decided who lived and who died at Auschwitz. Best known for vivisecting humans and injecting dye into kids' eyes, he always took time out of his busy schedule to greet every shipment of prisoners. The SS doctor "selected" the fate of every man, woman and child who arrived by cattle car with a brusque wave of his right hand: right meant a slow death from starvation and overwork, left led straight to the crematoria.

In America, the selection process isn't as brutal, but it's just as arbitrary. First- and second-grade teachers armed with IQ exams disguised as "aptitude tests" mark kids as college—or 7-Eleven—bound within the first few months of school. From that point forward, the fate of American children is virtually predetermined. Nonetheless, college-tracked students are expected to spend the next twelve years preparing for the college application process. Even for the fortunate who have been selected, a minor slip-up can lead to developing an intimate knowledge of deep-frying.

"College-bound" students devote their childhoods to the hope of receiving a thick letter from a college admissions office. They join cheesy activities they don't really like: student government, marching band, Latin Club, yearbook. They invest hundreds of dollars on test-prep courses for the PSAT, ACT and SAT. Then they take the tests again—as many as four times—to raise their scores. Plagued by "senioritis" and burned out after more than a decade of college prep, some may be tempted to let their guard down, but it's best to keep their Junior Council on World Affairs membership dues paid up through commencement. After all, students listen with a shiver, colleges have been known to react to a drop in senior-year grades by rescinding their acceptances.

So you've gotten into the school of your dreams? Don't ease up now! The same vicious atmosphere of competition prevails here—you'll need the right grades to get the right college recruitment offer from the right company, or even to make it to graduation. Given up on the job market? You'll still need at least a 3.5 GPA to get into a good graduate school! The treadmill never stops.

Until the day your heart stops beating, people will ask you where you went to college. Your answer to that cocktail-party question will often determine what people think of you, what jobs you'll be considered for, whether or not you'll be promoted, whether your in-laws will approve of you. If you're lucky, your glowing personality, savvy wit and stunning achievements can overcome an education deficit ... if you're lucky. You won't even be safe from the cult of college when you die; your alma mater will rate a prominent mention in your obituary.

Not everyone buys into the The Promise. Dan Hassan, 31, found that dropping out of an Ivy League school after just a year hasn't prevented him from rising to a management position as a director at a Manhattan ad agency. "Very little that you learn in a liberal-arts education is ever used in the workplace," he says, but admits that his in-laws still nag him about finishing his degree. Dave Schulman, a twenty-six-year-old Duke graduate, told me, "College is complete bullshit. I owe $40,000 in student loans, and for what? So I can make $28,000 doing data entry?" Everyone's so busy saving money and getting good grades to go to school that they never ask the most fundamental question of all:

Is It Worth It?

Once you cut through all the hype, the financial and emotional sacrifices Americans make to send their kids to college just don't yield the payoff that many of them are looking for—financial security. Some people figure out they've been had after the fact. Allan Feuer, a twenty-seven-year-old freelance writer says, "I don't think it was worth it. I haven't seen a financial payoff." Feuer dropped out after three years and returned after a five-year hiatus: "I'm glad that I finished, but it's more for personal reasons."

Politicians from Labor Secretary Robert Reich to Federal Reserve Chairman Alan Greenspan blame our current economic problems—downsizing, increasing income disparity, the trade deficit—on the need for more education. Why are these people lying to us?

Jared Bernstein, an economist with the Economic Policy Institute, finds no correlation between education—even a technical education—and increased income. The best-educated, most computer-literate workers do no better in the seventeen-year-old climate of downsizing than anyone else. "We are seeing wage declines for the vast majority of workers," says Lawrence Mishel, Bernstein's partner at EPI. "Workers in every industry you look at, including those that are the most technologically advanced, have been losing ground."

Despite dazzling innovations like the Internet, Bernstein and Mishel say that new technology is entering the workplace at the same rate it always has. Contrary to popular perception, American workers haven't suddenly been rendered obsolete by sudden technological improvements. In fact, the United States already has the most highly educated work force in the world—25 percent of our workers are college graduates. Logically, we should be kicking the most ass in the global economy, but we're falling way behind. Blame our economic problems on the decline of unions, greedy CEOs, excessively free trade, a regressive tax structure, the absence of an electric fence along the Rio Grande, whatever you want. But it's not caused by insufficient education.

Certification, Not Education

We take for granted that a four-to-eight-year stint at a college or university is required to mold an American into a well-rounded, educated, *Homo modernis*. In ancient Greece and Rome, the relationship between students and teachers was personal, customized and intense. Today's colleges and universities are anything but.

First of all, American colleges are not a filter. Only about 50 four-year colleges reject more applicants than they accept. About 200 more admit 50 to 90 percent of all who apply. The rest let in anyone with a high school degree. One of the best-educated people I know is a UC San Diego dropout. He sneaks into the first day of classes at San Francisco State, grabs syllabi to snag the reading lists and reads the assigned books on his own. On the other hand, an acquaintance of mine with a B.A., M.A. and Ph.D. in physics from Columbia is a total moron who can't read a map. She knows nothing about history, politics, music or literature. In her case, a college degree does not equal an education.

At Columbia, I met countless student-idiots: kids on football scholarships who passed classes without attending them, children of wealthy alums, pre-meds who cheated on almost every exam they took. One time, when I was working as a math T.A., I tutored a calculus student in the "help room." We kept breaking down a question until I found the problem—she didn't know her multiplication tables.

Although America's universities are churning out a steady stream of brain-dead simpletons, our society relies almost exclusively on college credentials as the central determining factor of social status and employment opportunities. "A college degree is a signal to employers that you can do what people tell you to do for four years," Patrick Barkey, Ball State University's Director of Business Resources says.

If I were hiring for Microsoft, I'd be much more interested in related work experience than in a Stanford degree and a GPA. But it ain't that way.

College Tuition or Mutual Funds? Name the Better Investment

Our society devotes enormous resources to the quest for a college diploma. The United States is the only industrialized country that relies on individuals to foot most of the bill for higher education.

At any given time, roughly 8 million full-time students each pay an average of $19,000 per year in tuition and board fees—a total of $152 billion. This is equal to more than half of the federal budget deficit. During the '80s, health care prices rose 110 percent, an increase that sparked the current health care fracas. Meanwhile, the cost of attending college rose 109 percent for public schools, and 146 percent for private schools, but no one's panicking. They're just writing out checks.

As with most things that Americans buy but can't afford, they borrow the money. They take out $19 billion per year in guaranteed student loans. "The shift in emphasis of federal student aid from grants to loans threatens to create a generation of debtors," says American Council on

Education president Robert H. Atwell. Actually, it's already happened—in the late '80s, 23 percent of student loan borrowers defaulted.

And the program is only getting bigger. In 1992, Congress removed the ceiling from a program that allows parents to borrow up to the total cost of four years tuition and created a new, unsubsidized loan option that permits undergraduates to borrow up to $10,000 annually—without considering financial need. Rates are higher, too—up to 13 or 14 percent from the old 9 percent.

It's More Than Just Coed Dorms: The Financial Advantages of College

If, like most Americans, you consider a college education as a certification process—a means to a high-paying job—there are reasons to take out big loans to pay that bill (tuition, books, housing, food and other expenses typically total $25,000 a year for private four-year colleges and $15,000 for public institutions):

You're less likely to be unemployed
In 1993, 3 percent of college graduates were on welfare, compared to 8 percent of the mere high-school grads. (No one seems to keep track of college drop-outs.)

You'll make more money
Young men with college degrees in 1993 earned a median income of $35,000, compared to $23,000 for those with high-school diplomas. The difference shrinks to $27,000 for women with degrees and $18,000 for those without.

You'll make more money over time
In the recent past, those who have completed more education are not only likely to earn more, but also more likely to earn much more as they get older. Nationally, B.A. and B.S. holders can expect lifetime earnings of $1.4 million (in 1992 dollars). High school graduates will receive career earnings of only $800,000.

More degrees means more money!
Masters degree holders earn an average of $1.6 million over their lifetimes, and doctorates chalk up $2.1 million.

There's no doubt that our society rewards those brave souls who have met Milton, Thucydides and Einstein on the academic fields of battle. For one thing, your old college pals can hook you up with good jobs later in life. But you liberal-arts majors won't share in the spoils. The degree differential pays off almost exclusively to those who go the professional route—particularly in engineering and medicine.

A year after graduation, members of the Class of 1990 earned an average of $23,600, compared with $21,000 for high school graduates five years after commencement. But humanities majors earned only $19,200—less than workers of the same age without any college education. Biology majors didn't see a dime of payoff for passing those brutal organic chemistry exams—they earned $21,100. The winners were the 20 percent of students who majored in health care ($31,500), engineering ($30,900) and math, physics and computer science ($27,200).

That $600,000 difference in lifetime earnings between B.A. and high school grads evaporates when you focus on liberal-arts majors.

Unless you're planning to become a doctor, engineer or programmer, there is little financial inducement for attending an American college or university. The 80 percent of college students who are liberal-arts majors are getting screwed—or screwing themselves. And if you're majoring in something like art history...

It gets worse. In 1991, the last year for which information was available, unemployment for liberal-arts majors exceeded the national jobless rate of 6.2 percent. Those irritating health care majors had a low 1.0 percent jobless rate, engineers 3.2 percent and computer scientists 5.1 percent. On the other hand, 6.7 percent of psychology majors spent their afternoon watching "Ricki Lake." History majors were the kings of the dole at 8.2 percent. Hey Mom! Guess what I finally majored in?

College and Education: Are They Related?

My alma mater is very proud of its "core curriculum," which is a long list of required classes that every student must complete to graduate regardless of his or her major. Every Columbia student is required to demonstrate a well-rounded knowledge of all of the liberal arts. Molecular cellular biologists read de Beauvoir, art history buffs memorize arpeggios and future French lit professors struggle through two years of calculus.

In some ways, I benefited from Columbia's approach to higher education. Although I hated spending time and money on classes I didn't choose (despite being fluent in French, I had to take it to fulfill the foreign language requirement), I would never have learned about the architectural significance of the Seagram Building, John Donne or Soviet innovations in astronomy if they hadn't been shoved down my throat. As Dan Hassan says, "The primary advantage of college is that you learn how to look for what you want to learn." But that could be taught in a year or less.

On the other hand, most of school is a waste of time. For full-time students, classes take up perhaps fifteen hours a week. If they're diligent, they may study and work on assignments perhaps another fifteen hours. The rest is down time. I fondly recall numerous naps, soap operas on TV, marathon sex sessions and learning about drugs from my friends. Not that sex and TV and sleeping are bad or anything, but should we spend four years of our lives screwing and sleeping?

Arguably, most classes are worthless too. Many are rehashes of topics you already studied in high school; others move too slowly to offer an intellectual challenge. Still others are taught by inept graduate students or professors with no interest in teaching. Few classes are devoted to intellectual exploration or problem-solving. English lit students parrot what they suspect their professors want to hear: "I'm really happy you assigned this book..." Chemistry professors jot formulas on the chalk-board; students are so busy copying them into their notebooks that they don't have time to think about what they mean. The real work will occur at night when they try to unravel the stuff on their own. Grades are capricious and therefore worthless. When I returned to Columbia I discovered that uttering the following statement to my professor vastly improved my chances of landing an A: "I'm an A student. Could you tell me what I need to do in your class to get an A?" It worked—I went from a 2.4 to a 3.8 GPA in my second incarnation.

Worst of all, most college students learn to regurgitate information rather than think for themselves. They take notes as their professors blather on and on, but rarely question them out of fear of getting low grades. They read books outside class, then they come in to be told what they mean. They've been programmed for employment.

In an ideal world, education would be customized to the needs and desires of every student. In reality, college students work through codi-fied curricula that fit a school's lowest common denominator. This rote regurgitation that passes for thought is excellent training for working as a corporate drone, but it's not an education.

You're Gonna Pay: The Costs of a College Education

You're 17 years old. Your decision to head off to college—rather than a first job—is going to cost you a hell of a lot more money than mere tuition. Sure, tuition is a bitch. You'll pay a school like Bryn Mawr $30,000 a year in tuition, fees, housing and food, and that's before next year's tuition increase. Attending Ohio State will save you a substantial chunk of change—the home of the Buckeyes only costs about $15,000 per year.

Let's assume $28,000 to attend a private school and $16,000 for a public one. Both figures are rough averages of the total of tuition, fees, books, room, board and sundry expenses. So that's $100,000 and $60,000 over four years, right?

Not exactly. First, the average pupil takes a nice, leisurely pace to earn that B.A. or B.S. Only 43 percent of college students finish in four years or less. Another 23 percent need five years and yet another 9 percent take six. Forget the wankers—25 percent to be exact—who need even longer than six years to get their bachelor's degree. Maybe they're so busy working to pay tuition that they keep failing all their classes. In any event, five years is typical, so tuition et al. totals $125,000 and $75,000 for private and public, respectively.

Then there's lost income. That's right—instead of arguing over keg duty at the Beta house, you could be out earning a living. If you're a typical high-school grad, you would have earned $20,000 a year, so that's $100,000 in lost income.

If you go to a private school, you're out $240,000. If you opted for a public school, you've lost $190,000.

The Gift That Keeps on Giving: Student Loans

Student loan rates currently range between 9 and 14 percent. Because loan interest is compounded exponentially (you pay interest on interest on interest), at these rates you'll eventually repay more than three times as much as you borrowed. At 9 percent, you make $8,000 in payments to repay a $2,500 student loan.

The standard repayment period is ten years. A typical debt burden for a graduate of a moderately priced institution is $20,000. Unless you default, you'll send in $500 a month until you're out $60,000.

The student loan system destroys Americans under 32 years of age both financially and emotionally. You'll never qualify for a home mortgage as long as you've got the Student Loan Marketing Association chasing you down every month. This works out well because you probably can't afford a house anyway. Because of my own crushing debt burden—once $32,000, accruing $3,400 a year in interest—numerous career options were ruled out. I couldn't intern, join the Peace Corps, work in publishing or music, volunteer at a soup kitchen or work on a political campaign. Money-grubbing is your only choice when you're a slave to your loan coupon book. People who have to take out loans are relegated to whatever stupid job will pay their bills, defeating the purpose of getting a degree in the first place. Four years of English lit to become a PR whore? Four years of history to file loan applications? Why?

In an economy in which high-paying entry-level jobs are rare, even forgoing idealism isn't a simple solution. You won't even get a car loan if you default on a student loan. Crushed by college debts, a lot of college grads consider personal bankruptcy, but student loans are "grandfathered debt," meaning you have to repay them even if you file Chapter 11.

Pulling Your Strings: The Secret Life of an Admissions Officer

I've seen the Rubik's Cube of college education from virtually every possible point-of-view—applicant, problem student, honor student—but my perspective wouldn't be complete without the other side of the process. After I finally graduated with a bachelor's degree in 1991, I worked for two and a half years in an undergraduate admissions office at Columbia. I handled hundreds of admissions and financial aid applications, proctored and graded entrance exams. I saw the application process from a person's first request for a catalog to their first registration for class.

What I saw made me wonder why employers are so ready to rely on a college degree as an indication of ability. Admissions and financial aid in particular were subject to a nasty witch's brew of nepotism and politically correct maneuvering. The school's highest need-based scholarship ($7,500 a year) of 1993 - 94 went to a woman whose annual income was $36,000—in interest earnings from investments. She got it because she licked the dean's ass, which I suppose was good training for life in the workplace. The dean justified it because the student was a woman. Meanwhile, we turned away poor kids from the Bronx because they couldn't pay their tuition.

Admissions was no different. First, as at most universities, there aren't any admissions committees. Applications are divvied among the admissions officers, who make 99 percent of acceptance and rejection decisions individually. Most students' fate are decided based on their GPAs and test scores, in that order. In marginal cases (at Columbia, a GPA of 2.5 to 3.0), extracurricular activities come into play, but it's rare. Affirmative action policies are formalized. Admissions officers multiply test scores by factors based on your race, further muddling an already dubious process (for example, a university might multiply GPAs with a formula like Caucasian=1, African-American=1.3, Hispanic American or South Islander=1.1).

Most of the educational bureaucrats who make the Big Decision are poorly paid, third-rate losers who are too untalented to do anything else. Because admissions officers receive low pay (around $28,000 to $34,000 at Columbia) and few chances for raises or promotions, the job attracts unambitious older slackers. They like the low workload and outstanding benefits of working inside Ivy walls—free gym, generous retirement plan, no dress code, access to attractive young students.

Atypically, my division was blessed by two admissions officers who were perceptive, amusing geniuses. The third, however, was an insufferable, cheesy, moronic hardass. Aware of her predilection for arbitrarily rejecting people, we *üntermenschen* gave her all the admissions applications of students whom we didn't like. If we had it in for someone, we could misplace their file until it was too late for a decision to be made for that term. Alternatively, we greased the skids for our friends. We'd go to the dean and give her the old "his grades don't reflect his abilities" speech, or supply our pal with essay tips. This often made a big difference.

Even the lowliest clerk (I was an office assistant) affects admissions decisions. If someone gave me a lot of shit over the phone, I'd mark them a "20" (do not admit/pain-in-the-ass) or "19" (insane). Their application wouldn't make it past my file drawer. A lot of applicants are transfer students with several transcripts from various colleges, often of varying quality. If I liked someone, I could pull their unfavorable transcript until after they'd gotten admitted, then drop it back into the file so they'd still get their transfer credits.

If you didn't get into the school of your choice, don't worry about it. The decision process is so screwed up that admissions and rejections don't say anything useful about the people getting admitted and rejected. American colleges turn out hundreds of thousands of total idiots every year, and millions of geniuses are working the night shift at Arco. Truly educated people learn on their own—at school, at home, on the bus. Everyone else is just going through the motions. It's too bad your next potential employer doesn't know this.

The Prestige Differential

Assuming that you've decided to pursue an undergraduate degree, where should you go? Differences in the quality of education are subtle. Professors at Dayton, Ohio's Wright State University are just as likely to have earned their doctorates at Yale as are professors at Yale itself, assuming that that makes them better teachers. At state universities, instructors tend to be less accessible due to large class sizes, especially for your first two years. However, the big-name schools' small class sizes tend to get canceled out by the pressure on professors to publish and do research. By your junior year, it's essentially the same deal, whether you attend City College or Cornell.

To be sure, attending a "prestigious" school has its advantages. Many of your classmates will be rich, influential fucks. Conceivably, these people could help you later on. Among my classmates at Columbia were a Moroccan princess, Martha Stewart's daughter, Dan Rather, Jr., and a rock star's live-in girlfriend. I tutored the princess in calculus, attended Dan's well-funded parties and spied Martha's tax deduction in the cafeteria now and then. Making it to Harvard won't grant you acceptance to the American aristocracy, but it will put you on a first-name basis with it.

On the other hand, opting for a lower-cost state school will save you about $40,000, which makes up for the reduced snob appeal. If you're willing to seek it out, you can get just as good an education at Eastern Kentucky State University as anywhere else.

Attending a not-quite-Ivy institution like NYU or Amherst offers the worst of both worlds. You'll wallow in rush weeks, pep rallies and date rapes, and still shell out $25,000 a year for a degree that won't even raise an eyebrow at HR offices of a snotty law firm.

Life Deferral Alternatives: Graduate School

Clearly you must go to law or medical school if you want to become a lawyer or doctor. (In many states, including California, you don't have to have a law degree to practice law—you only have to pass the bar. But firms won't hire you without a law degree.) But most people who go to graduate school do so to escape having to look for a job. "There aren't any good jobs," a friend told me a few years ago about her decision to apply to grad school in Asian Studies. "And my student loans will be deferred while I'm in grad school!"

"Yeah, but what will you do when you finish?" I asked. "You'll still owe the loans from undergrad, plus your new loans for grad school."

She shot me an exasperated special-ed-teacher-staring-at-her-idiots look. "Then I'll go for my doctorate. Obviously. Duh!" This philosophy works well for people with deep pockets. For everyone else, it's a road to ruin, or to a life as an assistant professor. These poor people, having entered college unsuspectingly at age eighteen, will spend the rest of their lives trapped in academic oblivion. These pathetic souls will never have lived real lives, but will delude themselves into thinking they made a lifestyle decision. In fact, they never made any decision at all—they were hoodwinked by the higher education swindle.

College and the Winner-Take-All Phenomenon

Robert Frank and Philip Cook argue in their book *The Winner-Take-All Society*, that "winner-take-all" markets, where more and more people compete for fewer and fewer prizes, add up to enormous differences in economic rewards for negligible differences in performance. For instance, an Olympic silver medal winner is very nearly as good an athlete as a gold medalist, but doesn't receive nearly the same amount in endorsements and prestige. Frank and Cook found that although degree holders tend to earn more money than non-degree holders, education only accounts for 15 percent in the difference of wages. "Human capital"— people's personalities, abilities, physical appearance and intelligence— account for the vast majority of the variance in wages and personal success.

The use of college degrees to screen applicants for jobs and petitioners for marriage leads to social and economic instability by discouraging and disenfranchising non-degree holders. Given how secondary schools, the admissions process, financial concerns and academic curves randomly prevent countless brilliant Americans from obtaining college degrees, it's insane to rely on them as a qualifier.

There is no proof that holding a degree from an accredited educational institution makes you a smart person, yet that's a central assumption in our society. So people chase more degrees. And yet a bachelor's degree is now worth what a high school degree was a few decades ago. In most companies you need a master's to be considered for a middle-management job. Soon you'll need a doctorate. As degrees become devalued, the only winners are university trustees, who invest their skyrocketing endowments in the financial markets so they can afford to pay themselves six-digit salaries.

Why play along? If you really need a cumbersome bureaucracy to teach you what they want to teach you because you're too unimaginative to learn on your own, and the idea of a four-year vacation from life appeals to you, start rounding up recommendation letters and application fees.

Otherwise, bear in mind that The Promise, whatever its merits during the '50s and '60s, is a quaint anachronism dating to an unwritten social contract that has long since been revoked. Inexplicably, our politicians and pundits are trying to turn the U.S. into France, where Sorbonne graduates drive taxis and collect unemployment. Trained for an elite without openings, these people can't find it within themselves to do what they want— start their own business, write books, write software, sell stuff on the street—whatever it takes to survive in a world without guarantees. They bought into the notion that a college degree is everything. They expected to coast through life after graduation, so they focused all their energies into the day when they'd walk down a long aisle in alphabetical order and collect a diploma. They lived for that moment, and once it passed, their lives were over. They'd wasted years of their lives and lost infinite opportunities.

At least they didn't pay for the privilege. ▪

HEIDI POLLOCK

The Sudden, Unsavory Ubiquity of Faux Caesar Salad

Caesar salad is everywhere and in its ubiquity our doom is writ. Not that it's a bad salad, mind you. Crisp, green lettuce, jaunty croutons, tangy sauce—in and of itself it's charming culinary delight and a graceful accompaniment to any meal and has long been one of my favorite treats. Once it even saved a relationship of mine. My boyfriend and I spent five weeks driving across the country, during which we had a wide variety of mechanical work done on our 1977 Cadillac. Two weeks into the deep South, Caesar salad saved the day. Now, I am not a healthy eater by any-one's standards, but fourteen days in a region which considers french fries to be a vegetable was more than I could take. As we waited on the new brake line, any number of unmentionable atrocities which I was certain to inflict upon my boyfriend were forestalled by my fortuitous con-sumption of fresh, leafy greens in Caesar salad form courtesy of Denny's. I was too busy eating to tear into that bastard. I tell you this only that you may understand my current fear of widely accessible Caesar salad is not merely an irrational whimsy.

I do not think I have been to a non-Chinese restaurant in the last two years which has not had Ceasar salad on its menu. I'm fairly sure that every time I eat out with a party of four or more at least one person orders this particular dish. Within a three block radius of my house alone there are at least four separate purveyors of Caesar salad and I do not, mind you, live in a tony neighborhood. As if I am not already deluged by this item, even my favorite coffee stand confronts me every morning with literally dozens of Ceasar salads all lined up in pert plastic containers ready for the devouring needs of an anonymous lunch mob. Frankly, I can't remember when I had my first inkling of Ceasar salad's omnipresence but I clearly recall being seized by an inexplicable panic when I realized that this onetime salad delicacy was being served to billions by none other than the McDonald's Food Corporation.

Formerly exotic foods appear seemingly from nowhere on a fairly regular basis. Remember pine nuts? It's a distant recollection for me too, but they did appear almost overnight to colonize salads, pastas, desserts and the salted offerings of better bar snacks everywhere. And who can forget the advent of the sundried tomato? Today you can't even go into a humble bagel shop without being confronted by the odd cultural aberration sold over-the-counter as "sundried tomato schmear." As if by magic, the most unlikely foods leap suddenly into our culinary awareness and run amok. Bananas did so nearly a century ago and I can hear the fiddle playing now as ginger challenges Caesar salad for the food trend throne.

It's almost beyond imagining that you can get anywhere in this world without advertising, but it's not as if there's a Caesar Salad Chefs Association adamantly pushing their drippy greens into our faces at halftime. Although what causes one food to attain supremacy over another is one of life's great mysteries, the fact that odd and unfamiliar forms of sustenance consistently consume the public imagination can be traced back to our most primal fears. Our fear of the Other is easily defeated as we consume that which is foreign and remake it in our form. Fear of loneliness is forgotten as we all eat the identical thing and pretend to have something in common. We deny our fear of the future by trying something new, thinking that it will demonstrate our ability to adapt and evolve. Unfortunately the problem inherent in Caesar salad's trendiness has nothing to do with its origin in our fears. Ceasar salad is unique amongst food trends in that what lies at the heart of its current popularity and accessibility is deceit. Fear is understandable and forgivable, but deceit is deadly. The Caesar salad of popularity is not in fact real Caesar salad. Real Caesar salad requires above all the three following ingredients: romaine lettuce, anchovies and raw egg. Done in by salmonella and squeamishness, only the most circumspect and unlawful restaurants still craft their Caesars with raw egg. Anchovies, something of a farce to begin with, harkening back as they do to the eating of live goldfish and the French, can still be found in chic restaurants despite the fact that most people are too plebeian to actually enjoy them. And while an absence of egg and anchovies is an unpleasant reality, the McDonald's Caesar is the ultimate abomination, lacking even the fundamental pillars of romaine lettuce. The tragic truth is that Caesar salad as served by the vast majority of establishments is entirely inauthentic. Inauthenticity and the degradation of the esthetic are commonplace in this historical epoch and hardly seems worth mentioning were it not for the fact that behind the beguiling facade of these deceitful salad imposters lurks a much darker truth. The proliferation of qualitatively diverse "Caesar" salads is part of a deadly phenomenon which in Kierkegaardian terms is known as leveling. Kierkegaard was obsessed by the dissolution of qualitative distinction and in his 1846 essay "The Present Age," he links the indecisive, passionless, ambivalent, uncommitted nature of his generational peers to their lack of qualitative differentiating power. It seems as if he is speaking directly to our culture when he states that "an age without passion has no values, and everything is transformed into representational ideas." One cannot doubt that qualitative distinction has been discarded when the collective cultural voice places a garden fresh salad replete with a still-warm-from-the-chicken raw egg in the same linguistic category as the oil-slimed iceberg pot found at the feet of the golden arches. Partaking of the Platonic ideal to differing degrees, these two forms of Caesar salad have nothing in common except a name. When we reference them both with the identical term we drag down the better salad to the level of the bad salad, abandoning our values along with our senses.

McDonald's "Caesar salad" is not a Caesar salad; it is merely the idea of a Ceasar salad, an empty signifier to that which once had specific qualities, relevance and import. When you abandon the raw egg, the primordial fish, the substantial lettuce, you are left not merely with a disgusting, tasteless salad but with the end of participatory culture, ethical deliberation, and impassioned existence. One salad is as good as the next, one president is a bad as the next, all choices are equal, all decisions meaningless. Participation in quality culture cannot be purchased no matter what the ads say. An imposter Caesar may allude to a rich and worthwhile life but this allusion is an illusion: You are no closer to living the good life than the Gauls were. ■

Shiny Adidas Tracksuits and the Death of Camp

take something and exagerate it

so silly that its cool.

I got my first Adidas tracksuit in 1980, sixth grade: shiny cream nylon, with the triple stripes in brown. Because I was fat, none of the suits at the store fit me at both waist and leg; I got one several sizes too large, with legs like stilted clown pants, and my mother hemmed them up. The first day I wore the suit to school a seagull in the lunchtime sky let drop a deposit that stretched in stark white and gray, flecked in black and redly threaded, from my right shoulder down nearly to my waist.

The stain never did come out entirely—that slippery fabric has an amazing ability to retain foreign pigment of any kind—but I wore the tracksuit anyway. My mother had prudently left several inches of pant-leg curled under at the cuff, allowing for alterations as I grew, and when the tracksuit finally disappeared from my closet, an event memory marks in the latter part of 1982, its knees and ass were rubbed pebbly from slides across the gymnasium floor, and the jacket had been permanently pink polka-dotted in the course of a slingshot berry fight with my stepbrothers.

Susan Sontag set out presciently to define "Camp" sensibility in an essay in 1964. It consists of a brief introduction and 58 observations, attempts to definitively pin down an inherently slippery term. The first and last of these are sufficient to provide a rhetorical base for my argument: "1. To start very generally: Camp is a certain mode of aestheticism. It is one way of seeing the world as an aesthetic phenomenon. That way, the way of Camp, is not in terms of beauty, but in terms of the degree of artifice, of stylization. 58. The ultimate Camp statement: it's good because it's awful … Of course one can't always say that. Only under certain conditions, those which I've tried to sketch out in these notes."

The Camp sensibility, which at the time of Sontag's writing was the sensibility of the cultural elite (whom she defines in Observation 50 as, "an improvised self-elected class, mainly homosexuals, who constitute themselves as aristocrats of taste"), is now the prevailing sensibility. Unfortunately the caveat at the end of Observation 58 is no longer observed, and what might have been the last refuge of good taste has been flooded and permanently polluted by the rushing tide of culture. Demonstrating this comprehensively is a task much larger than space allows, so I will seek to do it by metonymy, tracing the disintegration of taste, in fact the obsolescence of the very concept, "taste," by following the changing types of value we have placed on a single unit of cultural currency, the Adidas tracksuit.

Adidas tracksuits are designed by Germans; therefore we must discard their intended meaning altogether. Contemporary European or Canadian attempts at spiffiness are generally authentic Camp (which depends upon a divide between intent and result). But the popularity of Adidas tracksuits in America in the early 1980s was not Camp. By sheer luck, German designers had come up with an outfit that met our collective concept of modernity: sleek, shiny, tight. We liked Adidas tracksuits innocently. Now we feel differently about them.

Run-DMC wore Adidas tracksuits in 1984. Sontag divides the canon of Camp into two mutually exclusive subgroups: "naive" Camp (works earnestly intended) and "deliberate" Camp (works intended for a sophisticated audience, already privy to the joys of Camp sensibility). Tracksuits on rap artists in the early and mid-'80s can be construed as earnestly intended: they reinforced the connection those artists must have felt with African-American athletes, who had already achieved the cultural ascendancy to which rap artists aspired; and also tracksuits represented a type of snazzy leisure clothing which emphasized the prerogative to dress down, rather than the superannuated notion of dressing up as a privilege.

But related issues, issues not related to the tracksuits, but to Camp, intervene, calling that analysis into question: specifically, gold and Aerosmith.

My admittedly unconsidered view on whether Run-DMC were serious about the gold is, "Sort of." Many other people were quite serious, and killed each other on the street for it, as well as for fashionable shoes, but the Run-DMC aesthetic had as one of its primary components the Camp sensibility: consider also the bowlers and canes, borrowed either from an extremely outmoded, and therefore comic (and Camp) form of dandyism, or else from *A Clockwork Orange*, Kubrick's crucial contribution to the Camp canon.

As for Aerosmith: obviously a monolithic topic in itself. The initial Aero-sthetic was a version of '70s Rolling Stones decadence (in itself predicated upon Camp, so we're on shifty ground), but I think Steven Tyler et al. may be members of the genuinely retarded minority of culture producers whose earnest works comprise the most sacred Camp: they're "it," but they have no idea what "it" is. In this complicated fashion Aerosmith, who to my knowledge do not wear Adidas tracksuits, were and remain representative of the central problem of American cultural production today: we don't know when we're camping and when we're not. Run-DMC, in sampling the guitar from "Walk This Way," may have been obliquely mocking Aerosmith (and thereby deliberately camping). Then again, that's a pretty fantastic guitar lick; and Tyler is an iconic presence in American rock irrespective of his relation to Camp. So were Run-DMC camping with the tracksuits? No, but yes: as with the gold, an element of in-joke clowning was in shimmery evidence. The dissolution of Sontag's Manichaean divider between naive and deliberate Camp was underway (and incidentally, further evidence was provided for the thesis set forth nearly half a century ago by Ellison and Murray, that American culture is African-American culture, and vice versa).

The Beastie Boys, close on the heels of Run-DMC, are at once farther from their sources and more nakedly vulnerable to deconstruction. Before the recording of *License to Ill* they were a pimply hardcore band. As such they had relation to Camp, but not to Adidas tracksuits, so we will treat the Beastie aesthetic as it was posited at the time of *License to Ill*, and thereafter—tracksuits were in evidence from the release of that album onward. The function of the tracksuit in the Beastie aesthetic is deliberate Camp, of course—*License to Ill* was to rap albums what *This Is Spinal Tap* had been to rockumentaries. But the nature of the endeavor was retroactively influenced by two factors not present in the *This Is Spinal Tap* phenomenon, which were monumental (as opposed to widespread cult) success, and the youth of the performers themselves. Mike D, Ad-Rock, and MCA were in their middle teens at the time, and though they possessed a sophisticated humor and better rhythmic sense than the rest of us, they were no more capable of naming their sensibility than we were. Their explosive success effectively forced them to take an aesthetic stand, reductively, "Tracksuit." Sontag muses in her introduction that Camp is "unmistakably modern, a variant of sophistication but hardly identical with it." If millions of teenagers in the late '80s were capable of responding to *License to Ill*—which they (we) were—then at the time of our earliest exercise of independent taste, we were operating from a Camp sensibility. We leapt over conventional sophistication entirely, and landed in its farthest lagoon. That is not to say that the album was an insignificant effort, creatively or artistically—au contraire.

That single album, more than any other, defined the aesthetic which is ours: We knew, in our deep hearts, that it sucked. But we liked it. The same question applied to Run-DMC's mobilization of tracksuits (Were they camping?) can be applied to the Beastie Boys' mobilization of same, but with declining effect. The answer in this instance is neither Yes nor No, nor Sort of. It is, "What?"

In 1992 I bought another Adidas tracksuit. This one was powder blue and silver, but with the sweet old shine and stretch. I had just graduated from college, and it seemed the exact outfit I needed to express the relation I took to my past: distance, disdain for the self I had been (a fat boy with birdshit on him), but also a fondness for that self which would have been impossible any earlier. Sontag addresses this aspect of the Camp sensibility in Observation 31, as follows: "... It's not a love of the old as such. It's simply that the process of aging or deterioration provides the necessary detachment—or arouses a necessary sympathy." I had also noticed that among the sartorially attuned, Adidas tracksuits (which had never disappeared entirely) were enjoying a subtle renaissance. I am not overtly modish; that the joke component of my purchase might be underscored (as well as to prevent the hem from snagging in my bicycle chain), I cut off the pants around the knee.

Predictably, I received many compliments on my suit as well as a validating measure of derision from the uninformed, and was quite pleased with myself.

Around that time a friend of mine was an assistant to Kal Ruttenstein, the arbiter of chic at Bloomingdale's. My friend told me that as a birthday gift she and the other assistants had given Mr. Ruttenstein a black Adidas tracksuit, an outfit he wore happily about the office, smoking his narrow cigarettes through a tapered amber holder. I wasn't quite sure what to make of this information. Did it mean that I was independently fighting the same honorable battle of taste as fashion's foremost phalanx? Or did it mean something else altogether? I visited Manhattan to find out.

I found a store in the West Village with nothing but Adidas clothing, and the girls were all wearing those halters and long dresses which you remember from that year: skin tight and triple-striped. Obviously it was time to retire my tracksuit. I did so, but with a queasy feeling that I hadn't quite grasped the situation. Indeed I had not, though it took some time to realize exactly what I'd missed.

The 56 observations Sontag lovingly ticked off between the first and the last have evaporated as conditions for celebrating the odious. So have the examples of Camp—Tiffany lamps, Flash Gordon comics, "Swan Lake"—that she cited at the time. Her last observation, "The ultimate Camp statement: it's good because it's awful," is the only one that continues to operate, and even that has been reduced to the fond, "That sucks!" It's not the particular objects constituting Camp that matter, but the mode of appreciation we bring to them. And now that we all have access to that mode, it is cheap, as banal as the objects upon which it was originally turned.

A fatter target than the tracksuit, obviously, is that dull undying phenomenon, the Spelling television shows. Clearly, the shows are bad—that is not in question. I feel safe in estimating that there are three or four thousand genuine morons who appreciate the shows without the interpretive framework of Camp, but those people are an insignificant portion of the Nielsen ratings, and also unlikely to read this article, so we can forget them. I'm talking to you. Most of all I am talking to those of you who claim to enjoy the shows genuinely, that you really, really like them, or like one more than the other. Burying your head in the sand of Camp sensibility is a logical move for a cultural ostrich, but don't imagine that it's anything else. The same goes for interest in drag, aliens, Betty Page, etc., or the collection of lame artifacts, such as limited edition cereal boxes. It's a big bore now, and sadly the more kitschily available (e.g., N.K.O.T.B.) or deliberately arcane (medical treatises on schizophrenic scatophagy) the interest, the bigger the bore.

A measure of personal disappointment attends these realizations, of course, and it's more than disappointing that I can't wear my Adidas tracksuit anymore. I'm disgusted by my own mode of enjoyment, but it's quite difficult to imagine a way back to a more innocent type, pleasure in things simply because they are good.

Last night I went out to get some dinner, and in a not uncharacteristically creepy move I engaged a girl who looked about sixteen in conversation. She was wearing an Adidas jacket, hooded, silver and maroon. I explained that I was writing a piece on Adidas tracksuits—that I got my first one around the time she was born—and asked her what she meant by the ensemble. She didn't understand. Well, I said, do you like it because it's inherently good, or because it sucks? She gave me the look I probably deserved, and rejoined her companions at their table. ■

November, 1996

CHRIS HARRIS

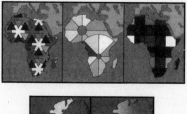

Design Intervention

Solving the world's problems with style

Quit kidding yourself: Looks are everything. Supermodels who can't act, sing or paint get paid fortunes for their acting, singing and painting. Companies blow millions testing product names like 'Olestra.' We haven't had a bald president for forty years. "And yet..." you murmur. Ah, no doubt you're thinking the same thing anyone would: "And yet... national borders pay no attention to image at all!"

So very true. Jagged boundaries, confusing shapes, and unfortunate names like "Greenland" pepper the globe. If nations were people— imagine Canada as your jolly drinking buddy, or Iran and Iraq as two bratty kids who should be kept away from sugar products—they'd be incorrigible slobs. Since image is so important to us, this blatant lack of regard for image—rather than poverty, war, oppression, etc.—must be the true source of much of the world's current malaise.

And why not? World maps are so common in this age, the simple act of constantly viewing these monstrosities—for example, some intestine-shaped country like Panama, or the massive spermatozoa we call Norway—has likely caused untold devastation worldwide. Consider the following scenario: *Little Johnny—or Johann, or Omar, or*

Chou—*sits in geography class, trying to memorize the countries. He looks at South America. Does Chile resemble a chile? No, it resembles a string bean. Frustrated, the child drops out of school and joins a neo-fascist terrorist organization.* A bit simplistic, perhaps, but be certain that the extent of damage our current system has inflicted cannot be overdramatized.

This must change. It's time to retire our politicians and economists and militarists and diplomats from the international arena and, knowing that they could hardly be less successful, let *graphic designers* try their hand at world politics.

Coincidentally, I happen to be a graphic designer. For the past six months I have labored over the international map, finding that even the most basic application of design theory to our nations' borders can markedly improve the global situation. Following I outline a three-phase plan to remodel the world.

Phase I: Current Disputes

First, a global makeover can provide immediate, effective and—yes!—pleasing-to-the-eye solutions to most of the world's current major conflicts. Consider the following examples:

Israel: The Homely Homeland

From an artist's perspective, the biggest problem in the Mideast is not the continued radicalism of extremists, or the status of Jerusalem, but the fact that Israel looks like a big, ugly fishhook. Hell, this was a *planned country*, and I've seen Rorschach tests with better layouts. However, if one "filled in" that ugly gap—with, oh, let's say, the West Bank—and likewise reattached that missing Gaza Strip, then Israel might look alluring, even sexy. And this nation's shapely neck benefits not at all from the protruding "Goiter Heights;" let it fall to Syria.

One need not have watched many late-night infomercials to understand the power of self-esteem. When residents—Jews and Palestinians alike—discover that their ugly duckling region has been transformed into Cinderella, the resulting *détente* will be nothing short of miraculous.

Northern Ireland: Peace, Gradually

Now, let us turn our aesthetic eye to Ireland—a quaint island nation, charming and rustic and backwoodsy and—ack!—Great Britain drips into its northeast corner! This is blatant sloppiness, reminiscent of a preschooler's coloring outside the lines.

But we cannot simply cede the whole area to Ireland; distinct boundaries cause trouble in areas of mixed loyalty—not to mention being harsh on the eye. Fortunately, we have another option: the gradient fill. Starting with 100 percent United Kingdom territory in the northeast corner, gradually blend in Irish sovereignty as one moves out radially so that Belfast is two-thirds the former and a third the latter, and one reaches full Irish rule somewhere around Monaghan. And the soft, gentle touch of fuzzy borders may also provide a solution to the ongoing Kashmir debate between India and Pakistan.

The Country Formerly Known As Yugoslavia

No doubt the greatest challenge to the power of the paintbrush lies in the former expanse of Yugoslavia. Death, discord and a general lack of manners persist across this region. Old-style politics and line-drawing have succeeded only in reaching a fragile compromise which is unsatisfactory for everyone. Equally horrifying, Croatia's borders stretch like a geriatric Pac-Man around a decomposed Bosnia-Herzegovina.

To most, the situation seems hopeless. But the fashion conscious eye recognizes just what this area needs: *polka dots*. Picture, against different background fills—Croatian in the Northwest, Bosnian Serb in the East, and so forth—lively circles of the other ethnicities' countries standing out cheerfully. Not only does each individual region (with some concession to a consistent pattern) get the nationality of its choice, but a fun, lighthearted feel is reinstilled across an area in desperate need of frivolity. Imagine how quickly tourism will pull these countries back to prosperity when families look at a world map and see the "happy clown countries" beckoning to them from afar.

Phase II: The Next Wave

Once these pressing crises are dealt with, the world can turn to correcting a number of geographic eyesores that undermine the entire globe's presentation.

For example, disconnected countries give the world a hurried, slapdash feel, like a magazine that's poorly laid out. To solve this, eliminate that broken-off wedge of Russia near Poland. Likewise for the similar part of Oman. And while we're at it, attach that Upper Peninsula to Wisconsin.

Applying this guideline, one might fear the loss of Alaska to our northern neighbor. But those who would worry about a new, resurgent Canada, fear not: Our primary goal, remember, is a beautiful world map. Canada, for reasons unclear, is always *pink* on world maps. Pink is a horrendous color, even for Canada. Alaska can never become part of Canada simply because it will increase that country's territory, and hence the overall pinkness of the globe. Better instead to grant Alaska full independence.

And maybe Quebec, just to be safe.

Going...Going...Ghana

One hundred and seventy-eight countries? Busy, busy, busy! One major task will be to clean out all the "dust bunny countries:" those redundant, cramped, and miniscule entities which serve no aesthetic purpose. To start, let's scrap Portugal entirely. And imagine how seldom Haiti will trouble us, once it's part of the new, improved Dominican Republic.

Malaysia, Swaziland, and Papua New Guinea will likewise no longer trouble geography students. You can say "later" to Lichtenstein, so long Singapore, and bye-bye Bangladesh. Does France stick too far into the Atlantic? Then perform a Brest reduction. Chop off the ends of Cuba so it looks more like a cigar. Give Kyrgyzstan some more shape, or at least some more vowels. Shake, shake, shake out Djibouti. Center Lesotho within South Africa. And—sorry, George—let Saddam have Kuwait.

Phase III: Macro-Reengineering

In the final phase I recommend totally renovating at least three of the world's larger areas. In Africa, we have a golden opportunity to once and for all throw out those antiquated, arbitrary colonial divisions with no respect for tribal boundaries, and replace them with a whole new set of arbitrary divisions with no respect for tribal boundaries. I believe a floral pattern of nations may suit this continent best, or perhaps a large paisley.

The other areas are Canada and Russia, two countries that could use some serious time on the StairMaster. I propose—contingent on their approval—their complete dismantlement, replacing them with a more dynamic montage. Imagine, in place of the former Soviet empire, a fifty-nation depiction of Picasso's "Guernica," stretching from Moscow to the Bering Sea. What a moving testimony this would be to the power of art!

Afterwards, only an occasional tweak here and there, or minor changes to fit the latest styles, would be necessary.

This global reworking may initially cause some concern, particularly in those areas where such quaint ideas as patriotism and self-determination still prevail over a sense of style. But the entire process can be accomplished smoothly and quickly as long as a good attitude and a touch of humor are maintained throughout. For example, what if Turkey really *was* shaped like a turkey? Or, with minimal adjustments, we redrew Germany into a beer mug? One mustn't forget that when drawing international borders, the key word should be *fun*.

In conclusion, I truly believe that these ideas represent nothing less than the world's greatest hope for solving its most difficult problems. Through their application, we will solve most territorial disputes, end war, increase happiness, support the arts, and probably solve the health-care crisis, although we're still working on those numbers.

Once its programs are in place, the United States of America Minus Alaska can then turn to solving some of its domestic problems in the same way. Our most glaring problem ("Hey, Rhode Island isn't an island at all!") can be quickly solved by switching it with Hawaii. Continuing on this glorious track, our descendants can then tackle the big questions, like: Is there any way to reattach that ungainly Baja strip? Or clean up Micronesia? Or does the ocean have to be blue—why not a deep burgundy? And why, for that matter, a sphere? ◼

May, 1996

Cool Like Me

(Are black people cooler than white people?)

I'm cool like this:

I read fashion magazines like they're warning labels telling me what not to do.

When I was a kid, Arthur Fonzarelli seemed like a garden-variety dork.

I got my own speed limit.

I come when I want to.

I maintain like an ice cube in the remote part of the freezer.

Cooler than a polar bear's toenails.

Cooler than the other side of the pillow.

Cool like me.

Know this while understanding that I am in essence a humble guy.

I'm the kinda nigga who's so cool that my downstairs neighbor bursts into hysterical tears whenever I ring her doorbell after dark. Because sometimes, but not always, I'm the kinda nigga she's afraid of. Three people live in that unit of the duplex, and the one we're talking about is a new immigrant who has chosen to live in our majority-black Los

Angeles neighborhood so that, I'm told, she can "learn about all American cultures." But her real experience of us is limited to the space between her Honda and her gate; thus, much of what she has to go on is the vibe of the surroundings and the images emanating from the television set that gives her living room a minty cathode glow. As such, I'm a cop-show menace and a shoe-commercial demigod—one of the rough boys from our 'hood and the living, breathing embodiment of hip hop flava. And if I can't fulfill the prevailing stereotype, the kids enroute to the nearby high school can. The woman is scared in a cool world. She smiles as I pass her way in the light of day, unloading groceries or schlepping my infant son up the stairs. But at night, when my face is visible through the window of her door, I'm lit only by the bulb that brightens her vestibule, and I, at once familiar and threatening, am just too much.

Thus, being cool has its drawbacks. With cool come assumptions and fears, expectations and intrigue. My neighbor wants to live near cool, to be exposed to cool, but she's not so sure about cool sharing her roof, having a key to the building, prowling around after dark. She'll learn better over the years, as she navigates the highways and byways of our American culture, but for now, what she fears is inimicably tied to what makes me so undeniably cool. During the day, she sees a black man; at night, what she sees in the shadow gliding across her patio is a nigga. I know there's a line, and I know where it is, and niggadom I can turn on and off like the lights. Black is all right, but nigga is cool, and I know the difference. It's this simple: I'm a nigga, and I'm cool. More like it, I'm cool because I'm a nigga. You can't have one without the other.

The question on the cover is a dumb one, and one that I imagine a lot of people will find offensive. In 1997 America, it's a pop-culture phenomenon, an intangible concept that plagues the minds of white people everywhere, especially those who know there's something to it but are too dumb to get it. But we know what we're talking about, right? We're talking about style and spirit and the innovations that those things spawn. It's on TV; it's in movies, sports and clothes and language and gestures and music. It's one part white fascination, one part white insecurity, and a few parts inescapable truth.

See, black cool is cool as we know it. I could name names—Michael Jordan and Chris Rock and MeShell N'degeocello and Will Smith and Allen Iverson and Charles Barkley and Snoop Doggy Dogg and Tupac Shakur and Mary J. Blige and Foxy Brown—but cool goes way back, much further than the superstars. Their antecedents go back past blaxploitation cinema, past Pam Grier, past Ike Turner to Muddy Waters, back to ghetto stars whose names you'll never know. Cool has a history, and cool has a meaning. We all know cool when we see it, and now, more than at any other time in American history, when mainstream America looks for cool we look to black culture. Black cool is imperialistic and ubiquitous.

And I should know. My being cool is not a matter of subjectivity or season. The way I am might one day run low in supply, but it won't disappear in any of our lifetimes. It's a matter of fact. At the Census Bureau, I'm classified as Cool-Ass American because I'm black. To be more specific, having lived as a nigga has made me cool. Let me explain.

Chris Rock jokes in his stand-up act that, in this era of the underclass being removed from W.E.B. DuBois' "talented tenth," there's a civil war going on between niggas and blacks. Once upon a time, little need existed for making the distinction between a nigga and a black— at least not in America, the place where niggas were invented. We were just about all slaves, so we were all niggers. Then we became free on paper yet oppressed still. Today, with as many as a third of us a generation or two removed from living poor (depending on who's counting), niggadom isn't innate in every black child born. But with their poverty rate still hovering at 33 percent, black people still got niggas in the family, even when they themselves aren't niggas. Folks who don't know niggas can watch them on TV, existing in worlds almost always distanced from blacks. Grant Hill is a black man; Allen Iverson is a nigga (for now). Oprah interviewing the celebrity du jour is a black woman; the woman being handcuffed on that reality show is a nigga. Negroes jumping around in commercials are black people; the ones flowing in rap videos are niggas. In one fascinating transformation, Will Smith went into Bel Air a nigga and came out a black. Definitely something in the rarefied air.

In my humble estimation, cool was born when the first plantation nigga figured out how to make animal innards—massa's garbage— taste good enough to eat. Hog maws and chitlins became good enough to cherish and long for wistfully. That inclination to make something out of nothing—to devise from being dumped on—and then to make that something special, articulated itself first in the work hymns that slaves sang in the field and then in the songs at the center of their secondhand worship. A mature version of the vibe would later reveal itself in the music made from cast-off Civil War marching-band instruments (jazz); physical exercise turned to spectacle by powerful, balletic enterprise (sports); and (my personal favorite) streetlife styling, from the pimp's silky handshake to the crack dealer's sag. In time, an amalgam of all of this and so much more would arrive in the form of hip hop culture. Cool is all about trying to make a dollar out of fifteen cents.

Cool derived from having to survive as far as can be imagined from the ideal of white culture, with little more than a spiritual dowry for support. It's about living on the cusp, on the periphery, diving for scraps. Essential to cool is being outside looking in. Others—Indians, women, gays—have been "othered," but until the past 15 percent of America's history, niggas in real terms have been treated by the country's majority as, at best, subhuman and, at worst, as an abomination. So in the days when they were still literally on the plantation—the original nigga neighborhood—they developed a coping device called cool, an elusive mellowing strategy designed to master time and space. Cool, the basic reason blacks remain in the American cultural mix, is an industry of style that everyone in the world can use. It's making something out of nothing, finding the essential soul while being essentially lost. It's the nigga metaphor. And the nigga metaphor is the genius of America.

Gradually over the course of this century, as there came to be a chasm of access between black people and niggas, so developed the elliptical nature of cool. The romantic and now-popular image of the pasty Caucasian who frequents a jazz club was exclusive. Cool, as a concept, was a privilege, not a promise—the reward to any white soul hardy enough to pierce the inner sanctum of black life and not only live to tell about it but also live to live for it. Slowly, various watered-down versions of this very specific strain of cool, black cool, became the primary means of defining American cool. Derived from music, the place where you can find the history of my people, it was blues, jazz, R&B, and then soul. And, though tasted in moderation by a slight slice of white America, it wasn't until Elvis, the hip-shaking Prometheus, that cool was brought down from Olympus (or Tupelo, Miss.) to majority-white culture. The rise of TV, and of mass media in general, did the rest. Next stop: high fives and chest bumps and "Go girl!"; Air Jordans and Tupac and low-riding pants. It took just half a lifetime for the vanilla paradigm that had been built for American kids to become rusted and unused by all but Mormons and kids raised on militia turf.

Once it reached their shores, white folks made the primary concern of cool—recognition of the need to go with the flow—a part of their living as much as it was that of niggas. But cool was an avocational interest for white culture. It hinged on too much go, not enough flow, and could never be the necessity it was for their colored co-occupants.

(Why are period send-ups like Austin Powers so powerfully funny? In part because they throw light on the artificial nature of white representations of cool. The grunge-era parody starring Jonathan Taylor-Thomas as Eddie Vedder—due out in 2007—will be a laugh riot.)

Some worked harder at it than others. Some had it; some didn't. As a result, the spawn of late 20th-century mainstream white culture has never come close to even defining cool, much less mastering it. Yet, as they come to understand coolness as being of almost elemental importance, they are obsessing on it, asking themselves on a daily basis, in a variety of clumsy, indirect ways, as confused and uncomfortable as Eric Weisbard at a Trouble Funk show: Are black people cooler than white people, and if so, why?

The answer to the first question is, of course, yes. And if you, the reader, had to ask some stupid shit like that, you're probably white. It's hard to imagine a black person even asking that question, and a nigga might not even know what you mean. Any nigga who'd ask that question certainly isn't much of one; niggas invented the shit.

And it's a good thing, too. Humans hold cool on a pedestal because life at large is a challenge, and in that challenge we're trying to cram in as much as we can—as much fine loving, fat eating, dope sleeping, mellow walking, and substantive working as possible. We need spiritual assistance in the matter. That's where cool comes in, because, at its core, cool is utilitarian. Cool is about turning desire into deed with a surplus of ease; at its outermost reaches, cool can be egalitarian. It's about completing the task of living with enough ease to splurge it on bystanders, to share with others working through their travails a little of your bonus life. In other words, because of cool, you can gain value in your life just by observing mine—and you don't even have to know me. Cool gave bass to 20th-century American culture, but I think that if the culture had needed more on the high end, cool would have given us that, because cool closely resembles the human spirit.

This crystallized for me at a party I threw a few years back. A friend of mine told an astronomer I knew: "You's a cool muhfucka!" And the astronomer, the epitome of a pencil-necked geek, shined like he'd just discovered a new star. (For he had—it was he!) Elusive as it is, cool keeps us going. Keeps us interested in each other when the terrifying emptiness of our workaday worlds might make us lose sight of why we're alive. The appreciation of cool leavens jealousy and opposes the inclinations to watch reality television and to fully embrace communism. Cool mediates.

Some white people are cool in their own varied ways. I married a secretly cool white girl. Raves reined me in during the same year I felt my first urge to riot. And you can't tell me Jim Jarmusch and Ron Athey and Tom Gugliotta ain't smooth. Beth Lisick is a personal favorite. (If you don't know who these people are, well, exactly.) There's a gang of cool white folks, all of whom exist that way because they find their essential selves amid the abundant and ultimately numbing media replications of the coolness vibe and the richness of real life. And there's a whole slew of them ready to sign up if you tell 'em where. They don't think they've realized King's Dream because they know the words to Nas' latest album. (Just cuz I have a PETA membership doesn't mean I don't go to the races.) Your average wigger in the "rap" section of Sam Goody ain't gone nowhere; she or he hasn't necessarily learned shit about the depth and breadth of cool, about making a dollar outta fifteen cents. She or he has just entered a doorway glimpsed by the same white folks who got hooked on Elvis. But, like I said, there's a whole gang of cool white people. Remember the movie *The Warriors*? Like that, maybe. A gang among many.

The problem with majority-American culture is that it processes cool so as to make folks think cool is something you can put on and take off at will (hence the snap-on goatee). They think it's some shit you go shopping for. And that's bad for everyone, black, white, and all the flavors in between. It taints cool, gives that mutant thing it becomes a deservedly bad name. Such strains aren't even cool anymore but an evil antithetic, one that fights cool at every turn. Advertising agencies, record-company artist-development departments, and over-art-directed dive bars are where such quasi-cool dwells.

There's a much larger gang of these white folks, and they're the reason why white culture in the present tense is so ridiculously spent, and why all documents of contemporary whiteness resemble postmortems on a way of life that's been spinning away from the sun since Satchmo first exhaled into a trumpet. American culture at large seems oblivious to its coolness shortage because it processes cool through a perspective of whiteness. Cool, as the unlikely cool muhfucka Elvis Costello put it, is like starlight—hardly even an indication of the now past-tense place whence it came. What passes for cool to the white-guy passerby might be—is probably—rote vibe duplication without an ounce of innovation. *Friends* is like watching a compendium of secondhand 20th-century poserdom from rat-pack Kerouac to post-Reagan slack. Howard Stern is a get-out-of-life-free pass. Icons emblematic of great swaths of white culture, these motherfuckers slouch toward cool—sometimes even purporting to be the opposite—but refuse to do the work, and just flat-out flaunt the fact of their sloth. I'm not feeling these people, and can't believe that anyone is, except on a superficial level based almost entirely on familiarity. What does it mean when the inversion of nigga metaphor gains cachet?

The vibe void created by the acceptance of clone cool is what makes hip hop the shit. It's what negates the hopelessness of the postmodern sensibility at its most cynical. The hard road of getting by on metaphorical chitlins kept the sons and daughters of Africa in touch with life's essential physicality, more in touch with the world and what it takes to get over in it: People are moved, not convinced; things get done, they don't just happen. Life doesn't allow for much fronting, as it were. And neither does hip hop. Hip hop allows for little deviation between who one is and what one can ultimately represent in expression. In an age of digital technology and PR, expression of the raw physicality of all life isn't getting a ton of support. Hip hop is rough, rugged, and raw in the face of all that. Its singular syntactical fidelity means a more realized, more true relationship between performer and listener. In that respect, there ain't much art out there that's as efficient and powerful, as cool, as hip hop.

Rap—the most familiar, and therefore emblematic, example of hip hop expression—is about the power of conveying through speech the world beyond words. Language is placed on a par with sound and, ultimately, vibes. Huston Smith, a dope white guy, wrote:

"Speech is alive—literally alive—because speaking is the speaker. It's not the whole of the speaker, but it is the speaker in one of his or her living modes. This shows speech to be alive by definition, as we see when we realize that it cannot exist—as can writing—disjoined from the speaker. It possesses in principle life's qualities, for its very nature is to change, adapt, and invent. Indissolubly contextual, speaking adapts itself to speaker, listener, and situation alike. This gives it an immediacy, range, and versatility that is, well, miraculous. Original wording breathes new life into familiar themes."

In other words, hip hop is cooler than words. And it don't get much cooler than that. That's a rap. And that's why it's become the most insidiously influential music of our time. It took a little while, but it's on every stop on the radio dial—Beck, the Beastie Boys, hell, even Ricki Lee Jones. Like rock, hip hop in its later years will have a legacy of renegade youth to look back upon fondly. But unlike that dynamic social force, hip hop will insist that its early marginalization be recognized as an undeniable part of its past. Them's the rules, and when the day comes that grandmothers are rapping and beatboxing as they might aerobicize now, and samplers and turntables are as much a part of accepted leisure time as channel surfing, niggas will be glad. Their expression will have proven ascendant.

I would argue that hip hop's terms of expression extend to other components of hip hop. Take, for instance, deejaying. Many have argued that back when the movement first took shape, hip hop was a reaction to New York urban-renewal efforts, and DJs were at the forefront of this movement. Back in the day, their role was akin to what the MC now represents. DJs moved the crowd and showed that one didn't need instruments, just a real connection to music, to do so. In the hands of one imbued with the brilliance of nigga metaphor, old records could renew epiphany—just like discarded instruments could give birth to jazz. Yet another way of making a dollar out of fifteen cents.

But it goes further than that. Developments in film (check the movement of Kevin Smith's *Chasing Amy* or the verbal flow of *Pulp Fiction*), along with more traditional pieces such as DJ Shadow's Entroducing ... and the last ad you saw that had a beat, have a dubious duality of possibility. They indicate the far-reaching possibilities of a young form, but also allow white folks, and others, to recoil as much as ever from naked nigga expression while still basking in its genius.

If white people were so cool with black cool, you'd more often put your cool with our cool to work shit out. I'm not talking about the people you break bread with as much as I am your cultural icons, your college radio, your indie film. Your Kurt Cobains, your must-see TV. You banish us to UPN, music videos, and sports channels, so you can visit whenever you like without being burdened by our difference. Most of the time, I think white folks really don't want to be a part of black cool. They'd just like to come out and see their boys do a jig once in a while, as long as they're still producing. And maybe even learn a few things, like DJ Shadow.

Josh Davis, aka DJ Shadow, grew up white in Davis, California, with a complete hard-on for the hip hop music he heard on the radio. A more suburban milieu than his would be hard to find, but Davis sought out the vibe that moved him, accessing Los Angeles pioneer station KDAY in the late '80s through AM maneuverings and making record store pilgrimages to the Bay Area. He first performed in public at UC-Davis' Black Family Day, a northern California institution whose name explains itself.

It's not the basic embrace of an aspect of black culture that makes Josh Davis cool. Such is the assumption that chops cool at its knees and hampers relationships between black and white America. ("If we could just appreciate each other for who we are, and wholeheartedly accept and admire what the other has to offer, then we could all get along!" What bullshit.) Black culture, hip hop in particular, meant so much to Davis that he immersed himself in it until the parts he derived directly from the culture and that which originated from within him were inseparable. In return for meeting the vibe more than halfway, he became one of the most naturally flowing and expansive DJs the world has known.

As the concept of deejaying grew, in both popularity and scope, beyond what the first wave of South Bronx innovators practiced deejays like DJ Shadow (and a trillion other "alternative" [read: not black] spinners) received an added bonus, one most never requested. The white pop establishment—the only pop establishment—lauded the shit out of him, making its embrace Exhibit A in how to distance itself from a black vibe that white power can only hope to contain, not stop. Captains of marketing and their lieutenants who edit music magazines crowned Davis America's first turntable God, as if DJ Premier had never happened, as if 500 innovative DJs hadn't sprung up wild and free on the West Coast in the wake of what the South Bronx wrought. Hearing themselves in the expanse of his style, the marketing people distanced themselves from the quality that gave Shadow access to greatness. The kid that hip hop cool saved was turned into a modern-day Bill Haley and used to slap down his spiritual father.

Cool's great secret is that the tastemakers and trend peddlers of mainstream America have a partnership in preserving this almost feudal arrangement, in which they continue to toil generation after generation on turf they've next to no chance of owning. But it's hard to hate Bill Gates and Clive Davis and Tommy Hilfiger when niggas give assists like a John Stockton in blackface.

Everyday life in black America isn't all Ellington and Rakim. Far from it, black life in its most mainstream forms can be especially mundane and tedious, full of bad TV and mannered mirroring of manufactured trends. There's a rote corniness to it, which shows—surprise!—that only a few black folks are responsible for cool. The rest copy and recycle. "But it's never pointed out," Chris Rock told me recently in a telephone interview. "At the end of the day, there are probably more Babyface black people, R. Kelly black people, than Ice Cube black people." Simply put, not all niggas are cool. In fact, most aren't. And coolness projects a notion of self-sufficiency that in an increasingly conservative society plays out as disregard. It's no accident that black men—who are seen by the mainstream as more threatening than just about anyone else—are held up most aggressively as icons of cool.

Of course there are more Babyface Negroes (or Rolonda Negroes or Puff Daddy Negroes), or else society would have long ago been turned on its head. At the historical core of the lives of blacks in this country is the understanding that deviation from the assigned limited life results in punitive sanctions: lynching, hunger, homelessness, and, maybe most psychologically stinging, the assessment among blacks that you're not onboard in the struggle, i.e., you're a Tom. More than a matter of social security, solidarity in this quadrant of underclass America is about genuine survival. Back in the day, if a black woman said, "This shit sucks—I'm taking a slow boat to Europe (or Africa or South America)," the entire extended family felt the repercussions. That person was more than an idealistic rebel; she was a figure of abandonment. Go back far enough, and someone was having to pay for the act in blood.

This fear of departing from the familiar is where the inclination to make chitlins becomes a downside. It's where the shoe-shine-boy reflex to grin and bear it was born, at the point of understanding that the circumstances of their lives couldn't justify something so flighty as deviation from the nightmarishly constructed social norms. And most black folks hold on to the ways of the past as though they're the last rungs of a ladder to escape. Slave-culture rebellion in America was never based on abstract, existentialist grounds. A bird in the hand, no matter how small, was damn-near everything. Status quo won't rape your wife or lynch your child. It's useful to remember that when civil-rights organizers traveled to the South, they came upon discrimination victims more eager for a bus trip North than for the confrontation that awaited them on home soil. Crusaders had to provide assurances that stepping forward to vote, or to get equitable customer service, or to be schooled, wouldn't result in their being beaten down worse than ever.

Today, when deviation from normalcy not only goes unpunished but is also damn-near demanded to guarantee visibility in our fast-moving world, blacks remain woefully wedded to the bowed head and blinders that made them great mudders in the past. Instead of bowing to massa, they slavishly bow to trend and marketplace. From this stems a hemming-in of cool, an inability to control the cool one makes. By virtue of their status as undereducated bottom-feeders, many niggas will never overcome this flawed way of being. But, paradoxically, black people—who exist at a greater distance from cool than niggas—can and will. That's the peril of the cool impulse.

Basically, niggas have forgotten how to make chitlins. They don't remember that the first guy who made chitlins probably failed—they probably tasted like the unsavory intestines they are. Perhaps it's unreasonable to expect that black people, at least a third less hungry than they might have been in the time when jazz was born, would want to go there, where people eat chitlins.

African origins deserve much props for American Negroes' role in the development of contemporary cool. (The characteristic that made Africans build the pyramids so well that they forgot how they did it—let the debate rage on!—is the same thing that makes your star NBA baller unable to deconstruct a magnificently complex dunk he put down moments ago.) But the secret weapon of cool has been the eye open to synthesis. Just about every important black cultural invention of this century has been about synthesizing qualities or elements previously considered antithetical. MLK did it with Eastern thought and civil rights. Chuck Berry brought blues and country music together. Michael Jordan showed that old-school ballers Jerry West and David Thompson could inhabit the same body. Those who think black opera star Jessye Norman a genius detect soul in her mastery of the classical canon. (On a more base level, the first kid to wear DKNY to Crenshaw High carried on the tradition.) Talk about making a dollar outta fifteen cents.

After music, sport is most powerful at manifesting this synthesis in the public realm. The basketball court, the baseball diamond, and the football field are where black and cool meet head-on, with pyrotechnical results. The three major American sporting pastimes are games designed and pioneered by white men and currently mastered by niggas. The psychology of white America ogling its nigga gladiators en masse is overwhelming. A more manageable study is available to anyone willing to dissect the emerging psychology and dynamics of sports commentary. I mean, if we're going to talk about ogling niggas and disseminating their collective cool, let's go to the source. Let's go to ESPN.

Like so many good Americans, I look to ESPN and Disney for answers about the future. Regular viewers know that on-air personality Stuart Scott ("Here's Karl Malone getting his swerve on!" "Ya know he's butta 'cause he was on a roll!") is the sports network's hot new property. Scott throws hip hop phrasing, black lingo, and undeniably contemporary energy into his broadcasting, devising a performance that, while sometimes shticky, is unlike anything sports television has seen before. It's journalism that reflects the spirit of the subject it documents. Scott's delivery makes his pairing with fellow sportscasters a dicey issue. I suspect the older, aristocratic Peter Gammons has a contract clause prohibiting Scott from ever interacting with him on camera—the genius is undeniable. Throughout the NBA playoffs, other channels' anchors and reporters black-vamped and funked as never before.

But while Scott does his thing, ESPN's other three black talents go the old-school route. Always amiable Mike Tirico mimics Bryant Gumbel to effective ends; Marc Jones does a mild take on Scott's game, with more inflection variation than whole 'nother thang; and David Aldridge, a *Washington Post* grad and ESPN's basketball analyst, brings a whole new meaning to whiteness, which, I suppose, is a kind of innovation in the hands of a black man, but mostly it's funny. (I know a twenty-three-year-old gay guy in L.A. whose whole social manner seems based on that of a thirtysomething suburban housewife from decades past—think Samantha from *Bewitched*. It's completely unselfconscious and totally hilarious.) David Aldridge, while not that funny, is just as compelling. His style achieves a kind of whiteness that's beyond what any real white person might convey, because it's based on a vague whiteness template rather than on any actual person's experience. When the reporter signs off in mannequin's tones—"I'm David Aldridge, Eee-S-P-N"—we suspect Replicants walk among us. But as we stare in fascination at this man, we also stare in horror. Because milquetoast as it is, Aldridge's act is a holdover from nigga shit. No person could have been raised to act this way. Rather, what we see in this man is the triumph of the system in its efforts to make a man bow down, forfeiting his own flavor and all that it might earn him. While Stuart Scott will get paid for his invention, get paid for projecting his being, Aldridge—and to a lesser extent Tirico and Jones—collect checks for putting on an act while inventing nothing.

Trivial though it may seem, Stuart Scott's idea is in keeping with storied black synthesis, no less true than Hendrix's marriage of blues and psychedelia. Not many Negroes could ever see the beauty of such notions, and in the rare event when they happen today, it is a fat cat such as Disney, ESPN's owner, that benefits most directly. Such stagnancy is the legacy of black conservatism.

Forgive me for seeing the notion of permanent, race-based differences in expression of cool as incidental COINTELPRO residue. As long as some black people have to live like niggas, cool, as contemporarily defined, will live on. As long as white people (and brown people and yellow people and so on) know black people to one degree or another, cool will continue to exist, with all of its baggage passed on like, uh, luggage. The question, "Are black people cooler than white people?" isn't appropriate. "How do I gain proximity to cool, and do I want it?" is much better.

Back to that immigrant neighbor whom I terrorized with my mere presence—you know, the woman who has an interest in, yet limited experience with, American Negroes. Well, relations have worsened, not just with the woman but with her roommates as well. We don't speak, unless my stereo is too loud. The once cooperative effort to move trash cans on garbage pickup day now hinges on blind intuition. Recently in the twilight, a light bulb fell from my second-floor porch, smashing onto her patio; I hesitated to tell my neighbors what had happened. Angrily, I suspect, they cleaned the mess up before dawn. Our landlord has become curt and suspicious, and my wife wants to move. With cool like this, who needs awkwardness?

Corny as it sounds, cool watchers will always be confused about cool, until they've already said that I am cool. Take the effort to step meaningfully into its world and truly know where it comes from. No dope white person has become such before demystifying the origins of cool so as to separate the earthy from the threatening and bring an end to the love/hate relationship with the unknown.

Out in the netherworld of advertising, they tell us that we're all Tiger Woods. Well, only one nigga on this planet gets to be that motherfucker, but we all swing the same cool, to whatever distant ends. The coolness construct might tell us otherwise, but we're all handed the same basic tools at birth; it's up to us as individuals to work on our game. Some of us have sweet strokes, and some of us press too hard, but everybody who drops outta their mama has the same capacity to take a shot. ■

Note: All chitlins in this article are strictly metaphorical. The author cannot stand the stench of animal innards wafting into his nose, much less the taste in his mouth.

June, 1997

Are You on the Bus or off the Bus?

It wasn't the first time the emperors had no clothes, and will hardly be the last time, but this time, they were young and good looking, so nobody really minded.

The first public appearance was a well-attended press conference at the Washington Press Club. Therese Heliczer, leader of a Washington coalition called Youth Vote '96, presided. She took her cues from a hired communications consultant leaning near the cameras in the back of the small room. Still, Heliczer seemed understandably nervous, what with ABC and C-Span taping her every move.

Youth Vote's goal is to celebrate this year's 25th anniversary of the 26th Amendment—which gave 18- to 21-year-olds the right to vote— by turning out a record twelve million young voters for the November presidential election. Calling the press conference to order, Heliczer announced that such a turnout would prove how people her age (she's 24) are concerned about public affairs, belying what she perceived to be a popular impression to the contrary. The point made, Heliczer introduced colleagues from a chorus of young leaders standing beside her at the podium, two ranks, most wearing conservative blue suits.

A few of these people came forward in turn to speak in favor of voting. Heliczer also presented two pollsters, Alexander Jutkowitz and Jefrey Pollock. Jutkowitz and Pollock had donated a free study to Youth Vote, which they released as part of the conference, claiming to have constructed a political profile of the 18- to 30-year-old American. Chief among their findings, they said, was that the standard 40 percent voter turnout among what they called, in pollster language, "the 18 to 30 cohort," did not represent proof of widespread disinterest in politics, but rather disaffection—a generational disgust with a lack of attention they say candidates and campaigns pay younger Americans. This would change in the 1996 election cycle, Jutkowitz said, because campaigns would realize they were missing a potentially potent block of voters.

Then the questions began, and even though the representatives from ABC, Associated Press, C-Span, the *Cleveland Plain Dealer*, and most of the rest of the Washington pack in the Edward R. Murrow briefing room were under thirty, the Youth Vote contingent took a lot of heat. The change in the conference's tenor from enthusiastic to defensive was not a matter of the Youth Vote speakers being inexperienced or inarticulate. They seemed neither, and they had that media consultant, Doug Hattaway, himself over thirty, helping. The problem was much more fundamental than reasonable nervousness: They just did not know the answers to most of the questions.

No one at the podium, it turned out, knew much at all about the 18- to 30-year-old Americans they purported to represent, and more, they seemed surprised to be facing specific questions from the press at the conference. Heliczer started to look panicky, stressed, her eyes getting a little too tightly focused. Jutkowitz in particular was getting hammered.

The Jutkowitz/Pollock survey, for example, said "crime" was the matter of greatest concern to voters under thirty, but Youth Vote cannot say why this might be so, how many young people suffer from crimes, or commit crimes, or what portion of the prison population they comprise. It was also unclear exactly what was meant by crime, though the assumption seemed to be violent assaults. A local radio reporter, older than thirty, asked Jutkowitz whether the Republican presidential candidates' downplaying of crime issues, in favor of concerns about jobs or social policy, meant that young people were having little influence on political strategy, in defiance of Jutkowitz's predictions. Few answers were forthcoming. Jutkowitz, who favors bow ties and walks with a slow, paunchy sway, looking a lot like the unfortunate spawn of Winston Churchill and Adrian Zmed, eventually foundered. Flummoxed, he deferred to Heliczer. As he stepped back from the podium, it was as if he had just realized that his poise had not distracted anyone from his apparent lack of actual information which, for a change, the assembled press seemed keenly interested in receiving. Heliczer jumped in to say that the poll was not intended to be definitive — an odd assertion since Youth Vote seemed to have constructed much of its message from the poll's results. Things were getting worse.

The Associated Press's 24-year-old reporter noted that the polling sample was 40 percent students, and wanted to know how many 18- to 30-year-old Americans in fact were students. Again, no answer. Finally some kindly reporters asked softball questions of the "How are you going to get young people interested in voting?" variety, and got relieved looks from the speakers, then packaged answers straight from the vault of lost "Schoolhouse Rock" lyrics — coy patriotism from Heliczer about "participation in our democratic system." When others returned to more pointed questions ("What is the average tax burden for people 18 to 30?"), they again got equivocations, or no response at all.

Among the questions left unanswered after Youth Vote's press conference, and interviews with the speakers immediately afterwards, were the following: How many 18- to 30-year-olds are there? (about 48 million); How many are in the national labor force? (31,286,000, or 24 percent of working Americans); How many are enrolled in two- or four-year colleges? (3,413,000 and 6,434,000, respectively, 9,847,000 total), How many receive some sort of student financial aid? (44 percent); How many own their own businesses? (about 1 million); How much of the country's prison population do they represent? (45 percent of federal prison inmates, 67 percent of state prison inmates, for a group from 18 to 34); How many have been victims of crime? (9 percent of 20 to 24-year-olds, 5.9 percent of 25 to 34-year-olds); How many live in major cities? (18 million); How many are unemployed? (2,855,000, or 8.3 percent unemployment); What is the group's average earnings? (about $20,000 per year); How many earn minimum wage? (2.7 million); How many live in poverty? (7,808,000 or 14 percent); What percent own homes and pay mortgages? (25 percent); How many say abortion should be legal in all circumstances? (37 percent); Or never? (9 percent); How many are in the military? (887,310 or 60 percent of the military).

By the time it was over, Youth Vote had demonstrated little beyond good will and an unexpected inability to make its own case. Leaving the press conference, I headed to K Street and the office of a friend, a reasonably successful twenty-nine-year-old environmental lobbyist. He's spent his late twenties accruing vigorous enemies in both government and private industry, rather than just a Rolodex of people who ignore him. I had every intention of forcing him to buy me lunch. He asked where I had been. I told him about the scene at the press conference. He smirked. I told him that he fit the target demographic of the Youth Vote survey and the get-out-the-vote drive. He held his hands a foot apart in front his body and moved them up and down, as if masturbating an oak tree. I told him Therese Heliczer is an environmental activist like he is, head of not only Youth Vote '96, but also Campus Green Vote, a voter education project. He kept moving his hands. We left. At the cafeteria where we ate, I was surrounded by more lobbyists and other political gadflies and functionaries, many of whom are roughly my age, twenty-seven. I bought the lunch.

Three weeks later I interview Heliczer at the offices of Campus Green Vote. Youth Vote is run from Green Vote's offices. I ask Heliczer about what she does for Campus Green Vote.

"Voter education," she says. About what? "Like, we tell them about the Clean Water Act." What about it? "What it does." What does it do? "Its name is descriptive. It cleans the water." How? She pauses. "I'm not familiar with the specifics," she says.

Heliczer adds that she is running "voter education" for Youth Vote similarly to how she does it for Campus Green Vote. It is therefore a bit troubling that she seems ignorant of the Clean Water Act beyond the sunny implications of its title. To confirm darker suspicions, and to get her back on the election topic, I ask her what she thinks of then-candidate Steve Forbes' plan to set up student IRA accounts as a way of creating private college funds. Youth Vote concentrates mostly on the "register and vote" message, but they also have a slate of issues they consider particularly appealing to young people, which they often speak on to spur interest. The environment, crime and health care are among these. Student loans is also one of them, and Forbes was the only candidate talking much about that on the Republican side. She hesitates, then again claims ignorance.

Heliczer, a self-dubbed election year political spokesperson, who just three weeks prior had been on national television representing, by virtue of her age, 48 million people, soon proves to know not the first thing about the platforms of the candidates in the election. Or about politics in general. Or, with no more specifics forthcoming since the press conference fiasco, anything more about her constituency than she did when the reporters ambushed her there. For a moment, sitting across from her, I stop being her inquisitor and become firstly her peer, offended by her dilettantism and frustrated by her arrogance. She gives no reason why anyone might look to her for leadership. Therese Heliczer is her own worst nightmare. She's professionally lazy, she's politically puerile, she's primarily identified by her age because she hasn't done anything else worth noting instead, and she seems convinced that packaging is more important than content.

Somehow, none of this seems to affect the public legitimacy of Heliczer or the group she leads. Youth Vote is funded by a six-figure stock of grants from the respected Heinz and Cummins Foundations, and is currently fishing for more money, which they expect to get. Their two-day organizing conference was held at Harvard University's prestigious Kennedy School of Government, and featured appearances by Clinton strategist George Stephanopoulos and Chinese dissident Harry Wu. Youth Vote has been the subject of editorials in the *Boston Globe* (written by a twenty-three-year-old) and features in the *Washington Post*. They bill themselves, or at least Heliczer defines them, as the premier coalition in the nation working to organize young people for the election.

As nicely as I can, sitting in her Washington office, I compare Heliczer to Ralph Reed of the Christian Coalition. Obviously that's a bit pejorative. But it's startling how similar she sounds: like the Religious Right leader, Heliczer says that she represents a silent majority that is offered no place at the Washington table, so her intention is to organize this dormant demographic into a voting bloc and steer it to affect policy. She wants to be a swing vote this year, to have the politicians respond to young people as a unified pressure group, and wants political concessions—student loan programs, environmental guarantees, health reform—in exchange for that bloc's support. "Voting used to be considered a civic responsibility. Now it's more of an activist tool," she says. It's a fascinating and depressing statement. She wants to package young people for political strategists of one stripe or another—though more likely Democrats, given her generally progressive concerns. "They wouldn't necessarily know that they're targeted," she says. "Most people outside Washington don't realize that's how politics works. I don't think they would resent being targeted because they wouldn't know it." She's read her Machiavelli.

"Why isn't the government speaking to younger people's issues, and are speaking to issues of interest to people of older generations?" Heliczer asks. If you accept her slate of youth issues—increasing student aid, national health care, raising the minimum wage—the answer might be because the general election hasn't started yet, and Republicans just aren't sympathetic to her generally liberal demands. Moreover, in the speeches that week surrounding the New Hampshire primary, the big themes seemed to be jobs, the deficit, taxes, abortion, and to a lesser but still notable extent, crime. It's unclear why these aren't central issues for people eighteen to thirty. Heliczer responds that the medium is the message. Candidates may talk about her sometimes, but they aren't talking to her. They don't come to young people's media, and stump in their forums. "They aren't addressing young people specifically," she says. Dole's appearance on MTV was a good start, but not much more. The conversation then turns odd. Heliczer suggests that young people are "particularly sensitive to marketing," but then returns to complaining about not being spoken to, not being grouped and aggressively courted by political strategists in a way she finds appealing. She seems to be saying that she's ready for solid food, but won't eat it unless they put it in a *Sesame Street* bowl.

The Choose or Lose bus is a garish extravagance that feels equally like a retired garmento's garage and a New Orleans bordello. Going on board makes you simultaneously want to do cocaine and wrap everything in plastic seat covers, have sex and drink fiber supplement. New York fashion designer Todd Oldham is the person responsible for the vehicle's interior. The ceiling is the color of Dijon mustard and feels fuzzy, with bent, baroque fleur-de-lys shapes imprinted on the fabric. The floor is fake leopard skin. Outside, the bus is painted red, white and blue with jagged letters reading "Choose or Lose," and stenciled political quotes from historical figures, politicians, musicians and actors. The top of the bus is anointed with a square MTV News hood ornament about a foot high. Dave Anderson, formerly a member of Clinton's White House administrative staff, now the manager of the bus, either doesn't know or won't say the price of the vehicle, beyond that it cost "a lot." ("I don't think we give out costs," says MTV spokesperson Andrea Smith). The driver is thirty-nine.

The bus is parked inside the Washington Convention Center for a promotional fair called Collegefest. Convention goers, mostly high school and college students, pay five dollars each at the door to enter a display of advertisements. The students fill out credit card applications, pick up free copies of *Spin*, take free shots of YooHoo, Orangina, and bottled water, get their hair cut for free at the mobile Hair Cuttery, get a free CD after waiting in long lines at the record store booths, slip free T-shirts over the clothes they came in, take in a free show by The Zimmermans (a D.C. art-rock band) and Jimmy's Chicken Shack (a D.C. Chili Peppers knock-off). They sign a Greenpeace petition, eat a chocolate swirl brownie from Planet Hollywood, rollerblade off an inclined plane, try on some snowboard boots, get a calling card, shoot a paintball rifle at a pie plate, receive literature and a button from an AIDS clinic, ogle a black Dodge Viper, and, if they visit the loudest, most impressive booth, the bus parked heavily on the clean convention floor, they register to vote with MTV and sign a promise to go to the polls on election day.

Onboard the bus, Rock the Vote's Jaime Uzeta is showing Dave Anderson a postcard from the nearby Americorps booth. Americorps, the Clinton administration's community service corps, would likely not survive a Republican victory in November, and they are doing a lot of PR work. Anderson finally takes the postcard from Uzeta and looks at it. It shows a cartoon picture of a smiling insecticide can labeled "You" spraying a dying bug labeled "Apathy."

"Oh cool," says Anderson.

"Yeah," Uzeta agrees.

"Americorps is so cool. I want an Americorps T-shirt," says Anderson. "Ask them if we can trade. Do we have any more T-shirts?"

Apparently not. A few moments later, Anderson is on a cellular phone talking to some sort of MTV mothership, requesting more T-shirts. "I need T-shirts bad," he says.

It takes a while to get the shirt order and a few tours of the bus for local radio personalities out of the way before Anderson and I can sit down and talk. Amid the confusion, Anderson proves to be a soft-handed manager of his crew, a pleasant man, affable, roundish and amiably goofy, a good egg.

Anderson talks about voter apathy, enemy number one for Americorps' spray can and Anderson's bus.

"Young people are certainly disillusioned. But young people aren't entirely different from the rest of the population. They have parents, they come from various influences. Apathy exists in every part of the population in some numbers. But I think disillusionment is the more significant trend." It's an unusual statement. Most organizers trying to get young people to vote are far less willing to parse motivations like that, to draw a distinction between thinking about politics but throwing up your hands in defeat, and not thinking about it at all.

Outside, the crowd appears to bear his point out. Most of the high school and college students are dressed like characters from a Peanuts cartoon, a melange of quotes from no one's actual childhood, polyester Pop Warner athletic shirts on the girls, or tiny T-shirts with corporate logos in the center, and gas station attendant uniforms on the boys. What I want to ask Anderson about is how the scene seems like a critique of consumerism. The people outside look harshly media savvy, in their T-shirts hawking products they may never buy and uniforms for jobs they would resent. Presumably they are also savvy to their politics being packaged for them.

If the disillusionment is in part due to the overcommercialization of the culture, the falseness of commerce beggaring any attempt to be genuine in politics, then MTV's heavily stylized bus campaign may help create the disaffection it seeks to counteract. Choose or Lose has the feel of an advertising campaign, not a political education effort; it's about persuasion, not information. Anderson could slap a different logo on the side of his bus and sell sneakers without having to change any other thing about his project ("Shoes or Lose," a friend suggests he could call it).

I ask Anderson about all this. He focuses on the back wall for nearly a minute. "This is out of my league," he eventually says. "You're talking about a level of intellectual discussion I'm not really qualified to comment on. I'm, like, I'm bus manager guy here. I mean, I've got opinions on what you're talking about, but it's not appropriate for me to comment on something like that." Anderson is MTV's spokesperson on the bus, which is why reporters are directed to him rather than any of the other MTV staffers on board. Of course a comment is appropriate, and of course Anderson, obviously a bright guy, can talk about it thoughtfully. That he won't is telling. Like Heliczer, he suggests the medium is the message. But unlike Heliczer, he seems to realize that his message, minus that medium, is a mile wide and an inch deep.

I ask him for some information on his audience. I am curious about who he is reaching, what they represent politically. What does someone who wasn't going to vote, but is persuaded to by MTV, act like on the whole? Anderson says there is a broad spectrum, but not one he can describe. Outside, the spectrum looks pretty narrow: Viacom Nation. It does not, for example, seem to include many fans of Garth Brooks. Everyone looks the same, just like everyone at the previous day's stop at George Washington University had looked.

That seems likely to continue. At the start of the presidential campaign, Anderson explains, the Choose or Lose bus route went from the University of New Hampshire, to George Washington University; to Collegefest in Washington; to the University of North Carolina at

Chapel Hill; to Emory University in Atlanta; to the University of Texas in Austin. Anderson is unspecific about whether they intend to stop at any military bases, community colleges, union halls, gravel pits, religious institutions, gas stations, country bars, Indian reservations, or other places that aren't four-year universities from the *U.S. News* Best Colleges list, but are nevertheless likely to have a lot of people under thirty present. "Yes," he says, "we'll go all over, army bases, shopping malls." He is adding army bases for my benefit, I think, because I keep harping on it. At that moment I would bet my life that he will not stop at Fort Bragg to talk to nineteen-year-old Marines while on the way to Chapel Hill to talk to nineteen-year-old students. Anderson's itinerary—colleges, concerts, malls—shows Choose or Lose pointedly going only where MTV's audience is, where the particular youth culture they reflect is found, reliably responsive and eager to see them.

As traffic in the bus increases, the interview breaks up. Serena Altschul, Los Angeles correspondent for MTV News, looks on blankly from the corner.

Mark Strama, Rock the Vote's program director, greets me with an elaborate handshake that is momentarily disorienting. He wears a leather coat. His hair is shoulder-length and curly; he looks a bit like the singer from INXS. His wristwatch has an MTV logo where the hands meet, the same logo that is embroidered on his bulging shoulder bag.

This is in the Manchester Holiday Inn, hub of the New Hampshire primary. Every floor is either rented to campaigns or converted to temporary studios by television news crews. Strama hung out in the Holiday Inn a lot; he was usually sitting in the lobby.

Strama can not define the youth vote, but says it is there. "There's no evidence to support that (young people) vote as a bloc," he says. "Polling is an imprecise science." He is referring to the Jutkowitz/Pollock poll, which he seems to agree is less than scientific. "But I think there are discreet issues that unify people because of their age."

Strama echoes Heliczer's point about candidates not speaking directly to young voters. "It's a sign of ignoring young voters when you don't go to their media," he says. "It's not objectifying. It's showing them respect. This is a generation that's grown up with marketing. We can smell a rat."

Nevertheless, Strama then starts to talk like one. "I think a constituency can be a group of people who vote the same way, but it can also be people who are reachable in the same way," Strama says. I suggest that such a concept is terrifying. He tells me to be realistic. "Look," he says, "there are these books called Arbitron books, and a sophisticated media buyer can look in these books and decide who they are going to target. Our demographic targets are according to music. We know music is a unifying thing." He seems very sure.

Across the lobby is Mike Evans, who is less sure. Evans, who is in Manchester with a group called None of the Above, an on-line political education effort, says he worked with Rock the Vote in 1992 at the party conventions and in New Hampshire. He later worked with the Clinton campaign. "I think what happens is people are, like, 'Vote, vote, vote,' but it's not 'Why?' It's like it's nothing to me. I was (he chants) 'Go out and vote.' Yeah, okay, but why'd I vote, what's the point, why does this affect my life?

"Yeah, I think a lot of it is fluff. A lot of people, they build these groups, they want to do this, they want to do that, and it's, you know, a lot of ego." He is talking in fast forward. "It's like telling kids to vote, but why are they voting?"

Two weeks later, Jaime Uzeta, who has Evans' old job, answers that with a non-answer. He says the why comes later: "First we get them to vote, then we educate them."

In New Hampshire, looking to ask someone under thirty who isn't a campaign staffer about voting, I follow a young woman with a half-shaved head into a coffee shop, and get re-directed to a somewhat more popular place called the Little Vegas, a competing coffee house where indeed everyone is talkative and young. The Little Vegas is four blocks from the Manchester Holiday Inn. Strama hadn't known about it, having not left the hotel much. The Little Vegas turns out to be the locus of his constituency in the city.

Before sending me to the Little Vegas, where she works the morning shift, the woman with the half-shaved head, Lisa Champagne, says Rock the Vote "will work for people who need to be told what to do, and who do what they're told." Champagne is twenty.

"They're trying to hit an audience that doesn't exist. If it does exist, it's only in music circles," says her friend Todd Doherty, twenty-four. Neither he nor Champagne, nor her twenty-one-year-old husband, she volunteers in his absence, plan to vote in the Tuesday primary. They don't like any of the candidates.

"You can't target a generation. It's like if you tried to target all plumbers," says Doherty. I ask what he does for a living. "Italian cuisine transportation specialist," he says.

The Little Vegas is filled with people in their early twenties who aren't going to vote. Everyone is pierced in painful places, tattooed, wearing bandannas on their heads or leather collars; they look like apprentice pirates. The coffee shop opened the same time the youth vote movement got going, around the start of the year. The proprietors are Joshua Palmer and Christian Skinner, 20 and 23 respectively. Both shake my hand normally. They financed the business with a $12,000 loan from a local bank, after first being turned down by the Small Business Administration. Two days prior to our conversation, Skinner had contacted Strama, and Rock the Vote had come to the shop en masse. Now mention them in the Little Vegas and angry remarks start quickly.

"'Oh no, I understand,' they kept saying, 'But, don't you think you should get involved?'" says Kristen Delude, nineteen, sitting at one of the tables made from telephone cable spools. "And they'd listen, but then they'd contradict everything you just said. And then they wouldn't understand the reasons why we didn't want to vote, they just kept saying to vote. They all tried to fit the scene, you know what I mean? The coffee house scene?"

"They were from MTV, what do you expect?" says her friend, Jacy Kelly.

"They were fake. They weren't real," Delude says.

"If they were coming into, like, a rave, they would have come in plastic skirts," adds Kelly. She speaks with a slight lisp. I notice her pierced tongue later.

Delude mentions Strama. "He was sitting there on his cellular phone. They were just preaching, basically. People went off. I think everyone here said, basically, 'Fuck you, I don't believe in this.' "

"They didn't really have any points to make," Rob LaFreniere, an auto mechanic, says a short time later, after he has taken Delude's seat. "They're all college level. By the way they dressed, the way they acted, the way they talked, it made them seem like they were looking down from their pedestal." He is wearing a leather collar, and takes a moment to volunteer some information about his S&M proclivities when I ask about it. Then he continues talking about Rock the Vote.

"After I've explained my politics to you, why would you keep trying to convince me? Personally, it bothered me. There were like thirty of them, and cameras. I come here to hang out with my friends."

"It's kind of threatening," says Heather Mims, next to him, drawing an eyeball on a sketchpad.

The comments continue over the night and some of the next morning in the Little Vegas. At about one in the morning, Dave Murphy, a drawn, twitchy young man who has dropped out of three art schools and was the butt of several heroin jokes, leaves for a moment and returns with lawn signs from the Buchanan and Forbes campaigns, three-foot-long wood stakes with the candidate's placards stapled to the top. He parades around the shop with them, then rips them up.

For a moment, what motivates people like Mark Strama, Therese Heliczer, and Dave Anderson becomes clear and difficult to dismiss. No matter how perverse it is to take on vast responsibility and a public persona as a way to find the fountain of youth, that's what they want. They want to matter, but they don't want to grow up, and while that doesn't work in the campaign, it makes sense in the Little Vegas.

In the morning, Dave Murphy and three others from the Little Vegas take me up on an offer of a tour of the primary. Adam Beers, twenty-one, and Michele Gelfand, eighteen, a couple who live together, end up spending most of election day with me, running around the Holiday Inn press facilities, seeing the C-Span studio, watching the picketers in front of the Buchanan campaign headquarters (a Jewish group protesting the candidate as anti-Semitic), and attending the various poll-watching events that night. We run into Strama in the lobby and take everyone's picture together. After the polls close, Beers ends up getting interviewed by MTV News at Pat Buchanan's victory party. The MTV reporter fairly seems, given the context, to assume that Beers has voted. But he hasn't; he is dismayed by the penal system, and won't support President Clinton because he signed the Crime Bill, which contains a three-strikes mandatory sentencing clause. Beers had made the same argument to Strama over a chessboard in the Little Vegas. He says Strama was a nice guy, but not convincing. "He said my vote is my voice," says Beers. "I said no, my voice is my voice." He means protests; Beers has visions of barricades that no one in the Youth Vote effort was able to dispel. Gelfand is quieter than her boyfriend, a serious person who looks very interested in everything that is transpiring over the hectic primary day. But she doesn't vote either.

After the Buchanan party, the two go back to the Little Vegas. After that they go home and sleep a while. Later, they go to afternoon classes at a community college. Then, they go to work. ■

MATTHEW GRIMM

The Zen Rub of Alcohol

I scream. You scream. We'd all scream if more of us realized the monumental conspiracy of pin-striped rodentia nibbling away at the remaining common sense in this goddamn country. Only the latest impetus to run screaming into the ocean is Corporate America's latest nefarious strategy to undermine what little remains of the independent will with which we can resist its sweet, facile wiles: the supplanting of booze by Jamocha Fudge Chip.

That, at least, is per the suits at Grand Metropolitan, an English mega-corporation that brings unto our marketplace Häagen-Dazs, Burger King and, in bitter irony, J&B, Amaretto and Bailey's. The latest ad campaign for Häagen-Dazs, courtesy of New York ad agency Partners & Shevak, recasts the product as the stuff that alternatively soothes the savaged yuppie or toasts his superfluous bourgeois triumphs. You've seen the spots:

"Your plane landed on time. Have some Häagen-Dazs," the voiceover says. "So did your luggage. In Bolivia. Have some more."

Or, your kids washed the car. Sweet creamy reward. They used steel wool. Sweet creamy escape from woeful reality.

Or, I don't know, it's your fucking birthday. Have some ice cream. You got cancer. Have some more.

Vanilla Swiss Almond, Lars, and make it a double. And none of that cheap private label shit!

Unless the Born-Agains are even remotely close to the estimate of their numbers in this empire, we've got ad agency smurfs treading dangerously close to what little sacred ground the unassimilated of us still recognize. The bar is the last bastion of democracy—that's the bar, not the club, disco, bistro or Ruby Tuesday's—because it is a realm without class, status or otherwise social pole position. All who enter are equally entitled to their nourishment of choice, their opinions, their differences, their problems, their solitude and even their usually misbegotten selections on the jukebox. All are free to navigate their own route, be it meditation path or roller coaster, toward oblivion, or even enter into that other realm wherein we are all truly equal, oblivion itself.

Versus the Evil Empire that bombards us with nebulous pastel paperdoll images of what our life and society should eventually resemble (be orderly, get credit, reproduce, buy insurance, reinvest), booze serves as a deprogrammer. This is the Zen rub of the Bar. What dogma protects, booze calls into question. It is a psycho-social turpentine, stripping away the layers of hype caked upon your oppressed head, the workaday crap you accumulate and fret over. It crashes the program of your gross rationalizations, kicks in the back-up of your serpent brain, putting all the stupidity of life into a context accessible by 1/0 binary function— good tingle, bad tingle, friends good, poverty bad, buying depressed guy a round good, Dole bad, sex really good, Dole and Nazis really bad. Yes, you truly love your girlfriend. Yes, your girlfriend is a tetanus-infected syringe jabbing your ass. Hell yes, you make your living selling products or services no one really needs. Hell yes, you might get hit by an International Harvester tomorrow and be denied even the time it would take to realize that your dreams will dry and crack, unfulfilled, like your blood on the pavement. Hell yes, the American Dream is a massive thought-bank to which you've made ever-increasing payments since birth with nary a flash of enlightenment returned on the investment. Hell yes, Alanis Morissette sucks.

Next time you get in a fight with the squeeze, see how easy it is to get it together down at the local Dairy Queen after ten or so Heath Bar Blizzards.

In need of dialectic injection? Hit the Friendly's for some Coffee Mint Chip and see how much the conversation with the bright, well-dressed, perky young couples with strollers goes beyond the weather and how old the screamin' brats are.

I'm not advocating the elimination of ice cream from your damn diet, nor am I encouraging you to get behind the wheel of your little Honda with a .17 blood-alcohol content and haul ass into a Gas N Sip—cabs exist for a reason, after all. I would contest, however, that downing a pint of Midnight Cookies 'N Cream versus a pint of Blatz as self-consolation is a psycho-social next step toward polite society, toward Donna Reed (sitcom period), etiquette films, Eisenhower, Reagan, bridge club and lawn care. Booze is not only irreplaceable—much less by some goddamn confection made in New Jersey—it is in fact a vital component for remaining scrutinous of the Evil Empire.

Get drunk. You might wonder what really lies beyond the pale of commercial reality, maybe make a mental note, do some reading—or maybe even do something.

Eat Häagen-Dazs. You might wonder if you should paint the shelves. ■

May, 1996

Jews in Rock

In the library of the Niles Township Synagogue there were two books worth stealing and it is I who stole them both. One was a Judy Blume coming-of-age story, of interest because it described a girl's first period in excruciating detail. The other book was about the greatest left-hander ever to hurl a baseball. Though he pitched his last game before I was born, Sandy Koufax was my hero because he was classy and strong and a little wild. But mostly because he was Jewish and had succeeded where few Jews had ventured. I would sit in Hebrew school and create all-star lists composed exclusively of Jewish players. After Koufax, Hank Greenberg, Rod Carew, Ken Holtzman (whom Cubs manager Leo Durocher once called a "gutless Jew" for refusing to pitch on Yom Kippur), and Harry Danning (who could pass for my twin), the pickings grew slim. Moe Berg and Sid Gordon would trot reluctantly out to their positions. Sometimes I'd field Irv Kupcinet and Sid Luckman in the outfield, hoping they'd play baseball better than they'd played football.

If one believes, as I do, that ethnic stereotypes are rooted in at least a kernel of truth, then the fact that Jewish professional athletes are so rare is not a surprise. For the most part, Jews are indeed bookish and cerebral. They have historically emphasized knowledge over muscle, the spiritual over the physical. To a boy who had little of the latter attributes but absolutely none of the former, the Jews who had subverted the stereotype were compelling role models. Thus when my interest migrated from sports to rock music, I naturally searched for Jewish rock stars. But if the list of Jewish athletes merits only a leaflet, the list of Jewish rock stars would surely fit on a postage stamp.

My first attempts to uncover satisfactory role models were unsuccessful. Paul Simon and Art Garfunkel were obvious. Billy Joel was too much of a wuss and even he tried to come off as Italian. An encounter with Leonard Chess left me awed but not enlightened and Bill Graham was so rich and ambitious that had he not existed, anti-Semites surely would have invented him. It was only upon spotting a buried Bar Mitzvah reference in a Manowar interview in *Hit Parade* that I began to sense an undercurrent of Jewishness in the more forbidding realms of dangerous rock.

I began to dig more deeply. For reasons ranging from self-hatred to self-promotion, Jewish rock stars often change their telltale surnames. Fleetwood Mac's Peter Green dropped the "baum," while Peter Feld became Peter Wolf before leading The J. Geils Band to the charts. As I pored over the names on my record jackets, I realized that there were far more rocking Jews than I had anticipated. Using a lineage system that would have made Hitler proud (I considered any rocker with at least one Jewish grandparent to be a Jew), I compiled a heartening list of Jewish rock stars. A pattern began to emerge.

As the fortunes of Israel shifted, so went the Jews in rock. Hear me out. Israel braces for the 1967 war, Dylan goes electric. Lou Reed—certainly the ultimate Jew in rock—penetrates the nation's hippest circles with full-blown acceptance, and Israel not only wins the 1972 Yom Kippur War, but humiliates surrounding Arab nations. Within two years, Kiss and the Ramones hit stages worldwide, their triumphant mugs plastered in bedrooms everywhere, newly assertive and unashamed of their ethnic faces. Yet they remain essentially Jewish, aggressively New York. Gene Simmons, former high school teacher, touts his drug-free lifestyle even as he indulges his notorious predatory streak in his search for lusty (and probably gentile!) groupies.

The dearth of Jewish women in rock is telling in a different way. While Jewish men have been allowed to show their faces on TV—albeit in a wimpy, Seinfeld kind of way—there's nary a Jewess among them. The same holds true in Jewish rock: I challenge anyone to think of one prominent Jewish female. OK, I'll give you Lisa Loeb—dubious in both Jewishness and rock stature—but I think the category begins and ends with her.

The invasion of Lebanon in 1982 marked a turning point for Israel and for Jews in rock. No longer content with the gains scored defensively, Israel became a bully. The next thing you know, the Beastie Boys are unleashed on pop music and the Chili Peppers' Hillel Slovak OD's and Perry Farrell goes platinum, becoming emblems for the new Jew in rock: obnoxious, drug-abusing overgrown children. Jews were suddenly not only refusing to apologize for, or obscure, their Jewishness, they were celebrating it with a newfound in-your-faceness. The son of staunch Semitic playwright Israel Horovitz turned up as King Ad-Rock, the very royalty of the name recalling a time when Jews walked the earth with straight backs, if not straight noses.

As with all assimilations, however, regression toward the mean has taken its toll. The culture that produced Jascha Heiftiz, George Gershwin, Irving Berlin and Vladimir Horowitz is now best represented by "Fight For Your Right (To Party)"—an anthem advocating a verb Jews have only recently embraced. In short, Jews in rock, like their Israeli brethren a world away, have become indistinguishable from their non-Jewish counterparts. ■

April, 1995

Paradigm for Sale

I'm not sure about the proper protocol for these types of things. When one defects from one political branch to another, are you supposed to send out a printed announcement? Register something with the county clerk? Get a form notarized? Call Apostates 'R' Us?

I figured the easiest way to make my conversion public would be to write an open letter and explain why I have decided to defect from the camp of leftist feminist journalists to the side of anti-feminist right-winger polemicists. It's not a question of values or principles or politics. I am pretty much still a feminist at heart, despite many of the well-publicized foibles of the organized movement. And yes, I know that "progressives" have much better parties, less guilt-drenched libidos, and cooler shoes.

It's simply a matter of money. The bottom line: I can no longer afford to be a leftist feminist.

After almost a decade of covering progressive social issues in a book, several mainstream newspapers and various outlets of the popular press, I have decided that this type of work simply doesn't pay. The Quicken-crunched numbers very clearly corroborate the same harsh reality. If I had an accountant, he would tell me to cut my losses, swallow the sunk costs and go right wing, or at least libertarian.

At least for authors, that's where the money is. You know you've found your sugar daddy when your patron is a foundation titled with vague yet staunch words like "heritage," "liberty," "enterprise," "freedom," or "concerned." Christina Hoff Sommers, author of the antifeminist 1994 book *Who Stole Feminism?*, received $164,000 from three such right-wing foundations between 1991 and 1993. In the opening pages of his 1991 book Illiberal Education, Dinesh D'Souza thanks his gravy trains, the American Enterprise Institute and the John Olin Foundation, for a similar sum. Robert Bork is now writing a book on the culture wars with the help of his $167,000 post at the American Enterprise Institute. Still a university student, my sister's boyfriend's roommate, who has never published anything, applied to receive $25,000 for seven years from a libertarian foundation to pursue his writing and research. His prospects look decent.

In contrast, leftists don't get squat. A scholarly friend of mine, John K. Wilson—deeply entrenched in leftist academic networks across the country—wrote a counterpart book to Sommers and D'Souza, *The Myth of Political Correctness*, and received only $1,500 from his university press publisher. While I received more to do my first book, *Feminist Fatale*, a journalistic documentary of young women's attitudes about feminism, I just about broke even with my living and research expenses during the six months I spent working on it. Now, older and working less maniacally, I have several months of writing yet on my second book for a bigger publisher, and the coffers are near empty.

Greed isn't my only motivation for wanting to dine at the patriarchal trough. I'm now twenty-nine, and my poverty tolerance threshold is diminishing. More than ever, I am having a hard time determining the difference between what I want and what I need. At wedding showers, I no longer dismiss the Crate & Barrel registry as a frivolous bourgeois trapping; instead, while the gifts are being opened, I find myself joining in the worshipping chorus of the other women in attendance by muttering, "Will you get a load of the detail work on that crock pot?" Each night at dinnertime, I long to eat at a restaurant with multiple forks.

But I should be especially attractive as a right wing convert; I come to this party bearing gifts. I have juicy insider stories, and I can't wait to dish them out. I'll scour my feminist memoirs for dirt: provocative tales of group cervical inspections on the summer solstice, nefarious replacements of the word "seminar" with the word "ovular" (as Sommers likes to point out), last names gleefully hyphenated into neverending phrases and sweaty indulgences of lesbian orgies in company conference rooms. In the time-honored tradition of other anti-feminist writers, from subservient Christian wife Beverly LaHaye to the young professional D.C-insiders of the "Independent Women's Forum," I could prove how "those feminists" have become an insidious threat to the family, education, morality, free speech, and the very fabric of democracy itself.

Long ago, in my foolish youth (two years ago), I hoped to avoid this path. I hoped to eke out a decent living as a feminist writer, especially after hearing so many conservatives describe the awesome influence wielded by the omniscient, omnipotent, omnivorous "feminist establishment." Writers such as Camille Paglia, Sommers and Elizabeth Fox-Genovese wax indignantly about its totalitarian monolithic powers for thought policing, political influence, and covert ideological warfare. Fox-Genovese builds them up in the title of recent book: *Feminism is Not the Story of My Life: How Today's Feminist Elite Has Lost Touch with the Real Concerns of Women*. "Elite?" I observed. "Hmmm… That means cash. There must be some money somewhere there for me."

So following their cues, I embarked upon a futile journey to find this supposed mother lode, the "feminist establishment," and collect my due. First, I looked for feminist books from the library. No endowments from feminist billionaires cited in any acknowledgements. Then I started to write letters to well-known feminist writers asking if they knew how I could locate this touted feminist establishment. Did they have any clues: an address, longitude coordinates, a Web site, an 800 number, a P.O. box perhaps? One famous feminist critic and author with a prestigious fellowship at an Ivy League school wrote me back and said that she couldn't help me; her own writings have yielded such meager sums that she can't afford even to have children.

Next, I thought that maybe the bold conservative writers who base their careers on confronting and tearing down this legendary establishment could provide some clues. However, they often describe this feminist establishment too vaguely. Paglia, for instance, derives much of her irreverent humor blasting the "feminists" without naming names. And books like Sommers' that are bulging with footnotes and examples pointing out plenty of supposedly deranged professors and activists don't offer much help; their targets are scattered, without enough authority or deep pockets or power to give me a free ride.

Since I couldn't find a centrally located feminist establishment, I decided to inquire with women's foundations, which have developed throughout the country in the '80s. Unfortunately for me, unlike the conservative and libertarian foundations, they have expensive social change to fund. They are so consumed with frittering away money on so many thousands of victim-centered activities in every city in America—like rape treatment centers and programs that help poor women get health care and shelter and start businesses—that they don't have the funds for the important matters, like PR. I could write reams of political dogma on the money they squander on just one women's shelter.

Unlike the conservatives, feminist foundations rarely fund personal projects; the bucks go to bona fide non-profit groups. After months of searching, I have found one small foundation in Brooklyn with the specific purpose of funding feminist writers and artists. But the grants rarely top $500, and competition is fierce. Actually, they do offer a less publicized grant to lesbians, which I did consider applying for. I still wonder, though, how they would check my qualifications.

Don't think that this conversion is easy for me. I do have many doubts and even some guilt (I'm going to get rid of the guilt before I switch over). Perhaps I don't have to defect for life; I'll just stay right-wing until I get the Visa bill and my new Body Shop card paid off. Money talks, after all, and I've finally found the strength to listen. And while my principles aren't actually for sale, I will admit that they can be leased. The terms, of course, are highly flexible, at least until I can get some new cutlery. ■

May, 1996

Green Bay

In Green Bay, Wisconsin, you could eat cheese and sausage for breakfast, lunch, and dinner—for a week—and it wouldn't be a big deal. By the time I arrived on a Friday evening in June, Scott, a college buddy, had nearly finished making dinner. He met me in the driveway, our handshake turning into a clumsy half hug. In the kitchen I could smell the bratwursts, boiling in a pan of beer and stringy white foam.

On the back deck the coals were nearly ready, Scott reported, reaching into a cooler for cans of beer, Classic Draft Light (by Old Style—$6.99 a case). We sat on patio furniture and looked over his lawn, shaped like a piece of pie. Here, in Ashwaubenon, a suburb of Green Bay, backyards drift into one another and property lines are determined by the pattern of lawnmower cuts. Scott went to the kitchen, and returned wearing an oven mitt, carrying a bowl of nacho cheese.

My intentions weren't purely to rekindle an old friendship. I wanted to discover why anybody would settle in the same small town where they grew up. I thought immediately of Scott, who in the five years since college had distinguished himself by becoming more and more firmly rooted in Green Bay. I needed to figure out why.

I convinced Lounge, another friend from college, to pick me up at the train station in Milwaukee and drive to Green Bay for the weekend. Lounge, who hadn't moved from Milwaukee since we finished school, was the one person from school who saw Scott regularly. While the bratwursts hissed on the grill, Lounge recalled his last visit, where all they did during the weekend was rent a Sega, smoke dope and play video games. Lounge liked to take it easy. "Not this weekend," Scott said to us from the grill, knowing the intentions of my visit. "We're going to soak up the flavor of Green Bay." He had an absurdly long pair of tongs and waved them like a wand over the lawn while he spoke.

It had been sixteen years since I'd been to Green Bay. When fifth grade let out, I was sent up to stay with Sean Lynch, my best friend who had moved north. On the bus ride I wasn't thinking maturely about how our friendship would be changed. Instead I was trying to figure out why the man sitting next to me had bits of toilet paper stuck to his neck. Sean and his older brother picked me up at the bus station. During the ride to the Lynch's I realized that Sean had become cooler than me. He and his brother talked about the best places to park with a girl. Girls came over to his house to hang out or play flashlight tag. In the mall Sean lifted an Oakland A's plastic baseball helmet, the kind that were so popular back then. He wore it backwards during my entire stay, reminding me that I had chickened out.

At Scott's, after our first bratwurst, we played croquet. The neighborhood had become quieter, as parents called their kids inside for bed. Lounge swung his mallet with one hand. Lounge earned his nickname freshman year by roaming throughout the dorm trying out different couches and chairs and beds, like Goldilocks. Scott used a practiced, between-the-legs stroke to knock Lounge from the game early. Lounge went inside to watch TV. Scott and I loaded our plates with seconds—bratwursts, mustard potato salad, sauerkraut from a can, nacho chips and cheese, and cold Classic Draft Lights. As we were digging in, Lounge called us inside to watch O.J. Simpson.

O.J.

We weren't going to "soak up the flavor of Green Bay" while the TV cameras tracked O.J. fleeing in the white Bronco. I felt like I was missing something, sitting on a cavernous couch, sipping from my can of Classic Draft Light. When someone read the suicide note for the second time in an hour, I suggested that we go out, watch the highlights later. "But we're watching live history," Scott said. A minute later Barbara Walters reported that O.J. could be put into the cell next to Lyle Menendez.

I rooted for tragedy, for the worst possible outcome. I wanted O.J. to shoot himself, or at least the dog that wandered in the driveway. The only promise of watching was that the gun could go off. Peter Jennings introduced a man on a cellular phone, reportedly just across from the Simpson driveway. I thought it was a local reporter until I heard the exaggerated fake black voice: "Peter I'm lookin' and all I see is Oh Jay ... O.J. be crouched over. He be lookin' angry, too..." Lounge and Scott remained glued to the television, but I began to break up, laughing with a mouthful of Classic Draft Light. I was trying to swallow when the caller said, "I'd be scared too with all these poh-lease around." I choked on beer, spitting it into my hand and laughing. Here was the terrifying moment when O.J. was going to kill himself, transformed into a farce by over-eager ABC airing a prank call. Scott and Lounge started laughing, and we all took turns imitating the caller. We laughed through O.J.'s surrender. I laughed until my throat hurt.

Cock and Bull

So we got out late, to a college bar called the Cock and Bull. We met Carrie, my friend from graduate school who was living with her mother in Green Bay until she had enough cash to move to Missoula. She and I teamed up to beat Scott and Lounge at three straight games of shuffleboard. We broke up the teams so I could stand next to Carrie. She told me she was leaving Green Bay because everyone was so stupid. "I know it makes me sound like a snob," she said, "but it's true. Look at this place." Three blond girls, hair stretched and teased and pulled out, crossed through the back. Heads turned and conversations stopped. One guy whistled above the din. The blondes all wore shirts that opened up to show their bellies. Even though it was late June, their tans looked an anemic yellow. At the far end of the shuffleboard, Scott and Lounge watched them cross the room. Lounge scratched under his ear, at the place where beard and shaved skin met.

The four of us got a pitcher and took a table in the corner. Smoke hung near the ceiling. I could feel the cigarette grime seep into my clothes. Carrie said she was experimenting with pills to stay off cigarettes. She left early. After we closed the bar, Scott, Lounge and I walked to the end of the parking lot, leaning on a wall, staring down at the East River. "The East River is the stinkiest, worst river in all of Green Bay," Scott said. The water smelled rubbery and toxic but looked poetic in the moonlight. Soon there was the obligatory spitting contest. Lounge's went the farthest, his white gobs outdistancing ours, floating and bobbing quietly downstream.

Scott kept the car keys under the passenger side floormat. "That's what we do here," he said. At home the garage door was open: Trek mountain bikes, a lawnmower, fishing poles, softball cleats, a bin for recycled cans, all free and open.

Green Day

We slept late. Scott was up first, making coffee like a real host. I sat at the kitchen table, reading the paper, sipping coffee, waiting for Lounge to finish his shower. In college I always tried to picture meeting my good friends five, ten years later. I imagined it nothing like this, and yet this all seemed perfectly inevitable. Scott's roommate played the new Green Day CD, so I told him that those guys had played in my living room in Oregon. Not to be outdone, Scott said his neighbor was Jackie Harris, all-pro tight end for the Packers. "We share a wall with him," he said, knocking on the end of his kitchen. "But we'll probably lose him to free agency."

Hall of Fame

The last time I was at a sports museum it was the day after Elvis died. I was in Troy, New York, and my grandparents drove me out to Cooperstown so I could see the Baseball Hall of Fame. I browsed through the many walls of bronze plaques, the way I do at art museums. Occasionally I'd read the biography of some "Lefty" or "Buck" or "Shoeless," but I was hurrying to the rooms with glass cases of colorful jerseys, mud-caked spikes, and video presentations. My grandmother crept behind me, took my ear between her fingernails, pinched and twisted. Ear lobe burning, I wriggled away from her grip. "Your father," she lectured me, "was so grateful when we brought him here that he read every word on every plaque." My ear stung, but I didn't touch it. I stood in front of each plaque for the proper amount of time, resolutely not reading another word.

At the Packer Hall of Fame, the boring part, the actual room of silver plaques, is tucked away in an annex of the building, almost an afterthought. When you pay the $5.50, you are directed upstairs to a series of rooms with glass cases holding old footballs, leather helmets, trophies, photographs of coaches in long coats and toothless linemen with crew cuts. The Packer Hall of Fame has three theaters and at least three video presentations. For fun, I started my tour by looking for some picture or video with O.J. Simpson in it, but all of the items, without exception, are Packer related. One of the more arresting displays features three pieces of splintered wood, the largest about the size of a pinky finger. A card explains that these were removed from a former Packer's groin, after he had played with the splinters for an entire season. The "Football Follies" theater shows an unfunny NFL film produced in 1969, a series of dullingly simple goofs—quarterbacks drop the football, tacklers slip on the mud—with stupid voiceovers reminiscent of those "Shark Attack/ Convoy/ Oil Shortage" collage records from the 1970s. The strangest, and most troubling folly, comes at the end of the film when the camera focuses on two adults with Downs Syndrome screaming from their front row seats. One of them waves a thin pom pom. "This is the wacky world of the NFL," says the voice. Then the image freezes and goes to black. Ha, ha.

I was told that you could kick field goals at the Packer Hall of Fame. I had imagined being allowed to run out to the thirty yard-line of Lambeau Field and try one soccer-style. The actual room, with miniature goalposts and tires mounted on the walls, is very much like a set from American Gladiators. The floor and walls are covered with Astroturf. Lounge scared all the little kids out of the room by punting footballs into the ceiling, ferociously, with an energy I've rarely seen in him. The kids scattered. Scott threw footballs at the tires, pretending he was Brett Favre drilling touchdown passes. I tried to find a safe corner where I could take pictures. I photographed Scott, while Lounge ricocheted punts off the ceiling at me. I put my camera away. Lounge and I threw balls at each other, seeing who could catch the hardest pass. We tried to break something, but the Astroturf, the cement ceiling, even the footballs were rubbery and indestructible.

Though he'd lived in Green Bay and loved the Pack for twenty-seven years, Scott had never been to the Hall of Fame before, to this shrine in his back yard. The Packers are the spiritual center for the people of Green Bay, for all of Wisconsin. The hundred or so visitors that day, families mostly, from places like Oshkosh, Stevens Point, and Pewaukee, serving as a profound testament of faith, walked with reverence and wonder through a museum built for a team that had only won a few championships thirty years ago.

The gift shop was packed, and everybody was buying. Packer troll dolls, Packer checkbook covers, Packer wrist bands, and Packer sand wedges. I tried on a foam rubber cheese-head hat. The smell was overwhelming, like airplane glue and rotting potatoes. Tomorrow was Father's Day, so Scott tried to find something for his dad. He settled on a mesh sun hat, with the famous Packer G stitched into a bandanna tied around it. He wore the hat for the rest of the afternoon, thinking aloud that he might get his dad something else.

Krolls West

Scott took us to a famous diner across from the stadium with promises of chicken bouilla (Boo-Yah), a chicken-based, everything soup. The restaurant smelled like cigarettes and frying cheese. Each vinyl booth had an intercom to call the waitresses, who were outfitted in plain white dresses and black shoes. Our waitress was young, wearing braces and Reebok high tops. She apologized that they were out of bouilla, but said the smelt was fresh and very good. Scott ordered the smelt plate and cheese curds. Lounge got a pizza burger and cottage fries and I tried a bowl of meat chili with spaghetti noodles and a hot dog. We all had dessert: pie and ice cream, and left with individual checks under five dollars. The cashier gave us extra Coca-Cola Hot Summer Scratch and Win cards. We set them on a newspaper box outside Krolls and used our toothpicks to push off the gray paint covering our magic numbers. Every card was a loser.

Fort Fun, You Ruined It

At Fort Fun, a mini-amusement park down near the bay, we played adventure golf. Halfway through the game I was winning. Lounge turned competitive and hostile, cheering when my ball fell off a bridge. "Water penalty, two strokes," he insisted. Scott joined him in heckling me, but I prevailed. When we finished, Lounge was tired and wanted to go home and watch ESPN. I was tired and sweaty also but insisted on seeing the rest of Fort Fun, the Ferris wheel, bumper cars, arcade, and the waterfront. Scott told Lounge we'd only stay for a little while. We wove through the kiddie rides; some families lingered in the early evening, while others arrived, the fathers holding strips and strips of ride tickets. The air smelled sweet, like caramel apples and cinnamon. A group of adult riders, mothers and older cousins, had jammed themselves into a kiddie electric train that slowly lapped the grounds. The conductor, a bored high school girl, sipped from a black and pink neon plastic bottle.

We climbed upon broken rocks lining the shore of Green Bay. The sky clouded out the sun, but the air was still wet, sticky. A breeze blew off the muddy water, cooling us. Scott skipped rocks. I took pictures. Lounge sat. I recognized his silent pouting and it irritated me. It had been a long day, but now it would be too easy to sink into a couch and find the remote. I looked for an authentic image in the camera lens. Scott poked a branch at a dead fish. It was a large, rotting coho. Another dead one floated in the waves, about fifteen yards out. Scott and I threw stones at it.

I tried to take a few more pictures, posing Lounge and Scott in front of Fort Fun, then by the water. Scott was jumpy. While I changed film, he and Lounge started back toward the amusement park. I looked around for something else to shoot, an island, the coastline, a jagged tree. Nothing was good enough. We should ride the bumper cars, I said when I caught up to them, At thirty cents, it's a bargain you can't pass up. Lounge told us to go ahead and sat on a bench in a cove of flowering bushes. Scott called to him when we decided to look in the arcade for Skee-Ball, but if Lounge heard us, he didn't answer.

There was no Skee-Ball in the arcade, only the clatter of folding chairs in an attached room. I peeked through the doors. Two high school boys cleaned a reception room, hired for the afternoon probably. One had a *Kiss Alive III* T-shirt on.

Outside it looked like it would rain. Popcorn cooked at the snack stand. The board said all ice cream was forty cents. A pudgy kid with a Mickey Mouse ice cream bar walked past us. I said hello, but he ignored me. "Elizabeth. Elizabeth!" he said, trying to get the attention of a girl who watched the Scrambler. "Elizabeth, you want something to eat?" he said, holding out Mickey's chocolate ear.

The girl turned, her face flushing. She screamed viciously: "You ruined it. Because you were too chicken! Now I can't go on this." Elizabeth pointed at the Scrambler. Her grandfather stroked her pigtails and she cried. The boy backed away, still offering Mickey as a way out of his cowardice, the ice cream face dangerously close to falling off its stick.

I wanted to take Elizabeth on the Scrambler. It only cost two tickets, twenty cents. But Scott and I were already making our slow way to the bumper cars. We'd kept Lounge waiting as it was, and besides, I couldn't take a little girl on the Scrambler. Who was I kidding? I hadn't showered in two days, and my hair was matted with dirt and sweat. Still, she cried, as the Scrambler began spinning again. She'd recover by evening, crying hot tears into her pillow until she fell asleep. By that time we'd be drunk.

"Frick You, Riznowski"

I wanted to stop at Kara's Czech Bar, a converted house, but I was alone in the backseat and the car kept passing slowly through neighborhoods and corner bars with Pabst signs glowing in the windows. Scott suggested we go home and order a pizza. Lounge's silence registered agreement. It was early evening and people sat on front steps, on porch swings or rusty lawn chairs, wondering if it would rain. Everyone seemed an extreme, either obese or cancer thin. At Bert's there was a group throwing horseshoes. I begged to stop. "Frick you, Riznowski," Scott called to the back. "Frick you" was a common Green Bay insult. Whenever I suggested that we stop at a bar or a park or an abandoned factory, Lounge said, "Frick you, Riznowski."

In DePere (another of Green Bay's five suburbs), Scott searched up and down Main Street, looking for Jake's Pizza.

"They must have closed it," he said. In McDonald's there was a large Help Wanted sign. "Or maybe Jake's is on Main Street, downtown. I can't remember."

Avoid the Noid

The delivery guy gave us a Domino's frisbee that had the old Noid mascot on it. Scott and I went outside to play catch. It was dark, but not pitch dark, and you could see the frisbee just as it came close. Rain fell, lightly, but we just kept chucking the disc back and forth. Lounge joined us, moving slowly to the ones out of reach. Lightning flashed in the sky, but we kept throwing in a triangle. When I thought that Lounge might be thinking I was trying to hit him with the frisbee, I became rattled. My throws faded right, rolling in an arc on the lawn. Lounge sauntered after them. Scott slapped at his shins, and then we all felt the mosquitoes on us and headed inside.

Christian Rock

A coal barge stopped traffic on the bridge to downtown, forcing us to pay closer attention to the FM radio in Scott's Chevy Cavalier. He had preset four stations: a heavy metal station from Appleton, a straight classic rock station, a top forty station, and a Christian rock station. Scott's fingers snapped from one to another trying to choose between Boston, Metallica and an Idle Threat interview on the Christian Radio Station.

"Why do you program this station if you never listen to it for more than two seconds?" I said.

"Sometimes there's a good rap song on here," he said. "Besides, these are the only four stations worth listening to." I made us listen to the Idle Threat interview. The singer explained how they had sponsored a national contest at Bible camps to name their band. On the heavy metal station, a DJ ranted above the rumbling engines from the dragway in Kaukauna. It was half-price admission to the races if you said "WAPL kicks ass" at the gate. I wanted to leave the bridge and head for the races, picturing myself in the bleachers with corn on the cob and a 16 oz. Pabst. This was summertime in Wisconsin, after all. But Kaukauna was thirty-five minutes the other way, and we'd waited fifteen minutes for the barge to pass. The boat sounded its low horn, and the bridge unfolded into place.

Speaks

The Speak Easy, or Speaks, is Green Bay's grungy bar. Inside it was dark and crowded, like a college party. The CD jukebox, four songs for a dollar, played at a deafening level. A short guy with muscley arms showed his buddies what appeared to be a new tattoo of the Red Hot Chili Peppers' logo. Scott shouted to me that the bartender had a sexy Cindy Crawford-ish mole near her mouth. I went for beer, bottles of Leinenkugel for a dollar. She carried four of them in one hand. I left a dollar tip on the bar and she rang the bell next to the cash register three times.

I gave Lounge a beer, a peace offering. It was too loud to talk. The Smashing Pumpkins poured from the speakers. The guy with the tattoo played invisible drums. I leaned close and told Scott that I was missing a secret Smashing Pumpkins show in Chicago. "But this is just as good," he shouted.

Conversation meant yelling and spitting into each other's ears. I rolled the beer bottle across my chest and thought numbly about happiness. Carl Sandburg said happiness was a Hungarian family, a keg of beer, and a Sunday picnic by the Des Plaines river. By comparison I imagined O.J. Simpson, alone in his cement cell. An alcohol-inspired truism occurred to me: Relaxation is the foundation to happiness. During the entire weekend, Scott never claimed he was happy, though I might have expected him to, since he knew that I'd come to write about Green Bay. I know few people my age who were ever more unflappable or relaxed than Scott, leaning against a post, drinking, swaying to the Smashing Pumpkins, and getting glimpses of the bartender when pockets in the crowd opened.

Four years ago Scott sent me a letter that tried to explain why he stayed: "My plan was to get a job, save some money and move on to a much more exotic, metropolitan locale, for surely, there I would find all the missing elements of my life. Then a very curious event occurred: Don Majkowski made a game-winning touchdown pass to Sterling Sharpe, and the Packers beat the Chicago Bears. While this in itself may not have been responsible for the turnaround of my attitude toward Green Bay, it did succeed in doing something that the first eighteen years of my life in Green Bay failed to do—it actually made me proud to be in Green Bay."

Lounge brought more beer, lingered, then went to look at the jukebox. Scott said he liked a girl at his work, had liked her in fact for more than a year. The problem was, of course, she had a boyfriend. So he wrote a poem, his first, and gave it to her. It was the nicest thing anyone had ever done for her, she had said, but she kept her boyfriend just the same. "She might come around," Scott shouted in my ear, waving to a group of guys he recognized coming in the back door. I wasn't sure if he meant that she'd show up here at Speaks, or if the poem would eventually inspire her to dump the boyfriend.

Drink for Three

We were surprised when another friend from college, Mike, came in with his girlfriend. After finishing law school in Utah, Mike returned to Shawano, the Wisconsin town where he grew up, and began to practice law. He looked exhausted, and it wasn't long before the volume in Speaks was overwhelming.

We all headed out on Main Street, walking to Patrick's, a sedate UW-GB hangout. A girl leaned out of a mini-pick-up truck and yelled something to Mike's girlfriend about pussies. Mike's girlfriend didn't seem too upset, so we tried to figure out exactly what she had screamed. Mike said he thought it was "Get her pussy, I did." Meanwhile, shirtless guys with tan chests rolled around in the back of another truck, hooting and chugging cans of beer.

"Drink for Three," the sign in Patrick's bar said. "Every Sunday from 7-12." Mike thought it meant drink for three dollars, but at the bottom it specified "FREE." It was our next riddle. "You gotta drink three times as much on Sunday," Mike said.

I puffed out my belly and rubbed it with both hands. "Look," I said, "I'm drinkin' for twins." We laughed until I remembered his girlfriend had a baby boy at home with her grandmother.

Mike told me why people get trapped in their own towns: "It's comfortable. You've got a job. Why bother looking for another one?" He considered for a moment. "But I'm going to move back out West, sometime," he said.

His girlfriend, who first met Mike on the bus when he was a seventh grader and she was a sophomore, said that she loved the safety of Shawano. "You never have to lock your doors, or worry. I can go any-where I want, and not get hassled." I didn't know if she was referring to the girl in the truck who had yelled at her earlier. I told her that Scott leaves his keys under the floormat. "In Green Bay?" she said, surprised. "I would never do that here."

Reservation

Though I spent most of 1990 teaching on the Pine Ridge Reservation in South Dakota, it wasn't until the bars closed on Saturday that I made my first trip to a reservation casino. The Oneida Bingo and Casino, and its accompanying seven story parking garage, sits in a grove of pine trees on the tiny Oneida Reservation, close to Scott's house and open all night. We met Mike there after stopping at Taco Bell. Everyone was eager, except me, but I figured it could lead to some good pictures. Just before we went in, Lounge told me they'd break my camera if I tried to bring it in. "What?" I said. He and Scott staggered through the revolving door. Of course, cameras weren't allowed. The doorman said I could leave it with the coat check girl, but I went to Scott's car, took the keys from under the mat and locked my camera inside.

I didn't play any games. I had about eight dollars and a handful of change left. I could have gotten a cash advance, but I wanted to watch. Mike played blackjack (all they had was blackjack, bingo, and slot machines). Mike said he had a system. I was trying to figure out what it was when the cart of coffee, Pepsi, and Mountain Dew arrived. I'm winning, I thought, taking a free cup of coffee, and wan-dering to the back. Even though lights flashed everywhere and coins jingled into slot trays, I felt as if I were at a party where I'd overstayed my welcome, the hosts patiently waiting for me to tire. A woman ran a vacuum cleaner down an empty aisle of slot machines. Lounge and Scott were the only guys in the next aisle, standing in front of a machine with a large, yellow twirling light, like a tow truck. At the far end of the casino, security guards filled green, blue and red buckets with quarters from the machines. Here and there, large Indian men, casino officials, sat on stools and counted thick wads of cash.

When I finally caught up to everybody, they were comparing their losses. Lounge couldn't believe I hadn't bet anything. "You didn't even play one lousy quarter slot?"

I patted my pockets and shrugged. "I was watching bingo," I said. I felt guilty, as if I was implying that gambling was beneath me, and refusing to play was an insult. With Scott it was easy to fall back into all our stupid college habits and joking, but Lounge acted like an adult.

Lounge wouldn't stay to play blackjack, he said, if everybody else was finished gambling. Nobody cared about staying later. I was eager to watch Lounge lose at blackjack. "We'll cheer you on," I said. But he had a bachelor's party the following weekend, and they were all going to a casino in Canada, so we left.

In the car, Lounge threw the extra burrito from Taco Bell back at me. "Here you go, Riznowski," he said, disgusted. I won the extra burrito because, by staying even, I was the big winner. I felt like a loser, a tagalong who had made the outing worse by not risking anything. I wondered how much of Lounge's weekend I had spoiled by insisting that we go look at Green Bay. Scott played Christian rap on the radio. I left the burrito next to me on the backseat, staying quiet, unclipping and reclipping my camera strap.

The Poetry of Patience

We all grew up Catholic, met at a Catholic university, and have relatives and friends who go to church every week. Even so, I can't remember the three of us ever going to mass together. In college, we would stay in Scott's dorm room, throwing darts while students filed down for Sunday night mass. Scott had rationalized skipping: "What good would it do? I'd only go to church to look for girls."

So on Sunday, instead of mass and the free doughnuts, we went to the Country Kitchen and ate Hungry Man's breakfasts.

Afterwards, while I packed up my bags, I thought about the best way to ask Scott for the poem. I didn't seem to have anything tangible besides a few notes about cheese and beer. I mumbled something.

"You want the poem?" Scott said.

"Uh, yeah. If you have a copy. Or you could send it to me," I said, leaving an escape hatch for both of us. Why did I want the love poem he'd written for the girl at work? I don't know. It was like I needed some evidence of Scott, more than just a souvenir cap or bag of string cheese. He darted up the stairs, and came back down with it, saying that the one he actually gave her was changed a little, but still about the same. I stood reading the poem while they watched me. My favorite line goes "And once I thought the answer was carried by the voice of someone new."

We made plans to go camping later in the summer. I got into Lounge's car for the ride to Milwaukee. Scott used a pitching wedge to loft dandelions from his lawn at the windshield. Lounge gave a lonely honk as we backed out of the driveway and pointed towards the freeway. I tried to find a suitable cassette in a box of Grateful Dead bootlegs. Lounge seemed happier now that he was heading home. He said this was much earlier and much less baked than he'd ever left for Milwaukee. "Yeah," I said, thinking that something important had broken between us. ■

February, 1995

JESS MOWRY

Wake Up America! There Are Gangs Under Your Beds!

Yes folks! We got trouble right here in River City! And that starts with T and that rhymes with G and that stands for GANGS! (The fact that T also rhymes with P and could indicate police and politicians is purely coincidental.) And unless we do something about it right now, it's only going to get worse!

If your children have contact with the minority races, they may have already brought a gang member into your home! And, while studies have indicated that Caucasian youth are far less susceptible to this insidious new social disease, you cannot afford to take the risk of your child contracting it! At the present time there is no known cure for gang-association syndrome. Like AIDS, prevention is the only defense! (And abstention is the safest prevention.)

Please be assured that a concerned government will do everything possible to eradicate this new menace to American Society and that the paid protectors of your life and property will spare no taxpayers' dollar so that more and tougher laws are passed and more and bigger prisons are built to deal with this threat to the American Way of Life.

Remain calm. Public schools, libraries, parks and playgrounds will continue to be underfunded and closed if necessary because these, after all, are the breeding pits for the juvenile sociopaths and murderers that make up youth gangs. Rest easy knowing that the most qualified and highly paid statisticians will work tirelessly compiling statistics, and that the finest, most highly paid experts are constantly in government employ doing research and devising new theories about the connection between disadvantaged children and violence in American Society. Be confident that the vast majority of these highly qualified and well-paid researchers come from middle- and upper-class white environments and have university degrees to certify that they can accurately assess the true personalities and problems faced by inner-city youth in America today. Be also assured that of these thousands of (highly paid) experts, at least a few have had real life experience, and some even possess actual children of their own.

Much research will also be done to determine if there is any parallel between the youth gangs of today and other anarchistic activities in American history. A similarity is noted both with the anti-war movement of the late 1960s and the Red Menace threat of the early '50s. In both instances, a segment of American youth expressed dissatisfaction with American Values and lack of confidence with America's leaders. Fortunately, the government reacted quickly and efficiently to suppress the problem, resorting to violence—as in the incident at Kent State—only when all other methods had failed.

But it is absurd to attempt to draw parallels between the inner-city youth of today and their historical counterparts. To suggest that one of Dickens' characters, from *A Tale of Two Cities*, was actually "tagging" when he smeared the word "blood" upon the wall of a public street in pre-revolutionary France is patently preposterous! It was simple allegory on the part of Dickens to show that a population (presumably young because life expectancy was short for slum-dwellers in those times) was so oppressed that it scrawled its anger in the streets. In this instance, the word "blood" was used to symbolize what was to come—when the people at last banded together and threw down the corrupt and uncaring government that oppressed them.

Of course, this could never happen today! If anything positive came out of the Rodney King riots, it was the demonstration that American Society has more than ample power to crush any mob of urban dissenters! And besides, the downtrodden peasants of France were able to revolt because they acted together and with one purpose, just as our own forefathers threw off the oppression of England. But, it may be easily observed through our impartial news media that these youth-gangs today fight only each other and will never carry their rage and resentment beyond the confines of the ghetto!

It is more than obvious to any decent citizen that these gangs of unwanted youth should be outlawed, and their individual members must receive the harshest punishments a just society can devise. New prisons should be built as quickly as possible. If America is to continue leading the world in portion of population incarcerated (South Africa used to be second), then we must consider this expense a small price to pay for our way of life! And how else could we possibly deal with these children and still call ourselves civilized? It is much kinder to lock them up at eight years old than to have them trying to compete in today's job market.

Legislation making it a crime for a child to belong to a gang would be simple to enact. There is no shortage of (highly paid) experts already on the government payroll who would have no difficulty defining a "gang" in legal terminology. And gang members are easy for our police to spot: They are mostly minorities, who often wear distinctive clothes or headgear. Some have tattoos, and police already routinely stop black and brown youth on the street and check for identifying marks (though one gang in Oakland had the arrogance to tattoo their posteriors). If these young people still persist in defying the law, the ruling on gangs could be tightened so that no more than three children could "hang" together at any one time in a public place, and their meeting in secret would be defined as conspiracy.

But of course this would only be enforced in the inner cities! ■

February, 1995

Never Fucked Anyone

Ah, the rock 'em, sock 'em, explosive art world of New York in the '80s. Could you stand the excitement? It was palpable, no? Auction prices ever higher, Japanese bidders snapping up Van Goghs for tens of millions. Speculation, speculation: Longo and Schnabel and Fischl selling paintings for $100,000 before they were dry. Yes, it was a heady time. Money and art and fame and even more money—as sexy as a David Salle diptych, and without the misogynistic aftertaste. Accordingly, it screamed novelization. But still, it's been over ten years and we've had virtually nothing. Seems a cinch for Tom Wolfe—collate *The Painted Word* and *Bonfire* and you've got something, easy. But no such luck. Instead, we have only the bizarre residual side projects of the period's A-list. Robert Longo's, um, darkly prophetic *Johnny Mnemonic*, Salle's movie that no one saw, Schnabel's *Basquiat* and the singing career, clearly a cry for help. To date, we have heard so little about the era itself, of lives lived in that lustrous time.

Until now. With Fernanda Eberstadt's *When the Sons of Heaven Meet the Daughters of the Earth*, released a few months ago, the Knopf publicists promised the first novelistic look at the culture of the art world's boom time. And though the canvas is a bit smaller than advertised—it really doesn't go too far into the market as a whole, and the references to actual people are clouded—it's still a good book. (Kind of a lame third act, but really great most of the way.) In it, we meet the Geblers, a Manhattan family of unconscionable wealth, whose matriarch, Dolly Gebler, presides over the Aurora Foundation, a nonprofit art space made possible by the family's fortune, created in Chicago by her father, in pharmaceuticals. Presiding over the foundation, Dolly is brilliant, domineering and coolly passionate about art. Her taste runs toward the minimal—she decorates her home with work by Stella and Agnes Martin— and her life is similarly ordered. She has settled into middle age with three teenage children and has come to terms with being attached to an infantile, adulterous husband. For fun she surrounds herself with artists and writers and such, and at her parties, everyone's fabulously rich and well-bred and articulate, and they all speak in wonderful, quip-laden prose. One finds "the Renaissance overrated," another deems "the young people of today so *censorious*," while another finds the pato negro "a bit gamey."

Meanwhile, across the city, we are following the plight of one Isaac Hooker, a rough-hewn castaway from New Hampshire, an almost-homeless painter of unrefined talent but great passion. He's also a Harvard dropout, and like all Harvard men, speaks like the brilliant rogue in a Victorian drawing room. When he is displeased with an avant garde opera about the Trojan War—one that Dolly, through Aurora, has sponsored—he lets a guest at the post-party know what he thinks: "[For] everyone to everybody to stand around gushing about the lighting is to accede to her meretricious pretentious gall in lobotomizing one of the most heartrending stories in Greek tragedy."

After 300 or so pages of setup, Dolly and Isaac finally fall in love. She is attracted to his intensity and becomes infatuated with his primitive and sensual artwork, full of allegory and religious imagery. He responds to her loving encouragement, and to some extent the allure of her money and power. Soon there are the Central Park walks, the weekends at the house in North Fork, the clandestine meetings at his dingy studio. For a fleeting while we are convinced that they are meant to be. Their relationship is lustful but tender and respectful, and we imagine that she's found a new life at middle age, and that he's found love and stability in Dolly, twenty years his senior. But then something happens on page 357, really deep into the novel, actually, that sort of sticks out, and changes the feel of things. The two have been meeting often, sometimes at hotels—"the St. Moritz or the Pierre"—and during one of their encounters, Isaac muses on his good fortunes: "[He] could not resist these wayward autumn afternoons decanting into evening. The delectable melancholy of lying on crumpled hotel sheets, watching ever-diminishing reflections of Dolly in the bath, and wondering if he couldn't fuck her once more before he dropped her home."

Did you flinch? I flinched. I flinched, and then I was troubled. It really came from nowhere, that word, "fuck," used as it was, as a verb. Isaac and Dolly are no doubt in some sort of love, and have a certain clear respect for each other. They talk endlessly about art and philosophy and literature, treat each other to various kindnesses. But when Isaac thinks of her sexually, he wonders if he can "fuck her once more before he drop[s] her home." And so I wondered why it was that Isaac wanted to "fuck" Dolly, wondered what Eberstadt meant there. Had I missed something in their relationship, in Isaac's character? I guess he was supposed to be sort of tough, kind of unrefined in his manners, but essentially he's a sensitive, intellectual artsy type. So then, um, why does he want to "fuck" her? Nothing in the text until that point led me to believe that Isaac would, while having an affair with a fifty-year-old heiress and mother of three, look at her and hope to "fuck" her. It leapt out.

And after that, reading the book for me became about trying to decipher the meaning of that word's appearance, and the other times when Eberstadt used words like "pussy" and "prick" and "gash" in the middle of her otherwise genteel prose. And just as the book became about that word, so will this essay, which really has nothing to with Eberstadt's book, or novelizations of the '80s the art world. It's about that word, "fuck," and I guess what I'm saying, and will use the next 5,000 words to say in a really plodding and meandering (I won't say peripatetic, you're welcome) sort of way, is that I have a problem with using that word. As a verb.

Every language must have its profanity, and "fuck" is our most astringent and versatile specimen. I use the word all the time, really, all the fucking time, actually, heh heh, but its use as gerund-acting-as-adjective seems to me wholly different than its use as verb of choice to indicate copulation. Now, when I use it to strengthen a point I'm making, as in, "I'm really fucking hungry," I'm using its inherent abrasiveness to indicate, as all such words do, the serious immediacy of my need. Its power comes from its gutteral sound, its status as profanity, its (admittedly, often mild) shock value. I really don't want to have to go into the etymology here—Mr. Safire, for one, traces the word to the "Lower

Dutch,"—but I think we can all agree that without exception, its sundry applications are all of the negative nature, uniformly unpleasant. To be "fucked over" is not desired. To "fuck someone over" is to do him wrong. To be in a situation where one is "fucked" is to be in a bad situation. To "fucking hate" someone is to hate that person a great deal. To want to "fucking kill" someone shows that if you ever get a chance to kill that person, you will do so with extreme predjudice, as it were. And, see, I've said all these things, used all these ways of employing this word, "fuck." I've said "fucking" this and "fucking" that. I have gotten "fucked up," and have had a "great fucking time," have been "really fucking pissed," and "so fucking mad." While driving, I have told other motorists that if they don't get the "fuck" out of my way, that I will "fucking" [do something bad] to them. I have told people to get the "fuck" out of my house and my office, and that if they didn't, that I would "fucking" [make them]. When playing my slow white guy version of basketball, I have told opponents to "fucking" get that shit "outta here." I have been "really fucking tired," "really fucking confused," "really fucking depressed," and "really fucking happy."

But I've never fucked anyone.

I have done what people are talking about when they use that verb. But I'm really pretty sure that I have never done what that verb conveys. And it does convey something different than the other words and phrases available to describe what we're talking about. What does it say? Let's think aloud for a sec. On a basic level, it implies that the sex was down and dirty. That it was sticky and raunchy, maybe sweaty and smelly and raw. And all that is, of course, great — sex can be/should be down and dirty and sticky and sweaty and raunchy and raw — but then there is another aspect of the word, the negative aspect alluded to above, that comes with it. It more than comes with it, really, it overwhelms it. Due to a combination of the oomphy, clipped sound of the word, and its many other applications, "fuck" carries with it, inevitably, the force of violence, the weight of the I'm-doing-something-to-you aspect. And it doesn't matter much, really, whether it's being used in the cooperative sort of way, "we fucked," or the more common "I fucked him/her" sort of way. Any usage, no matter what the context, actually, carries with it meanings and signifiers, even in trace amounts, that reduce sex to something sort of base, something not profound, something unequivocally trivial. And so the hypothesis here is this: "Fuck"'s increasingly widespread usage, conversationally or in books or whatever—and what I can only see as the fast-approaching time when it's interchangeable with more benign terms like "to have sex with" or "to sleep with"—is, I think, one of the sadder things going on in these happy times, blessed as they are with a robust economy and so many action movies starring Nicholas Cage. It seems clear, to me at least, that every time a person uses that word, every time a person has sex and afterward decides that he or she has "fucked" someone—there's that gap between the two things, it seems, between being with someone and having sex, and later naming it with that name—every time that happens, when the choice has been made and that term applied, the act named "fuck," it seems to me that that's where, a little bit, the world crumbles.

I have a friend, who we'll call Buddy, who does not openly proffer news from his own sex life, but who heartily enjoys hearing about the activities of others, including mine. And invariably, when I tell him that I had been out with someone/had been recently romantically involved with that someone—quite often someone he knows well—his reaction is always the same. His eyes will narrow on me, his eyebrows will do a Jack Nicholson kind of thing and he'll lean forward in his chair and ask, "Did you fuck her?"

And at that point the conversation goes cold, because though I sort of want to tell him about the events in question, and really have no qualms recounting such things in detail, I find myself unable to go on with it. Even if my night was kind of uncivilized, even if by his standards (and we're talking about a pretty odd duck here; I mean, Buddy's a sick fuck, really) "fucking" is exactly what I had done, I've lost heart. I feel like the wind's been knocked out of me.

At those times, and when reading Eberstadt's passage mentioned above, I've considered it, thinking back, from partner to partner, trying to recall a time when the sex I've had could be called "fucking." But even when taking into account the most creative activities with old girl-friends, even the most random one-nighters (not too many, but still), even the times in closets and crawlspaces and parking garages, I haven't been able to make the word "fucking" stick. Even when I've been drenched in sweat, when it's dark and humid, even when I've been poked and scratched and we're making completely ridiculous sounds and ugly faces and have to slow down periodically to catch our breath, even when condoms are breaking and we're trying positions that are clever but sort of unfeasible in the long term, even when things are red and sore and soaking, soaking wet, even when I was last visiting New York and was out and met someone at a party at Rebar, someone who was some vague friend of a friend, and I talked to her for a few minutes, and almost immediately was touching her, knowing from pretty much the start that something was going to happen, it being summer and Saturday and everything, even when we went to that club in the meat-packing district where you dance to bad Billy Idol music and where we made idiots out of ourselves, mashing on the dance floor, groping and everything, even when we finally decided to go home and then walked entirely too far to her apartment and then made some half-hearted pre-tense of talking on her bed but then really kind of right away we were wearing nothing and I was watching her above me and knowing that I didn't know her really at all, and knowing I probably wasn't going to ever see her again, and/but feeling her body and her incredibly taut skin, so perfect everywhere—as far as I remember, anyway—so smooth-ly stretched over munificent curves... I mean, even then, when we were whispering purple-y stuff to each other and making outrageous requests, and when we got sick of the rubber and tossed it at the win-dow and gave our lives away to those minutes in the dark—even then, even then, friends, I can't say it was "fucking." (By the way, hi, Lenora.)

Honestly, I'm not sure what to call it. The other terms aren't much bet-ter. To "make love" always carries with it that sort of dopey New Agey stench, in the same earnest-but-stupid vein as calling a boyfriend or girlfriend your "lover." There are the funny words—"boning," "pork-ing," "screwing," etc.—that are relatively harmless, used lightly as they are, usually in anecdotes told by fraternity men and/or people who fish. The main one, "to have sex" is a pretty pedestrian way of putting it, and really without its own baggage; it's clinical and acceptable in almost all situations—dinner conversation, junior high health class, perky sit-coms featuring Brooke Shields and Judd Nelson. And therein lies the dissatisfaction, I guess. It's too common and plain, and has been stripped of its power to evoke. And so there isn't really any way to talk about it that conveys the sensuality of it, without sounding dorky and without implying a do-er and a do-ee. We're at a loss, really, except I have to say that the phrase I really like, right now, just because it's so devoid of content, is "To sleep with." As in, "I slept with Lenora, whose last name I don't remember but who I know works at some ad agency." The phrase has some dignity, however colorless, and it manages still to hold some sort of mystery/aura about it, I guess drawn from the "sleep" part. (Sure, it's not always accurate, like when you don't actually sleep with the person afterward, but still.) It's not poetry, but it's something. And it doesn't for a second imply force, or an act bereft of meaning, or worse, a combination of both.

———————————

If you think I'm annoying and preachy now, you should have known me in grade school. I was a third-grade moralist, a strange mixture of Regular Popular Kid, Bully, and Voice of Virtue. Living in a fire-and-brimstone Catholic household, I was not allowed to swear (or even say 'God' out loud; if a sibling slipped and did so, I would tell on him or her by saying that they had said "dog backwards." Really.) And so I enforced my code of propriety in the playground, determined to curb the growing propensity of my peers to swear during recess. I would confront offenders: "What, do you think that makes you sound cool?" I'd ask, rhetorically. "Because it doesn't. You're not impressing anyone." And the odd thing is they usually bought it, partly because I was the sort of person they might be trying to impress in the first place, and partly because I sometimes punched people in the stomach when I felt like it would help make my point.

And so I'm about to force a comparison between the kids-trying-to-impress-other-kids-through-swearing and another group of people with stunted social skills: purveyors of contemporary literary fiction. Now, for some reason, seeing the word "fuck" in print, in fiction in which its appearance is incongrous, seems to exacerbate the problem with the word. Just as there's dissonance between the higher aspirations of sex and the something-you-find-in-the-plumbing sound of "fuck," there is dissonace in seeing the word used among the refined prose of books like Eberstadt's. There, other words stick out, too—really any of the "alternative" words that can be used to describe sex and the body parts involved. "Fuck" has bedfellows in words like "cock," "pussy," "gash," "ass" and "prick" (which, by the way, is always the wrong word. "Cock," maybe, but "prick" implies a blood sample—and a small one at that).

Some history: A kind-of educated guess would point to D. H. Lawrence as the pioneer of the use of naughty language in literature, but even his stuff was mild by contemporary standards, and of course his descriptions of romance and desire and sex are unequaled in their sensitivity. (Responding to criticism of *Lady Chatterly's Lover*, published in 1918, he said the book was "verbally improper but very truly moral." (It was originally titled *Tenderness*.)) Things changed irreversibly with

Henry Miller's *Tropic of Cancer* (published in Paris in 1934 and in the U.S. in 1961), which wasn't so concerned with any such appearance of moral structure, and which of course made "fuck" and "cunt" the household words they are today. Then there was Miller's biggest fan, Norman "call me Jehovah" Mailer, and then Philip Roth and a host of other writers for whom Miller apparently broke down some long-reviled barrier. In general, the '70s were pretty big for "fucking," and also marked the emergence of the word in the lexicon of women writers. Maybe the best example is Erica Jong's *Fear of Flying* (1973), in which she longs for what she calls the "Zipless Fuck." The "Zipless Fuck," she explains, is sex with great passion but no obligation, and necessites that "you never get to know the man very well," that the encounter be brief, and that "anonymity [makes] it even better." And since, the word has steadily increased its appearances, making its way into countless novels, and of course into every other issue of *The New Yorker*.

But how often is it the right word? Pretty much never. Let's use as an example Kathy Acker, one of our most prolific "fuckers," who really doesn't use any other word when talking about sex. The strange thing is that, however nihilistic Acker's work seems on the surface, in much of it, particularly the openly autobiographical stuff, there is a soulfulness that betrays a sort of deeply-felt love of life, just under the thick skin of her tough and stylized writing. In *Kathy Goes to Haiti*, the first sentence tells us that Kathy "doesn't believe in anyone or anything." On page 17, she's in bed with the cabbie who drove her from the airport. "Kathy grabs the man's cock. As soon as it's hard, she sticks it in her cunt." The cabbie wants to take it slow, which frustrates Kathy. "The man refuses to fuck the girl." Sure, it seems barren of sentiment, and Acker's work would seem to be a place where the word "fuck" would seem as appropriate as anywhere. But consider this: The narrator, at twenty-nine, has flown to Haiti alone, for no reason other than to get away, to see what will happen, an undeniably romantic idea. Almost immediately, she's sleeping with the cabbie, and if you look at it one way, far from meaning nothing, it indicates a yearning—for affection maybe, for sensual pleasure maybe, but more, I think, a yearning for something deeper, a bridge between herself and the strange new country and its people, a way to communicate profoundly with some random fat guy in a far-away place. I'm probably stretching it a bit there, but it's really a beautiful notion, if you buy it even a little, and it embodies the most romantic aspirations of what sex is all about. As opposed to something between two people married and/or in love, the word "fucking" is used more often when referring to the union of two strangers, like in *Tropic of Cancer* or Jong's "Zipless Fuck," to indicate its primal physicality and fleetingness. But that's only part of it, I think, because you see, when it's with a stranger—with a Haitian cabbie or with Lenora, the New York media planner—there is so much risk involved, with two people naked and strange and at their absolutely most vulnerable, all in the interest of finding pleasure and fulfilling desire and staving off loneliness and maybe feeling wanted and possibly even sharing a bed for a night, that far from being random and unimportant, it's so often the bravest and most existentially hopeful thing we can do. And thus it means everything, completely.

Try this: another common application of the word "fuck," maybe the most common usage, actually: When something really doesn't matter, when someone really, really doesn't care about something, there's one expression that conveys, more than any other, the utter throwaway meaninglessness of that something: "I don't give a fuck."

But I have lately felt besieged. Exploring this issue of the word "fuck," I've come to feel like a Midwestern Rip Van Winkle, like I've just woken up and can't find common ground with my contemporaries. Even though I look and act the same as the other Young Urban Hipsters, with my mini-goatee and thrift store clothes, this word, alas, has cast me adrift from my peers. Example: I recently ran into My Gay Friend Ron at this deli-convenience store-restaurant near my office. We were waiting for our food and so I asked him, as I had lately been asking just about everyone I knew, about the word "fuck."

"It's the word of choice for gays, definitely," he said, adding that it's his word of choice, too—the term that he uses more often than any other. I asked him why that is. He thought about it for a second, folding his arms and leaning back against the window. "I don't know," he said. He cited the ineffectiveness of terms like "make love" and "have sex" and "sleep with." He doesn't like those terms because they sound "corny and outdated." He said that "fuck" works for him because sex is often just that, a "fuck," that there often isn't a whole lot of caring and tenderness involved, and that if it's quick and physical and pretty much anonymous, that "fuck" fits the bill. I wasn't going to get into the quick and anonymous part with him, so I just zeroed in on where I figured we'd find common ground. I set up a scenario: He's seeing someone, and he cares about that someone. After a number of times going out, after some buildup, during which they get to know and like each other a lot, they finally have sex. Then, let's say the next day he and I go to lunch, and I ask him what happened. I ask Ron—and this is really the big question, I tell him—when he thinks back on the previous night and the new and giddy romantic encounter with that someone, some-one he cares for, does he look back and think, "We fucked"?

He didn't skip a beat.

"Yeah."

We went around on it for a while. I told him that I couldn't help but associate the word with violence, that saying that "I fucked" someone would be only a few slippery steps short of saying that "I raped" some-one, that both imply something being done to someone, whether will-ingly or no. He granted me that.

"But you know," he said, "maybe it's a white hetero male thing." Huh? "It's a Guilty White Male hangup," he said, "where it's like all the frat boys and everyone who's used the word before have made it taboo for you—where you can't use it because it's your crowd that's given it the bad name it has now." On the other hand, he said, people like him, Ron the Progressive Gay Guy, could be free to use it without shame or guilt—trangressively. With his usage, there was irony maybe. And any-way, he said, the gay sex thing doesn't suffer as much from the stigmas of rape and date rape and violence in general, so there isn't the threat-ening aspect that "fuck" takes on in male-female relations. A nice new wrinkle, sure, but it didn't really solve the whole problem of him using it instead of something kinder and gentler. I was about to press him on it again when Sarah, a coworker of his and friend of mine, came in and joined the conversation. In contrast to Ron, who seems to have been born streetwise, Sarah was obviously raised in the suburbs, and tilts her head sometimes when she's thinking hard. The question was posed to her. Do you "fuck" people?

Her answer was quick. "Oh, definitely."

For her, it has a lot to do with using the word politically. "It's such a male thing, 'to fuck,' so when a woman uses it, it's a source of power." She might use it, she says, when talking to another woman, because she likes the content of it, the implication that she was in control of a par-ticular encounter. Fine, fine, using the word as a socio-political weapon is fine in certain contexts, but she wasn't answering the big question. Does she think that what she has done with people—[okay, full disclo-sure here, I had had sex with this person, Sarah, in a sort of random way,

the way friends end up having sex when on vacation together, especially in a Nevada desert]—does she think that what she's done with people (read: me) has been "fucking?" Here, like with Ron, I figure that I've
cornered her into a place where she can't help but find her true, soft
heart, where she'll know that the right answer, for the sake of my feelings and in a larger sense, for the sake of the world and the crumbling
discussed in paragraph nine, is "no." She wouldn't call what we did
"fucking," would she?

She did the thing where she tilts her head.

"Yeah."

There is a book out called *The New Good Vibrations Guide to Sex*. For
those who haven't seen their ads, which occur in 1/8 page slots in better magazines all over the country, Good Vibrations is a retail and mail-
order sex equipment store based in San Francisco. The company prides
itself on having really any sex toy and erotic device imaginable, and
they appeal to a wide market, without any specificity of gender or sexuality. They are often lauded for their "sex-positive" attitude, and for
dispensing information and products frankly and, according to one
reviewer, "without lasciviousness."

And so they've just released this new book, the revamped second edition of the popular guide that orginially appeared four years ago. It is
quite educational, written with perfect clarity and candor, without
overdoing the safe-sex message or getting too political about anything.
Throughout the text, though, there are short quotes from Good
Vibrations customers, italicized and meant to illustrate the attitudes of
average people to whatever topic is being discussed. And while reading
it, I felt how a grandfather must feel listening to his granddaughter's
hip-hop albums. I honestly felt like the world had passed me by. These
quotes from the chapter called "Penetration": "I much prefer oral sex
over fucking. I do love both, but the fucking part is mostly for my hon-
ey so he can come inside me"; "I like being fisted, if they listen to my
instructions to make the little duck thing before jamming their whole
hand up my cunt"; "Psychologically, I dig just about any hard and rapid
fucking." And this from the authors: "Sexual orientation is not defined
by how you fuck, but who you fuck." And the thing is, I really didn't
have to go looking for these quotes. Pretty much every page, every
chapter has someone—I guess someone sex-positive and hip and everything—talking about how/where/with whom they like to get "fucked,"

and what they like done to their "cock" or "pussy."

Because the Good Vibrations people are nice people, and because I was pretty sure that they would have really well-thought-out answers to my questions, I called them up. I was quickly on the phone with Cathy Winks, one of the book's two authors. I told her of my troubles with the language in her book, and she seemed interested, but more in the way that a therapist would be interested—in a caring, concerned way. I asked her why she thought people quoted in her book liked to use the word. "I don't know," she said a handful of times, to that and related questions. I told her I thought the word "fuck" implied anger and force. "I think the word has a lot of friendly potential," she said. We were quickly at an impasse, with neither of us wanting to buy what the other was selling. She did say this, which makes some sense: "fucking" is really the only expression that uses an active verb, and that the other expressions, including to "have sex" are too passive, sounding like keeping something in the cupboard, with the cereal. ("Do you have sex?" "Yes, would you like that dry, or with milk?")

The Good Vibrations angle is an interesting one. In the interest of swinging the pendulum away from the problems brought on by sexual ignorance, they appropriate a word associated with animosity and disrespect. One friend, who uses it sometimes, says this: "There's always a split second beforehand when you feel bad about saying it. But the taboo aspect is part of the appeal." But for the makers of "sex-positive" manuals, isn't it counterproductive, while trying to rid sex of its taboos, to employ a word bursting with negative content? Isn't is odd, while bringing sex into the open and making it acceptable for polite conversation, to use a word that isn't? And isn't it strange, while trying to make sex seem healthy and wholesome, to choose a word that undeniably implies the opposite?

Another Gay Friend, my Gay Friend Dan, is an AIDS educator who specializes in getting safe-sex information to young at-risk men in San Francisco. A few years ago, in such an effort, he and I had tried to come up with a narrative cartoon that would dispense safe-sex information in a "hip" and "funny" way. We never really finished the project, but in the meantime he had helped produce a book called Faggot Sex/Sissy Speak, a safe-sex resource guide written for young gay men. The educational material inside, designed using all those tricky fonts and photo overlays that are popular among the kids today, is complete and informative, but studded, far more prominently than the Good Vibrations book, with the words in question. There are sections titled, in large bold type, thus: "Fucking," "Butt-fucking," "Finger Fucking," "Fisting," and "Sucking

Dick." The text is equally, brutally coarse. The "Butt-Fucking" section explains: "Some people fuck frequently, while others do it occasionally … You can be a top (the person who sticks his dick in the ass) or you can be a bottom (person whose ass gets fucked)." Elsewhere, there are really no instances of another term other than "fucking" being used. Invariably, a penis is a "dick" or "cock," a butt is an "ass." When they discuss the probability of HIV transmission through various boldily excretions, there is "sweat" and "blood," but also "piss" and "shit." The whole book is sort of relentless, really.

"We have to use plain, street language to reach young men," says Dan. "This is the way they talk. If we get all geeky and clinical, they stop listening." And because he is the educator, I have to believe him. I really don't know exactly what's on the minds of the gay youth of San Francisco, anymore than they know what's in my medicine cabinet. Still, I can't help feeling that with all the "fucking" and "fisting" and "eating ass" in the book, mixed as it is with warnings, everywhere, about AIDS and STDs and watching out for gay bashers and Jeffrey Dahmers, that it doesn't make sex sound like all that much fun.

And that's a big part of the problem, I guess. The lack of fun. "Fucking" doesn't sound like fun. And using the word sort of takes so much of what's essential about sex, out of it. "It just reduces it to the basics," says Dan.

The question is: Is that possible?

————————————

Last year, while my thirteen-year-old brother and ward (I am his guardian) was in seventh grade, he came home one day and, while we were cooking dinner, told me about the day's special science/health class assembly. A man and a woman from a nearby college had come to his private school to talk about safe sex and AIDS. In the course of about twenty minutes, the educators had described in rather graphic detail the death that awaits sufferers of AIDS, and then, without further ado, they had passed around to the children a large dildo, encouraging the twelve-year-olds to apply condoms to it.

My brother came home sort of freaked out. He hadn't previously known what a dildo was, and his idea of a condom was relatively vague. He had a cloudy notion about the mechanics of sex in general, and only a newspaper-headline sort of knowledge of AIDS. Why? Mainly, um, because he was twelve. He was, I thought, entitled to that sort of ignorance for as long as it had nothing to do with his life. And up to that point, it didn't have anything to do with his life. His seventh grade class was slow, socially; there was no dating going on. Thus, there was no sex, no kissing, no hugging, no known instances, in fact, of seventh graders even holding hands. Nevertheless, in twenty minutes or so, in the interest of really getting all the facts out there to the kids at a young age, etc., my brother's class went from knowing little to nothing about sex to associating it immediately with dildos and death.

And I thought this was sort of too bad.

———————————

There is something that you learn early on in painting class at the more academic art schools, and that is that in accurately rendering life, the use of black is unacceptable. When creating volume, darkening an edge or underside to indicate three-dimensionality, black is not to be used, should not be on the palette, because, being black, it has the effect of flattening the image. Various alternatives are offered—burnt umber, blues, reds, browns, etc.—and combinations thereof are encouraged. The point being that black, being a tone and not a hue, stands out and makes a painting seem two-dimensional when used amidst an other-wise wide range of color. In using browns and blues and such, you are using the subtleties of the palette, creating more depth in the picture, using colors to make colors (what happens when you mix them all together? Brown.), making a more convincing representation of life.

What am I saying? This: I think "fuck" is black. It flattens.

———————————

Maybe it's a Bay Area thing. I'm beginning to think that the "fuck" thing, the crassness, is kind of weirdly prevalent here, weird because San Francisco can be so puritanical about some stuff, and thus many of its residents find it necessary to do superficially provocative things to prove they're loose. It really doesn't seem like anybody's having all that much sex with anyone around these parts, but still there are so many of the sex-lit luminaries living in the area—Acker, Nicholson Baker (*Vox, U & I*), Barry Gifford (*Wild at Heart*, etc.). And there's the recent, almost-mainstream popularity of S&M clubs. And then, of course, there was the Jack Davis Incident.

Remember the hulabaloo about the party thrown by Jack Davis, the big political consultant? You may remember, from Only-in-San Francisco accounts of the event that appeared in the *Times* and *USA*

Today and everywhere else, that at the fete, which was to celebrate Davis's fiftieth birthday, some strange things happened. There were various leather-wearing people walking about, a topless woman with a mustache, an area where you could have your nipples pierced and have weights attached to them. Of course, the part that everyone heard about involved the performance of the chubby Satanist guy. Wearing only a leather loincloth and a mask, the chubby Satanist guy got onstage, and first read an expletive-filled version of the Declaration of Independence. Then a dominatrix-type woman joined him onstage and, apropos of nothing, cut a large pentagram into his back, with a knife. Bleeding profusely, the chubby Satanist guy then got on his knees and arranged himself so the dominatrix woman could pee down his back (She did.) Then, for good measure, he stood up and drank a mixture of the urine and blood. Finally, he turned around, bent over, and she sodomized him with a bottle of Jack Daniels. Oh, and then he rubbed the Declaration of Independence in the blood on his back.

The event was in the news because Davis and his party-planning minions had invited the mayor and the press, and the place was full of local politicos, all of whom later denied being there during the activities in question. But I was there. My friend's band had been hired to be the loud raucous punk band, and I had tagged along, both to watch them and to see what Davis, somewhat notorious for his parties, would put together for his fiftieth. So my friend's band got on first, and played some of their songs, which are loud but probably not punk. After maybe fifteen minutes, they were unceremoniously pulled, clearly not satisfying the organizers' overarching interest in putting forth a show with real cutting-edge shock value.

Anyway, as I watched the Satanist guy getting carved up, and witnessed the urine-drinking and the bottle up the butt and everything, I really, more than anything else, wanted to be somewhere else. Despite the A-plus effort they put forth to terrorize the unsuspecting audience, the whole thing was really sort of boring. Though everyone was watching the proceedings, they were still ordering drinks, eating at the buffet, chatting. When he was doing the Declaration of Independence, you couldn't really understand what he was saying. When they did the sodomizing, you couldn't really tell exactly what was happening, or if it was even real. The whole thing—which was, we later found out, supposed to have been protesting the U.S. government's treatment of Native Americans—was so muddled and heavy-handed that it had no real effect on its viewers. Artless as it was, it convinced no one of anything.

I sound like a grump, and you tire of me. If you aren't already covering your ears and humming, then get ready, because I'm about to quote the Bible. There's an expression that you never hear anymore, but I think actually works better than "sleep with," endorsed earlier. It's the expression "to know." As in, "She knew him, in the Biblical sense." The phrase works on two main levels: First, like "to sleep with," it has a certain poetry to it. Sleeping and knowing are a few of the best things we humans have at our disposal, evoking as they do a wide range of happy thoughts, having to do with rest and contemplation and dreams and such. Second: In a remarkably brief manner, the expression addresses the fact that when you sleep with someone, you do make a huge leap in, um, knowing that someone, even if you pretend that you don't know them and that you don't care and that sex is vaporous and anonymous. The only catch with using the expression, of course, is that to avoid confusion in print, you'd have to use italics, and worse, in conversation, you'd always have to wink or raise an eyebrow to get the point across. Which brings us back to the problem with sick fucks like Buddy, and also to his kin in the Good Vibrations book. One of their more interesting testimonials goes like this: "I like it when a man slowly introduces his tongue in my mouth and fucks my mouth with his tongue the exact same way his cock is fucking my cunt."

I'll just say this: I for one do not want to "fuck" that woman's mouth, and I don't want to "fuck" that woman's "cunt," and, as a matter of fact, I really don't ever want to run into that person in a dark bedroom. I don't want to know that person, and I'll certainly never *know* that person, and if that person wanted to take the dental dam out of her mouth and complain that in the absence of "fucking" that there really wasn't any way to truly put it into words, I'd have a little revelation and say you're damned right, because shit, woman, unless you're into God or aerobics or heavy drugs, sex is pretty much the best thing we've got going, the closest thing we've got to rapture, to an experience that could be called religious, and if there's no way to describe it, no shorthand way to name it, then Jesus Fucking Christ, maybe that's the way it should be. ■

August, 1997

Babylon by Bus

We had checked with the State Department. We were assured that there were no travel warnings for Ecuador. We were told time after time that Ecuador was one of the most peaceful and stable countries in all of Latin America. But perhaps because it is nestled in between Colombia (a nation torn to shreds by drug warlords) and Peru (a nation torn to shreds by Shining Path Maoist guerrillas) what the State Department meant was, travel in Ecuador is peaceful compared to being bludgeoned to death with a wooden mallet by the Shining Path while on a nature walk. That kind of peaceful.

I went to Ecuador over the Thanksgiving holiday with my girlfriend, a twenty-two-year-old Bronx native of Cuban and Puerto Rican heritage with an alleged fluency in Spanish, and my cousin, a Jewish doctor also from New York, who specializes in neurology and neuroses. Our plan was to canoe in the northern Ecuadorian jungle waters and to drive two hours north of Ecuador's capital, Quito, to visit the great poncho markets of Otavalo.

We landed in Quito late on a Saturday, rested all Sunday and arranged our trip to the jungle the following day. We were anxious, and when we found it was too late to catch the next plane to Lago Agrio, our jungle embarkation point, we decided to take the bus instead of spending another day in Quito. Admittedly, this decision was made at an altitude of 8,000 feet. But in effect, of our own free will, we decided to take a nine-hour bus ride through the mountainous Ecuadorian jungle instead of waiting one day to take a twenty-five-minute plane trip. This was our decision.

We headed to the bus station on foot, stopping only to buy water and bread, which turned out to be one of our better decisions. The bus terminal was only twelve blocks from our hotel, but the searing equatorial heat combined with the altitude made even that seem an odyssey. Our gentle jungle travel agent had assured us we would be sitting in seat numbers 14, 15 and 16 on bus #94 to Lago Agrio. We walked sluggishly through the bus, sweat running in little rivulets down our backs, our mute co-passengers staring at us. We were the only non-South Americans aboard. Three of said mute passengers were in our seats. The temperature was kiln-like, the seats contorted by the heat into perverse shapes that looked to provide all the comfort of a melted surfboard. Everyone—small children, infants, everyone—was chain smoking. Speakers blared viciously distorted mariachi music. We moved to the back of the bus.

The road between Quito and Lago Agrio is a narrow one-lane affair that snakes along the Andes Mountains, up one side and down the other. It is comprised largely of pebbles and red clay, paved in some parts, packed dirt in others. The edge of the road descends thousands of feet in a steep death-drop. When two vehicles pass each other, one has to pull to the side and allow the other to squeak slowly by. Each bend offers the possibility of a head-on collision and a quite scenic—but absolutely fatal—fall from the Andes to the tropical valleys below. The driver of our bus apparently felt skillful enough to drive about 40 mph. For the record, 40 mph is too fast.

About two hours into our trip we blew a tire. A half an hour later, we stopped again after a man shouted something to the driver. The man walked off carrying a little girl. He placed her down on the side of the road directly outside my window and pulled her pants down. She proceeded to projectile-blast a stream of mustard-colored liquefied feces while simultaneously pissing on the man's shoes. He then wiped her and carried her back on the bus, where they sat directly behind us. His hands dangled over the back of my girlfriend's seat. I couldn't tell if I could actually see the molecules of leaping bungus turds, baby cholera and typhoid stools slathering across the hard vinyl seat and into my girlfriend's perfumed hair.

Two hours of mariachi, punished buttocks and exhaust-induced nausea later, we stopped for "dinner." We decided against the local delicacy of fried pork rinds and dug into our suddenly tasty bread and water before heading back on the bus for what we were told would be another five hours to Lago Agrio. It was explained to us that Lago, as the locals called it, was an oil town with all the appeal of a toxic dump and the feel of a lawless frontier outpost. The thought of enduring five more hours on the bus to arrive at such a destination was akin to being told that hanging by your scrotum would occupy the five hours preceding your castration.

I began playing mental games to make the time pass. An hour went by grudgingly. It began to rain. Another hour passed, like a gallstone. The distorted mariachi began to transform itself from incessant Latino party music into strains of reggae, klezmer, and old Negro spirituals, but always back again to a tinny salsa jangle. The rain poured. The windows rattled. The bus careened. Night fell. I began meditating, trying to snap my attention from the intricate modulations of fear, discomfort and the horrible veering of the bus. Only one windshield wiper was working. The music never stopped.

Perhaps because I wanted so much for the final two hours to pass, about forty-five minutes later I latched on to the belief that the lights I saw ahead in the road might be Lago. I was buoyed when I noticed a few people in the bus beginning to stand up and collect their belongings. I rose to my feet with a huge grin. I was wrong. The people were not standing because we were arriving; it was to get a better look at the fire raging in the middle of the street. I was so utterly let down I didn't stop to think—how strange, there's a bonfire of burning tires in the road. The bus driver apparently wasn't too concerned. He drove around the conflagration as if it were road kill, paying no mind to the possibility of our gas tank igniting and sending us all into the dark roadside like bits of charred gristle.

We drove a few hundred yards further into the town of Cascales before seeing another tire-burning roadblock. But this one had a crowd of men waving sticks and shouting, *"Regresa! Regresa! Regresa!"* And these men were heading toward the bus.

The bus lumbered backward and pulled to a stop. There was a policeman sitting in front of me and when he got off to see what was going on, most of the men followed. My cousin and I did not. My cousin's eyeballs seemed to be protruding several inches from his skull and were darting left to right like goldfish in plastic sandwich bags filled with water. The policeman—who had been serving as a kind of cork for all my bottled-up fear—had been gone for about fifteen minutes, but he'd left his duffle bag on the bus with an old carbine rifle sticking out. That rifle had been serving as my nightmare's pressure-release valve. If the crowd stormed the bus, I actually thought, I could always go for the gun. I began pacing, asking questions—in English. "Is it safe to stay on the bus? Should we try to make a run for the woods?" My only answers were cow-like gazes and unintelligible mutterings. Then the policeman returned, momentarily hiking my spirits, only to pick up his bag and rifle and walk off the bus. I felt trapped, desperate. I began to sweat like a fat salesman in a polyester shirt, in Daytona, in August.

Outside a man was yelling through a loudspeaker. It echoed down the one-street town with surreal, ominous resonance. At first we thought he was trying to disperse the crowd. But after a few minutes of constant references to "Los Estados Unidos," it became painfully obvious that he was rousing the crowd, and that this was a very bad thing for us.

Finally, three soldiers in fatigues arrived with M-16s and a yellow Caterpillar plow. It seemed our little brush with South American realpolitik was going to be brought to a nice, crushing end. But then the gunshots started. My cousin needed to be physically restrained and earnestly convinced to stay on the bus. I found a can of tuna and opened the top, creating a make-shift weapon which I figured would surprise some anti-Yankee Imperialist-basher, and slice his neck up good in the last moments before the crowd dragged us off and hacked us to death, Sendero Luminoso-style, with wooden hatchets. But about an hour later the army returned with a plow and thirty soldiers, who held the crowd at bay while the bus passed. We ducked down in case rocks were thrown and the windows shattered, but the people just shouted.

Forty-five minutes later, on the outskirts of Lago Agrio, we encountered another fiery roadblock. Flames 30-feet high licked at the sky from a gas-drenched barricade that spanned the entire width of the road. The bus pulled to a stop in the middle of a caravan about twenty vehicles long. We were about ten lengths from the fire, without the possibility of going forward or backward. In a freakish well-spring of bluster and bravado, I mentioned something about getting off the bus and kicking somebody in the sternum. But my anger quickly smoldered back to fear when the bus driver gestured that I should lower my voice, and whispered that we might already be surrounded by Colombians. Significantly more timid, I asked if we could take our bags and walk the rest of the way. He just shook his head and drew his index finger slowly across his neck.

It was 1:00 A.M. Most of the people on the bus had gotten off. The bus driver went to sleep on the floor. There were a few Ecuadorians, mostly invalids and old women, still left on the bus, and they seemed to be resigned to sleeping as well. The driver woke up twice to reprimand someone for snoring. The rain increased in intensity, and I began to watch the height of the flames go down from thirty feet to twenty, from twenty to ten, mentally willing them lower and lower. Another hour passed. The flames went out. I whispered to myself, mantra-like, that the fire had gone out. Moments later somebody poured gasoline on the embers and the bonfire raged again.

I saw silhouettes of people walking in front of the fire. The rain was coming down in thick sheets. It would have been almost pretty if it weren't for the very immediate prospect of rape, larceny, murder and mutilation. Finally, around 5:00 A.M., we began to see the lights of vehicles from the other side of the fire, and the blaze began to go down quickly. Plows and bulldozers were clearing the way. We pulled into Lago Agrio about fifteen minutes later. It was everything we'd been told, and more: Run-down buildings with bars on the windows and steel security gates on all the doors, families with children sleeping on the street in groups of five or six. We got off the bus with a unique sense of purpose that only comes with extreme weariness, drunkenness or righteousness, and strode into the barrio looking for the Hotel Machala.

At the Hotel Machala the pillows reeked of urine and the bathrooms stank even worse. I found a bucket of water under the sink, rinsed myself and got into bed. I made love with my girlfriend like a sad, crazed animal and fell asleep with the lights on and a clean sock over my eyes. Two hours later I was downstairs having eggs in oil for breakfast. It was time to go to the jungle. As we left, I noticed some horrid-looking white people enter the place, but when I tried to ask them about travel in the region they responded, in surly German accents, that they didn't know anything.

It was still raining. Twenty soldiers stood in front of a dilapidated building outside our hotel. We put on plastic ponchos, loaded our luggage and ourselves into our guide's small pickup truck and drove off for the jungle. I didn't wave good-bye. Almost four hours later we arrived at a riverhead and loaded all of our belongings onto a long, thin wooden canoe. For the next three hours we wound our way down a tributary of the Amazon, through dark green, molasses-like water. None of us had life preservers; none of us could swim. Our guide, Alejandro, said that didn't matter. The water was rife with caiman (small crocodiles), piranhas, and anacondas anyway. Then there were the schistosomiasis, haematobium and mansoni, eager little parasitic worms that like to drill through that little webbed space between your toes or swim up your urethra and burrow bloody caverns in your bladder. Or, you could be smitten by cysticercosis, in which case you'd end up back in New York three months later, reduced to a howling vegetable in a neurology ward, being fed soup by a hunchbacked Jewish mother.

But our time in the jungle was guided with terrifying confidence by our guide. He pointed out every manner of flora and fauna, every insect, butterfly, bird and poisonous plant in paradise. He navigated the splintered branches of the river effortlessly. He cooked us sumptuous meals. He taunted us for not wanting to bathe with him in the lagoon. He told us that, unfortunately, our cabanas—the "paradise huts" promised by our gentle jungle travel agent, with the long-awaited showers, electricity, private bathrooms and hot water—did not, in fact, exist in this part of the jungle. We would not be sleeping out in the open, though. There were some wood planks on the ground and a thatched roof; alas, walls were not available.

By day, Alejandro took us on jungle walks and forced us to drink white pus from a tree he split open with an unwashed, salmonella-infested machete he'd used to butcher jungle chickens. He went piranha fishing, and held the jaws of the fish open, stuffing bits of chicken meat down their throats for breakfast before returning them carefully to the lagoon. He was a gentle guide, but cruel.

I had trouble sleeping in the jungle. I kept thinking about being eaten by a jaguar. My cousin had difficulty adjusting to jungle life as well. One morning I woke up to the sound of just how much difficulty he was having.

"Everything hurts. Everything hurts. Everything hurts. Typhoid, cholera, hepatitis A, vibrio, scrofula, yellow fever, extra-pulmonary tuberculosis, leishmania. Trypanosomiases, schistosoma japonicum, lepromatous leprosy. The dreaded dengue. Tophaceous gout. Crystal deposits in my joints. God knows what virus I've caught now. Certainly something I've never been exposed to. Generalized immune response. Tabes dorsalis. Foot drop. Loa loa. Thick black dirt underneath my fingernails. Thick black dirt. Thick black dirt. Backache. Stench. Mildew. Mold. Fungus. Spores. Runny nose, congestion, minor sore throat. Put me in autoclave."

After three days in the jungle, we packed up our belongings and prepared to return to Lago Agrio. We had plane tickets to Quito the following morning. On our way back up the river we encountered another canoe with three Israeli tourists aboard. They told us it had taken them several hours to escape Lago Agrio, and they had been driving since 4:00 A.M. Every road had been blocked and it was only when they obtained a military escort on the road toward the airport that they were able to leave the city. They said the airport was closed. They said they had seen a hotel owner beaten in the street because he had not obeyed the boycott against tourists. They said four people had been shot by soldiers. We smiled and thanked them for the news.

We resolved that no matter what happened, no matter what our guide told us, no matter what—we were not going back to Lago Agrio. We kept repeating that phrase, "We are not going back to Lago Agrio," like a mantra, less to convince ourselves than to mentally prepare ourselves for the inevitable confrontation with our guide, a man who had already proven he had the steely will to force us to suck white salmonella ooze from a tree.

We decided that although we'd already paid for plane tickets out of Lago, we'd forfeit the cost and bypass the social unrest by looping down into another jungle region called Misaluoui, on to the city of Baños and then back to Quito. We were pleased with our plan and sat smugly in the canoe.

When we arrived back at the riverhead, three English tourists who were preparing to head down the river told us that the airport was open, but that under no circumstances should we go into Lago. They said that the people there were delivering random beatings to anybody with North American features, and that there were fires on all the roads. When we confidently told them of our plan to just go south, they told us that the troubles had extended to all of the Amazon region of Ecuador. The entire Oriente, as the jungle region is known, was paralyzed by a highly organized national work stoppage.

I felt a crushing implosion of anxiety, an almost phobic reaction to information I couldn't accept. I wanted out of my skin. I wanted to disappear. We couldn't wait and hide where we were, because we were out of clean drinking water. We couldn't go to Lago or we'd be stoned by angry Ecuadorians. And we couldn't go south because of the roadblocks, gasoline shortages and total disruption of what few basic services had been in place. It was a nightmare that was unwinding with Hitchcock-like precision. And I hadn't evacuated my bowels in three days. I was consumed with panic, dread and distrust, and I had to make dookies like a bandit.

Somehow, our guide forced us to get into a yellow pickup truck. He was very insistent that we go to Lago Agrio, and took grievous offense if we even asked what his plan was. All he would say was that he had friends and he knew the roads well. He grew livid when we didn't immediately place our trust in him, as we had in the jungle. Not wanting to alienate the only person in Ecuador we actually knew, upon whom our lives completely depended, we had no choice but to get in the truck and head back to Lago Agrio—a place I remembered to be very much like hell.

While we drove, and I attempted to hide from the locals, Alejandro explained that he felt we could cross through the town on foot and arrive safely at the airport. I suggested that maybe we should sleep in a small, safe town until the whole thing blew over. He drew a map of the region for me and came to the conclusion that the only real option was to go back into Lago and meet a friend of his who would sneak us out of town and into southern Colombia. From there we would take a seventeen-kilometer canoe ride to Colon, a nine-hour bus ride to Pasto, and then catch another two-hour bus ride to Quito. This, he said, would require three days of travel and the likely possibility of rapid exsanguination leading to total necrosis, i.e. bleeding to death from any number of causes, mostly relating to the absolute drug-crazed lawlessness in southern Colombia. (Our guide book said that no gringos had ever made it from Lago Agrio into southern Colombia alive, and asked that if anybody did, would they please write in and tell the author.)

The equatorial sun was reducing my brains to *mofongo*. I peeked my head up to get a little air and look at the surrounding countryside and a low-hanging branch hit me in the forehead. My sunblock now mixed with sweat and blood. We stopped at the home of the mother of the fellow driving the truck. I got out to pee. It was while peeing that I began, if you will, to get ahold of myself. I realized that I had to die one day, and it might as well be then. The thought calmed me.

When we finally got to Lago we found a roadblock on the outskirts of town. There was no fire, just a pile of tree branches, dirt and rocks, and about thirty soldiers with M-16s keeping the crowd in check. We got out of the truck, unloaded our luggage with bent heads and nervously prepared to walk into the city. Our fear showed on our faces. A soldier walked toward us and a few members of the crowd followed him. He spoke quietly, saying that we could pass on foot if we wanted, but it was likely that we would be stoned into horrible pulps once inside the city. We decided to sleep at the airport.

Despite Alejandro's insistence that he could sneak us into the city and get us a room in a "nice" hotel (where, he titillatingly reminded us, for the first time in four days we might shower and sleep on a bed), we reloaded our bags into the truck and drove a few minutes to the airport on the outskirts of town. I was having visions of the evacuation of the American Embassy in Saigon and the fall of Phnom Penh. In fact, it was more eerie than that. When we arrived, the airport was deserted. It was clean and empty, but there was no gate, no fence, no security. The fact that no other foreigners were waiting for a flight did not bode well. It was very quiet. There would be nobody to hear our final anguished screams.

It was Thanksgiving Day. A few soldiers of the Ecuadorian Air Force were playing soccer in a field nearby. Some of them began to drift over and we made small talk with them. We learned they were stationed nearby, protecting a U.S.-installed radar device against possible terrorist attacks, and that there were a few U.S. soldiers there. My cousin instantly became overjoyed and started saying that once the American soldiers found out about us they would helicopter us to safety. He began trying to get one of the Ecuadoran Air Force captains to call the U.S. soldiers with a walkie-talkie.

Meanwhile, I laid a plastic tablecloth on the ground and ineffectually demarcated a square with Raid to ward off bugs. We'd been hoping that airport security would let us sleep on the floor of one of their air-conditioned offices in light of the unusual risk, but no. Insects and arachnids swarmed over my girlfriend and me while my cousin sat watching, telling us that the Americans would take us to sleep in their barracks and that they'd surely have turkey and cranberry sauce just like you always see on CNN.

Two U.S. soldiers, a man and a woman, finally showed up. They were scary, emotionless robots who answered our questions with almost comic evasive generalizations. They said they ate rice and beans for dinner because all of their supplies were trapped inside the city at their hotel. Although they had guns, they had been instructed not to shoot anyone, and when they tried to drive around, their truck was pelted with stones. They went away, but took our names down in case we were mutilated in the night.

Soon after, Alfredo, an Indian friend of Alejandro's, came running into the airport. His pant legs were all wet and he was shiny with sweat. He had run from the locals who tried to stone him, he said, and had waded through a small river to bring us a bottle of Orange Fanta and some food. I almost cried. It was the best Thanksgiving meal I ever had.

In the middle of the night an Ecuadorian doctor and his wife arrived, with a baby and an old man. As the sun rose, more and more people arrived at the airport. The surly Germans came (having also waded through the river) and told us the night in the town had been a horror of screams, sounds of glass shattering and the smell of things burning. Finally, at about 11:00 A.M., Ecuadorian military men armed with automatic weapons lined the runway and a plane landed. We were quickly loaded on and before we knew it were safely in the air.

Within twenty minutes we landed in Quito. The next day was the beginning of the great poncho market in Otovalo, and we resolved to take a cab the entire two-hour distance instead of boarding another bus. We were feeling like big spenders, the way people who have had near-death experiences are wont to. We wandered around Quito until late afternoon, buying pastries and feeling good to be alive. That evening we decided to see a movie, but as we were walking to the theater an Indian gestured for me to follow him into an alley. Under the spell of some foolhardy Nietzschean precept that what does not kill a man makes him stronger, I followed him. My companions lagged behind, resigned to the fact I'd be kidnapped and never heard from again.

The alley opened up into a small courtyard, surrounded by several small stores. I followed him into one, a tiny space in which his two daughters and young son worked at sewing machines. The room became even more cramped when my cousin and girlfriend finally joined us. There were beautiful sweaters and ponchos and felt hats, and handwoven knapsacks and embroidered dresses and wool caps and silk scarves. Everything was handmade and designed in the traditional bright colors of the Ecuadorian Indians. Perhaps as a subconscious act of reaffirming life and the prospect of living for a long time, we went into a buying frenzy and bought several hundred dollars worth of goods.

Feeling warm and happy, and wrapped in our new ponchos, we headed back into the street. The sun had set. We turned a corner when suddenly we heard shouts and the sound of feet pounding pavement. To our right we saw a crowd of about a hundred people charging toward us with sticks and rocks. To our left about thirty people ran screaming. It looked like the running of the bulls in Pamplona—without the bulls.

We took off like rabbits down the street, toward our hotel. Two blocks later I palm-heeled the front door of our hotel open and we ducked inside to cower and shake while listening to people's shouts and the sound of gunfire and tear gas explosions. We decided to leave Ecuador the next morning.

Unfortunately, when we got to the airport we found that, independent of the rest of the world, Ecuador had decided to move their clocks forward an hour that day to save electricity, so we missed our flight. But we managed to arrange for an Ecuadorian airline to honor our tickets, and boarded a flight to Miami. As we taxied down the runway and pulled up into the sky I wept with joy and sadness at the horrible chaos of life. The Yamaha Indians of Bolivia have a word for this kind of thing—*pachakuti*, the disruption of the universe. But pachakuti also implies the inherent resumption of cosmic order—*nayrapachar*—which, as the sun rose out the plane's window, seemed nowhere in sight.

■

April, 1995

ZEV BOROW

The Old Man
and MTV

Never refuse a dinner with Kurt Loder. He smokes, but he buys. "Don't worry about the check," he says before the napkins are even unfolded. "I work for MTV."

He orders bottles (plural) of expensive French red wine, practically commands you to order pricey appetizers, and sometime after the main course alerts the waiter to the fact that coffee and cognac, perhaps two, will be required. If you happen to be at his favorite restaurant in New York—Café Josephine's, a velvety theater-district nook half a block from the studio where Loder tapes his MTV News segments and "The Week in Rock"—he will even introduce you to his friend, the owner, one of Josephine Baker's adopted sons. He'll tell you delicious tales of giving Madonna shit and of doing drugs with Hunter S. Thompson. He'll make fun of himself and the people he works for; quote people such as Oscar Wilde without sounding ridiculous; and say mean, funny things about people and institutions that deserve to have mean, funny things said about them. Afterward, maybe he'll invite you back to his hardwood-floored downtown pad to listen to weird country records from the 1930s, or obscure '70s punk bootlegs over a few glasses of chilled apple juice. Like I said, he smokes, a lot, but you'll eat well, drink well, engage in interesting, if not always deep, conversation, and probably go away thinking Kurt Loder is a pretty OK guy—even if you never wanted to.

I never wanted to. Before dinner, to say nothing of drinks, I had decided I didn't really like Kurt Loder and probably never would, pretty much the same way it's easy to dislike—or rather, sneer at—most things associated with his employer, MTV. Loder was too smug, and he wore mustard-colored sport jackets. He had that icky, aging rock-and-roll hanger-on vibe. If nothing else, he was definitely guilty of too much screen time shared with Tabitha Soren. Plus, I knew his past. Loder was an editor and writer at *Rolling Stone*, and for over nine years (of that magazine's better days) was responsible for a slew of sharp, well-written articles. He'd written a regular column for *Esquire* and co-authored Tina Turner's impressive autobiography, *I, Tina* (from which the film *What's Love Got to Do With It?* was adapted). This guy was a writer. What the fuck was he doing as a talking head on MTV—doing remotes with the Spice Girls and plugging the release of Howard Stern's new movie from his Popemobile. He should know better. He should do better.

"I remember my agent called me up and asked if I'd like to work at MTV," he says in his signature undulating drone. "I think I said, 'I don't think so. What would I have to do?' My agent said, 'Not much. Can you read?' Suddenly, it dawned on me that I should take the job. I hadn't actually seen much MTV at the time. Of course, I had the usual snotty attitude that it was all garbage, which a lot of it is, but so is a lot of rock and roll. But, you know, television is the American form, and writers really don't get a lot of appreciation for what they do, and they're certainly underpaid. They look at me and think, 'You make nine times what I make, and you do nothing.' And they're right."

Kurt Loder is 52 years old. He has been the anchor of MTV News for the past ten years. In that time he has proved to be the most permanent fixture of a network that is, by design, in a perpetual state of metamorphosis—easily the oldest on-air personality at a network whose very currency is youth, and perhaps the most ubiquitous face on a channel that makes its living off the concept of heavy rotation. Loder can be seen as often as five times a day on MTV News updates, on the weekly hour-long news wrap-up "The Week in Rock," and on numerous

"MTV News Presents" specials devoted to topics ranging from the violent state of hip hop to alien abductions. There isn't a politician alive who wouldn't (and, more likely, doesn't) spend big money for the name recognition Loder enjoys among the 18- to 34-year-old demographic. Thanks to the indelible mark (some would say scar) MTV has made on a generation of culturemongers, he has come to occupy a singular niche in the American-pop pantheon, somewhere between Dan Cortese and Wolf Blitzer.

Bring up Loder's name in mixed company, and you'll discover there is something of a Cult of Kurt. People who you never thought would even admit to watching MTV—let alone gush that Loder is their favorite thing on the channel—wistfully coo that they've "always wondered about him." It's strange but perhaps understandable when you consider the stark contrast between Loder and the rest of MTV. He's old and wrinkled and dry, whereas MTV is young and taut and, often, wet. But it wasn't until attending a taping of "The Week in Rock" that I began to understand his appeal. Loder sat on a swivel chair in front of the amply art-directed (tastefully neon) "Week in Rock" set and, in between chain-smoking cigarettes off-camera, played anchor. He began by introducing a segment from MTV News correspondent Jon Norris on The Fugees' "homecoming" concert in the group's native Haiti. The show is taped in order, with Loder actually watching, often for the first time, each of the taped stories he segues to and from. While viewing Norris' piece, which attempts to sum up Haitian political, economic and social strife in about twelve pithy seconds, Loder slowly begins to shake his head, first conveying something like minor discomfort, then something closer to scorn.

"What?" he exhales, still off-camera. "Well, so far not one of Haiti's problems has been even remotely addressed." Then dryly, almost under his breath: "Political commentary without a trace of political commentary, hmm?" The three guys working the cameras in the studio titter awkwardly, then one of them flashes a finger at Loder, who, on a dime, straightens up and begins a story on an Oregon woman suing two small death-metal record companies.

Back on air, the derision is toned down, but it's not entirely gone. It never is—Loder manages to hint at it throughout, with a crooked eyebrow here, a carefully calibrated inflection there, and always an expression just shy of a smirk. But watching him turn it up and down for the camera seemed to answer the question one Loderphile told me summed up his allure: "I just want to know if he's really laughing at the whole thing. I want to know if he really gets it."

It seems he does. But in distancing himself from the MTV fray, he perches himself on the narrow ledge where a smart, clever guy manages to deftly celebrate dumb, banal stuff. There's not a lot of room to maneuver. One misstep and you're Bryant Gumbel. But it's not so clear that Loder "gets" this.

"I think the proper attitude to have about MTV is to kind of be fascinated by it, and terrified by it, and in awe of it, all at the same time," he says. "It's amazing, really. Dumb-ness as a concept is not necessarily stupid—look at 'Beavis and Butthead.' It's absolutely the best rock-critic show of all time."

But if Loder does not necessarily laugh at MTV, he certainly laughs at himself. "I've got a really easy job," he says, "especially compared to people who actually work. My father was a housepainter with an eighth-grade education. I could never do the job he did. He has heroic stature in my mind. Most people are poor and unhappy. I feel immensely privileged to be interested in what I do. And I am genuinely interested in showbiz. I see it as something distinct from rock and roll. Showbiz is the American culture. The fact that people really identify with showbiz, with its shmaltziest and cheesiest aspects, fascinates me.

"We're doing this special on alien abductions," he continues. "Now, I'm amazed that there are actually people who believe this crap, but it's a great pop subject, like rock and roll itself, all a lie and pretty much for fun … Why not?"

Kurt Loder is ghostly pale and, like all people on TV, shorter than you would think. As opposed to the studied splashes of color that rule the day elsewhere at MTV's mammoth Times Square corporate lair, Loder's office is positively cavelike, with the blinds permanently drawn, lights permanently off. "I don't especially like being in an office," he says. In person, he comes off much the same way he does on TV—as something of a cross between a disheveled intellectual and a cool, but not entirely un-creepy, uncle.

He grew up in Ocean City, New Jersey, a small beach town on the South Jersey shore. As he puts it: "In the winter it's like someplace out of an Ingmar Bergman movie." He always wanted to write and, after hearing black music for the first time in the late '50s and early '60s, realized he wanted to write about music. Today, his musical knowledge is encyclopedic, his tastes eclectic and not necessarily bent on golden oldies. He's as quick to enthuse over Notorious B.I.G.'s latest as he is about a re-release of a 1965 album by the Black Monks, "a pop garage band with an insane electrobanjo player."

Loder left Jersey for college in Oklahoma, but dropped out after two years and was drafted. "They said if I signed up for an extra year and went to Army journalism school I could go to Europe instead of Vietnam. My cowardice won out, but I will say that Army journalism school teaches you all you need to know about journalism in two months, without the four years of tuition. I was very impressed by that." After the Army, Loder wrote stories around Europe for the *Overseas Weekly*, a paper run by ex-GIs. He returned to the United States in the mid-1970s to work for the now-defunct glossy paean to heavy metal, *Circus*, and then joined *Rolling Stone* in 1979.

There, his forte became cover stories. Over nine years he wrote profiles on people ranging from Bob Dylan to Devo. He began a column, "Off the Charts," for *Esquire*. He was named to the nominating committee of the Rock & Roll Hall of Fame. At the time he joined MTV in 1987, the network itself—let alone MTV News—was still very much a work in progress, its future as a cultural juggernaut far from decided. Still, his wasn't exactly a leap of faith.

"Of course it had a lot to do with money. I have a clothing allowance now," he laughs. "I know people looked at it as a sellout, and I'm sure a lot of them gave me shit for it. But nobody ever came up to me or said something to my face. It's been my experience that every writer wants to be on TV. They flock to it whenever they can."

"Besides," he says, now well into a second glass of cognac, most of the dinner crowd at Josephine's off to the theater, "there seems to be something missing with magazines. When I go to magazine offices now they tend to seem really quiet. I go to *Rolling Stone* and I never even hear music playing. *Esquire* seems like a once-really-bright magazine now put together by half-bright people. *The Village Voice* has just gone down the toilet. And Bob Guccione Jr.? He has a fake British accent. What's that all about? I still love magazines. There are just not enough good ones." He cites *The Economist* as his favorite, and has a copy of *American Spectator* with him, which he gives me to take home.

His criticisms of the magazine biz smell a bit hypocritical in the face of his "it's only rock 'n' roll" attitude toward MTV, but it's clear he feels his former industry has become lifeless and irrelevant—two things, he claims, MTV is not. And while his work on the channel may not enjoy the cachet of his magazine pieces, his spots are, more often than not, put together and delivered with wit and intelligence. He doesn't shy away from poking fun at bands, celebrities, MTV, or himself. A recent "Week in Rock" story on a Rage Against the Machine European concert tour was particularly striking. After segueing into a clip of Rage's rocking Marxists in some Eastern European town square railing against capitalism, Loder came back to tell viewers that the American band would tour its "evil homeland" this summer, tickets starting at $30.

And Loder's arsenal of smirks and asides often manages to convey opinions that buck the PC-at-all-costs themes traditionally embraced by MTV. His audience may not always realize it, but he does, at times, flirt with the subversive. "I actually try to restrain myself," he says. "But sometimes the stuff is just so stupid I can't resist. The whole politically correct worldview is something that people just get fed all the time. If you substituted a few actual thoughts for people's platitudes, it would be a major stride. I try to do that a bit. I don't think MTV worries about it too much anymore. I think they used to worry about me saying mean things about Michael Jackson, but have gotten over it."

The self-proclaimed King of Pop has indeed been one of Loder's more frequent targets. "Look, Michael Jackson is a maniac," he begins. "Nobody is disputing that he's talented, but he's a child molester. I find it offensive. It doesn't take a lot of courage to say that."

But there have been more prickly topics. Take drugs; Loder has. His MTV News special on drugs was anything but an endorsement of traditional "Just Say No" dogma. "It was a libertarian approach to drugs. I mean, drugs shouldn't be illegal. Whose business is it what you put in your body? It's not wise to come out and announce it, but I really feel that. It was my idea to do the show that way, because the way these things are always presented is: Let's do a story on the 'drug problem.' I'm always saying, 'What is the drug problem?' Alcohol hurts more people in this country than drugs. But the standard TV starting point is: Let's have both sides of the story so it says nothing."

Loder's hands-off politics—he reviles both textbook conservatism and liberalism—get to the heart of his dismissal of the notion that there is anything "wrong" with him working for MTV. "I think most Americans just want to be left alone and would rather leave other people alone," he says. "It's the ancient American vibe." We're back at his place now. It's messy and big. Various pieces of faux pop art stolen from MTV sets lie against one wall. Loder is scanning what looks to be no fewer than a couple thousand CDs stacked haphazardly against another wall, and he's still talking politics. It's questionable how much his views influence his audience ("not at all," according to him), but it's worth noting that the political instincts of most young people, whether they know it or not, lean toward a Loder-like libertarianism. He tells me: "The idea that people shouldn't smoke, shouldn't drink, that there will be someone to take care of you all your life—I hate that." Your average sixteen-year-old would probably agree, and might be more willing to accept the fifty-two-year-old Loder because of it. "Of course," he adds, "that forces you to take responsibility for your actions, which nobody really wants to do."

It's an interesting point, especially if you consider the question of whether or not Loder deserves to shoulder any responsibility, if not for himself or for MTV News, then for the millions of viewers who, as MTV News editorial director, Michael Shore, admits, "realistically may not get their news from anywhere else." If Loder is indeed a Tom Brokaw to some, then maybe he should be held to some of the same standards. He was quick to dis the vapid report on Haiti, but never raised an objection to anyone but the camera crew—and willingly disseminated it to millions. It's one thing to have a "why not?" attitude about leaving glossy culture magazines to cover showbiz for MTV. (Really, what's the difference?) It's another when you take into account Loder's on-the-couch-for-the-afternoon audience.

"I don't know if I buy that kids are really stupid, more so than they used to be, and that they don't get news from other places," he says. "I think they probably get less news from other places than ever before, but I don't think about it that way when I'm writing. I try to put a story together clearly, highlight some things I'd like to get across, and hope that a normal person will understand it." Notably, Loder did not desire to be part of MTV's political coverage. He is in favor of the channel covering politics but wasn't comfortable playing a large part in it, saying it's "Tabitha's thing." (For the record, Loder will not utter an ill word about his most prominent—and most often castigated—colleague, even after a couple of cognacs.)

"I don't really have any TV aspirations," Loder says, regarding the differences between him and his on-air counterparts at MTV. Having finally found a CD featuring the country stylings of the singing Carter family (of Tennessee circa 1930), he sits down on a black leather couch in his cluttered living room. "Most of the people in TV really want to be in TV. I just don't object to being in TV. It kind of precludes having a lot of friends, though; makes it impossible to go out. My life has been pared down to listening to records and watching movies."

Not that you should worry about his lifestyle.

"I get in at around ten-thirty, leave by six. I have to wear hairspray and makeup more than I ever thought, but I don't usually work weekends. I do write all my stuff—you have to, or else they'll try to sneak things in —but there are people that do all the actual work, get all the facts."

In many ways, Loder mirrors the stereotype of the MTV viewer. He's hedonistic, pop culture-obsessed, a bit lazy—and deeply cynical. His sly, detached stance toward the channel is easy, like his decision to go work for it—the path of least resistance. Most of which Loder freely admits. He does take responsibility for himself and his job, which he does well. It's just that he doesn't necessarily take either job or self all that seriously. Fittingly, when I ask him if he misses, you know, real writing, he quotes a sitcom actor.

"Writing is very hard," he demures. "I think Jack Klugman once said, 'I miss having written; I don't miss writing.' I guess I should do something, though, a book or something, so I can feel like an honest person again. But, you know, a job where you get to deal with what you've always loved and get to take potshots at people you don't like, it's heaven right here on earth. Besides, where would I move on to? Writing sitcoms? Work for ABC? I couldn't work for any real TV; that would be too awful." ■

June, 1997

HEIDI POLLOCK

This Thing About Men and Nail Polish

At first I thought it was the next, new trend. And then it seemed like maybe it was only last year's trend. And then I remembered it had been trendy around the time I was twelve. But when I started asking around it began to look like not a trend at all. And then I became confused. It is just not possible for such a thing as men with painted toenails to be anything other than a trend, right? Surely it must be part of that whole modern primitive-tattoo-piercing movement? Or maybe it's some kind of fin de millennium outburst of hedonistic androgyny. At the very least it has to be a statement, a critique, a commentary on modern society and branded marketing, gender roles and sexuality.

But it's not. It's just your basic, average, uncontroversial, boring non-event. Doesn't mean a thing. Really. Nope. No way. "I just did it because I wanted to," is what they're telling me. Men—straight men—normal, mature, employed men—are cropping up everywhere with painted toenails and pretending that it's not a big deal. Acting all casual about it. Too casual actually.

I've seen this casual act before. Last Saturday night if you must know.

In a bar. He had slicked back hair, Dockers and a micro-brew in hand. I'm sorry, let me be clear: this toenail painting phenomenon? It's one, big pick-up line.

Not only is it the latest in a long and ridiculous string of bizarre methods whereby men attempt to bag the babes, it actually appears to be working. The men in question seem to think that it's working because it's an indication that they are comfortable enough in their manhood or sexuality not to care that they might look like, ahem, you know, *gay* people. And, the reasoning goes, since they are so self-assured and at ease then they must be good in bed. Yeah. Sure, boys. Whatever you say.

The reason painted nails works as a pick-up line has nothing to do with manhood. It's a sisterhood thing. The reason it works, when it works at all, is because having painted toenails means that the painter was recently in the presence of a female. A female who, out of fondness and affection, allowed the hapless male to borrow some of her nail polish. And what this means, listen up here, is that the male in question now bears a stamp of approval from the girl world. Well, maybe stamp of tolerance is more accurate. As practices go, I wholly approve of it. Short of setting up a Web site or an 800 number, sisterhood approval by way of nail polish will have to do.

Of course, like all acts of camouflage, there is more to this movement than meets the eye. To begin with, it's nice to know that men are taking an interest in grooming. But infinitely more significant is that insofar as we choose to deem these nail polish-wearing men to be cool or hip the badge of coolness is, as we have noted, something which emanates from the female world. Nail polish is and will always be a girl thing no matter how many men end up adorning themselves with the product and the fact that polish is being used, however tentatively, to indicate some level of hipness means that girl things are publicly cool.

For the most part, accessories of hipness have come primarily from traditional male worlds. Combat boots, flannel shirts, athletic gear, wallet chains—all of these things have at some point indicated that the bearer or wearer of the object is less uptight than the next person. And yet all of these things belong to the traditional world of men. I have a number of theories for why the supposedly cool gear tends to stem from stereotypically male dominated realms—theories which range from the fact that women are less concerned with appearances than all those magazines tell us we are to the fact that men are obsessed with paraphernalia and toys to a truly disturbing degree—which I don't wish to delve into at the moment. The point is that by utilizing a girl thing, nail polish, in a cool fashion, the entire world of girl things is being openly acknowledged.

This may seem like a trivial thing but in a subjective world, there is nothing more important than recognition. In a very real sense the recognition of the secret inner boudoir of female life makes that world real. It's that whole the tree falling in the forest thing—if no one hears it, does it make a sound? If you aren't in the girls' room, does it exist? Of course it does. Always has. It's just that now it seems we finally don't need to argue the point any more.

None of this is to say that femininity is defined by nail polish. Or even that the present nail polish fad is even remotely feminine in the first place. In actuality one of the only reasons men seem to be engaging in the practice at this point in time more so than in the past seems directly related to the current abundance of decidedly non-feminine colors. In truth, these shades of un-pink are the primary reason *women* are wearing nail polish again. No matter whose standards you apply, it's just not cool to admit that the shade of polish you're wearing is "Sunset Blush." But being able to say, "Why thank you. It's 'Uzi' by Urban Decay," definitely has that cutting edge kind of sound that beauty products traditionally lack.

Of course, butch colors have been around for as long as I can remember. Certainly men with polished nails have been showing up at events from Adam Ant straight through to the Chemical Brothers and beyond and there doesn't seem to be anything spectacularly different about this year which would cause the polish trend to spill out of the nightclubs and into the daylight. In fact, there isn't anything different about this year. We are just as burdened and overwhelmed and oppressed by branded product this year as any other year and therein lies one of the possible clues to the seemingly sudden popularity of nail polish.

Simply put, there are very few avenues left for brand-free personal adornment in this era. Pretty much everything has that damn Swoosh on it and that's not the half of it. The common practice of brand adulation cum scorn has turned into one of the most terrifying, autophagic processes imaginable, rendering self expression, even via cynicism, almost entirely impotent. Our bodies have been billboards of cultural commentary and cultural critique for so long that we seem to have finally reached nirvana, ripped away the veil of maya, and are saying nothing more than, "This color blue is kind of cool, don't you think?"

Not that anyone is thinking about this when they paint their nails. And even if they did think it they probably won't admit it. Case in point, people will rarely even admit that they enjoy *having* painted nails; they will only tell you that they enjoyed the act of painting them. Which makes sense in a roundabout way. Men, naturally, are wildly reluctant to admit that they enjoy having festive, decorated toes. Initially I expected to discover that the thing the men enjoyed the most about their painted toes was having women do the painting. I could not have been more wrong. The story my friend Paul told me was that he was just lounging around in Tahoe, watching his female friends paint their nails when the urge to paint his toes struck him out of the blue. He said that the women offered to do his nails for him but that he declined. "Because," he said, "I didn't want them done so much as I wanted to do them, know what I mean?"

Well, no, I don't really know what he meant. I suppose it's fun to paint your nails but it tends to be something that I and my female friends enjoy having other people do for us. Just last week I went to a slumber party (no kidding) and the women did each others nails while the two guys (who we did not allow to spend the night) insisted on doing their own nails. Frankly, I have no idea why men are suddenly insisting on painting their own toes. I have polled a number of men— normal, average, bring-me-home-to-meet-the-family straight men with painted toes—and they have all, without exception, said the exact same thing: "I just wanted to do it myself."

Paul's experience captures this strange take-charge spirit perfectly. After having successfully painted his toes that weekend in Tahoe his "number two pencil" colored polish eventually began to chip. (Welcome to world of beauty maintenance, Paul. Can you say 'top coat'?) While staying at another girl's house he not only removed the chipping silver polish but actually painted his nails again. This time he chose an apple green. "Females tried to advise me on color but I went with the one I originally wanted." You go girl!

The thing is, Paul is not the kind of person who would strike you as a toenail painting kind of guy. Well, maybe he is a toenail painting guy but he's not a let's-redo-this-in-a-different-color-toenail painting guy. Or at least that's what I used to think. But that was before listening to his lengthy exegesis on the intricacies of chipping, fading polish and the merits of cool versus warm tones. That incident has forced me to re-examine my belief that men are engaging in this activity as a one-time only act of counter-culture rebellion.

I had thought that these men were proud of their avant garde foray into the less arcane body arts. I really had no idea that so little thought was actually being given to the act. One of my oldest friends proved this point just after telling me that, "Oh no, I was proactive in painting my toes. I knew exactly what color I wanted and had Ellen buy the polish for me." Yes, I know he said "proactive," but that isn't part of the point. The point is that Rob is in venture capital and what's strange is that not five days after painting his toenails with an admittedly lovely light blue opalescent polish, he simply forgot about it. He went up to the Bohemian Grove, one of the most exclusive and most powerful men's only clubs in the world, absent-mindedly leaving behind his nail polish remover. One simply does *not* cruise around with George Bush whilst sporting light blue toenail polish. Rob had to spend the entire weekend making sure he didn't leave the cabin unshod and ruin the family name.

The only explanation for this account is that painting his toes was a purely esthetic event for Rob. Some men are claiming that painting their toes was an act of whimsy and desire while others are rationalizing it by citing the apparent sex appeal of owning painted toes. And of course there's that whole deconstructive, non-branded self expression rhetoric. But the only thing which seems certain in this burgeoning new era of esthetic evolution, and the surest indicator that this phenomenon whereby average straight boys are painting their toes with nail polish is in reality a new radical paradigm shift, is that the cooties are dying off.

It's very simple. Nail polish is a girl thing. Girl things have cooties. If boys are wearing nail polish then, quid pro quo, cooties must no longer be a threat. They must be dying. This is no small step for mankind. Cootie spray has been deemed unnecessary and Wal-Mart simply can't move their inventory no matter how much they cut their prices. Wall Street shrugs.

No. But seriously. Boy things have cooties too. When you get right down to it, almost everything has cooties regardless of apparent gender affiliation. Cooties are an inconsequential, nonexistent substance deemed meaningful only to those people who acknowledge their power to cause damage or discomfort. But in all known history cooties have never been seen to harm their supposed carriers. For that matter, in all known history, cooties have never been seen. Cooties are a purely subjective toxic experience and as soon as we recognize the stupidity of having our esthetic practices, values and desires influenced by rumors of arbitrary ickiness, the sooner we can get to work on the world's truly ugly problems. Like male pattern baldness. ■

August, 1997

PAUL TULLIS AND ZEV BOROW*

Fare Thee Well, Gentle Friend

The sad, untimely, perhaps even tragic
death of Adam Rich

The mass of ice plant that grows along the California coast just up
from Malibu is particularly plentiful, and Billy, Will and Jared's
favorite spot at the water's edge is covered with it. Its dense, pulpy leaves
cover the ground like a dank blanket, and seem to swallow the sounds
around it. Today the usual sounds—sea lions barking, waves crashing
up against the shoreline—are joined by the voices of these three
teenagers. It is the song of mourning for slain actor Adam Rich.

"He was just so real, so honest with his emotions—in every one of
his roles," says Billy, 18, whose weathered blond hair blows softly in the
coastal breeze, as he skips rocks into Santa Monica Bay.

In a flannel shirt and Converse All-Stars, his bowl cut half-shadow-
ing his eyes and his cheeks still pudgy, it's nearly impossible to miss the
resemblance between Will, 19, and Nicholas Bradford, the character
Adam played on the seminal '70s family dramedy, *Eight Is Enough*.
Indeed, Will could be his hero's reincarnation. "I was real young when

---

* *This piece was originally credited to "Christopher Pelham-Fence," a pseudonym created for no
reason that we can remember now.*

it was on, so I've only seen it in reruns," he confesses. "But I swear, even though I was an only child, it was like Nicholas could've been me."

"I never actually saw the show," offers Billy, "but he still meant everything to me.

"I can't believe he's gone," adds Jared.

But ask Will and his friends just why Rich is gone, and the reply comes almost in unison: "Short temper."

Not since Kurt Cobain, Brandon Lee, River Phoenix, James Dean, Jimi Hendrix, Jim Morrison, Lord Byron and Shannon Moon has the sting of remembrance been so bittersweet. And yet, this time, the memories seem to be shared on a more personal basis, as thousands of fans gather in spontaneous outbursts of mutual feeling and shared recollections. Indeed, Adam Rich's untimely death was largely ignored by the national media. But when Betty Buckley takes the stage in *Cats* tonight to sing her signature rendition of "Memories," it will resonate with new meaning as she mourns her slain former *Eight* co-star. For she knows, as well as the thousands of others who've found out through word of mouth in the past weeks, that here in the City of Angels, on the city's most famous avenue, outside a club, in a parking lot, Rich was killed in a senseless act of violence that has become all too familiar in urban America.

The details remain sketchy, but this much has been confirmed by the LAPD and unnamed sources close to Rich and the case. At 1:04 a.m. on March 22, Rich walked out of the swank Asp Club on Sunset Boulevard and headed for his car parked around the corner. The street light in front of the club was out. It had been raining. And 5/8 of the way to his 1986 Porsche 911 Turbo 20 feet away, Rich was confronted by a mysterious stranger—who has since been identified as 29-year-old unemployed dinner theater stagehand Tad Michael Earnhardt. Earnhardt brandished a gun and demanded Rich's wallet, which the actor reluctantly handed over. Then, displaying hints of the short temper Billy and his friends speak of, Rich offered a sarcastic— but according to Earnhardt, pointedly accurate—remark. The short, rotund Earnhardt, whose beefy frame belied a hypersensitive and trigger-happy teddy bear within, responded by shooting him three times in the chest. Earnhardt was picked up by police minutes later in a movie theater.

At the time of his death, Rich was hard at work producing an independent film whose plot, title and cast remain shrouded in mystery. Rumors say that it was a genre-bending blockbuster in the making, incorporating multimedia and interactive elements—the type of film propelled by a raw personal vision that comes along perhaps once in a generation.

The cast and crew of Rich's mystery film (known in *Variety* gossip columns as "The Squatter Project"), and nearly everyone in the small beach community of Venice where he made his home, were shocked by the tragic loss of one of America's finest young acting talents. Yet the Los Angeles police remain coolly—some might say cruelly—indifferent. "That kind of shit happens around here all the time, especially in parking lots," said LAPD Sgt. David Vigliano in a prepared statement.

If you believe in destiny, that we are all just derelict Chinese spy satellites hurtling through the atmosphere on a plotted trajectory toward a final flame-out, then Adam Rich was destined to die in a senseless and completely unpredictable way. The ultimate irony is that Rich, infamous for his short temper, would be sent to meet his maker by one with an even shorter temper than his own. For while Adam Rich is uniformly remembered as a kind, giving and effusively charming soul, nary a single recollection is absent of his somewhat darker side.

"I can remember the first time I met him," recalls Kentaro Tanizumi, an animator who brought Rich's voice to life as The Wizard in the cartoon TV series *Dungeons & Dragons*. "We were talking motorcross, trading wipeout stories, you know, friendly as could be. Then all of a sudden he was flyin' off the handle because it was too humid."

"It was like fire and ice with Adam," says Heather Locklear, who starred on *Dynasty* when it was shot next door to *Eight* on MGM's Culver City lot. "One minute he was charming the pants off you—like, literally—and the next minute he's totally berating you about your shoes. But I was just like, 'Adam, they're just shoes.'"

"I've never seen anyone so totally embrace a role," says Lorne Greene, who worked with Rich on the short-lived ABC series, *Code Red*. "But he'd be running lines with you on the set, and then, totally out of the blue, he'd be tearing his trailer apart. The tiniest little thing could set him off."

"He'd be playing with G.I. Joe, happy as a clam, and then for no apparent reason, he'd order Joe to run commando mission on his sister's Barbie dolls," recalls Rich's mother, Francine. "He was like that since the day he was born."

That day was October 12, 1968, and the place was Brooklyn, New York. Francine and her husband, Robert, moved Rich and brother Wayne out to California when Adam was five. Though nobody in Rich's family is an actor or even a producer, he demonstrated a precocious proclivity for the life of a thespian, and his future as an actor seemed predestined. "Oh, he used to put on little shows when family would come over," says Francine. "He'd write down whole scenes that he'd seen on TV and act them out. Then after about three months of him bugging me, I finally let him go to acting school." Rich's talents were the biggest sensation at Beverly Hills School of Performing Arts since its opening in 1971, and they were so taken by his gift that the instructors brought in the top child-actor agent at the time, Iris Burton.

Those who knew Rich early in his career would attest to his unadulterated innocence. "Adam was like a baby seal," says Jules Wandermann, director of BHSPA. "He fucking shimmered in the sun."

Rich's talents—along with some fast talking from Burton—got him cast opposite Hollywood patriarch Henry Fonda in a long-running commercial for GAF viewfinders. "Adam's youth and enthusiasm seemed to invigorate Henry," recalls Wandermann. "And if I'm not mistaken, it wasn't long after they started working together that he saw the script for *On Golden Pond*." Of course, soon after the commercial stopped running, so did Fonda. He died at the apogee of his career, as did Rich.

But one of the millions who saw the GAF viewfinder commercial was Lorimar Productions producer Tim Hamilton. After five callbacks and two screen tests, he instantly recognized Adam's innate talents and cast him in the role of Nicholas Bradford for Lorimar's one-hour pilot of *Eight Is Enough*, based on the best-selling family saga by author Thomas Braden. Braden passed away soon after writing the screenplay. Now Hamilton is dead, too.

On March 15, 1977, the newly formed cast of *Eight Is Enough* assembled in director Kent Morris's Beachwood Canyon bungalow for the ABC debut of the hastily edited pilot of the show. When the clock struck eight (a coincidence?), a nervous energy emanating from the cast and principal crew crackled in the Hollywood living room like kindling. They gathered and stared at the television with increasing tenseness, brought together now by their shared doubts: Could a show about a family with eight kids make it on American television? A show about a family with eight kids that lived in Sacramento? A family with eight kids that lived in Sacramento whose father was Dick van Patten? The odds seemed stacked against them.

But Rich would later tell friends that he could see his destiny laid out before him that night from his seat in a beanbag chair by the ficus. Just eight years old at the time, he was perhaps the only one present who could see that the show would be an instant success. The precocious youth stood up as the credits rolled and proclaimed, "It's a hit! A palpable hit!" The room stared at him in disbelief.

Rich was right, of course. *Eight Is Enough* went into immediate production as a one-hour series, and for the next four years established itself as a Wednesday night institution for millions of American families. And from this cast of over seventeen regular players, it was Rich who leapt into the collective heart of America. Within months of the show's debut, Adam was featured on magazine covers and morning wake-up shows nationwide.

But despite the show's wild success and Rich's universal popularity, problems developed between America's latest pre-pubescent darling and the rest of the cast of *Eight*. Even at the age of ten, Rich was prone to bouts of self-imposed solitude and moments of unpredictable, gale-force rage. One time on the set, he threw a bowl of catering-truck macaroni salad at costar Willie Aames, who played brother Tommy. Another time, in a discussion with an unsuspecting gaffer, he pulled a knife.

"Back then, people had this impression of Adam being this adorable little pip-squeak, and he was ... most of the time," says Susan Richardson, who played Susan. "But he had a dark side you just couldn't imagine, unless you were quite imaginative."

"He scared me. Scared me bad," confides *Karate Kid* Ralph Macchio, who had a small part on *Eight* as Nicholas's friend Jeremy. "I'm glad he's dead."

Rich had an entirely different feeling about his next show, *Code Red*, an emergency drama that attempted to combine the formulas of hit shows *Emergency!* and *CHiPs* with the family-oriented, tug-at-your-heartstrings allure of *The Waltons*. *Code* featured Rich as the adopted son in an extended family of fire fighters headed by Lorne Greene. Greene once said in an interview that Rich learned everything there was to know about fire fighting and was always lecturing the cast and crew about smoke detectors, fire-resistant pajamas and other safety devices. "It was something else," said Greene of Rich's fire-safety hyperawareness. "I mean, you'd light up a Marlboro or something, and he'd stop, drop and roll."

But Greene also admitted that Rich eventually began to take the role too seriously. Legend has it that Rich had heard on late-night TV somewhere that eating vitamin C tablets could actually make your skin fire retardant, and took to chewing the tablets constantly. "He had orange, cherry, tangerine—it was ridiculous," Greene told *Esquire* in 1988. "Couldn't get enough of that ascorbic acid. If the caterer ever ran out, he'd go bananas and start throwing those moist towelette packets all over the place."

Despite Rich's safety lectures—and short-tempered outbursts—
Code bombed anyway. Publicists said the ABC program—which was
produced by disaster maven Irwin *The Poseidon Adventure, Towering
Inferno* Allen—was a victim of a noble but failed experiment to merge
two successful formulas. But the truth is that Rich's star quality wasn't
enough to carry the weight of the soon-to-be-dead Greene, a Canadian.

Later that year, before the cancellation of *Code*, Rich co-starred
alongside Bill Cosby in Disney's paranormal-family-comedy film, *The
Devil and Max Devlin*. Unfortunately, the publicity it generated for
Rich couldn't prevent *Code* from joining *Eight* on the beach of the isle
of castaway television series. The film gave way to *Dungeons & Dragons*,
an animated TV program that aired at the height of the adventure
game's popularity with future engineers and computer programmers;
Rich enthralled audiences as the voice of the Wizard. (Willie Aames
also co-starred.) Along the way came guest appearances in such TV hits
as *The Love Boat, Fantasy Island, CHiPs* and *The Six Million Dollar
Man*. After *D&D* came a role on *Gun Shy*, a CBS series that lasted just
six episodes, and then Rich's star faded from the television firmament
like a fizzled-out comet whose tail burned too long and bright. At age
fifteen, he could only hope his star would come back, at least before
Hyakutake.

It was the years between 1984—when *Gun Shy* was prudently canceled—and 1994, when he turned up in an interview centered around
his shoes that appeared in this magazine, that remain the most enigmatic of Rich's short life. There were, of course, appearances on the two
Eight reunion shows, but cast members recall it was as if Rich were coming out of hibernation. "He'd show up late, unshaven, shirt halfway
unbuttoned, and immediately start slapping around some grip for no
reason whatsoever," recalls Aames. "You could tell he really didn't want
to be there; he'd just sit in his trailer, chewing that vitamin C."

Fortunately, Adam soon found another outlet for his emotions:
painting. While re-creation of family life in Sacramento wasn't enough
to bring Rich out of his funk, art was. He'd developed into a skilled
artist by the time of his early death. But no one will ever know just how
talented he was because of what transpired in the early morning hours
of a fateful Sunday in June, 1993.

It was then that Rich went into his penultimate short-tempered spi-
ral. A Brentwood gallery had opened the first exhibition of Rich's can-
vases earlier that night to great success. Shy about showing his work,
Rich had previously rejected numerous offers of exhibitions at respect-

ed galleries in New York and Los Angeles. Only a select few of his closest friends ever saw his paintings. "It was really weird with Adam's paintings," says Rich's personal trainer, Andy McBain. "Because he was so proud and showy when it came to his work as an actor—well, most of it, anyway—and yet he'd never let anyone come near his art."

The work was said to exhibit "an innate compulsion of solipsistic agony," in the words of the exhibition catalog. At the show's opening, Rich's self-taught virtuosity was lavishly praised. But praise wasn't enough for Rich; he overheard an ambivalent comment uttered by an artistic neophyte and stormed out of the gallery, his short temper ablaze.

According to court documents obtained by *Might*, Rich returned to the gallery sometime after three a.m. with a pilfered key, a matchbook, five gallons of kerosene and some tinfoil. After drenching each painting in the flammable liquid, he set fire to them all. The gallery burned to the ground, but owner Claudia von Claudia, moved by what she saw as "the ultimate act of artistic license," declined to press charges. "The place was way overinsured anyway," she told *Buzz* magazine.

If the world is a less beautiful place without Rich's paintings, perhaps we can take solace in the fact that this manifestation of his ill disposition seemed to pre-empt all future ones—until the one that would result in his death. For in the flames of destruction, Rich found redemption. After the gallery fire, Rich continued to paint, but would burn each canvas almost as soon as he finished it.

"Just having the work around long enough for the paint to dry was agonizing for Adam," says Rich's chauffeur, Ron Russell. "And if you're a painter, you know that acrylic dries in seconds." Russell pauses, staring straight ahead at nothing in particular. "He'd just sit there chewing his vitamin C and blowing on the painting," he says. Rich would regularly close the blinds in his apartment and go into what he called "lockdown," according to Russell and other sources, doing nothing but smoke cigars and paint, smoke and paint, smoke and paint. Then, when satisfied with what he saw through the pale, hazy light that crept through the blinds' slats, Rich would start a fire. "Sometimes he'd actually use the cigar to burn the painting," says Russell. "But that was real slow, so usually he'd just throw it in the fireplace."

Ironically, the habit may have pacified Rich in his final years. After about a year of frequent "lockdowns," Rich began work on the highly secretive "Squatter Project." Rich's tattoo artist, Mark Mahoney, says that Adam had never seemed happier than when he was talking, albeit obliquely, about "Squatter." "Adam was, like, a tattoo artist's wet dream," says Mahoney. "All his tats, which were inspired by 'Squatter,' had such depth."

In an act typical of his more generous side, Rich introduced his communications specialist, Ken Gold, to Harrison Ford and Nicolas Cage, who are rumored to have been just two of the many Hollywood heavyweights involved with "Squatter." "He was finally so happy, and not eating so much vitamin C," says Gold. "That's the real tragedy here." Since Rich's death, Gold confides, business has been slow.

The only other thing that seemed to effectively calm Rich's soul during these last years was motocross. A hobby of his since before his *Eight* days, Rich owned two bikes. And though both were in need of some minor repairs, friends say he was constantly talking about getting them running again.

"Sometimes we'd ride bikes together out in the desert," remembers fellow motocross enthusiast Jon Palumbo between bites of an In & Out Burger. "It was nice. Too bad he's dead."

On the day of Adam Rich's funeral, a soft breeze whispers through the rain-flattened grass of Holland Hill Cemetery. When the service is over, and the white enamel casket has been lowered into the ground, about twenty-three people gather in a circle to share their memories and their grief. Gloria Hazen, Rich's first girlfriend, reminisces about how, after his family moved from Brooklyn, he used to walk down to the beach at sunset to throw large rocks at seagulls. "He was so pissed to be living away from his friends," she says. In the harsh morning light, she looks frail and timid, a mere shadow of her former self when Rich was alive.

"That's totally bullshit," yells Kathy Williams, a former girlfriend of Rich. "He hated Brooklyn!"

"Whatever, Kathy. How would you know anything? He only took you to the Golden Globes," says Cindy Hansen, another former girlfriend. "But he totally loved L.A., even from the start."

"No, he never really found himself here," corrects Sapphire Hermann, Rich's junior-year prom date. "And he never really knew his mom."

"He was a goddamn angel, that's what he was," sobs Mary Barnes, another girlfriend.

As the grief session advances into the afternoon, it is clear that the enigmatic Rich was too complex to be understood by any one of those around him. But it also becomes clear that he not only touched the hearts of those who knew him well, he actually touched many of those who knew him less well. This was his nature and the facet of his personality that gave his acting an electric spark: to love, to share, to touch —but to keep a little something inside, a little something held back.

Mary Barnes sits quietly in a corner of the circle, meticulously pulling apart a dandelion. "I thought he liked seagulls."

Today and every day since Rich's death, small charred stick-figure drawings, some of them small as cocktail napkins and paper plates, along with a motley collection of cigars, vitamin C tablets and motocross patches line the alley outside the Asp Club. Go there at sunset and inevitably a crowd will have formed, a mishmash of motocross enthusiasts, struggling painters and actors, small children and older, inconsolable *Eight Is Enough* fans. They usually mingle for a while, lighting candles and laying flowers around a makeshift memorial of trash aligned to spell "Adam." It's a group similar in makeup to the dozens that attended Rich's memorial/rally/barbeque on Venice beach the Saturday after his death.

There, a tape recorded by Allison Hughes, Rich's girlfriend of the last three weeks of his life, was played to the assembled mourners. She urged the fans to be strong, and quoted one of the ten moving tips Rich gave this magazine's readers in 1995. "Just turn on some Superchunk, throw your stuff in a box and move it!"

To show up in person would have been the most difficult of moments for Allison Hughes, a dancer. "I just couldn't face standing up in front of all those people, you know. It's not like I have a lot of black in my wardrobe, so I'm not entirely confident about how I look. But hearing about it later, it just hit me—they really loved him. Wow."

Hughes suggests that Rich was largely a misunderstood figure. "He never stormed out of any restaurants, or got mad at his dentist, or cursed. All that shit about his so-called short temper came from you faggot Nazi journalists." She makes little quote marks with her fingers when she says the words "short temper" and "journalists."

Looking out at the waves that extend endlessly into the horizon from this ice plant-covered coastal chaparral in Ventura County, the life of a talented young actor may for a moment seem small compared to the Pacific Ocean. That is, until the silence is broken by one whom that actor touched so deeply with his life and art—Ron Russell. Ron has come to share some of his remembrances of Rich with these three fans, Billy, Will and Jared. He points to a single episode just after pre-development meetings began on the "Squatter Project" that may have signaled what was to come.

"We were going to get some more vitamin C from the 24-hour GNC one night after working late," Ron relates to the young fans, who hang on his every word. "A guy came over to Adam and asked for the time. Adam just lost it. He snapped at him, 'Do I look like a fucking clock?

Do I? Am I Big fucking Ben to you?' I was like, whoa, Adam, settle down. I had to hold this guy back from taking a swing at him. I remember Adam just glared at me," he says. Ron's eyes glimmer like the ocean before him as he continues. "He glared, and glared, and glared, and glared, and glared, and—glared. Then he glared for a few more minutes. Of course, by now the guy was long gone. But it was really weird."

Billy, Will and Jared sit silently for a moment. Finally, Will speaks. Still cherubic at twenty-two, he embodies the type of kid who related to Rich, and his pain now is somehow beyond all the glowing eulogies at the funeral the day before, or the somewhat less flattering anecdote Ron has just told. "That doesn't sound like him at all," says Will, incredulous. "I mean, remember when Nicholas ran away from home and made friends with the bum in San Diego? Does that sound like the type of guy who'd throw a temper-tantrum?"

When one who has shone so brightly to so many is snuffed out with terrifying finality, the pain comes in waves that seem to lap at the toes of individuals, even as it crashes onto the beachhead of society. No, there will never be another quite like Adam Rich, and while his memory, to both his fans and those who knew him, is immortal, what really are we left with?

Questions. What was Tad Michael Earnhardt, a well-off, albeit unemployed, dinner theater stagehand, doing in that parking lot that night? What made Rich race to meet his destiny outside the Asp Club's doors? How do you finish a movie when the producer and principal actor has been killed during pre-production? And, finally, what will Ron and company do for a job now?

It is said that to fly too close to the sun is to have your body turned into stone. In the weeks and months that follow, an industry and a generation will have to mine a new quarry. ■

May, 1996

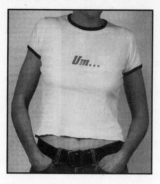

The T-shirt: More Problems of Signification in American Low Couture

Or, what am I saying? *tony-stylish*

During a brief stint in a psychiatric ward, I met someone who seemed perfectly "normal," so I asked him why he was there. He said because he was always late. I said, Oh? And he said, Yeah, I was never making it to school until way after my first class. Sometimes not until after lunch. And I asked, How come? You were sleeping? And he responded, No! I wasn't sleeping—I'd set my alarm for seven in the morning, six in the morning, after a while I was just like fuck it and didn't even go to bed! I'd start getting ready as soon as I got home! So I said, What are you talking about, dude? What was the problem? And he said: My shoelaces.

Your shoelaces?

Yeah, I'd tie them, and then they just ... Somehow they just didn't look right, you know? First I'd do it the bunny-ear way? You make the two bunny-ears over the first knot, and then you tie them, the bunny-ears, in a knot. But it wouldn't look right, so I'd tie a double knot, like tie the bunny-ears again, but it would look even worse. So I'd undo it and try the other way, where you tie the first knot, and then you make a tree with one end of the lace, and you wrap the other lace around it, loopy, and stick it through the hole it made in itself. But that didn't come out right either. I mean, it would stay tied—definitely, it would stay tied. But the way the laces wrapped around each other, the particular way one overlapped the other: I'd look at it and think: No. That's not quite right. What does it mean, to have the knot like that? What am I saying? I didn't know. So I'd start over.

His problem, however cruelly compounded by an obsessive-compulsive disorder, was the central problem of contemporary representation: "What am I saying?" What he needed was a system to simplify the question, to narrow the scope of his inquiry. (What he needed was a pair of slip-on Vans). In another essay I examined this crisis of signification by following the changing values we have placed on the Adidas tracksuit. Now I march straight to the gnashing vortex of fashion's gory battleground, and type with my nipples bare to the wind. Above me flutters my own system, my uniform, my flag of false truce: my plain white T-shirt.

There is an excellent book on the subject of white T-shirts already. (*The White T*, by Alice Harris, introduction by Giorgio Armani. Umbra Editions, 1996.) It tells about how the fabric and cut of the modern T evolved over decades of military testing. The garment's purposes initially were dual: to insulate, and to hide unsightly chest hair. But sailors in the tropics found that the light, smooth, stretchy qualities of the T, in addition to the UV protection it provided the shoulders (earlier undershirts were sleeveless), also made it an excellent choice for deckwork—sans the customary V-neck jumper. In the Pacific Theater of the Second World War, the T-shirt became the unofficial emblem of bellicose manhood. Prior to the war, the T-shirt was also worn by factory workers in the North and sharecroppers in the rural South, which lent the garment grease cred and dirt cred but marked it as definitively prole. After the war, soldiers and sailors continued to wear their T-shirts; this was in the days of universal service, so rich men as well as poor men owned them. At first the garment, worn alone, indicated naughtiness—Brando, Dean, the King—but when young Senator John Kennedy was photographed relaxing in a T-shirt at his summer pad, the garment achieved legitimate swank cred, while retaining Beat cred and butch cred. A miracle was in the making. Hippies sported Ts because they could paint designs on them and tie-dye them, homosexuals sported them because it was manly, feminists sported because Gloria said to. T-shirts were mufti for the Revolution, but squares still wore them, black people, you name it, this book has pictures of everything.

Rewind. In 1959 someone invented Plastisol, a durable, stretchable textile ink. Prior to 1959 most printing on T-shirts was done with cloth letters or flocking, fuzz stuck to gooey glue. The Smithsonian Institute's oldest printed shirt dates from 1948: "Dew-It with Dewey," a relic of the New York governor's unsuccessful presidential bid; but at that time printing was mainly found on military or collegiate-athletic gear. The invention of Plastisol made massive print-runs possible. Disney had already hit on the idea of T-shirt-as-souvenir; several artists had made small runs of screen-printed or airbrushed (with house paint or spray paint) automotive designs.

In 1962 a young man named Rick Ralston moved to Hawaii and started a company called Crazy Shirts, based on his notion of decorating T-shirts with surf designs. Later in the '60s a T-shirt appeared with a bottle of Budweiser printed on it. Other corporate logos soon followed. In 1972 Winterland Productions began selling rock merchandise at shows in San Francisco. In the '70s, printed T-shirts came to be casually accepted as a means of stating one's identity: I like this beer, I like this band, "I'm with Stupid (arrow)." It hardly seems remarkable now. In fact, it's quite difficult to picture an alternative modern world, one without printed T-shirts. The concept resists the imaginative faculties—it's like trying to imagine an alternative modern world without television or nuclear weapons: No way.

But printed T-shirts—especially logo-printed T-shirts—are weird! Here is the idea: I put my product logo on a T-shirt; you pay me for it; and then you wear it. That's a good deal better than free advertising for me—it's doubly profitable advertising. Markup on a stylish printed T (such as those Winterland still produces) is in the neighborhood of twenty dollars. What is the T-shirt buyer buying, exactly, aside from a layer of clothing? A twenty dollar share in the advertising campaign? That sounds patently ridiculous. And it is. But then again, it's not. Let's use the example of the Nike Corporation, since it will reverberate in several fun directions. Nike spends hundreds of millions on advertising, hundreds of millions of dollars to say: "Nike stuff is cool." You pay twenty-four dollars for a "Just Do It" shirt, and at—relatively—little expense you partake in a global program asserting that you, by association, are cool. Not bad.

On the contrary—it's ludicrous. And you already knew it; subversion has been in the works for a good ten years now. Winterland Productions started out hawking Grateful Dead merchandise. The Grateful Dead, like them or not, remained down for the common (wo)man—even after making gabillions of dollars themselves—and they pulled no Eddie Vedder puking-and-cancellation fits to prove it. Instead, they allowed nearly unrestricted commerce among their fans, at least until the parking lot souk itself came to resemble a T-shirt industry trade-show. Grateful Dead iconography—skulls, lightning bolts, teddy bears, etc.—comprised an alphabet of quasi-secret symbols whereby Deadheads could identify one another on the highway (bumper stickers) and on the sidewalk (T-shirts). The merchandise sold inside venues by Winterland and other licensees was imprinted with official copyrighted symbols, and the parking lot goods with bastardized versions of the copyrighted symbols, which served the same purpose of mutual identi-fication. Deadhead culture, while deeply rooted in American capitalism, nevertheless considered itself to be in direct opposition to that system; one mode of printed Deadhead T-shirt that came into vogue in the late '80s was the encoded parody of a mega-campaign, such as Nike's. A "Just Dew It" T-shirt, with Nike's trademark swoosh tweaked into a Deadhead lightning bolt, began appearing at concerts in Northern California dur-ing the acme of the "Just Do It" campaign. (The pun is on the title of the Grateful Dead anthem, "Morning Dew"—this may mean nothing to a non-Deadhead, but oh! what joy of recognition for the faithful. (And what a workhorse of a pun—see "Dewey" above.)) That the brisk sales of this particular shirt partook of Nike's gigantic expenditure, is an attendant irony which must be addressed.

Irony itself must be addressed first. Irony is defined adequately by Webster, but more elegantly by handsome belletrist Ethan Hawke's Troy Dire in *Reality Bites*: "Irony is when what you say is the opposite of what you mean." Remember the Denny's imbroglio? In the spring of 1993, the Denny's restaurant chain was accused of (among other codified vio-lations of law and common decency) implementing a policy demanding that African-Americans pay for their food before eating. My friend Dave already owned a Denny's T-shirt (chrome yellow, Denny's logo in red) which I already coveted for its ironic value, as well as for its intrinsic aes-thetic value. The ironies functioning pre-imbroglio were as follows: 1.) Denny's is a big dumb company, and wearing the logos of big dumb companies on shirts is fun, because I know the companies are big and dumb; 2.) Denny's is a crappy fast-food restaurant, representative of the kind of place where it's fun to pretend I might work even though I grad-uated from an Ivy League university, so I'm wearing this shirt. I mentioned that I coveted the shirt pre-imbroglio. (My personal uniform, my system—brown pants, plain white T-shirt—was still in development; I still owned some printed T-shirts.) When the scandal hit the papers, I stole Dave's Denny's shirt.

The person selling the "Just Dew It" shirt at Grateful Dead concerts had only a vague understanding of the forces he was manipulating, and the forces manipulating him. How do I know? This is fun: because he was me. At the time I had dropped out of school, and was working as an artist at InMotion, a screen-printing shop in Sonoma, Calif. My talent as a visual artist and my entrepreneurial acumen were both quite limited, so I went back to school. I went back to school extremely sick of screen-printed T-shirts, but highly sensitized to the fact of them. A company called Fresh Jive was in its nascency; this was 1990. I remember very clearly seeing its flagship T-shirt: white, with the Fresh Jive logo (one version of the Fresh Jive logo) emblazoned large on its chest.

The Fresh Jive logo looked like this: concentric circles of neon yellow and orange, with the word "Jive" in large blue block letters rising from the left side of the target to the right. "Fresh," in the same typeface and color, was printed at the same rising angle, but smaller, at the top. It was a parody of one of the most recognizable (and effective) logos ever designed, that of Tide laundry detergent. The "Fresh" was in the place where, on a Tide box, you would see "New" or "Ultra" or something like that—I couldn't remember, exactly, but I knew the composition and color were perfect matches. Nice! I thought. What was Fresh Jive? I wondered. Nobody seemed to know. I didn't get on the phone, or go to the library, or peek into the still-mysterious Internet to find out, but I did ask around. Most of the people wearing the Fresh Jive shirts seemed to be ravers or skaters—maybe it was a party promoter or deck manufacturer? Even the people wearing the shirts didn't know. They were just wearing them. The obvious never occurred to me—Fresh Jive was nothing at all. Or rather, it was itself: a brand, pure and simple, existing only in the abstract world of pre-existing brands, logos, names.

Rick Klotz started Fresh Jive in his family's clothing manufacturing warehouse in 1990. The warehouse is in Los Angeles. Rick is now 29, and richer than you. Exactly how rich is top-secret, but rich enough that I couldn't get him on the phone. I got a publicist named Sherry MacDonald, who is either afflicted with a cognitive disorder of her own, or is a great publicist, which is how you can tell someone is a great publicist. Here is a sampling of her work, when asked the question, "What is Fresh Jive?"

"Fresh Jive is its own thing. Its own entity. You can't explain it with just T-shirts alone. For me Fresh Jive has that Fresh Jive feel no matter what. For Rick, it's what he sees... Everything to him is a logo. He sees stuff, and he goes, 'I can make a logo out of that. I can make a T-shirt out of that.' He's like an Andy Warhol type of guy. He's really nice, and shy."

It's journalistically unkind to jumble someone's quote. In this case it was unnecessary; that's what Sherry said while I was looking for a pen. The Fresh Jive logo is unique in that it has no identifying feature but the words themselves—it achieves recognition by taking corporate shapes already familiar to us. The Peter Max style is big from Fresh Jive this season, and also Sad-Eyed Girls ([?] That one was lost one me, but Sherry assured me that if I saw them, I would know them). To Rick's credit—and Sherry's, for passing the information along—Fresh Jive has extremely high manufacturing standards: for instance, if you are buying a shirt imprinted with a Fresh Jive design deriving from a '70s logo design, your shirt will be cut to '70s specs (tighter, wider neck). Fresh Jive merchandise is available in 300 domestic stores, and 17 foreign countries. Fresh Jive now has dozens of imitators. Right. Think about it.

The ostensible subtext of the Fresh Jive aesthetic is disgust (or, if we take Elvis Costello's tack, attempted amusement) with capitalism, or at least with its monster embodiment, the Corporation. This notion rang dimly in my head as I took the hippies' money for the "Just Dew It" shirt—the disgust/amusement was a precondition of the shirt, but not necessarily one that could be articulated in connection with the shirt. At the time, I just knew people would want the shirt—there was something funny about it, and it answered the requirement of providing a marker for mutual identification. (I also knew, just as dimly, there was something deeply lame about my "Just Dew It" shirt.) Rick the Andy Warhol type of guy—I am definitely more a Valerie Solanis type of guy—was obviously more clued in, or an artist/capitalist idiot-savant (see "great publicist" re: problems of category). But once you understand that Fresh Jive, itself, is exactly what it hates, except even spookier because there's no underlying product—even with Nike, there were shoes before "Just Do It"—can you still wear Fresh Jive? If you do, what do you mean?

I can think of one way to wear Fresh Jive, right now: like the Denny's shirt. But with a dangerous extra somersault that would put me at risk of rejoining my friend with the shoelace problem. It's not worth it. I'm too scared. I will wear my system of simplification, my plain white T-shirt, which signifies only that I am a millionaire straight fag broke cultural critic, a little bit country, and a little bit rock and roll. ■

Pardon Me, Mr. Senator...
Will You Please Give Me
My Goddamn Money?

The two hundred senior citizens in this room will not sit still. As they listen to various witnesses give testimony to the Commission on the Social Security Notch Issue, they play the part of the disgruntled audience, trying intently to disrupt the hearings. It is an inspired performance. They fidget. They cough. They mumble sarcastic observations to each other. Then, in beautiful, unrehearsed unison, two hundred senior citizens collectively lose their shit.

Jumping from their seats, pointing fingers and shouting at commission members and hearing witnesses alike, the audience does a fairly competent job of making a lot of noise without making any sense. "It was like being in the room," said Richard Thau, one of the hearing's six testifying witnesses, "with a bunch of old people on angel dust."

The 257 million people living in the United States—save a small group of senior citizens on an emotional crusade—couldn't care less about this issue. The "notch," as it has come to be known, is political shorthand for a disparity in Social Security payments created by the Social Security Act of 1977. In that legislation, the formula to compute Social Security benefits was revised to correct payments to individuals that had become mistakenly and disproportionately large. When the law went into effect, the revised formula was applied only to those born after 1916. Predictably enough, those born in the transition group following this cutoff (1917-1921)—frequently referred to as "notch babies"—claim not only that their recalculated benefits are too low but that they are being intentionally swindled by the government.

The problem, however, is that they're wrong. And it's all Dear Abby's fault.

Abigail Van Buren, author of the wildly popular "Dear Abby" advice column, writes on a wide variety of topics. She covers, perhaps, a little too much ground. In late 1983, she penned a series of columns that brought the relatively obscure and technically intricate notch issue into the public debate. Unfortunately, Van Buren was not fully versed in the subtleties of the problem. According to the Congressional General Accounting Office report on the issue, "The 'Dear Abby' column was found to be misleading and likely created some mistaken impressions about the notch and who was affected by it." In fact, it had the unfortunate consequence of announcing to millions of benefit recipients that, quite possibly, they were being ripped off every time they received a Social Security check.

The facts are a little more complicated. Though the notch babies are receiving smaller benefits than the small group of people born before 1917, they are still receiving proportionally larger benefits than the rest of America. They refuse to acknowledge the reason for the 1977 legislation: The benefit payments to certain individuals were calculated incorrectly (i.e. too large). A graph of Social Security payments to this age group looks, more or less, like a mountain: those born in 1916 are at the top, the notch babies are just below them to the right, and everybody else, both older and younger than the transition group, are down below. Nevertheless, the notch babies may see a neighbor—someone who was born in 1916 and who had the same earning history as their own—get a monthly Social Security check for $100 more than theirs, and this makes them furious. A hundred dollars is a lot of money to someone on a fixed income. A hundred dollars is worth a letter to a

Congressperson.

During the '80s, given that the notch had become an immediate concern for an increasing number of registered and active voters, Congress began the laborious process of debating whether or not they would actually do something to fix it. In October of 1992, the Commission on the Social Security "Notch" Issue was created. Finally, 11 years after the Dear Abby alarm had been sounded, the commission brought its traveling public hearings show to the West Coast. The official purpose of the commission—and its $2 million budget—is simply to gather testimony from around the country. The testimony will then be used by Congress to make an informed decision on the notch. However, as many involved in the issue openly speculate, the real purpose of the hearings is to stall the notch babies—whose median age is 76—until either they are too exhausted to make a fuss or they have all died.

The date is November 17, 1994. Many hoping to speak with, listen to or grumble at experts on the notch have gathered in the walnut-appointed Metropolitan Room of the ANA Hotel in San Francisco. The group at hand is comprised of the 12-member commission, 6 testifying witnesses and the aforementioned, 200-strong senior citizen audience. The proceedings revolve around the commission members seated at a long wooden table set near the front of the room. They are all blue-suited, white-haired white men except for one woman who is dressed conspicuously in red. They call on the witnesses, ask an occasional question and pour each other glasses of water. For the most part, the commission seems bored.

With the commission looking on, the hearing progresses through the first three witnesses: a spokesperson from Social Security Notch Babies of Montebello, California; the commissioner of the San Francisco Commission on the Aging; and a private citizen named Mildred. Their respective testimonies are centered, of course, around the injustices of the notch. No surprises here. While the audience generally nods in support, a few individuals begin to look restless. They have heard this rhetoric before; they have come to speak. In the corner of the room, near a stack of unused chairs, a yawning cameraman captures it all on video.

The hearing is barely sixty minutes old, and Richard Thau would rather be anywhere else. There are three people in the room under age fifty, and Thau, a co-founder of Third Millennium and the fourth witness to be called, is one of them. The mission of Third Millennium, a political advocacy and education group, is to raise awareness of the

156 ■ David Moodie

United States' sundry long-term problems—many of which relate to
the ever-expanding budget deficit. Third Millennium testified last
February before the Bi-Partisan Commission on Entitlements and Tax
Reform. This oration earned Third Millennium—represented by
Thau—an invitation to speak before the Notch Commission and a
flight to San Francisco at taxpayer expense. Thau is here in hopes of
persuading Congress to address the ever-expanding cost of federal enti-
tlement programs, starting with Social Security. Needless to say, he is
not a popular witness with the audience.

In fact, Thau is actually booed and hissed. The audience has come to
hear how and when their individual benefit checks will be increased.
They have no interest in hearing about the faltering future of Social
Security. The Commission, painfully aware of this fact, uses Thau's testimony to cozy up to the crowd. After he is done speaking, the commission members demand answers to a number of questions,
apparently striving to challenge Thau's testimony. At one point, the
chairman of the commission, Alan Campbell, gazes solemnly down
upon Thau. "How many members does your organization have?" he
asks. "About 1,300," replies Thau. "I see," the chairman says, with a
smirk curling the corners of his mouth. Thau is finally told he may step
down. He immediately leaves the room.

If the audience is a bit rough with Thau, they are downright rabid
when the next witness, Patricia Dilley, a professor of tax law at the
University of Seattle, begins her statement. She is knowledgeable,
thoughtful and respectful, but her agenda, like Thau's, is to speak of the
serious problems that Social Security faces ahead. She has hardly begun
when the audience explodes. There is, at first, merely a loud murmur
from the audience. But it rises in volume until a small handful of senior
citizens are actually out of their seats and shouting at Dilley. "We came
here to talk about the notch, not the system." "We've been waiting
twelve years for Rostenkowski to get booted so we can get our money!"
yelps a woman in the front. "We're gonna be dead soon!" moans another. The loudest and perhaps most straightforward exclamation comes
from an elderly man in a bow-tie and beret: "We don't care about the
future, we just want our money!" There are many other exclamations.
Most cannot be heard over the din of the crowd, and others, sounding
eerily like Grandpa Simpson, are downright incomprehensible. It takes
the chairman nearly five minutes to quiet the audience.

The audience's ability to summon this fury is both impressive and
unexpected. It makes for exceptional drama. And theatrics or not, the
notch babies are genuinely convinced they are not getting what is owed

to them. The members of the commission, however, feel otherwise.

On December 29, the commission delivered its final report to Congress. The 36-page document recommends that no action be taken to compensate the transition group or otherwise modify any existing payment formulas to individuals. In short, the commission advises maintaining the existing policy of doing nothing. The report states, "To the extent that disparities in benefit levels do exist, they exist not because those born in the 'notch' years received less than their due; they exist because those born before the 'notch' years... continue to receive substantially inflated benefits."

Though it took the commission two years and $2 million dollars to submit this recommendation, the notch babies will presumably maintain that their benefits are too low. Eventually though, they will realize that the issue has been decided, and any further protests are in vain. After all, their quest was doomed from the start: Old age and hostility will always lose out to youth and bureaucracy. ■

February, 1995

ERIC WESTERVELT

The Glorious Climb of the Affluent Recreating Professional

Anxious and bored. Really bored. Bored to the point of—yes, it's true—ennui. That's how segments of the upper and middle classes felt in the waning years of 19th-century America. The rushing onslaught of rapid industrial change and its sundry creature-comfort by-products had cast over them a kind of disorientation one historian called "weightlessness." Nothing was real anymore. The rugged individualist that once made America great, they moaned, had given way to a class of sissy automatons. So they turned to bicycling, camping, tennis and horseback riding, and the search for "authentic experience" was on.

A century later, amid our own technological revolution, the cult of experience is back, embodied by a new class of well-off but spiritually restless Americans. Sure, they may spend their days anchored to a PC, but when the weekend comes they head straight to the slopes, the trails or the river. Of course, these days, authentic experience comes with a price. Nepalese trekking excursions, Moab mountain biking trips, whitewater kayaking runs and helicopter-assisted ski vacations are a little more costly than a week at the coast, and whatever they do, today's outdoor elite feel the need to do it with style. Which means they've got to have the gear. Which means they've got to have the cash.

Move over crass '80s self-indulgence. Today's on-the-go consumerists have put on an outdoorsy face, eschewing BMWs for Range Rovers, overpriced art for camping equipment, bad suits and powder cocaine for head-to-toe Lycra and spirulina smoothies. These days, America's favorite free-spenders are not Yuppies but Arpies: Affluent Recreating Professionals.

Depending on where a person falls on the age curve, Arpies are either aging ex-Yuppies or their younger equivalents. She's the fortysomething marketing VP with the kayak rack on her Ford Explorer. He's the late-twenties software consultant with the windsurfer and rock-climbing gear cluttering his apartment. Whether fending off mid-life crises through public acts of accessory-laden exercise, or, for the younger professional, trying to prove to their contemporaries that despite fat salaries and uptown addresses, they're "totally into nature" and not at all like the Yuppies they so readily mocked in school, Arpies are united by a knack for having caught the right bandwagon at the right time. Oh, and they recycle.

Yuppiedom to Arpiedom is, in part, a brilliant adaptation to today's corporate climate. Embodying a new "discipline" lacking in Yuppie self-indulgence, the Arpie obsession with exhibitionist recreating better suits the calculated, cautious mega-mergers of the '90s that have displaced the hostile takeovers of the Reagan '80s. Arpiedom underscores Protestant values of hard work and endurance more suited to the '90s business world. Like astute changelings, the '80s Yuppies have metamorphosed, through vigorous sporting—or at least the appearance of it—into models of moral uprightness. The scorned are now praised. This crisis of confidence in the face of technological and cultural changes is as American as credit cards and manicured lawns. And once again, the search for true experience is fused with consumerism itself.

"Outdoor exercise seemed the perfect antidote to…excessive mental work," in late 19th-century America, writes historian T.J. Jackson Lears in his cultural history, *No Place of Grace: Antimodernism and the Transformation of American Culture*. "Said to recapture preindustrial vigor without sacrificing the benefits of industrial progress, sport revealed a strain of careful primitivism." The movement's most prominent booster was Theodore Roosevelt, whose hard-charging hunting and fishing outdoor ethos exhorted the nation to "just kill it."

Today, Arpies don't take up bike-riding just to get fit or enjoy the outdoors (which would require only a pair of shorts, sneakers and a Schwinn). Instead, they need to show the world that their participation in an activity indicates a lifestyle choice, and that their degree of seriousness about that choice can be measured according to how much high-priced gear they've accumulated to support it.

Any bicycle shop would be glad to put it all on your Gold Card. With Lycra shorts running at $80, shoes up to $220 and some bikes more costly than a Yugo, it's amazingly easy to rack up $5,000 in gear before leaving the store.

Pop culture and commerce openly encourage—and are encouraged by—the trend of conspicuous recreating: in loud, who-knocked-the-cameraman-over TV spots, Volkswagen offers a free mountain bike with certain leases; Gatorade tells us "Life is a sport, drink it up;" the heroes in a new USA Network show, *Pacific Blue*, are California cops on (you guessed it) mountain bikes; the ads for Ralph Lauren's Polo Sport line ("Accessories for outdoor adventure") feature models clutching ice axes.

At The North Face, a predominately wholesale business selling outdoor gear to retailers, sales rose 36.3 percent in 1995—a year in which overall retail sales declined. Recreational Equipment, Inc. (REI) opened two new stores in 1995, and a 100,000-square-foot flagship store this September; overall sales were $448 million.

Also telling of Arpie insurgence is the incredible rise of the indoor rock climbing gym. According to DeAnne Mousolf, an editor at *Rock & Ice* magazine, there were three rock climbing gyms in the U.S. in 1989, and today there are 500, with another 250 expected to open by the end of 1997. Ironically, in their search for real experience, Arpies can't escape today's desire for convenience. "You get a workout and can take a sauna and an espresso at the same time," says Sharon Urquhart, author of *Mock Rock: The Guide to Indoor Climbing*. The rock gym is a safe, urban place to go to see and be seen, a chance for a fashionable one-on-one communion with faux rocks. What's next? Well, indoor skiing is huge in Japan.

Which is not to say that Arpies don't crave real dirt—or at least the means to get to it. Witness the advent of Chrysler Corporations's "Camp Jeep," a two-day training camp held every summer near Vail, Colo., and Range Rover's "Worldwide Adventures" held in the Rockies, Moab, Australia and Morocco—an exoticized, consumer-friendly Outward Bound for those approaching middle age. Even though sport-utility vehicles feature lower pollution-emission standards and anemic gas mileage, car manufacturers market them as the one step necessary to morph from typical suburbanites into a make-believe frontier family.

But sometimes these would-be adventurers end up looking more like the Donner Party than Lewis and Clark. Arpie zeal turned tragic in recent years as several affluent, inexperienced climbers died trying to buy their way to the top of Mt. Everest, the world's highest peak. That's nothing new. Nineteenth-century narratives are littered with tales of rich American thrill-seekers who perished pursuing what they thought of as a "noble conquest" of rugged mountains.

Since Arpie civic engagement isn't local or national in focus, but is usually specific to their favorite recreating corridor, it's hardly surprising that Arpies sometimes place their leisure above other concerns. At Devil's Tower National Monument in northern Wyoming, recreational climbing has shot up dramatically from just 300 climbers in 1973 to more than 6,000 today, according to a National Park Service spokesman. Long considered sacred by Native Americans of the northern plains, the Park Service asked climbers "to voluntarily refrain from climbing during the culturally significant month of June," when some tribes conduct religious ceremonies at the majestic rock butte. While many obliged, some climbers refused. Near-perpetual climbing and the placement of hundreds of metal climbing bolts has, the Park Service says, "affected nesting raptors, soil, vegetation, the rock's physical appearance, and the area's natural quiet."

Oops!

In their unconscious belief that moving from the nightclub to the mountain top acts as penitence for the excesses of the '80s, Arpies benefit from the socially acceptable façade of environmentalism associated with outdoor activity. But Arpie culture will inevitably be seen for what it is: recreating as an end in itself, a singles club for the Lycra class, a temporary antidote to personal anomie, a vain attempt to find indentity. Even so, Arpie culture is as spiritually vacant as a stair-climber. Popular scorn eventually shamed Yuppies into conversion or hibernation. The only question for Arpies is, who's going to buy all those used Pathfinders? ■

November, 1996

EDITED BY BOB MARGOLIS & DAN KING

The Way We Were

Outtakes from the Haldeman diaries

As H.R. "Bob" Haldeman anticipated, the publication of the diaries he kept as Chief of Staff to Richard Nixon has provided an invaluable resource for both the historian and the cyclist. Chronicled in exquisite detail is the full tragedy that was Nixon, from his first-term accomplishments and landslide re-election through April of 1973, when the author was forced to resign in Nixon's desperation to avoid impeachment. And we see it from the insider's perspective, for Haldeman worked more closely with Nixon than perhaps any Chief of Staff in American history. Haldeman had Nixon's complete respect and trust, and was the only man from whom the President would tolerate the nickname "Peaches" (shortened to "The P" in the diaries).

The published version of the diaries, as Haldeman explains in his foreword, is edited down by approximately 60 percent from the full text. Whatever his motivation (to boost sales of the full text? One last coverup?), Haldeman has omitted some of the best stuff. Here we see Nixon at his worst, beheading a schoolchild for talking during his famous "Recess Address," and at his best, reaching out across party lines to locate and destroy his enemies. *Might* is proud to disillusion one and all with this small sampling of the missing entries.

Wednesday, February 19, 1969

The P called E, K and I in for another organizational meeting, but it never got off the ground. The P lit his pipe, then became concerned that though he had succeeded in setting fire to the pipe's contents, he had perhaps not lit the pipe in a way that could really move people, win over new voters without alienating our base, really turn the tide our way in several key swing states. He called in E and Colson and initiated a long discussion of the subject.

The three lit and relit their pipes in various attitudes, looking for the best, while I raised the point that, this being largely a cultural problem, different states might require different approaches. Eventually the clouds of smoke set off the fire alarms, at which point I fled the scene, but the P couldn't move, being too full of smoke, I think. E and Colson dutifully sat by his side, and the three were thoroughly doused by the Oval Office sprinkler system. Pretty funny, but the P was concerned that the whole thing was wrong, that they had not been doused in a way that spoke to the average American. Chuck and E winced as I ordered the sprinklers back on, but this time there was even less water than the first time and the P became very upset. We finally arranged to dump a 55-gallon barrel of ice water on him, and that settled him down a bit, but not before a series of phone calls to the Secret Service (re: the sprinklers) and the BATF (re: manly methods of pipe-lighting).

Friday, April 11, 1969

All day in the Garden again. We went over the lettuce and cukes and everything seems to be in place. Got to the carrots and discovered not only were they not planted, the seeds had not even arrived yet. P took it surprisingly well, calmly said, "Well, I'll get to work on the radishes then." I called Mitchell and got him over here with a back hoe so we could at least get the tomatoes going. P very concerned that his corn be knee-high by the Fourth, thinks it's critical to his re-election. Wanted me to check with Connally whether we plant squash now, or wait until after the midterm elections. Lots of follow-up on the weevils, and a plan to bug the Democratic Pea Patch, discover the secret of their spinach.

Monday, June 17, 1969

P again with no schedule, had me in all afternoon on his plans to convert the bowling alley (in the White House basement) into a dry cleaners. Thinks we could do all dry cleaning for staff and foreign dignitaries and turn a tidy profit by taking in outside work on a contract basis, maybe rid Washington of some tough ground-in stains and help balance the budget at the same time. Then said no, scratch the whole thing, let's make it a pizza parlor, one that does weddings, and get right on it. So I spoke to Loggins and Messina, and had that worked out.

Friday, July 11, 1969

P on again about need for better PR, more positive news coverage. He liked my idea of using other media, perhaps producing lavish Broadway musicals or delightful film comedies on Administration policy, as a way to end run around all the goddamn Jews who control the media. We took a break for some diplomatic credentialing and afterward the P called and said he never wanted to be interrupted again to receive some dirty foreigner from some backass little nation on the other side of the moon. So I'm to work that out.

Then back to the bowling alley, which we had started converting to a pizzeria, but now he wants to make it a Cyclotron particle accelerator, knows it may be rough, hasn't been invented yet, but says got to go ahead and do it, got to take the lead on this one.

Wednesday, December 3, 1969

A busy morning. P had another satisfying bowel movement, then called me and Ziegler in to ask why hadn't we gotten out the story of Nixon the Man, that rarest of world leaders who has excellent bowel movements, is more regular than de Gaulle or FDR. Points out that he is doing this every day, but never gets any credit for it. JFK never had a good shit in two years in office, but the point is people think he did. People don't know the extraordinary number of healthy dumps he takes.

Monday, March 16, 1970

Spent the morning working out some bugs with respect to Operation Breakfast, then met with the P regarding Operation Cambodia. *[Operation Breakfast, the plan for the bombing of Cambodia, turned out to be relatively simple in comparison to Operation Cambodia, a double-tippy-top-secret initiative to land the P some really good grub, first thing in the morning. Except for one slightly overcooked sausage, it was one of the first term's great successes. —ed.]* He had a long list of items—be sure the chef uses American-made eggs, wanted to know what E was ordering, etc. While I was in with him, K called and elaborated his belief that Rogers planned to order before him, and order his (K's) favorite. This would force him to either go with his favorite, and give the impression he was imitating Rogers, or order something else, and eat an inferior breakfast. Tough one, especially since the P also favors a poached egg, which Henry does not know.

Monday, June 15, 1970
Day started out pretty bad. Huge flap between Jorgen and Carlos, two of the office boys, over some desk supplies which came up missing from Carlos's desk, and were apparently found in Jorgen's. Then the P called, his PBJ was MIA, pulled K out of NSC and had E call the FBI, wanted the PBJ at the EOB on the q.t. I was too busy primping, called Mitchell to handle it, but he fumbled in his own end zone, gave up the safety and got hurt on the play. Then the Jorgen-Carlos thing flared up, as Carlos went directly to the P, demanding that Jorgen be fired, that he couldn't work under these conditions, and really got the P on his side. P finally stepped in to settle it, which he did masterfully, then complained on and on how he always has to castigate the officeboys, so from now on I'll take on more of that.

Rogers and Laird, meanwhile, have been substituting creamery butter for shortening in all of State's baked goods, and this is driving Henry up a wall. Said it may extend the war another year, wanted me to call the P which I did, and the P just muttered, "Let's get those bastards, really screw 'em, the ones who tried to screw us," and then we went over several small things, three or four midsized things, and one just really big thing, one of the biggest things I've ever been over with him. *[Portions deleted to titillate conspiracy freaks—ed.]*

Friday, August 21, 1970
Then made the point that this should show all those weak little bastards that anyone who fucks with Nixon gets fucked, and anyone who doesn't vote for us will get nothing from us. That goes for everyone: all the goddamn peaceniks who couldn't understand that Nixon is the true Man of Peace; Muskie, Meany, McGovern and Maud Adams, wouldn't know what hit them. Anyone who votes against us gets a ten-foot steel pole rammed *[portions deleted for national security reasons]* ... and that this was the reason ducks have bills, while other birds have beaks. Then off to Camp David for the weekend.

Sunday, July 22, 1971
A day off today and I used it to get away from the grind. Jake and Butch brought over a 12 and we threw darts for a bit. Then jumped in J's truck and headed for the reservoir, stopping on the way for a couple cases and some tequila. Then parked, cracked beers and cranked up the tunes. Spent the afternoon diving off the old tower, laying in the sun, shoot-

ing cans with a .22. B twisted up a huge fatty, which was nice. Then P called, which I had dreaded, but turned out to be OK. He was on a bit of a bender himself, went on and on about some damn football game. Then asked what that loud rock music was in the background (it was The Who), said how much he loved it, thought we might turn that driving beat to our advantage somehow, use it against the Democrats in the Senate. Don't know what he's been into, but it sure loosened the old fart up.

Friday, April 16, 1971

P had no schedule today, as usual filled up the day with trivia. Had me in for three hours about how he really hates those bastards, how he's really gonna cream the guys who're sticking it to him right now. In the second term he'll be able to go ahead with his plans to round up all his enemies, cut off their hands and feet and exile them all to one state (probably one of the Dakotas). Then called E and K in for homemade fudge and "Patton" again, then off to Key Biscayne.

Wednesday, December 8, 1971

P ran in screaming C'mon, let's do something, something of great historical import, then let's hurry up and get the line out on it, emphasizing all our points and trouncing theirs, a really vicious attack, really cream the sons-a-bitches, then let's get some follow-up and three polls, I wanna see them numbers jump through the roof! The P then circled the room, gesturing furiously and screaming in broken Swahili, the general thrust again being the need to stay up all night crushing our enemies, to see them driven before us, etc. He then strapped on his "wings" (two Disney kites adapted for the purpose) and leapt out the window, flapping furiously but with no effect.

I felt the P was way off on all this, he's obviously off his rocker, and I told him so. He was stunned, then his face lit up and he came over the desk and stuck his tongue in my mouth, which is the first time he's ever done that. Said Bob, you're the only one I can trust, come away with me to the South Pacific with Bebe and Sinatra, run the show for me.

Saturday, March 10, 1973

P back on the bowling alley again today, wants to add an eleventh pin to all the lanes to jack up his scores, then get the line out on his terrific improvement. Also wants a new staff member assigned specifically to apply anti fungal powder to his feet. Guess there's a bit of fungus there. Then back on Watergate. Suggested rounding up the Ervin committee and having them shot. Then softened, decided to pelt them with water balloons at the next hearing, come at the little peckersniffs with all sorts of streamers, sirens and silly whistles, to divert attention from the investigation as much as possible. It's crazy, but it just might work. Problem is how to pull it off without giving the appearance of a cover-up, or insanity. ■

September, 1994

JASON ZENGERLE

Is Michael Moore the Last, Best Hope for Popular Liberalism in America?

And, more importantly, does he have a sense of humor?

Michael Moore, reputedly the great satirist of the 1990s, has been only sporadically funny this decade. His crowning achievement, the humorous pseudo-documentary *Roger & Me*, which heaped a steaming pile of populist scorn on General Motors and its chief executive officer Roger Smith for destroying Moore's hometown of Flint, Michigan, was released in 1989, so it doesn't count. The material Moore has churned out since then—presumably the material on which he stakes his claim to exalted status—is remarkable only for its unevenness.

His 1992 short *Pets or Meat: The Return to Flint* is a tired replay of his attacks on corporate America. His 1995 attempt at feature film-making, *Canadian Bacon*, is akin to a slapstick-less *Spaceballs* that not only manages to squander the considerable talents of Rip Torn and Steven Wright, but utterly fails at the easiest of tasks: satirizing the Gulf

War. Even *TV Nation*, his award-winning newsmagazine which aired off and on for two years on NBC and Fox before being put "on hiatus," is a bit of a letdown, mixing some funny pranks—a trip to Newt Gingrich's federal-spending-rich congressional district to drum up support for Newt's call to cut public spending—with the offensive— protesting the private beaches of lily-white Greenwich, Connecticut, by importing an unwitting group of Latinos and African-Americans from Brooklyn for a day of fun (and racially tinged abuse) in the sun. Worse, Moore has packaged his most recent comedic misstep in the form of a book, *Downsize This! Random Threats from an Unarmed American*, in which he fantasizes about bedding Hillary Clinton and tries to make funny about the Holocaust.

Although he has never lived up to the promise he displayed with *Roger & Me*, Michael Moore is continually fawned over by the media, which typically hail him as an "irrepressible new humorist in the tradition of Mark Twain" or grants him "a working-class voice and an irreverent intelligence." Bill Maher invites him on "Politically Incorrect"; "Comedy Central" airs reruns of "TV Nation" in prime time; and Anita Gates, writing in the *New York Times Book Review*, dubs *Downsize This!* "delightful, outrageous, sometimes irrefutable..."

The book, more than any other single example of his work, demonstrates how willy-nilly and ill-informed his politics are, and yet its popularity proves how solidly his ideas strike a chord with a mass audience. This is, perhaps, a dangerous combination. Michael Moore is probably the best-known openly liberal media figure in America, and as such he has the ear of millions of the country's "progressives." But a close reading of his work begs the question: Does he have any idea what he's talking about?

Downsize This! spent three weeks on the *Times*' bestseller list and has sold well over 200,000 copies. Random House sponsored a 47-city book tour for Moore last fall, when he played to standing-room-only crowds, filling college auditoriums and factory-town civic halls. The tour even provided Moore with his next project: He filmed the whole thing for a documentary ("the first concert film of a book tour," he's calling it), coming this summer to a theater near you.

I caught Moore's act when he brought his road show to a Harvard Square movie house a week before the election. Even though Lawrence Levine, the celebrated defender of multiculturalism and author of *The*

Opening of the American Mind, was debating Dinesh D'Souza—of *Illiberal Education* and *The End of Racism* fame—down the street at Harvard's School of Education, the liberal vanguard of Cambridge had chosen to turn out en masse for Moore's appearance. And so I crowded into the Brattle Theatre along with them, sitting through what seemed like an interminable one-hour talk while waiting patiently for the promised question-and-answer session. When the time came, I raised my hand high and hoped for the best, anxious to pose the query that begged to be asked: "How do you explain your success as a political humorist when you know nothing about politics and you're only occasionally funny?" Unfortunately, Moore did not take more than a handful of questions, and looked in my direction just once. A woman one row in front of me was called on, only to gush, "Would you please run for president?"

As I was unable to ask Moore my pointed question at his Cambridge appearance—an episode an enterprising film editor could easily splice to parallel the scene in *Roger & Me* when Moore is rebuffed by Roger Smith at the GM shareholders' meeting—I decided that I would have to embark on a Mooreonic quest of my own. Public appearances and prearranged interviews be damned, I was going to track Moore down and surprise him on his own time, because, as I've learned so well from his oeuvre, there's no such thing as a stupid question if you make a story out of trying to ask it.

Although Moore constantly boasts about his Flint bona fides so that he can present himself as an "emissary for working Americans," the author's biography in *Downsize This!* explains that he lives and works in New York City. The bio provides a New York post-office box number and an e-mail address (MMFlint@aol.com; even in cyberspace he's true to his roots), but I eschewed these impersonal means of communication. Why go through the proper channels when you can just play dumb and show up unannounced on a person's doorstep for an interview? Of course, to do this successfully, you need to be able to find the correct doorstep.

Upon arrival in New York, I met up with my friend Morgan, who agreed to put on a gorilla costume and accompany me as Morgan the Gorilla. (We tried, but couldn't come up with a cool name like the one Moore invented for his anthropomorphic compadre on "TV Nation": Crackers the Corporate Crime-Fighting Chicken.) I assumed that a quick glance at the business part of the phone book would furnish me with the requisite info. But there was no listing for Moore's production company, Dog-Eat-Dog Films. A call to 411 proved fruitless as well. I had wanted to maintain some semblance of decency and ambush the man at his place of work, but his failure to list his office's phone number and address with the proper authorities left me with little choice; I would have to find Moore at home.

I had read somewhere that Moore lived on the Upper East Side, so I was happy to find a couple of listings in the phone book for Michael Moores in that area. We had our marks, so Morgan and I readied for the encounter. He put on his gorilla mask, and I opened my audiobook version of *Downsize This!* and put it into a Walkman I had hooked up to a megaphone. Armed for battle, we hopped on the 6 train at East 23rd and headed uptown.

Needless to say, the denizens of the swank Upper East Side did not particularly appreciate my friend's costume or my megaphone-amplified cries of "Michael, where are you?" interspersed with choice tidbits of *Downsize This!* read aloud by its author. Where bike messengers downtown had stopped us to ask if we were from "Letterman," strolling couples uptown ducked into their doorman buildings to avoid passing us on the street.

The doorman at our first stop, a modest postwar building on East 69th Street, confirmed that a Michael Moore did indeed reside in his building. But when I produced a copy of *Downsize This!* to show him the author's doughy face gracing the cover, he swore that he opened doors for an entirely different Michael Moore. I played him a snippet of the *Downsize This!* tape through my megaphone—the part where Moore lustfully describes Hillary Clinton as "one hot shitkickin' feminist babe" and chides Republicans who "immediately go limp at the thought of a strong woman"—to see if Moore's voice might possibly ring any bells, but the doorman was quick to shake his head so that I would turn the tape off, lest its contents offend any of his building's tenants.

Another doorman, this one working at a luxurious apartment building on Park Avenue, stood in the entrance and would not even let us into the lobby when we came calling to ask if he opened doors for the Michael Moore. "No," he snapped when I asked if he recognized Moore's face. I began to play my tape for a quick voice analysis, but he cut me off. "What are you doing?" he asked peevishly. "Let me close the door. Do you think this is funny?" And with that, we were left out in the cold.

My humorless but class-signifying exchange with the Park Avenue doorman—in which the doorman, the haughty authority to my underdog-championing Michael Moore, started to make things more clear to me. Moore isn't popular because he's funny, but because he's socially relevant. While Al Franken won the eternal gratitude of liberals everywhere for *Rush Limbaugh Is a Big, Fat Idiot*, his somewhat intellectual bent—he's fairly fond of reminding people he went to Harvard—makes him ill-suited to do real battle with a populist firebrand such as Limbaugh. To combat Limbaugh and his ilk, liberals assume that they need their own big, fat idiot, and in Moore they think they've found him. Like Limbaugh, Moore loves crude rhetoric and stupid pranks. He's equal to Limbaugh in his arrogance and is more than happy to stoop to Limbaugh's level and fight dirty. One of the few funny chapters in *Downsize This!* describes Moore's entreaties to the Secret Service to arrest conservatives such as Jesse Helms, G. Gordon Liddy, Oliver North, and Limbaugh for violating the federal law prohibiting threats against the president. But this is a rare stroke of genius. Moore, sadly, is not Limbaugh's equal. He's simply not as cunning or as skilled a propagandist. While both men have made the bestseller list and have adoring fans, only Limbaugh is capable of helping to instigate a voter revolt like the one in 1994 that ended 40 years of Democratic majorities in the House. While Moore was invited to make speeches for Jerry Brown's delusional 1992 presidential candidacy, Limbaugh was made an honorary member of the 104th Congress' Republican freshman class. Limbaugh is evil and brilliant; Moore is simply bumbling.

The more apt comparison with Moore is not Limbaugh but another, less obviously political funnyman: Yakov Smirnoff. Much the way Smirnoff's "what-a-country" shtick drew laughs in the '80s, when America was engaged in the Cold War and the Soviet Union was still around to be feared, Moore's lame jokes win him a following because Americans are nervous about corporate downsizing, income disparity, and wage inequality. By constantly decrying life in his former country and celebrating his new home, Smirnoff made Americans feel good about themselves and strengthened their resolve to fight the Cold War. Similarly, Moore's attacks on corporations and his encouraging words for the working class come at a time when many Americans are confronting a new sense of economic insecurity. The only difference is that while Smirnoff was subjecting Americans to his baleful sense of humor, the American government was hard at work backstage trying to defeat the Evil Empire. In Moore's fight for progressive causes, he's essentially out there on his own.

On the night I saw him in Cambridge, when he shuffled onto the stage decked out in his standard uniform—plaid shirt, jeans, navy windbreaker, and baseball cap—he didn't waste much time cracking wise. Rather, this media darling in schlump's clothing capitalized on his status as the liberal chic's posterchild for workers' rights and lectured the crowd about the "vanishing American dream":

"I've been real encouraged by the crowds that have turned out, the places I've been," Moore said, his voice swelling with nasally uplift. "We're really not alone out there. It's not just you in Cambridge feeling this sense of despair. It's a majority of Americans. That's the big lie of the media, that there are only 100 of us, that we're marginalized. We are the majority!

"But most working Americans don't like liberals," he continued. "I'm here speaking as their emissary from Flint, Michigan. Working Americans think that liberals are wimps, that they don't have the courage of their convictions. Right-wingers are proud of what they believe in, but liberals run away from the label. We have to stand up for what we believe in!"

And Moore certainly has never been bashful about proclaiming his liberal beliefs. His candor is in many ways refreshing, but just as Moore isn't consistently funny enough to be a good comic, he's not smart enough to be a sophisticated and effective political thinker. He basically spouts the same warmed-over, left-wing nostrums (labor is good; big business is evil) that have been falling on deaf ears since before the Reagan Revolution. In his book's first chapter, he cautions the reader, "I have no college degree, so take what I say with that in mind." That's hardly a difficult task when you read his trenchant observation about a homeless man—"Why was it him standing there like that? Why not me?"—or his keen insight (circa 1996) into the character of Bill Clinton—"He reminded me of that wonk who ran for senior-class president and was so ambitious about winning that he'd say or do anything to get elected." Moore's take on the failure of the Clintons' health-care initiative isn't much better: Rather than consider that the Clintons might have doomed their plan from the start by appeasing industry at the expense of cultivating grass-roots support for universal coverage, Moore blames the whole affair on "a bunch of men whining" that the plan's creator—Hillary—"was the proud owner of two ovaries." Moore seems to think that if only some proud owner of two testicles— Ira Magaziner perhaps—had been given Hillary's prominent role, every American would have access to decent health care.

And for someone who ostensibly wants government to run more smoothly and thus be better able to help the downtrodden—he is fond of praising "Big Government," and slags Clinton for pledging to end it—Moore is ridiculously partisan. One chapter of *Downsize This!* is called "Democrat? Republican? Can You Tell the Difference?" In it, Moore presents a series of quotes from various politicians, and challenges the reader to guess their source—Republican or Democrat. There is a quote wishing well to Ronald Reagan, which we are supposed to be shocked to learn came from... Bill Clinton! There is a quote praising the Democrats for ending segregation, which we are awed to find came from... Newt Gingrich! And while staking out a position left of the vaunted "vital center," is a good thing, the message Moore is sending is something like this: If elected officials fail to live up (or down) to our most grotesque caricatures of them—if, say, Clinton wishes well to Ronald Reagan shortly after Reagan is diagnosed with Alzheimer's disease, or if a Republican legislator favors planting trees—Moore throws up his hands and gives up on Washington. Voter apathy, he insinuates, is a natural response to all these politicians refusing to fit into neat columns of Good Guys and Bad Guys. At the end of the chapter, Moore offers this sage advice: "Congratulations! You've completed the quiz. If you scored less than 50 percent and decide not to vote on Election Day, we'll understand."

Moore's ideas are as notable for their mild hypocrisy as they are for their naiveté. He is surprisingly complimentary toward Bill Clinton for, of all things, his draft dodging. While it does no good to refight the Vietnam War by vilifying Clinton for what Moore charitably calls his version of "Alice's Restaurant," it is odd that Moore doesn't harbor any resentment toward a man who used his privilege and connections to escape service. After all, while Clinton was enjoying his time at Oxford, weren't Moore's autoworker buddies from Flint, most of whom didn't have the option of a Rhodes scholarship, fighting in his stead?

But such occasional blind spots on class don't prevent Moore from frequently rubbing his fans' noses in their elitism. At his reading in Cambridge, Moore urged his audience to get off its liberal high horse, end its "left-wing circle jerk," and get out in the "real world." "Corporate America has done the organizing for us," he insisted. "They've made working people so mad that they're ready to go. It's just that we need to lead them." Ignoring, for a second, the implication that the Harvard set would be the "we" leading the blue-collar "they," the question he begged of his listeners was "Yes, Michael, of course. But how?" As Moore paused for full effect, his audience eagerly awaited the inspirational words that might signal the dawn of a new progressive era. "We need to let the working class know that we don't think we're better than them," Moore commanded. "I want you watching *Friends* every single week. I want you listening to country music." Here, Moore was actually funny. The sad thing was, he was trying to be serious.

After striking out in our efforts to find Moore on the Upper East Side, Morgan the Gorilla and I decided to head to the only other address we had for him, his P.O. box. We hailed a cab and vamoosed across town to the Radio City Station Post Office, where we staked out his P.O. box for a good half-hour. I asked some of the postal workers if they recognized Moore from the cover of *Downsize This!*, but none of them had ever seen him picking up his mail there before. We decided it was time to leave when a post-office policeman, carrying a sidearm, asked us if we were aware that tampering with the mail was a federal offense. Outside, two Japanese tourists gave Morgan the Gorilla twenty-five cents to have their pictures taken with him.

If we couldn't locate Moore through the normal channels, I thought, we might find him by contacting some of his associates. In his four pages of acknowledgments in *Downsize This!*, Moore thanks his agent, Andrew Wylie, for all his support and assistance, so we made a call to directory assistance and procured Wylie's office address. A brisk walk to a building on the corner of Eighth and West 57th, a quick dash past its security guard into a waiting elevator, and we were on the twenty-first floor where Wylie—known in publishing circles as "The Jackal" for his ability to procure stunning advances for his authors—works his singular magic. I told the receptionist that we had come to Wylie's office in the hopes of finding Michael Moore, and she asked us to wait while she checked into something. A few minutes later, a nice, young man came into the reception area and informed us that Wylie's agency had ceased working with Moore two weeks earlier, and that perhaps we could find what we were looking for at the offices of Random House, Moore's publisher.

Another cab ride across town, and we were in the publishing giant's marbled atrium, where a beefy security guard greeted our arrival with a less-than-welcoming "Oh, this is perfect." I informed the guard of our quest and of our wish to visit Moore's editor at Random House, so that I could perhaps find Moore's address and ask the editor a few questions about Moore's book. "Are you media?" he growled. I sheepishly admitted that I was, and he replied, "All media requests go through Publicity." He called upstairs to Publicity and put me on the line with a woman who told me that Random House editors did not do media interviews and that since Moore had finished his book tour, Random House had stopped coordinating his media schedule. "Do you know how I might get in touch with him, then?" I inquired. "Oh, no problem," she replied, and gave me the phone number for Dog-Eat-Dog Films.

We left Random House and headed to a pay phone. My call was answered with a cheerful "Dog-Eat-Dog Films," and my heart fluttered. "Hello," I said in my best businessman's tone. "I'd like to courier a script over to Michael, and I was wondering if I could get your address?"

"And what's your name?" the voice replied. I gave my name, and he asked if I could hold. A minute later, he came back on the line and gave me Moore's PO box. "But I was really hoping I could have it delivered to him," I pleaded. "I'd like him to get it as soon as possible, and I don't really trust the mail with it."

"I'm sorry," the man said somewhat mysteriously. "We just don't accept deliveries. Send it to the P.O. box, and everything will be fine." And with that he hung up. At least Moore knew that to find Roger Smith, all he had to do was show up at GM world headquarters.

I had been thwarted again. I couldn't very well call up Dog-Eat-Dog and tell them I needed their address so I could ambush their boss. How was I ever going to ask Michael Moore my question if I couldn't even find out where he worked or lived? I was so close, but I needed to know Moore's precise location. I whipped out my megaphone and started begging for information from random passers-by.

"Have you seen this man?" I asked all who could hear, brandishing my now-tattered copy of *Downsize This!* "I'm looking for Michael Moore. Can anybody tell me where he works?"

People passed by, generally trying to ignore me. A homeless person asked a meter maid to write me a ticket. A teenager approached Morgan the Gorilla and mockingly did an ape dance. A woman, seeing the book and apparently assuming we were with "TV Nation," asked if it was Michael Moore in the gorilla suit. Two Hasidic Jews strolled past as my megaphone was blasting Moore's theory that the German tourists murdered in Florida ("Jerries") were actually victims of local Jewish retirees ("Moskowitzes") who also happened to be vengeful Holocaust survivors. Things were looking bleak. But then I realized that I was not totally helpless in my quest. I had a friend who knew someone who worked at another magazine that had interviewed Moore; maybe she would know the location of the shadowy Dog-Eat-Dog Films. Kicking myself for not having thought of this earlier—but also aware that Michael Moore would never settle on such an easy and obvious solution to his problems—I gave her a call.

"Oh, sure, you mean Michael Moore's office?" she asked. "That's in a building on the corner of 7th and West 57th." Before she could ask me why I wanted to know, I hung up the phone. Morgan the Gorilla and I hailed a cab and headed back across town for our rendezvous with destiny.

We jumped out of the cab at the corner of 7th and West 57th and pushed through the corner building's revolving door and into its small lobby, where we asked the earinged doorman for the floor number of Dog-Eat-Dog Films. "You got an appointment?" he asked. "No, we're just here to see Michael Moore," I replied. "Which floor is he on?"

The guard just shook his head: "No one gets past me without an appointment." I asked if he could call upstairs to Moore's office and tell them that they had visitors, but he remained steadfast. "You can call him from the street, and if he agrees to see you, you tell him to come down here and escort you up himself. I don't want any trouble from this."

With that, we were back on the street and back on a pay phone to Dog-Eat-Dog. This time a woman answered their phone. I explained to her my situation: the gorilla, the day-long search, the desire to ask Mr. Moore a few questions, the fact that I was on the street outside their office at that very moment. None of this seemed to impress her.

"Well, what do you want to interview him about?" she asked.

"I want him to explain to me why he thinks he's so popular."

"And you want to ask him right now?"

"Well, yeah," I said innocently. "Isn't that how he does it?"

"Yeah, but I mean it's not the same thing," she protested. "We're just a little office. We're all really, really busy here."

I was tempted to ask if she thought the corporations Moore ambushed had a surfeit of people available to field his queries, but I demurred and played dumb. "I just want to come up and ask a few questions. From watching Mr. Moore, I thought that's how these things were done."

She asked me to hold, and two dollars worth of quarters later, she got back on the line. "I'm really, really sorry, but Michael can't see you now. He's not doing any interviews."

"But I've come all the way from Massachusetts just to talk to him," I pleaded. "Can't I just come up and ask him a few questions. It'll only take a minute or two."

"No, no, I'm really sorry, but he's not doing any interviews now. He just finished his book tour, and he's kind of made an across-the-board promise to not do any more interviews. If we let you up, we have to let everyone up."

I scanned the block to look for other megaphone-wielding individuals accompanied by animal-costumed friends making their cases into pay phones. "Well, could I maybe ask you my questions then, just so I can get something?"

"No, no, you don't want to talk to me. I'm really not very funny. You really want to talk to Michael. He's going to be doing a bunch of interviews in March when his paperback comes out. Why don't we set something up for then?"

And with that she hung up. It was a tender kiss-off, but a kiss-off nonetheless, and what's worse, it came from a man who fashioned a career out of getting indignant over being stiffed in the very same way.

Still, his hypocrisy aside, it's hard to fault those who like Michael Moore. It is a scary time for liberals in America. Even though a Democrat is beginning his second term in the White House and Gingrich and his self-styled revolutionaries have beat a chastened retreat from the stridency they displayed after their 1994 triumph, moderate Republicanism seems to be the governing philosophy of the day. Even liberal icons like Mario Cuomo and Jesse Jackson have been co-opted, but Moore remains an obstinate holdout. While Cuomo and Jackson unabashedly campaigned for Clinton's re-election on the premise that only he could fix the welfare law he himself had signed into existence, Moore was titling a chapter of his book "If Clinton Had Balls." In Cambridge, when I saw him, Moore elaborated a bit on this idea. "Bill Clinton signing the welfare bill was an evil, evil act," he said. "It's what's going to prevent me from voting for him next week."

So Michael Moore will continue telling liberals that they are not alone in their current disenchantment. And liberals will continue to flock to his appearances, rent his videos, watch his TV shows, go to his movies, and buy his books—eager for the inspiring dose of re-affirmation only Moore can offer. Ironically, this cycle will make Moore a rich man—just as much a beneficiary of downsizing as the CEOs he reviles.

When the Soviet Union finally collapsed, whether from its own weight or from pressure applied by the United States, Yakov Smirnoff's career toppled right along with it (a frequently overlooked aspect of the peace dividend). Unfortunately, politicians don't appear to be as concerned with wage inequality and income disparity as they were with the Evil Empire, so the economic problems that give Moore his act seem here to stay. For that very reason, it will be a good day for America, not to mention comedy, when Michael Moore plays to an empty room. ■

March, 1997

Listener Appreciation

Soul Coughing front man M. Doughty takes a long hard look at his fans

My band has recently gained a rung of notoriety. I've rocked from the depths of the non-rent-paying, fully untelevised but respectable position of being one of those whose band's name is printed in larger typeface in the *Village Voice* club listings, to the dizzying pinnacle where I now occasionally bump into some guy in Hamburg, who asks in an awed tone, "Didn't you wear that same shirt on *Beavis & Butthead*?"

Yes, friends, I'm a Minor Rock Celebrity. I have bought Actual Shirts and paid Actual Rent with Actual Money. I am routinely addressed as The Internationally-Renowned, Award-Winning M. Doughty. There's at least 150 people in Philadelphia who'll pay five bucks to see me. I have been known to enjoy smart cocktails with the cream of society in the posh watering holes of the glittering Lower East Side. I have quipped on the third page of *Rolling Stone*'s Random Notes. I have indulged in Rampant Corganism. Why, right now I'm writing this from a glamorous lounge in a Holiday Inn thirty miles outside Ghent, Belgium, surrounded by Flemish conventioneers all agape at my Fabulosity.

You, who probably never heard of me, might be asking: just who are these people to whom I am Actually Famous? After all, in the bong-filtered atmosphere of a college dorm, there's little qualitative difference between the respective celebrities of, say, Gabe Kaplan, Oasis's "Guigsy" McGuigan and that girl from the Noxema ads that was murdered after marrying Dylan on *90210*. So, to the four dozen people who've listened to a Soul Coughing record more than twice, but may have rented *Repo Man* the night that *90210* episode aired, I am what the French term Le Mack. And I live to love them back.

Remember, future Minor Rock Celebrities of America, LL Cool J drives a leased Accord; even if you do leap from "120 Minutes" to the rarefied air of "Alternative Nation," chances are your constituents will be your chief reward. And, chances are, they'll break down into these easily recognized types:

1. The Dude-You-Rocks
You're rummaging through the back of your band's van, behind the converted seafood restaurant you've just rocked in West Virginia. The Dude-You-Rock approaches.

"Dude! You rock!"

"Thank you. Uh, no, you rock."

A complex fumble-through of whatever approximation of a late-'70s Jive Turkey handshake that's locally in vogue ensues.

"No, Dude! You fuckin' rock! I mean, that one song you do? With the thing in it? Dum-dum-dum-dum-OW!"

"You mean, uh, 'Bus to Beelzebub'?"

"Yeah! Dude! That song fuckin' rocks!"

An offer of bong hits generally follows, which is great, because, hey, you know, free bong hits, right? However, if you've just spent an hour and a half rocking Portchester, you might be kind of tired, or it might be time to head back to La Quinta Inn to call your girlfriend, to list the many reasons why foregoing a normal relationship with someone else who's actually around is amply rewarded by the natural transference of Minor Rock Renown she'll receive.

The guy, of course, is disappointed, but understanding. The Dude-You-Rocks always understand.

2. The White Girls Bearing Bad Poetry
Being lip-synched to is one of the richer rewards of the Life of Rock. Because, invariably, the song that that weird-eyed but not-altogether-unattractive girl with the Veronica-from-The-Archies streak in her hair

usually likes is the ponderous ballad you wrote after Tanya Lippey ditched you junior year. Well, ha ha, Tanya Lippey! Who's got the upper hand now?

What better way to thank the lip-synching girl than to graciously accept the fat stack of verse and the flattened orchid she offers you. You may want to decline the marriage proposal though, if only because you remember the time Tanya Lippey produced a mysterious manila envelope and vanished for twenty minutes after that Galaxie 500 show you saw with her in 1990.

3. The Phone Stalker

If you're like me, you're not famous in any real sense and no one particularly wants to kill you. A listed phone number may be the right thing for you. Your answering machine will be grateful for the hang-up calls—I myself used to dial up the then-listed John Zorn and listen to him say when he was getting back from his tour of Japan. Sadly, though, there's no way a stack of poetry can be handed to you, so be quick with your P.O. box or you're in for a reading-and-critique session. It's always nice to know you are a Dude that does, in fact, Rock, and who knows? Tanya Lippey, who subscribed to *Spin*, may have seen the not-unrespectable "seven" rating your record got and decide it's time to dial 411 and reverse the impulsive mistakes of the early '90s.

4. The Backstage Promo Hag

She fought her way through the cutthroat world of college radio, and now she's working at the Tennessee Valley Branch Office of the distribution wing of a record label you're not on. She may never have heard of you before, but she's got a friend that works for the promoter, and if you politely act like more of an Enigmatic Rock Legend than you actually are, she'll tell all of her friends at other branch offices that you're Gonna Be Huge. And that's as good as money in the trunk of a leased Accord. Plus, who else will drink all the Diet Pepsi in the backstage icebox?

5. Other, Slightly Larger Minor Rock Celebrities

They're playing the same town in Wisconsin that you are, but at the larger venue—the one that's not a sports bar on weekdays. You heard their single six times on the interstate, on the station that plays All Modern Rock. They gave you props in their *Details* feature. If you're lucky, they'll show up for the final third of your set, stroke your ego, grin and feign humility, though you've probably never heard their record in its entirety. They'll tell you which song of yours they covered at a gig in Duluth.

Pray they become Actually Famous—if so, Dude, you don't just Rock, you Rock Influentially. And if that cover they did in Duluth ends up on their next record, you could well end up playing Tom Waits to their Rod Stewart. Which will blow all chances of the singer from that Britpop band you opened for talking to you after the gig.

6. People Who Actually Remind You of Your Friends

They're out there. You can see them in the audience—seemingly witty, attractive and cool. You can imagine talking to them about the short stories of Denis Johnson, or explaining the ever-so-multi-layered metaphors in that one song, the one during which you saw them stifling a lip-sync. Will you ever actually speak to them? Doubt it. Most people that are actually like you think bands are too cool to talk to them. ■

July, 1996

Any Further Questions, Mr. Mayor?

Jess Mowry is the author of two novels, Way Past Cool *and* Six Out
Seven, *and* Rats in the Trees, *a collection of short stories. An Oakland res-
ident, Mowry writes about the kids who are growing up in his hometown,
particularly those known as "youth at risk." What follows is an epistolary
exchange between Mowry and Thomas L. McClimon, an assistant at the
office of The United States Conference of Mayors, who writes Mowry
hoping for his help in addressing the problems plaguing urban youth.*

Jan. 3, 1994

Mr. Jess Mowry
c/o Farrar Straus Giroux
19 Union Square West
New York, NY 10003

Dear Mr. Mowry:
   I had the opportunity over the holidays to read your book, *Way Past*

Cool, and found it to be enlightening, informative, but at times depressing. As a youngster growing up in a small Midwestern town and now a somewhat "yuppie" in Washington D.C., I have been fortunate not to have lived the lifestyle of your characters. I look forward to reading your new book, *Six Out Seven.*

The lives of the young children you write about—Gordon, Lyon, Ty, etc.—and their world of loss, hope and opportunities, guns and violence are the very same things which many of our nation's mayors are trying to find answers to. I believe you capture and convey clearly many of the messages that our leaders need to hear from our young people.

I believe that those who practice in the arts and literature fields can help the mayors to find some of the answers they are looking for. Our Arts, Culture and Recreation Committee has begun a process to work more closely with businesses and organizations in the recording, television, sporting, film and video game markets to address the problems of at-risk youths. In short, to use mediums kids are into as a way to reach them.

I believe you can play a role in helping the mayors not only to better understand the world of the children of the inner cities, but also help them find some answers. Possible avenues of your assistance might be through speaking to the mayors at some future meetings or having the mayors read selections of your writings. I would welcome any ideas you might have along these lines.

Again, my congratulations on your fine works and I look forward to hearing from you.

Sincerely,

Thomas L. McClimon
Managing Director
Office of Program Development & Technical Assistance
The United States Conference of Mayors

1-24-94

Mr. Thomas L. McClimon
The United States Conference of Mayors
1620 Eye St. Northwest
Washington, DC 20006

Dear Mr. McClimon:
    Thank you for your letter of 1-3. I'm happy to hear that you found

Cool to be "enlightening and informative." I have to say that this always amazes me because all of my writing to date has been FOR inner-city kids themselves and was never intended to "educate" what, for a lack of a more subtle tag, I call the "white world."

Speaking of subtlety, I'm afraid it's never been my forté. I say this to you because, while I don't intend to be offensive, I find it sometimes looks that way. You'll understand what I mean when I say that if you found my book "at times depressing," imagine what it's like to actually LIVE it.

Mr. McClimon, believe me I WISH with all my heart that I could actually do something more for these kids than just write stories for them and try to slip in a few positive messages. The cold fact is that Black people—particularly young Black males—are constant targets and victims of what is, after all, a racist society.

Now, please don't take me for some kind of crybaby. If you've gone ahead as you mentioned in your letter and read *Six Out Seven*, I hope you'll see that I don't hesitate to point out that we have got a long way to go toward helping our own selves. Anyone who really WANTS to get out of the ghetto, can. But, it takes SO much more will, determination and courage for a young Black man to "make it" in this society than for even the poorest white.

As for your saying I could possibly help mayors "better understand" the world and lives of these kids—I say to you that, in my life-experience anyway, the powers that be don't WANT to "understand" and, more importantly, don't WANT to do anything about it.

Case in point would be our own mayor of Oakland, who happens to be Black. His answer to violence is simply MORE violence. His "Violence Suppression Program" is in reality just another "violent repression program"—something that Black people in this country have been victims of for generations.

Would it be unreasonable to suggest that one only has to watch ANY network TV news to see how Black people, and by extension Black children, are portrayed to the "majority" in this country? Or to suggest that the same holds true for all other forms of media and entertainment? And that is only ONE aspect of the problem. Not only (as the old saying goes) does it "walk like a duck, talk like a duck, and look like a duck," but after enough of being told it's a duck it begins to believe it is a duck! Are people—in this instance Black kids—any different?

To say that I have little respect for the law would be putting it mildly. Respect is something that has to be earned. This government rules by fear alone, and fear is not a substitute for respect. I'd say this is a pretty basic premise, wouldn't you? This society loses the respect of ALL its kids, not just Black kids, at a very early age, because it lies. Would it be absurd to say that our current president is not only a liar, but not even a very convincing one? Taking it from the top, so to speak, need we wonder why, when we reach the bottom—the "ghetto"—no child has anything but contempt for the first visible figure of authority, namely the police. That child KNOWS he will be lied to and bullied... all the good any P.A.L. project can accomplish in years of working with kids can be wiped out on the street in a minute. And, I won't even mention the damage the Rodney King incident did for a generation!

I have known only one cop in my life that I had any respect for... and he had the good sense to quit Oakland P.D. He's now chief of police in a small Oregon town where, as he says it best, "I'm not THE police, but THEIR (meaning the communities') police." Perhaps when THE government starts being OUR government, things will change. Although my work is fiction, every incident involving police has more or less actually happened in the manner and circumstances portrayed... but I suppose you'd have to take that on faith.

Assuming the mayors actually do want to "help"—a concept I admit I find more than a little hard to swallow—my only suggestions would be to take a long, honest look at what history has shown DOESN'T work. I think I can safely state that both statistics and history clearly show that discrimination in any form doesn't work. That segregation in schools enforced or otherwise, doesn't work. That closing libraries doesn't work. That underfunding schools and education doesn't work. And that continuous passing of ever more binding, restrictive, convoluted, and just plain silly city laws and ordinances doesn't work.

So, what hasn't been tried yet? How about something as absurd-sounding as putting kids, who are after all the future, FIRST for a change? Seems like schools, libraries, and general education would be a nice place to start. Who needs freshly paved streets and sidewalks if the people are scared to use them? How about some real police reform—like weeding out cops who've gone sour, and REAL annual evaluations by INDEPENDENT review boards to make SURE a city has only "the finest"? While we're at it, how about offering the people of a community a few rewards for doing "good" instead of just punishment for being "bad"? How about some neighborhood watch programs that actually have the power to do something about large-scale drug dealers and crime—even if it shades into vigilante justice? Seems to me that we in our 'hoods know what's really going on and who's doing what to whom. If that sounds too much like Boy Scouts with Uzis, then how about just some honest and INFORMED judges with real-world experience who know the difference between a "repeat-offender" and a kid on an unlucky streak?

While we're on that subject, how about a local media that has the grace to mention a repeat offender's previous crimes were littering and smoking in the boy's room instead of just saying a "long list of prior arrests." How about youth programs in which the kids really have some power? How about a few major drug busts "uptown"—where the REAL money is? How about an extensive campaign to find a LOT more GOOD foster homes and families to take on juvenile-offenders instead of "youth-camps" that are really just kid-prisons.

I was on the *MacNeil-Leher News Report* following the Rodney King beating trial. One of the other members of the panel—a writer oddly enough—put forth the promise that "we must protect the law." Seems to me that the Rodney King trial was a matter of protecting the law at the expense of justice. All the suffering people went through—not to mention the COST—came at the expense of a city government unwilling to properly slap four bad cops on the wrists. I wonder how many schools and libraries could have been funded at the cost of those "riots"? Think about it, mayors.

A couple more how-abouts: Have some real-world experts re-evaluate the existing child-labor laws so that a kid who genuinely needs money has legitimate and real alternatives to crime. This might tie into tax-incentives for inner-city businesses to provide REAL employment to kids who are either in school or graduating from your properly funded schools and colleges.

"Sweatshop horrors?" No system is perfect or ever will be. One size will never fit all, but I'd much rather see an eight-year-old digging a ditch and getting paid for it than lying dead in the gutter.

That's about all I can suggest. And it always comes back to putting kids first. Seems to me that any society that doesn't care about its children—or makes war in its kids—deserves to fall. We here on the bottom wonder what's holding it up now!

Again, thank you for your letter.

Ever,

Jess

Quit Your Job.
Work Is a Sham.

The Rolling Stones sold out, most recently, to Bill Gates, to the catchy tune of $12 million. Bill Clinton sold out from the start. Kurt Cobain started to sell out but blew his brains out, ensuring himself a high place in the pantheon of the principled. What constitutes "selling out" for some people—working for a big corporation, changing one's image or work to conform to an accepted norm, being nice to people you hate—is mere pragmatism to others.

More often than not, selling out is associated with work. Usually, those accused of selling out are the ones who have taken jobs that pay well but compromise their professed beliefs. The equation is: Money over Principles = Hypocrisy. But it's a mistake to emphasize only the style of work. Work itself is never called into question. We take for granted that everyone has to earn a living doing boring stuff, except for the few people, like children and bureaucrats, who survive by living off other people's work.

But the fact is that most of the work done by most of the world's people—from the beginning of time and now more than ever—constitutes a monumental sellout. Why? Because almost no one really likes their job. Because almost no one would go to work if they didn't need the money. Because everyone is all too willing to buy into and adopt the following Assumptions About Work:

- Assumption #1) The work you do is somehow necessary
- Assumption #2) Your work won't be fun or interesting
- Assumption #3) Your work will be performed in uncomfortable clothes, in a depressing setting, with people you don't like
- Assumption #4) You will receive wages that will barely pay for your food and housing, ensuring only that you will be healthy enough to continue working
- Assumption #5) You will do said work under said conditions for two-thirds of your life, after which point, if all goes well, you can stop working, play golf, and die.

This is all a bag of shit. When Thomas More, Chairman Mao and Jerry Rubin suggested that work might not always be necessary, they were not talking about their own times, but rather of some period in the far-off future when technological progress and better social organization would allow everyone to sit around watching TV, building model airplanes or whatever else their little hearts desired. They thought that time was a long way off, but now it's here. Now there are options.

If you don't like doing something, but you still spend most of every day doing it, then you're cheating yourself. If you hate your job—and you probably do—and fantasize endlessly about quitting, then you should quit. Quit the job you hate. I'll say it two more times: Quit the job you hate. Quit the job you hate.

In August 1994, I got a job as a financial analyst at a San Francisco consulting firm, The Spectrem Group. (The name was purposely misspelled, to avoid confusion with another company where they were familiar with English.) Spectrem's clients are banks looking to increase their profitability, either by raising their fees without their customers noticing it or by merging with other banks. It's a very '90s company.

Before I was hired, my boss told me that I would set my own hours, take vacations whenever I felt they were justified and dress however I wanted. In short, the only thing that mattered, she said, was that my work—mainly cranking out spreadsheets and charts—got done. In return for my services, I would be paid $32,000 a year. As a cartoonist whose big break wasn't yet on the horizon, I took the job in a windowless, airless office.

After I started, my boss told me that while I could set my own hours, I would have to be in by 8:30 a.m. and leave no earlier than 5 p.m. Vacations were greatly encouraged, except when you actually asked for a day off. Despite the company's rhetoric and quarterly New Age-style retreats where a licensed therapist "analyzed the company's dysfunctionality," in reality what I had was a generic, full-time job.

At first, I had a difficult time learning where everything was and how the computer system worked. But after a few months, I found that I could finish all of my work in about two hours a day. This came in handy because I could use much of the remaining six hours engaged in far more personally satisfying activities, like calling newspaper editors, sending out faxes, talking to my friends on the phone and masturbating in the restroom. I learned to schedule my Spectrem work at times when the nosy office manager was around or when my boss wasn't on the phone. I got work done and no one ever complained about my output.

My experience at Spectrem was, I believe, typical of work in the United States insofar as style far outweighed substance. I soon noticed that my superiors at Spectrem—baby boomer former middle-managers who'd been laid off from various banks in the late '80s, especially Bankers Trust—also worked roughly two hours a day. They used their six-plus hours of "face time" engaged in such pursuits as dealing with their spouses and children, gossiping with one another and planning trips. Unlike the few jobs that require constant attention, such as answering phones or waiting tables, most desk jobs can be completely finished in a few hours a day. This is America's dirty corporate secret. Even well-paid executives, including an $800,000-a-year managing director I know, admit that their real work day is much shorter than the official 9-to-5.

Still, I'd get up at 7 a.m. to be at Spectrem by 8:30. I'd never be home until 6:30. I'd go to sleep at midnight. So I'd spend 10 of my 16 waking hours—nearly two-thirds of my life—at work or commuting to and from work. I spent six messing around, doing my own shit. Only my weekends were truly my own. And that's not even getting into the moral implications of my job: contributing to mergers which cause massive layoffs and bank fee increases that hurt consumers.

In short, my work was a giant waste of time.

I have always suffered from an excessive awareness of my mortality. I feel every second, every minute of my life slipping by, bringing me closer to a horrible death, with the attendant gasping and the wheezing, on some dirty and crowded sidewalk. Once you can taste your own mortality, and how fleeting it all is, you realize something that should be obvious—that there is no greater sin than wasting your time. You will never, ever get it back. Wasting one's time is usually associated with idleness, but my working at Spectrem was just as bad, probably worse, than if I had used that time to, say, draw all over my body with a ball-point pen. What could be a worse sellout than squandering your life-force five days a week, fifty weeks a year?

That's what I was doing, that's what most people do, and you're a sucker if you buy into it.

The Buck Is Not Stopping

Employers are starting to catch on to the fact that not a hell of a lot of work occurs at "work." Across the United States, big corporations are laying off one worker every twenty seconds. The official unemployment rate hovers around six percent. That number doesn't include "discouraged workers," people who don't even bother looking for work anymore. It doesn't include part-time workers who would rather be working full-time or people who are "underemployed," such as college graduates working as secretaries. Full-time workers have become part-timers; professionals have become manual laborers. The fastest-growing jobs in this country are janitor, nurse and food service worker.

Much of what passes for politics these days concerns placing blame and proposing solutions for a shortage of decent jobs that dates back to the 1970s. Lefties blame greedy, short-sighted corporate executives whose tireless search for cheap labor causes them to shrink their payrolls—and therefore shrink the pool of disposable consumer income. Conservatives cite excessive government regulation, taxation and weak public education.

The Left believes corporations have an obligation to employ people they don't need. They don't. The Right and their corporate allies want a more educated workforce though they can't challenge the workers they already have. Both sides refuse to adjust to a world with fewer jobs.

Jobs are disappearing without reducing productive capacity. The technological advances predicted by 19th-century utopian philosophers have finally occurred; the trend of increasing un- and underemployment ensures that we're all going to have a lot more idle time, whether we like it or not. Under such conditions, working for a corporation isn't what makes you a sell-out. The real dilemma is how to learn not to do stupid work when you don't have to.

Resentment Grows, Wages Fall

In 1957, the socialist philosopher Fritz Pappenheim defined alienation as the state of mind that occurs when people are separated from the fruits of their labors. For example, working on an assembly line is alienating because each worker only sees a small component of the final product, and doesn't see each specific item as it's sold and used. My analyst job at Spectrem was a classic case of worker alienation. I only got to see a small part of the final product—my three pages of charts in a seventy-page report. I wasn't told what the presentation was for, and I never met the client. When I was able to piece together the overall purpose of the project I was working on, I'd usually discover that it was an effort to reduce the expenses of some huge banking corporation.

I resented every single second I spent working at the Spectrem Group. I felt robbed of the few hours I spent actually working. Getting paid to do someone else's work always breeds resentment. Your employer takes away time and energy you might have invested in yourself. Working for a company is like renting—you earn money to pay your bills, but afterwards you've got nothing to show for it. All that time, that huge, screaming chunk of your life—two-thirds, remember—is gone, with nothing tangible or meaningful left to prove you were there. You've poured your soul into a company that sells something you don't care about to people you don't know, and at the end of the day, at the end of the year, at the end of your life, there is nothing to show for it but someone else's profits. You have learned little besides how to best sell a product. Your mind hasn't grown, you've scarcely been challenged, because the decisions you make require little vision or innovation.

Working for yourself, on the other hand, is like buying equity in a house.

The only person at Spectrem's San Francisco office who really worked full non-stop days, evenings and weekends was the chairman and founder. And why not? She owned the most stock, got her picture in the paper and her name at the top of the letterhead. She was the only one there working for herself. Everyone else was just a wage whore.

Worker Alienation

In 1973, 57 percent of Americans said they "derived no enjoyment" from their work. By 1992, that was true of 64 percent of us. If our work is boring, it may be because so much of it is utterly useless. In fact, the number of workers who felt their jobs were not important to society increased from 58 to 68 percent in those same twenty years. Most workers feel that nobody would be any worse off if their occupations ceased to exist overnight.

Productivity occurs when value is "added" to raw materials. Wood, for instance, is worth very little, but when used to make the frame of a house, its value-added component—from the architect's design, the builder's skills and other factors—increases dramatically.

In the new post-manufacturing economy, we don't make things, we move them around. Bankers collect fees on checking accounts and loans. Car salespeople are paid commissions for every car they sell. Their soul has nothing to do with their success, only their ability to convince people to buy products—like checking accounts and cars—that they obviously need anyway. Competition between brands spurs innovations in non-value-added fields such as marketing and advertising, but don't cause substantial improvements in the products themselves. In the vast majority of new jobs, there is no relationship between ingenuity and reward—people collect the same paycheck every other week whether or not they make an effort. People sense that they don't add value and lose their enthusiasm for work.

People who sell things feel a special form of alienation. Service-sector workers arbitrate the movement of things from one place to another. They don't make anything and they don't consume anything—they collect fees.

Huge segments of our economy operate in a similar manner. Bankers, stock brokers, travel agents, advertising executives, middle managers, real estate brokers, tax assessors, notaries, and auditors are all examples of professions that add little value; they merely shuffle paper back and forth and skim fees off the top. In other words, jobs are becoming more generic, less satisfying and less interesting. There are a lot fewer reasons—and less opportunity—for selling out than there used to be.

My analyst position at Spectrem was a classic no-value-added job. Most of the time, I was paid to fuck off. My contributions to the tasks were minimal at best. In fact, the company itself added no value—the banks that were our clients could easily have written the same reports themselves. We relied on information supplied by our clients to write our stuff. Arguably, our banker clients added no value either. My employment was nothing more than a four-level Ponzi scheme.

Get Paid More—Work Less!

When I was seven, in 1970, my father bought me a box of Cracker Jacks. The prize was a little booklet about how life would be in 1980. In 1980, it said, people would be scooting around in hovercraft instead of cars and working ten-hour weeks. What happened? In 1949, the average work-week hovered around thirty-eight hours, labor unions talked of bargaining for the thirty-hour week, and the military-industrial boom of the 1950s and 1960s was still in the future. Now we're working forty-eight-hour weeks, labor unions are all but gone and we're still not seeing the difference in our paychecks.

There is a lot of talk about improving the efficiency of workers in the United States. In fact, both per capita and overall per-hour productivity of American workers is by far the highest in the world. Productivity has more than doubled since 1949, mostly because of advances in technology.

This is not the story that the media is telling us. We hear horror stories of the United States losing trade wars with Japan and other countries because of lazy American workers. Regardless of the motivations behind the slacker myth, working longer hours for fewer wages will not resolve the fundamental issue of increasing unemployment caused by technology. All that this accomplishes is the sacrifice our personal lives—the ultimate sell-out—and starve other would-be workers in the process. The answer is for us to work less, not more.

As Juliet Schor, author of *The Overworked American*, says, society could have taken that gain in productivity in several ways:
• We could all have double salaries.
• We could be working twenty-hour weeks.
• We could work six months a year.

Instead, some of us are working multiple jobs with absurdly long hours for low wages while others can't find work at all.

The money generated by that hidden boom in productivity didn't disappear. The vast majority of it went to create an unprecedented upper strata of wealthy Americans. The U.S. now has the greatest chasm between rich and poor in the industrialized world—one percent of the population owns 40 percent of its wealth. We live under a corpocracy that pays $10 million a year to CEOs and $8 an hour to file clerks. Unless you are part of the fraction of one percent of Americans in this new elite, your hard work is benefiting some rich white guy—not you. The more you work, the more you contribute to this increasing disparity of wealth and its resulting social instability. At least in the old days, when you sold out, you got paid for it. Now you don't even receive a bigger paycheck.

Work Is for Suckers
As big business continues to lay off people, eliminate jobs by attrition and downgrade existing positions, the message has become clear: They don't need us.

When the local TV news interviews some putz, the network sends two guys out—a teleprompter operator and a cameraman. These days, the cameraman is actually doing three people's jobs—two years earlier, there would also have been a sound man and an electrician. The cameraman can handle all three jobs him- or herself—shooting the camera, checking the sound levels and stringing the wires and watching for power surges—because the equipment has dramatically improved. However, he or she can handle fewer assignments per day because each shoot takes a lot longer. Despite the reduced efficiency, the network prefers to cut its staff because payroll is the biggest expense in any company.

And, from a strictly business point of view, the savings from layoffs are almost always worth it. Instead of fighting to hold onto antiquated jobs, why can't we accept that our services are simply no longer required? We demand that companies hire people they no longer want or need, that the government subsidize employment programs and that other countries somehow stop competing with us to cut us some fiscal slack. Why can't we take a hint? It's over. Computers are replacing us at the office. Robots have our jobs at the plant. The company picnic, the gold watch and hanging out by the water cooler are all part of an anachronistic lexicon that people of the 21st century will struggle to remember while playing trivia games. They don't need us anymore, but there is hope: You can't sell out if they won't buy you.

Is Work Good for You?

We have been programmed to believe that work for work's sake is an intrinsic human virtue. We have always defined ourselves by our work. When Americans meet, the first thing they ask each other is: "What do you do?" And the problem is that we usually don't really want to know what that person does. It's too depressing. And it's too sad trying to explain to someone what minor, negligible role you play in making sure that the right slogans are screened onto hamster sweaters marketed to East Coast divorcées. We should be defined, it could be argued, by the way we spend the majority of our lives, but who wants to be defined by something they'd rather forget? We've taken jobs we don't like, bought ourselves into the dependency of consumerism, and have found ourselves trapped. "I'm a financial analyst," you find yourself saying, always tempered with, "but I'm going to quit." This sort of conflict—the way we see ourselves and what we want to be violently disagreeing with how we actually spend most of every day—causes us to lose our sense of self-worth and of feeling rooted in society. Now that searching for self-fulfillment through one's work is like fishing in the woods, holding onto antiquated ideas of the importance of work makes no sense.

In New York City today, 2.8 million people work and 1.1 million are on welfare. As that 5-to-2 ratio continues to shift toward idleness, the social safety net created by FDR and LBJ is being dismantled. With total income tax rates already close to 50 percent of gross income in some cities, politicians are no longer willing to tax middle-class workers to pay welfare to those who will not or cannot work. At the same time, our socioeconomic system will disintegrate unless we find some way of dealing with the jobless.

Rather than view it as a social ill, Americans should embrace widespread de-employment from traditional jobs. This is the fruit of our long struggle to improve the way we live by developing new technology. Provided that a new class of people aren't needed to work anymore, why should we call the unemployed lazy? And from the perspective of the young, salaries and benefits are low, the work is boring and advancement is nonexistent. In short, there is little financial inducement to work. There are several options for dealing with the new, permanent jobless class. Here are some alternatives to condemning people to work insane hours at stupid jobs while others starve:

• Reduce the work week. GM workers in Michigan recently went on strike due to excessive overtime. Although they earned much more money putting in those extra hours, they missed their families and were totally exhausted. Meanwhile, GM and other companies are continuing to lay off workers, as part of a strategy to maximize working hours and minimize health and other benefit expenses. Maxing the work week at a fraction of the current forty-hour week, including for salaried, white-collar employees, would slash the unemployment rate overnight, as well as provide health benefits to more Americans. This would impact corporate stockholder profits, but those profits have been coming out of employees' backs for years anyway.

• Mandate more vacation a year. We could join the rest of the world, where eight weeks of vacation is considered the norm, and perhaps go even further. This is essentially a variation on the shorter work week, but would suit people who like their time off in chunks.

At Spectrem, these options would have translated to, respectively, hiring me for the ten hours a week I actually worked; giving me eight months vacation a year; or, best of all, accepting that my job was utterly stupid and in no need of being done.

Money for Nothing

A national "de-jobbing" program would be extraordinarily expensive to a nation that prides itself on its habit of throwing used-up people out with the trash. Paychecks in the hundreds of billions of dollars a year would have to be issued to people whose jobs are deemed unnecessary; obviously the government does not have enough money to do this.

Corporate stockholders do. In 1994 the value of outstanding U.S. stocks increased from $4.01 to $4.68 trillion. That increase alone— $673 billion—is enough to feed the entire nation for a year, or pay every American worker $5,100. Stockholders have been the primary beneficiaries of increased productivity since World War II; clearly they could stand to be taxed more. Regardless of how it's financed, it is vital that society begin to confront the reality of work's obsolescence. Given that our government would rather debate school prayer and flag burning than anything that really matters, it's up to us to take action by refusing to do stupid work.

The Payoff

Sooner or later, the United States will have to acknowledge that work as we know it—the forty-plus-hour a week variety—has become obsolete. Economic and technological trends ensure that the ranks of the un- and underemployed will continue to grow in the foreseeable future. If we continue to ignore this demographic shift, social disintegration is inevitable.

Regardless of how one defines selling one's soul, what could be more corrupt than to work longer hours at a meaningless job? Not only do you sell yourself to a machine that doesn't care about you, but you contribute to the decline of society as you do it.

But waiting for the government to wise up isn't necessary. It's up to individuals to make the decision not to work. In my case, I got fired from Spectrem because of my bad attitude. Apparently I hadn't kept my personal phone calls, faxes and side projects sufficiently secret (not that my employers knew the half of it). My instinctive response to getting canned, as someone who has worked my entire life, was to start looking for a job.

But I didn't. My wife and I decided that rather than start looking for another day job, I should concentrate on my own work—cartooning. I had been doing okay as a cartoonist before, but giving eight hours a day to Spectrem had squelched my ability to make cartooning work for a living. I had won an award earlier this spring, some newspapers picked up my stuff, and I'd gotten some favorable press during the summer. To make up some of the $500 a week of post-tax income I used to get from Spectrem, I'll have to seek out freelance illustration work, so we're moving to New York where there are more magazines. I started working on a comic book and a new weekly column. And I filed for unemployment, which I'll use until my own work pays my way.

No more day job for me. I just wish I'd thought of it myself.

Now my time is my own. I spend a typical day—about seven hours straight—drawing, writing, calling editors and preparing mailings. I actually work a lot longer and harder, because it's all for me. I lose track of time. I forget to eat. I have a serious fire under my ass; if I don't make things happen, no one else will. So I keep my phone calls brief. And every second, every minute, is mine—not stolen by working for some stupid company.

I suspect that for some time I'll be making less money than I did at Spectrem. Maybe in New York, where the cost of living is so much higher, it'll be even harder to get by. But I sure don't have time to wank off during my work day.

We should stop whining over lost jobs. We don't want those goddamn jobs anyway. You've only got one chance to spend your life doing something you believe in. Quit the job you hate and start over, before you're too old and too stupid and it's too late to take a chance. We are on the brink of realizing humanity's oldest dream for the first time in history—the ability of the vast majority of people to stop selling themselves out. I can't wait. ■

June, 1995

The Future of Indentured Servitude

The big talk at the end of 1995 is about the reinstitution of slavery. This starts during the "first 100 days" of the Newt year with a game of bipartisan one-upmanship around "ending welfare as we know it." With unwed welfare mothers being blamed for crime, drugs and the impoverishment of our military, measures that were once dismissed as draconian, such as orphanages and forced sterilization, are now just trade-offs in a debate where the bottom line is "two years and you're off." A Republican-backed bill that includes all of the above and calls for an end to all welfare grants by the end of the decade appears to be headed for easy passage.

At this point President Chameleon trumps them. After much pondering with his advisors, he offers his final solution—The Sponsorship Program. Citizens with the financial means can become Sponsors of welfare-dependent persons. They can volunteer to take Sponsees into their homes and give them, as the President says, "a new life—one that guarantees them a roof over their heads, three squares, and above all, a good, steady full-time job." Sponsees can leave their poverty and uncertainty behind, and become "household helpers" to comfortable, well-off families in nice neighborhoods. Household heads who take on helpers will be given stepped tax exemptions—those who take two or more helpers are completely exempted from personal income tax and may even receive a small rebate.

Special community-based programs are set up to research and test "persons under public care." Those who have an appropriate profile are connected with sponsors. Sponsors are likewise processed—their homes and places of work are vetted, and they're required to attend a seminar on the treatment of their new employees. The Program mandates that household helpers must receive daily nutritional requirements, and must be appropriately clothed and sheltered. Sponsors may not physically abuse or touch helpers in a sexual manner, and they must encourage helpers to attend religious services and visit their children. Helpers' children are admitted without restriction to newly-endowed boarding schools, where room, board and school uniforms are provided free of charge.

With welfare coming to an end, employment shrinking, and life on the streets increasingly harsh and violent, it's not surprising that many welfare recipients agree to servitude. During the first several months of the Sponsorship Program there are rumors of abuses of every imaginable sort against the new helpers. There are also stories of helpers turning on their sponsors, in what is called "mau-mauing" or "fragging."

Despite this, the political spin is that Sponsorship is working. Happy newly-extended families appear in lifestyle columns and parade through daytime TV. Cynical or frightening articles in the large urban dailies decrying the "Return of Slavery" have little impact on public opinion. A CBS show, *Thank You Mr. Vanderbilt*, features an intellectual, slightly effeminate, formerly wealthy white man who is Sponsored (and mildly abused) by a barely middle-class family of Roseanne-style "white trash" Korean-Americans. The show becomes the top-rated sitcom.

At year's end, with what is now popularly called The Slavership Program a proven success, Newt Gingrich moves to put his own stamp on the reforms he helped engender. Since unemployment, homelessness and street crime remain a blight on the Newt World Order, he proposes a whole string of labor- and tax-law amendments that would allow sponsors to accept helpers also from the (non-welfare receiving) ranks of the unemployed and the homeless. In a striking extension of the Republicans' push to privatize government functions, Gingrich's legislation would allow sponsors to take on helpers remanded from the courts. The newly sentenced can work off their fines, or—for certain crimes—even work off their prison terms. (In a special case, DEA agents might be empowered to keep a violator's property *and* the violator.) Furthermore, special long-term tax breaks will be offered to those who take on "high risk" sponsorship contracts. These would take into account the sponsor's self-protection, allowing such privatized high-security measures as lock-up, shackles, "Singapore spankies," saltpeter, and sedatives. The plan appears headed for easy passage in 1996. ■

February, 1995

MARC HERMAN

Slow Boat to Grenada

R ecently, I had the opportunity to travel across a small section of the Caribbean by sailboat. Sailing the Caribbean has been a favored activity among foreigners for centuries, from explorers and competing colonial powers to the more recent influx of yacht owners and U.S. government functionaries. If you own a boat, or happen to work for the government, please be apprised of the following logistical, maritime and cultural information.

Seeking and Securing Passage

Caribbean harbors may be thought of as truck stops for the well-to-do. Unless it's hurricane season, people sail to and from each island fairly regularly, spending a day or several months anchored a few hundred yards offshore. They emerge and come to land by dingy, only to restock supplies, go to the movies, shower, get drunk together, or do laundry at facilities set up for them at the marina.

When not running errands, these people, who call themselves "yachties," can be seen lounging on the decks of their ships, which range in size from 24-foot runabouts to 100-foot floating white mansions that look like lost icebergs. The people who own the vessels are per expectation: Colorado architects enjoying early retirement; fifty-two-year-old French industrialists with thick heads of white hair; their nine-foot-tall naked girlfriends/boyfriends/daughters/sons sunbathing on the foredeck; senior citizens who decided against the RV and seasonal shuffleboard at a KOA campground in Yuma, now mending things about the vessel into eternity; children of means badassing around paradise after getting thrown out of boarding school, cashing in the trust fund and buying a thirty-six-foot sloop; Danish air-conditioning-repair technicians taking the winter off to do some scuba diving in Tobago; earthy Swiss Families Robinson managing onboard-schooled feral children; former merchant marines who read Dianetics at just the wrong moment; Stellas getting their grooves back and the drifters who love them. Notably, few of the people in the harbors of the southern Caribbean are in fact of Caribbean extraction, except those who repaint the boats or serve drinks in the bars.

Informed of your presence and intentions, a surprising number of yachties will turn out to need an extra hand on deck, or at least be willing to let you subsidize some of their expenses in exchange for passage to wherever they loll next. I inquired at Peaks Marina in Chagaramas Bay, Trinidad, a landing purportedly built by the U.S. military during World War II. At first I mostly hung around the bar. When that failed, the novelty of eating french fries surrounded by waiters with mellifluous accents soon passed, and in the resulting brainwave, it became blindingly obvious that the hundreds of striking white yachts anchored nearby were probably all registered somewhere, at a post office or boat repair shop or some such. This registry—basically a list of boats and their shortwave radio frequencies—turned out to be kept in a nearby office called Peaks Yacht Services.

The office had a radio and a bulletin board announcing news for the sailing community: "Nearly new fo'sail for sale," "Passage sought to Panama," things like that. In the corner of the board was a badly drawn picture of an old schooner surrounded by random, scarablike shapes; rays of sun; and a list of places the ship in the picture, the *Cassiopeia*, would go the following month. It took me two days to find the captain, Harold, by radio. Harold wanted $200 to take me to the Virgin Islands, a 7- to 14-day trip. Four others had already signed on with the sixty-two-foot boat under similar arrangements. It seemed fair. A week's sailing lessons would have cost more in the States, as would living on land for a week or two.

I met Harold the next day near the dock. He was in his late thirties, tanned and barefoot, with long hair, strong opinions, a captain's certification from the U.S. Coast Guard, his 1978 converted fishing schooner, and not much else. He said we would leave that Saturday. We shook.

Intervention and Interdciton Vis-à-Vis "Territorial Waters"

Prior to setting sail, I spent a week touring Port of Spain, Trinidad's capital. I went to the beach and to a cricket match. I also went to the parliament building and to a newspaper office where I caught up on regional events.

Though the term "police action" went out of vogue in America following the various military mishaps in Asia, policing the Caribbean has in fact been a major feature of U.S. policy for some time. Cuba aside, U.S. involvement in Caribbean affairs seems to originate mostly from the notion that the region is a too-conveniently-located source of both narcotics and cheap labor, commodities for which officials in Washington, D.C., regret their citizens' appetite.

The present Democratic administration, continuing the supply-side approach to drugs and immigration popularized in the '80s, has apparently decided to fault the Caribbeans for this. Currently, the parley has taken the form of a document, not quite a treaty—let's call it a firm suggestion—titled the Shiprider Agreement. It empowers some Americans, usually those piloting speedy U.S. Drug Enforcement Agency boats and Coast Guard destroyers, to enter the territorial waters of Caribbean partner nations to catch drug smugglers. Essentially, the agreement, which goes into effect on each island as its government assents to it, eliminates the notion of territorial waters when it would interfere with American drug interdiction efforts.

The imposition of the agreement on the region is currently under way, and though you probably haven't heard of it, it was front-page news in Trinidad during my stay there, usually interpreted as either bullying gunboat diplomacy or reasonable realpolitik. The Port of Spain government agreed to the idea and received a pleasant, if somewhat condescending, letter from U.S. Attorney General Janet Reno applauding its cooperation. However, reports from other Caribbean islands suggested misgivings. The prime minister of Barbados, Owen Arthur, for example, said that though he realized he wasn't a particularly powerful global player, he was nevertheless stuck on the notion of sovereignty. Revealing himself as a man to be reckoned with, the prime minister went so far as to say the whole plan sounded like something Brezhnev would have proposed to Eastern Europe in, maybe, 1974.

The Shiprider Agreement follows a $2.5 billion effort by the Bush administration, paralleling the better-known drug war and refugee-abatement efforts in Colombia and Haiti, to stem shipment of said contraband through Miami. The success of that effort is now believed to have redirected drug smuggling efforts elsewhere while barely reducing American drug imports. Rather, it led to the raging popularity of American intervention in Haiti and to the apparent growth of the other major drug entry point to America from the south: Mexico, recently the subject of many unflattering headlines to that effect.

Seafaring Knowledge Is Essential

We left two days late, after waiting for a hard wind to calm down. It hadn't by Monday, but everyone was impatient.

Immediately past the harbor's mouth, the ship became a demon funhouse. Ropes wiggled like spiders, and sounds like cannon shots came from strange directions. The deck lurched uphill to a 40-degree angle, and Captain Harold, at the helm, suddenly began speaking in tongues. His palm was surprisingly loose on the tiller, a 10-foot spar of elegantly finished wood that looked like a whale's rib, but his voice was desperate. The angle of the deck got steeper. As the boat heeled, I looked up. ("Heel" is when the boat tries to flip over as the wind pushes on the sails.) The mast was drawing Jackson Pollack shapes on the sky. There was an obvious difference in the size of the mast, the tall pole that holds the sail up, and the keel, the much-shorter vertical wing that keeps the boat upright from beneath the waterline. I tried to decide if the ocean was larger than the wind. The wind was winning. Harold told us to "blow the jib," so someone untied the frontmost sail at its rear corner and let it flap around, spilling the air out. Boats are like suspension bridges—massive tables of counterbalancing stresses. They therefore creak a lot. The boat eased up and settled at a final angle, the mast now stuck like a needle on a gauge. Harold, ignoring the sounds, set the tiller on a course and lashed it to the rail with a sail tie.

He went below deck and returned with a bottle of tequila, knocked some back, and poured a shot into the sea, a toast to King Neptune. The bottle was now empty. An empty glass bottle on a boat is a pain in the ass. Crewman George, a FedEx guy on vacation, had an idea. We put a note in the bottle. "Send more tequila," Harold wrote, adding his address on St. John. We corked the bottle and sent it overboard. The bottle disappeared into the waves. Everyone cheered, though I doubted the bottle—much less the shot—would reach its intended destination. We headed northwest and were soon out of sight of land.

Commercial Shipping in the Caribbean

During my stay in the Caribbean, the Coast Guard intercepted a merchant ship off the coast of Venezuela. It was carrying several dozen Chinese people, apparently would-be U.S. immigrants. After being intercepted, the people were quickly returned to their most recent port of departure, Guyana, a Caribbean nation on the northeast coast of South America. Coast Guard officials, perhaps realizing that the coast of South America does not fall under their jurisdiction, explained that the Chinese refugees were on their way to U.S. waters and clearly intended to enter the country illegally. This nevertheless seemed to strike many Guyanese—themselves uncertain why the emigrants were not being shipped back to China, if anywhere—as unnecessarily forward-thinking of the Coast Guard. One fellow joked that he'd not realized it was a violation of U.S. law for Chinese people to sail past Venezuela on Guyanese boats.

It was never clear what the Chinese people were doing in Guyana. They were trying to get to the United States, sure. But it seemed like an unlikely route. Also, they failed. Last I heard, they were still there.

Locating Paradise

After thirty-two hours at sea, we passed Grenada and arrived at Cariacou, where we pulled in and weighed anchor to sit level for the night. We were anxious to see Cariacou. In the harbor, Harold said, was a smaller island straight off a postcard—a literal desert island. It had palm trees and a perfect beach, he said. It had been a long trip, and we were anxious to see it.

Leaving the harbor in Trinidad had been a bad idea. The wind was too strong, and the seas were high, with two- to three-meter swells. Swells, Harold explained, are measured from sea level to their peak. But the sea, it turns out, is rarely at sea level. A three-meter swell means a wave three meters high—nine feet—followed by a three-meter depression. Together, this means the boat travels eighteen vertical feet with each wave, every seven seconds or so. The resulting effect is surprisingly similar to a cartoon image of a boat's progress—up the front of the wave and down the back, then up the next one. Meanwhile, the wind is blowing the boat off course, and currents are tugging at it. Sailboats, for all the talk of navigation, are not a very precise way to travel. At best, they manage to bob in a vaguely consistent direction, more like balloons than steered vehicles.

The surface of the water itself was also a problem. The common cliché of "crashing through the waves" is surprisingly apt. Rather than slicing elegantly through the water, *Cassiopeia* occasionally came to an unexpected dead stop as it sailed, like we'd hit a curb in the middle of the sea. We continued only after waiting for the wave obstructing our progress to go on its way. It was in this fashion, wave by wave, that we had proceeded with difficulty to Cariacou, usually slightly sideways.

Cariacou has a population of about 3,000; a volcanic, sawtooth profile; and a lagoon that contains the previously mentioned paradise island. Sandy Spit was, indeed, preposterous: 50 yards of perfect beach with a small grove of palm trees surrounded by water the color of a blue eye. Dave, an entomologist from Massachusetts who had been on board a month, hurried on deck with a snorkel and admired the island. He then told George, his friend from home, and James Brown, a bartender from Kentucky, that the island is famous as a location for fashion-model photo shoots. The sun was setting. Ashore, some other boat's crew was having a barbecue.

We ate on board. We had caught a large, green fish by trailing a line off the back of the boat that morning. The first mate, Julie, a troublingly perky person while the boat was anchored but serious as a shotgun under way, had landed the fish. Our first meal out of the wind was blackened mahi-mahi steaks that were not half bad. After dinner we went on deck and waited for the people on the beach to become naked by torchlight. In the water, blind jellyfish the size of baseballs reflected the moon. A wash of stars fell to the horizon.

We did not actually make it onto the island itself. We left the next morning and made a two-hour trip to Union Island, larger than Sandy Spit but smaller than Cariacou, filled with ever-more-expensive yachts and even-better-looking naked people. We parked in the harbor, a tricky bit of anchoring. It was crowded. We still had yet to encounter anyone actually from the Caribbean. The boat directly beside ours had a crew of trim, white sailors in smartly tailored white uniforms, complete with epaulets. Another boat, just off our bow, flew a French flag and seemed to be transporting Goldfinger himself, plus two escorts clothed only in snorkels. A third yacht, to port, was infested with Austrians in Speedos who kept leaping on and off their boat enthusiastically, as if they couldn't quite decide if it was on fire.

Everyone was having a carefree time. Back in Trinidad, a local hot-dog salesman had explained that the Caribbean was more than just a giant bar and sex club, as many from outside the region thought. But at Union Island, that's exactly what it was. The harbor was filled with nubile exhibitionists drinking from bottles labeled "Very Strong Rum" and pointing excitedly at multicolored parrot fish that inspected the coral in small, thoughtful groups. Ashore, the story was a little different, but not much. The small town on Union Island, officially one of the Grenadines, had its share of shacks, and indeed, the locals did not seem entirely enchanted with the tanned gentry coming off the boats to pick over their town. But this was, for the most part, ignored by the yachties.

How the Caribbean Got its Name

The Caribbean is named for its former residents, the Carib Indians. The Caribs were skilled seafarers who believed strongly that the best defense was a good offense. Following the arrival of Europeans to their waters in about 1500, they regularly traveled through the islands attacking the various settlers. By the 1700s, however, they were rounded up by the British and forcibly resettled in Belize. The sea is still named for them. The British are mostly gone, too.

Prices and Pirates: Vacation As a Lifestyle

The harder parts of the Caribbean were, we knew, to be avoided. Port of Spain's troubled neighborhoods had murder rates and drug trades to rival those of Washington, D.C. Guyana, the other place I had spent time, was the second-poorest country in the hemisphere (behind Haiti) and looked it. With the veil pulled back slightly, even only as far as reading the local newspapers (murder, murder, trade dispute, murder, racial tension, scandal over a concrete factory, murder), sailing the Caribbean seemed horrendously opportunistic, a quiet payoff for a few hundred years of Europeans carving up the place.

I think it was a sense of this that made Harold usually try to separate the *Cassiopeia* and its crew from the rest of the yachting community. He tended to refer to himself and us as "schooner trash"—scavengers for yachties' nuggets, a pirate ship to their royal fleet. Harold was a Texan, a former national-champion sailboat racer, a carpenter by trade, and an architect by training. He seemed to have come to the Caribbean for the sailing, then stayed on a libertarian-granola jag. "We've chosen vacation as a lifestyle," he frequently said, smiling at Julie, who lived with him on the boat. The *Cassiopeia* was their VW bus, a vessel of aimlessness. Two years earlier, he'd blown it up with bug spray. The former first mate, also his former girlfriend, had prepared the boat for a seasonal debugging while Harold was ashore. She accidentally left a pilot light burning in the galley stove. Harold then came back and emptied two cans of mosquito spray in the aft cabin; the fumes wafted over to the stove, and kaboom. The resulting concussion blew out the deck and tore the boat's cabin to splinters.

Harold somehow escaped injury and soon started rebuilding the boat, which now is seaworthy, though far from finished. At Union Island, he was proud of the incompleteness, the vaguely tattered look. The boat was clearly a work in progress, a far cry from the sparkling, million-dollar yachts bobbing around us.

The pride was understandable but strident and sometimes pathetic. A few days into our voyage, for example, the toilet suddenly broke. Harold explained this to us with a mix of regret and gritty realism, the way people with old cars sometimes talk about recurring breakdowns. We would now be using a bucket, he said. But there was an odd survivor's arrogance in his tone: *Cassiopeia* was worked honestly and kept afloat with skill and wit, plus some help from favorable exchange rates now and again. This was different than buying vacation as a lifestyle. For Harold, it was what made us legitimate—schooner trash rather than snotty yachties.

Maintaining Supplies

On board, food must be packed in ice, which is incredibly expensive. Ice does not naturally occur in the Caribbean, any more than charcoal briquettes do in Greenland. Still, mechanical refrigeration, like phones, is technically difficult to have on boats, so many travelers settle for ice and large coolers. Ice therefore sells for $8 a bag in the Caribbean, making it more expensive, pound for pound, than fish. Fish, after all, are plentiful. The problem is that you are on a boat, and there are so many fish to catch that you cannot possibly keep all of them, lest they spoil. The problem is often solved by wasting a lot of food, usually within sight of obvious poverty on many of the less-toured islands.

Protocol

The morning after arriving at Union Island, I was taking in the view from the foredeck while crapping into a bucket filled with a small bit of the sea, when I realized the boat in front of us had not been there the night before. The naked person on board the new boat waved, then noticed I was sitting on a bucket while wishing her a good morning. She scurried below.

An hour later, her boat began to drift. It was not anchored well. The crew of the *Cassiopeia*—Harold, Julie, Dave, George, James Brown, and I—stood on deck and waited for the new boat to smash into Goldfinger's nearby yacht. After five minutes of righteous giggling, we realized the wind had shifted and the badly parked boat was now heading our way. We shuffled closer to the bow to judge the threat. The distance closed. Three of us decided to head for the stern. Shouting began. *Cassiopeia* was firmly anchored, lashed down like Gulliver. As collision became inevitable, Harold leapt, piratelike, from our bow to the other boat and attempted to commandeer its steerage. Too late, he returned as it crashed into us with a little pop. The captain of the other boat was not on board, and the naked people he'd left behind did not know what to do, so had done nothing except put on bikinis before the catastrophe. Harold stood on the bowsprit fuming, but announced there was no damage. The other boat sloughed off with the current and languished a few feet away. Colorful insults began flying between Harold and the people on the other boat. They sounded Belgian.

"Fak yeau!" yelled the people on the drifting boat at Harold.

"Fuck YOU!" yelled Harold.

Watching all of this was a local water-taxi driver. He began yelling a string of English Creole. At first he was ignored. Harold and the Belgians argued loudly from their boats about anchoring strategies.

"You stop this!" yelled the taxi driver finally.

Everyone looked at the taxi driver for a moment.

"You have no respect, you have no respect for this island," said the taxi driver plainly. Harold decided to make his case against the Belgians to the taxi driver. The taxi driver yelled back that he didn't care. The Belgians rested. Harold pleaded some more with the taxi driver for his support. Then the Belgians got into it. Everyone yelled at the taxi driver. The taxi driver gave up and sped away, dodging around the Austrians, who were watching the scene from their starboard rail before starting the day's leaping exercises. The taxi driver stopped out of earshot and idled in the center of the harbor, racing his motor frustratedly.

"Why'd he get involved?" asked Julie.

Beautiful, Friendly Grenada: Now Open for Business!

The trip ended for me in Grenada soon after. It was not supposed to. It was supposed to end in the Virgin Islands, but things do not often seem to work out as planned in the Caribbean. Plans, in fact, are a mistake.

On Grenada it is difficult to ignore that the U.S. invaded in 1983. Though it's hardly remembered in the U.S., most people there seemed to appreciate the war, which included troops from several Eastern Caribbean nations as well. Today, Grenada is a beach destination like any other Caribbean island. Commercial planes now use the airstrip the Cuban army had built; the length that gave it away on satellite pictures as designed for military purposes now makes it perfect for 747s carrying tourists. It's how I got home that night.

Before leaving, I toured the capitol. Walking around an island your county once blew up is disconcerting at first, even if the people are not hostile (which they weren't). But it also feels a little like a place under a second invasion. Grenada is beautiful and poor and subject to northern largess. In the capitol of St. George with its horseshoe harbor and steep, colonial streets, the professionals are dressed to the nines and don't look at you, while the merchants smile and try to sell you nutmeg, which Grenada supplies most of the world with, dirt cheap.

You pay a few dollars for it, understanding that you are simultaneously paying their rent and ripping them off, and then you go swimming, knowing that any ambiguity surrounding the transaction immediately dissolves in a school of bright fish. ■

June, 1997

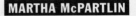

Ever Closer to the Flame

Ten days on tour with David Hasselhoff

A s the star of the world's number one television show, he's seen each week by over a billion people in 140 countries. He's a universally respected and accomplished actor and a platinum-selling singer. He's easily one of the most recognized faces in the world today.

He also happens to have a new record released here in the U.S., and if you're trying to break Hasselhoff to the American record-buying public, there's really only one place to go: the mall. I, Martha McPartlin, set up and accompany him to these appearances as a representative of his record company. This is my story.

Saturday, June 3 — Boston
To kick off the tour with a bang, David's first appearance is at a concert in Boston. It will be David's debut singing performance promoting his new record here in the U.S. Staged by a local radio station, it's an annual benefit concert to raise money for the prevention of birth defects. It includes over thirty artists, lasts for twelve hours and draws about ten thousand people. David is slotted to perform somewhere between Human League and Duran Duran.

2:30 P.M. I'm already at the venue when my boss calls from the limo and tells me they are on their way. David's not performing until 8:15 and his early arrival means there is no dressing room ready for him, his wife, his assistant and his producer. I have the stage manager get working on a solution and fifteen minutes later he produces a 6' x 8' cement-walled office, transformed (by the addition of a folding chair and a fruit platter) into a dressing room. I immediately declare it unacceptable and insist on one of the Winnebago trailers for him and his posse. They can pawn off that room to the guy who plays Donna's boyfriend on *90210* (who is also playing today) but not to David Hasselhoff. Needless to say, maneuvers like these are why I get the big bucks.

3:00 P.M. David and entourage arrive. Kisses all around.

3:30 P.M. Press! Backstage we do interviews continually for the next four hours with everyone from *Entertainment Tonight* to the *Cape Cod Times*. Though the competition is stiff, David is the biggest star here today and everyone wants him. We run into Chris Isaak in the press tent and within minutes David has him committed to do a cameo as a surfer on *Baywatch*. The rate at which David hypes his show is astonishing. Before the day is out I am convinced he could get the Pope to do a walk-on.

4:45 P.M. We're off to tape David's emcee spots for *ABC in Concert*, who are filming the entire event. David can't decide whether to wear his black button-down and vest or his sleeveless sweatshirt. His wife and I both vote for the button-down. He wisely agrees.

5:00 P.M. VH1 comes to the trailer to interview David. They spend ten minutes setting up the shot so that they will spontaneously knock on the trailer door and he will pop out while they film it. The interview goes something like this:

VJ: David there's something I've always wanted to ask you.
David: OK, what?
VJ: How tall are you?
David: Six-four.
Silence.
VJ: Oh.

That's going to make for some exciting television.

6:35 P.M. David's wife wants to see Tom Jones perform so I volunteer to take her to the side of the stage to watch. I'm not sure why, but David decides it would be a good idea to have VH1 tape a conversation between him and Tom Jones. I don't question it, leave his wife chatting with Amy Grant, and try to track down VH1 again but I can't find them. Luckily he doesn't mention it to me again.

8:05 P.M. Ten minutes to show time! David's assistant pokes his head out of the trailer and asks me if I can find an iron for the shirt David's going to wear on stage. David's wish is my command and I have one in my hands three minutes later. I knock on the trailer door and enter to see that they have instead wet David's shirt, and his assistant and his wife are each taking turns blow-drying his arms. Obviously my services are not needed here.

8:15 P.M. Show time! David walks onstage to a screaming crowd of ten thousand. He lip-synchs two songs; during his new single "Fallin' In Love" he jumps off the stage and into the audience. Naturally, they go nuts and surround him. He grabs one girl and sings a chorus right to her. The show is, by my assessment, a success, and I would even venture to say he's won over at least one or two of the skeptics. So to his query backstage afterwards of "How was I?" I happily and wholeheartedly say, "Great!"

Sunday, June 4 — Newington, NH

For those who have not yet had the opportunity to work on a national mall tour with a major television superstar/heartthrob, I will provide a synopsis of the schedule/general proceedings for our mall appearances:

1. Arrive at mall
2. Walk on stage while singing to the CD (5 minutes)
3. Question & answer session with audience (20 min.)
4. Onstage autograph signing (40 min.)
5. Press backstage (30 min.)
6. Meet and greet with radio station contest winners (30 min.)
7. Leave

12:40 P.M. Inspired by the radio station's benefit concert the previous day, David has been talking with his producer and assistant about a *Baywatch* episode tying in the concepts of both the charity (this one for birth defects) and a radio station concert. In minutes he has created an entire plot, plus a subplot based around a homeless pregnant girl. Seconds later he is on the mobile phone to one of his writers, getting them to work on it. An episode is born. I take the opportunity to admit to his assistant that I've really only seen one *Baywatch* all the way through and it had to do with a midget. Interestingly, I have to clarify further because, as he informs me, "We do a lot of work with midgets."

12:50 P.M. In the limo, we turn on the radio to listen to the station that's covering the appearance and what song is playing right that second but "Fallin' In Love" by David Hasselhoff! I crank it and we all have a moment. When it ends David's as giddy as a schoolgirl, since this is the first time he's heard his music on the radio in America. He's huge in Germany, though.

1:05 P.M. I get my first taste of the magnitude of David Hasselhoff's fan base. After the fact it would rank as one of the least frenzied of the malls, but as it's the first it strikes me as sheer craziness. The mall manager meets us, hands out our "backstage pass" laminates, and the local cops and mall security lead all of us through an entrance at the back of the mall. There are about 800 people mobbed around the stage set up in the center of the mall. Naturally, the majority of the audience is female but there are a few well-adjusted teenage boys, comfortable with their masculinity, dispersed throughout. The age range represented is nine months to ninety years and there is a somewhat ... dated look to the crowd.

2:00 P.M. Backstage (in the mall office) we have our Polaroid and autograph session with the winners of a local radio station's Hasselhoff trivia contest (one of the winners knew the name of the character he once played on *The Young & the Restless*—Snapper Foster). The mall staff, decked out in official "Hassel Free Summer Tour" tees, herds the winners in one by one to meet David and get their picture taken. One frail woman of about forty is so shaken by the experience she can barely approach him. He puts his arm around her to take a picture and she's about to collapse. Finally she must be led from the room by two "Hassel Free" attendants.

2:30 P.M. David and crew are off to the airport. I'm staying in Boston a few more days so I stick my head in the limo to say my goodbyes and thank him for his cooperation all weekend. He plants a kiss on me and says goodbye. I walk away from the limo relishing the envy of all the female mall employees who witnessed it. My hard work has paid off— David loves me!

Saturday, June 17 — San Francisco

6:55 A.M. I meet David and his assistant on the plane. They inform me that they almost missed the flight due to a grizzly roadkill accident on the ride to the airport. It seems their limo driver hit a skunk at full speed on the highway, and because of the overpowering stench that immediately filled the car, was temporarily blinded and missed the exit for the airport. They still smell of the unfortunate creature. I hear this story about sixteen times over the course of the weekend. The rest of the world has the privilege two weeks later on *Late Night with Conan O'Brien*.

7:00 A.M. David eyes me up and down and asks if I dyed my hair black. He is the first person who has noticed since I did it a week ago. I smile demurely, slightly blush and say, "Why yes, do you like it?" He says yes but exchanges glances with his assistant and they chuckle patronizingly. I am an enigma to them, or maybe just a joke. Probably the latter since my hair, clothes and the Dorothy Parker book I'm holding will prove to be a never-ending source of humor for them over the course of the weekend. I'm hardly surprised, because the last time I wore my Dr. Martens they called me "lumberjack." I exit first class and head back to 27F.

9:33 A.M. In Salt Lake City, we check into the hotel and get plenty of stares, partially thanks to the odor that follows us. David goes off to nap and work out and I check out the town using a map of the local churches that the concierge gives me.

1:05 P.M. Thirty minutes out of Salt Lake City lies the mall, a gleaming oasis in a sea of Sears vinyl siding.

1:09 P.M. David hits the stage and starts to greet the crowd but the mike isn't on. In a moment of utter panic I grab the nearest person, who honestly looked like a sound guy, and scream at him to turn the mike on. A split second later it goes on and I find out I'm grabbing the collar of the DJ from the local radio station who's hosting the appearance. Oops.

1:10 P.M. While eyeing the proceedings I get called to the side of the stage by a security guard. There anxiously awaits a woman with a mission. She begins by asking me extensively if David sincerely cares about the environment. All I can think to say is, "He seems pretty sincere to me." This seems to be good enough for her.

1:15 P.M. David fields questions from the audience and signs items passed up to the stage. Highlights include "Would you take off your shirt?" and two Knight Rider lunch boxes. David's assistant offers the holders of the lunch boxes $250 cash for either one, but they decline.

1:55 P.M. I'm standing innocently to the side of the stage contemplating the continually astounding thought processes of the audience, when David grabs me and shoves the microphone in my face.

"What's your name?" he says.

"I'm shy," I say, hoping that will be the end of it.

"How do you like my album?"

O.K., I'm game. "I love it, it's my favorite," I exclaim.

"What's your favorite song?"

"Fallin' In Love," I squeal.

Though I am obviously "with" David, and this exchange is blatantly bogus, my performance is still met with a smattering of applause from the audience.

2:05 P.M. The fifty-plus mall contest winners are led onto the tiny stage for their grand prize—a group photo with David. Naturally, mayhem ensues. People from the audience begin to pour on stage at an alarming rate. Mall security gives it a shot but all control is lost; we are caught in the throng of fans. A strange man appears in front of me and asks to "touch me, just for a second." I'm beginning to fear for my personal safety when we finally extract David and escape through the back of Wilson Suede & Leather.

2:25 P.M. Meet and greet time with ten lucky radio winners. It's your basic Polaroid and autograph session with the exception of one daring young gal who, while David's bent over signing something, gets her picture taken touching his ass.

4:15 P.M. We're heading back to the hotel. Our limo driver tells us that he is dropping us off and going to pick up Pearl Jam, who are playing in town that night. Apparently Salt Lake City is experiencing some sort of limo shortage. David takes the opportunity to write a note to the guys telling them to "have a great show" and autographs it. He includes our hotel's phone number, but, oddly enough, we never do hear from them.

Sunday, June 18 — Cincinnati

2:10 P.M. In the airport, a woman standing near us stares at David and says "Aren't you someone?" He pretends like he doesn't understand and says, something in German. She's pissed and knows he's messing with her but she can't do a thing because she still can't place him. Eventually he can't resist and whips out a pre-autographed photo out of the stash in his back pocket and gives it to her.

2:20 P.M. In efforts made by each mall to impress David, we are constantly subjected to what is apparently considered the height of luxury in each city. This one has outdone itself with our limo. Though it appears fairly basic on the outside, the interior is a dazzling sight to behold. Everything is white and a huge mirror covers the entire ceiling. Miniature lights encircle the mirror, controlled by a dial labeled "mood." The driver sees us admiring our surroundings and proudly informs us it was custom-made.

2:45 P.M. We are led through the service entrance, down a series of winding corridors and up two stories in an elevator to finally wind up remotely near the stage. I make a *Spinal Tap* reference and yell "Rock and Roll!" But no one gets it.

3:00 P.M. Pretty much a repeat performance at the mall here. The only perceivable differences are that the crowd is slightly calmer and the food backstage is better. Highlights onstage include an emotionally charged fan who's "life David has changed" (though she doesn't say just how) and another who "carries her Knight Rider poster around with her everywhere." Later, I find out that David has been getting letters from the first one almost every day for ten years.

3:20 P.M. David sings! With a little persuasion from the crowd, David gives a spontaneous rendition of his new single. He rocks the mall.

4:00 P.M. It's Father's Day and I call mine from the mall conference room. He tells me to tell David he says "hi." I relay the message later in the limo, and David writes out one of his pre-autographed photos to him—"Dear Ed, We've got your daughter. Sincerely, David Hasselhoff." I send it to him.

7:05 P.M. We're back at the airport with twenty minutes to kill before the flight home. Naturally, we hit the private lounge. We're not members, but the woman working the door lets us in because she "likes his show." I drop my bags and before I reach the bar David has secretly persuaded the bartender to card and hassle me. I'm in the middle of giving him my sign and social security number when I realize what's going on. I'm humiliated; David's howling at the other end of the bar.

Sunday, July 9 — Denver

1:50 P.M. Bad sign—there's a crowd outside the mall waiting for the limo. We weave through the crowd, both inside and out, and arrive at the main stage area. David takes it upon himself to break free from security and take off into the masses, circling both levels of the mall, the whole time singing. The security people follow him up and down the escalator and through the screaming crowd. After going to all the trouble and worry to provide adequate security, the mall managers are going insane. David's assistant and I have long since learned to let David go wherever he wants whenever he wants, so we just stand back and watch the whole scene. They eventually round him up.

2:00 P.M. Q-and-A time! I'd love to be able to say that this audience/mall/city differed at all from the previous ones but, alas, I can't. To summarize, there are only so many times a person can stand to hear the question "Boxers or briefs?" posed to David Hasselhoff. Here's a shocker: briefs.

2:20 P.M. We begin what becomes over an hour and a half of autographing. I stand next to David at the table, collecting the items from the fans and passing them to him. I am more than a little frightened to see a middle-aged woman slap down a copy of a Cosmopolitan centerfold from the early '80s of a mostly nude David. His unmentionables are covered only by two strategically placed puppies.

3:45 P.M. We finally we cut off the line and hightail it out of there. All of the malls have some sort of escape route mapped out, but unfortunately this mall office/backstage is located on what may as well be the other side of the state, at the rate the crowd is running after us calling his name and waving his picture. They are closing in fast when we slip up the stairs to the office. Mass hysteria may be something you can get used to, but call me green—I'm still scared shitless.

4:00 P.M. The winners, waiting not-so patiently backstage are, to say the least, upset. I can't blame them; not only are we two hours behind schedule but their "winner's buffet lunch" consists of a deli platter, a box of rolls from the supermarket and a cooler containing only cans of Diet Sprite. Since we have to get the press out of the way, I go in to appease them and buy some time. I introduce myself, apologize for the delay and tell them it will only be ten more minutes at the most. My little speech is met with ten cold, silent, blank stares. Finally, one particularly vocal woman pipes up and informs me she had "somewhere to be" a half-hour ago. The temptation to ask her why she doesn't just-get-the-hell-up-and-leave-then is strong, but I resist and apologize again. I know why she doesn't leave because I understand the power David has over people. It's bigger than all of us.

4:10 P.M. David walks in and has 'em won over in a matter of minutes.

4:30 P.M. The local cops on hand for security all want their picture taken with David before we leave. A group photo is taken of them pretending to handcuff and billyclub him.

4:35 P.M. We try to quietly exit the premises but the crowd is still there in full force. The security has mostly everyone held back and the three of us have a fairly clear path to dive in the open door of the limo. We grab a couple of Bud cans from the mini-bar and take a quiet moment to reflect, as the limo pulls gently away from the pressed faces in the windows for the last time. As usual, people are staring at me, obviously wondering why I have the unbelievable fortune and esteemed privilege to travel with David Hasselhoff. After five cities, four malls, one concert and thousands of screaming fans, I can't say the thought hasn't crossed my mind as well. ■

June, 1995

Falling Down

The rise and fall of Down Boye,
America's first angsta rapper

In hindsight, some people may argue that a rapper with low self-esteem was a product of the zeitgeist, that any society in which people scrambled after victim status was bound to produce someone like Down Boye. They'll say it was only a matter of time before every genre, even one usually known for its swagger, would offer up someone who'd been in touch with his inner child and didn't like him.

But they're wrong. He was special. "All I ever did was take my pain and make it rhyme," Down Boye once said. When the critics have finished him and the mainstream press moves on to the next phenom, maybe then we can appreciate Down Boye for what he really was—an artist who injected caution and conformity into a culture that was pulling apart at the seams. Instead of challenging us, why can't art uplift by allowing us to feel superior to the artist? Who better to speak to our strengths than someone who is weak? Time for a second look.

Most people are already familiar with the background of Down Boye (Nathan Jackson): his childhood in Watts as the youngest of six boys in a family of nine; his passage through school so unremarkable that few of his classmates can recall the chubby, diffident boy who always sat in the back and shied away from confrontation; his graduation into a series of nondescript jobs at fast-food outlets. Then, of course, the fortuitous decision one day when he was twenty-four to make a music recording, á la Elvis, as a birthday present for his mother, Denise. So much was left to chance—none of us would know Down Boye's name if his brother had not sent the tape to a radio station behind his back, if the *Los Angeles Times* had not covered the song in its Sunday arts section, if the national networks had not decided to run segments on the new singer as a gimmick on slow news days. From such caprice was a sensation born.

Down Boye's first album, *Invisible Boye*, was slow to gain acceptance among rap fans. Those used to Snoop Doggy Dogg and Ice-T weren't sure at first what to make of songs like "Tongue Tyed," Boye's lamentation that he stammered around attractive women:

Rollin' past the sisters
I see them check my stride
But when they're talkin' to me
I want to run and hide

or "OutKlast," his painful acknowledgement that a rival disc jockey was better at both song selection and crafting rhymes:

Ain't nobody give you
More rhymes to the beat
But when he's up there scratchin'
I know I can't compete

Sales were poorest among white males—a sizable portion of rap fans—who did not like their stereotypes challenged by contrary evidence. Down Boye's lyrics did not have the menace they craved to enliven their complacent lives, so what good was it? The least they expected from a rapper was that he be, well, assertive. But instead of aggressive songs like "Fuck Tha Police," here was Down Boye, giving them "True Blue," in which the singer begs an L.A. policeman to protect him from a rival gang member who has stolen his girlfriend and is now menacing him for money:

Can't you see me shakin'
So scared I'm gonna pee
Cause when he finished jammin'
He'll be comin' after me

A nineteen-year-old from Overland Park, Kansas, summed up the disgust of many suburbanites at the time in *Rolling Stone*: "I don't hear any street credentials in that sound. You can't tell me this is black music, because it's not."

Fortunately, the new sensibility appealed to people with influence. Music critics had a particular fondness for "Slack Attack," which *Spin* called "the best song about impotence to come out of L.A." Down Boye's low esteem, which was (allegedly) a new dimension to a rap singer, intrigued those on the watch for the next trend. In a profile of Down Boye entitled "Submission Accomplished," *Time* said, "Forget Clint Eastwood. Never mind Denzel. The 21st century American male, skimmed from the melting pot, wears his insecurity like a def badge of courage." *Vanity Fair* contributed its psychoanalysis, remarking that "it took a silent, imploded member of the dispossessed to voice one of the ironies of the human condition: getting rid of the ego gives room for the id to breathe." The accompanying photograph, staged by Annie Leibovitz, showed Down Boye standing on top of a stool with his head through a noose, eyes averted from the camera.

To compensate for Down Boye's shyness, Razor Records had paired him with flamboyant promoter David Schwartz, who told the public that Down Boye was writing songs that made all previous music irrelevant. At a press conference celebrating the ascension of Invisible Boye into Billboard's Top Ten, Schwartz told the media, "Everyone better wise up and realize that D.B.'s message transcends race and gender. People are going to have to forget about tokens if they want to catch this train." The comparison to Gandhi came the next week on NPR's "All Things Considered."

Invisible Boye was a seismic event, and the tremors sent everyone scurrying to cash in. One month later, another press conference was called, this time by MacKenzie Records, to announce the signing of White Flag, a.k.a. Adam Thompson. Although brought up in affluence in Grosse Pointe, Michigan, Thompson (who is white) proposed that his background was a source of great pain. "You don't know what low self-esteem is until you get the letter from the admissions office at Northwestern and see that the envelope is thin," he said. "You realize all the expensive toys you've been getting are just to hide the poverty inside." Despite brief renown that came with the hit "Livin' in Stocks," White Flag's popularity was mostly limited to white, pre-pubescent females.

The rest of America kept their eyes on the real thing. In September, Down Boye received his generation's stamp of legitimacy—an invitation to perform on *Saturday Night Live*. In an attempt to help those he could relate to, Down Boye set aside a block of tickets to be distributed by New York psychologists to patients experiencing problems with shyness and self-esteem. The fiasco that resulted from this made the idea seem foolish; therapists all over the city were flooded with requests for appointments by people with a sudden loss of confidence.

On the program, he unleashed "PussyFest," an idyllic song about hanging out with stray cats after being ostracized by friends. Suddenly, everyone was talking about this new singer, even those who hated rap music, and activist groups lost no time putting his work into perspective. Several days after the show, the Humane Society praised "PussyFest" as "a sensitive acknowledgement of our proper place in the interconnected web of the animal kingdom," while a radical feminist group deplored its "sly incorporation of male-centered pornographic terminology in a facile attempt to portray sensitivity."

Unlike many rap singers before him, Down Boye appeared completely devoid of anger or political posturing. Interviewers probed for his views on race, class, multiculturalism, Proposition 42, lead paint—but he pleaded ignorance and withdrew into himself. How did rap speak to the black condition in 1990s America? "Not really sure." How did he feel about his education in Watts? "Too many oral reports." One interviewer, after coming up empty for 45 minutes, asked Down Boye in desperation what he thought his best trait was. Down Boye fumbled for a few moments before saying, "I guess I'm pretty good about using seat belts."

The media were frustrated; Down Boye was ruining their chance to build him up and then destroy him. It turned out to be a moot point. Every trend is followed by a backlash. Down Boye's meekness ended up offending the wrong opinion leaders. A "Don't Be Down" movement began among African-American college organizations. In Miami, someone broke into a record store, smashed the entire stock of Down Boye's compact discs and left without stealing a thing. Even some of the highbrows began to turn. Stanley Crouch penned an essay for *The New Yorker* ("Tom-Foolery") in which he made the acid comment that "Rap has finally gotten what it deserves: self-abasement passed off as art by someone proclaiming 'I'm Black and I'm Cowed.' We can only hope they'll annihilate each other and not annoy us again."

The backlash crested soon after when Al Sharpton and Louis Farrakhan joined to denounce Down Boye at a rally held at the City College of New York. "It's no wonder white America has found so much to like about this traitor," Sharpton said. "He's the perfect black person for them—submissive and compliant, someone who denies his own manhood and asks those in power for permission to exist."

Finally, in November, Down Boye stunned the music world by announcing that he was giving up rapping forever. "I didn't go into this field imagining that I would hurt people's feelings," he said. "Besides, I know I'm not good at this; I never was. I want to be a hairdresser. I want to give people a sense of well-being I never felt."

Razor Records was more than happy to release him from his contract; Down Boye had become something of a liability. "We wish Nathan the best of luck," said CEO Harold Stannis, "and I hope his association with Razor Records has given him something to smile about when he's being so damned hard on himself."

He's already fading from memory. Go ahead and write him off as another passing fancy—the 1990s version of Jonathan Livingston Seagull—but do so at your own risk. The millennium approaches, the Eastern Bloc crumbles, and yet we feel more rootless, adrift and unfulfilled than ever. Forget about public victories; we know that our personal and private defeats remain with us forever. Like the sullen wallflower at a celebration, it was Down Boye who brought us up short and forced us to look into our souls. So next time you feel awkward at a party, or realize the memo you wrote at work is substandard, or learn about a gathering from which you were specifically excluded, then you'll see the timelessness, the real truth of what you dismissed as a fad. You tried to look right through this invisible man—and yet, who knows but that, on the lower frequencies, he raps for you? ■

November, 1996

DAVID EGGERS, DAVID MOODIE, PAUL TULLIS, ZEV BOROW, MATT NESS, JOE GAROFOLI, MARNY REQUA, NANCY MILLER, RACHEL LEHMAN-HAUPT

Virtual Enlightenment

There is a New New Age upon us, one where forces of spiritual alignment have joined to bring us a new era of enlightenment, community, enhanced consciousness and spiritual awakening. The young people of the world are again finding, through the use of alternative agents like raves, technology and non-Western religions, a long-suppressed but altogether beautiful and whole spirituality, one connected to the natural world but embracing of the healing and community-forming aspects of the cyber world. It is a new time, a new world, a great opportunity for us, the young, to shape our own metaphysical reality, and for that reality to take us, on its strong, feathery wings, into the glory of the New Millennium.

Or something like that.

It's unsettling about certain movements and ideas—just when you think that everything they represent has been discredited, laughed at, debunked, dismembered, embalmed and buried, they can somehow rise from their ashes, smirking through a new but oddly familiar visage, trailed by legions of new and hopeful followers. Communism, televangelism, trickle-down economics, novelty bands featuring three or more brothers: all silly, misguided notions largely proven unworkable, but still they find fresh disciples, new wide-eyed suckers born with each new generation.

And so it is with the New Age. Universally the butt of vicious jokes, openly mocked and largely abandoned by even its devout, its virus of mushy ideals and sentiments have found a new host—and it's us. It seems unfathomable—how can all that smarmy, ridiculous Shirley MacLaine-Yanni-crystal-wearing-love-and-community-Birkenstock offal survive—even thrive!—in these presumably cynical, post-postmodern times?

It's probably in the twist. The New Age way of talking about things—soft, earnest voices and fuzzy, Utopian messages—has been recast in the up-to-the-minute trendiness of the cyber/techno mentality. Take the New Age's loopy, air-head ways, filter them through technology (you know, like, e-mail them) and suddenly they are current, relevant, important.

To buy into it is to believe that raves are more than fun ways to spend a night—they are community-building be-ins, loving gatherings of future-people, warmth against the cold alienation of young lives. (Never has so much attention been placed on what is, essentially, a dance. Well, not since *Footloose* at least.) And while raves become the communal ritual, the internet becomes the Force that unites all with its transcendental interconnectivity. The soundtrack, of course, is some mix of techno, house and ambient music, the latter the demon love child of acid house beats and John Tesh synth washes. All this adds up to a new construct of "spirituality," one firmly rooted in the amorphous idea of "community," the word forever repeated, but seldom understood, by the New New Age practitioners. New New Agers are convinced that it all means something, that they are all riding some fabulous wave into The Future, and that most, if not all, of life's answers will come through their modem. The worst part is that they're serious.

And, more unfortunately, people are taking them seriously. Newt Gingrich quotes from the New New Age treatises of sci-fi political theorists Heidi and Alan Toffler. People read the columns and listen to the polemics of Arianna Huffington. New New Age books like *The Celestine Prophecy* sell in inuntterable numbers. Those people who were, five years ago, flaky, scorned outcasts of society are now its celebrated prophets. Credit is largely due to computers and, more specifically, to the internet. The fawning media, forever in search of any trend to which they can attach the prefix "cyber," have been willing accomplices in the lionization of any dorky notion powered by a microchip. And, unlike their predecessors, the torch-bearers of the New New Age are decidedly "hip." Forget the tie-dyes and sandals, New New Agers are younger, computer-literate, most likely professional-types who look like people you could trust.

Surely, among those who preach about The Future and what it should or will bring, there are some people with worthwhile, concrete things to say. At best, we are talking about those who seek to take apart cultural assumptions, making way for new ideas. But for every new and clearly articulated notion, there are a thousand dimwitted mumbles. And the worst of the bunch are those so convinced that they are architects of the New Paradigm, that they convert to a self-structured Religion of Newness. After all, religions have always been safe bastions for dumb ideas, a place where superstitions, hunches, and abject paranoia are welcomed, legitimized, often institutionalized. And there is no place more fertile for these ideas than in the "counterculture" and on the margins of established religions, inhabited by people with one eye looking for answers, meaning and a "sense of spirituality," and the other looking for the newest trend. Over many months, we have had the pleasure of observing, from varying distances, the New New Age phenomena—its most ardent goals and ideals, its most embarrassing follies and mistakes. We had fun.

––––––––––––––––

Like some unfortunate, fantastic conspiracy from the pages of an Umberto Eco novel, technology is licking the balls of the New New Age. Or perhaps it's the other way around. In any case, neo-paganism, the largest and perhaps most identifiable of the sundry New Age faiths, has benefited from a recent infusion of interest based almost singularly from an on-line, grass-roots, word-of-mouth exchange of ideas. Depending on who you ask, paganism is an umbrella placed over the heads of religions like Wicca, Druidism, hedonistic Satanism and neo-Shamanism, or a belief system analogous to these religions. Pagans are polytheistic, monotheistic or atheist, but all center around the "interconnection of living things and the cycles of nature," using rituals (candles, sage, room corners) to celebrate these beliefs. And yes, people who practice Wicca call themselves witches. In this day and age, witches can be young and wrinkle-free.

The recent popularity of paganism is an exemplary display of the capabilities for which the internet is so often breathlessly heralded. The only problem is that the ideas being exchanged here are not only centuries old, but, more often than not, bandied about by the same people who in high school carried around a twelve-sided die. They do, however, raise an interesting question: Does a hooded robe have a place to put a pocket protector?

In a genre of spiritual practices that traditionally places heavy emphasis on atmosphere, props and ceremony, a king-size suspension of disbelief is required for those practicing certain off-shoots of the pagan craze, the most striking being "techno-paganism." Though the glitches are currently being worked out — in the words of "Lebannen," a participant in an online rite, it's "hard to chat a pentagram" — there are people who not only participate in such rituals, but actually believe in them.

The following was excerpted from an hour-long log of a private chat room discussion of "Online Rituals," which occurred at 9 p.m. PST on 11/16/94, hosted by two people calling themselves "Nebet Het" and "Skyebrght." The original spelling and syntax has been left intact.

PStuart: Skye ... do you think energy transfer can be effective online?

Skyebrght: yes Nurien, but given time you feel a connection with those online and that helps the energy.

Nurien: (nodding) I imagine it does Skye. I've not yet attended a rite online.

Anwyn: Neither have I

Skyebrght: it can be a wonderful tool for beginners and solitaries who don't have contact with others

BrendaRoc: for me, the online ritual is good exercise for the astral temple building.

Rain Eris: is there a particular ritual being created tonight or are we just talking about the idea?

Skyebrght: There are people who haven't missed but one or two this year.

Nurien: Now THAT I'll go along with wholeheartedly, Skye!

Nebet Het: Rain, we're talking about the idea. We <could> attempt something very simple, if you wanted :)

PStuart: Eris... just talking about the idea

Nurien: Yes, Nebet...let's!

Rain Eris: ok

IvyCybele: that would be wonderful Nebet

Lebannen: are there rituals held on line somewhere?

Nurien: ::clapping hands::

Nebet Het: Okay, you'll all have to cooperate :) From this point on don't type.

Nurien: < — ready

Nebet Het: If you're in a ritual, you are listening to whomever is facilitating it, to "get into" the mood with everyone else.

Nebet Het: Okay. Everybody lean back from the computer, put your hands over your head and take a big stretch and a deep breath. :)

Nebet Het: When you're done, type a *

BrendaRoc: *

YUnUs: *

Nurien: *

IvyCybele: *

Lebannen: *

Rain Eris: a *

Skyebrght: *

HidesHands: *

Anwyn: *

Oaknivy2: *

Jarlis: *

EraserXXX: *

BIOVAMP: *

Nebet Het: NOW—when you did that, did the sense of being "in the room" change?

IvyCybele: yes, it changed for me ... felt everyone's energy

Lebannen: i did too!

BrendaRoc: Nebet, here's a drawback of online rituals: people who come into a situation and don't know what's up.

Nebet Het: Brenda—that's why rituals are held in private rooms at set times. We have never tried to do a ritual in a public room for that reason—it's too sporadic :)

BrendaRoc: well, someone recently did.

Rain Eris: <G>

Nebet Het: Really? I would advise against it. Too hard to keep concentration. It would be like having someone calling on the phone during a rite.

Nebet Het: Jarring.

BrendaRoc: i went to a gathering once in a public room, it was hard for those who didn't understand.

Nurien: ::shudder::

Skye's:...it's much easier when you know there will be no interruptions.

Anwyn: I usually put the phone off

Nebet Het: Just like outside of the cyber-world.

BrendaRoc: true.

Rain Eris: but it was an interesting demonstration

So, what's it all about? Alienation? Dissatisfaction with existing religious institutions? A spiritual quest? Maybe. Mostly, it's about inclusion, some way to find friends, some way to separate themselves from the rest of the boring, backward sheep that populate the world outside "cyberspace." And they seem to be willing to try just about anything. If it's not trying to resurrect some dubious ancient religion, it's attempting to revamp a rotting contemporary one.

In the center of a long rectangular room is an altar in the shape of a sun and crescent moon. A cup—OK, a chalice—sits under a glass pyramid on the altar. Dreamy ambient music bubbles through the club-quality sound system while soothing, blue lava-lampy images flow on a dozen monitors. Everybody's sitting on the floor.

A warehouse rave? A séance? A teenage girl's slumber party, replete with Ouija board? No, it's church. Like the kind your parents took you to, in a Gothic Episcopal Cathedral, no less.

Would you go to church if they played house music instead of that old fuddy-duddy Brahms? What if they projected trippy psychedelic images on large screens? And how about if they ditched that arcane churchspeak in favor of high-minded platitudes about environmentalism and consumer culture and referred to the Almighty as "Mother God"? What the hell is this, a Parliament concert?

Not quite. In this case, George Clinton has been replaced by a real, ordained Anglican priest. A group of 200 of the youthfully alienated, full of generational anomie, has been doing this for nine years in a place in England called Sheffield, and now they're bringing it here.

The Sheffielders are calling this service the Planetary Mass because of its concern about the future of the Earth, which is no doubt flattered by the attention. The group, which calls itself the Nine O' Clock Service (NOS), began with a group of young Brits who shared core Christian values and a desire to party, yet were turned off by the dusty language and music of the Mass and the Anglican Church's patriarchal indifference to feminism and environmentalism.

They deconstructed the Anglican Mass and redesigned it in a language they were familiar with—multimedia and techno music. They're fond of saying that they reclaimed the technology that was manipulating them.

Last fall, an anonymous donor flew thirty-five Sheffield NOSers to San Francisco to initiate rave church in the New World. They rented the basement of the largest Gothic cathedral on the West Coast and recruited 200 "spiritually aware" ravers to attend. Also in the house were Jerry Swing, Episcopal Bishop of California, nouveau spiritualist Matthew Fox, and two-time coma survivor, convicted felon and notorious speedball junkie Jerry Garcia of the Grateful Dead. (No, they arrived in separate cars). Jerry left early, but seemed to get into the spirit of things, despite taking smoking breaks between prayers. Swing also swung, saying afterward: "It will take the church fifty years to catch up to tonight." Too bad we'll be dead.

The service begins with several leaders (NOS is decidedly anti-hierarchical: "The posse is the priest" is the requisite mantra belying the white men in white robes who ran the show) holding white candles, inviting people to approach them and "use the flame to call the spirit." Moments later, the music kicks into a 140 BPM dance beat and several "worshippers" begin shaking their heinies. Others sing the words on the screen above. Dorothy, we're not at midnight Mass anymore:

Now we feel our Life-force sing!

Raise the passion ten times ten!

Feel the freedom pushing on!

Feel the freedom!

Feel the freedom!

Feel the freedom!

Then comes a little T'ai Chi exercise in which leaders ask everyone to raise their hands and "breathe in ... life, breathe out ... fear; breathe in ... passion, breathe out ... despair; breathe in ... hope, breathe out ... death." Ordained Anglican minister Chris Brian reads a quote from the Worldwatch Institute environmentalist group saying that the Earth's health is, of course, in serious danger. (New New Age-ism, like most religions, clings to certain vague assumptions in which followers must place blind faith. New New Age devotees, eager to lure environmentalists into their tent, must convince themselves of the planet's impending doom— any day now—not from the fumes from their '72 Volkswagen vans, but at the hands of some undefined corporate "other.")

"The Kingdom of God is not synonymous with the Church," the priest continues. "It's synonymous with all of life—and that means one thing: We all are saved or we all must die."

Next, in keeping with the conviction that something doesn't exist unless it's on television, there is a video montage of televangelists juxtaposed with the word "sorcery;" Bill Clinton and John Major with a movie clip of Judas betraying Christ with a kiss; starving Third World children with more starving Third World children.

The rave Communion replaces boring old bread and wine with water, air, fire and soil. Much more pagan. The priest washes his hands with the soil, which is supposed to symbolize his connection with the Earth. And instead of offering "the body of Christ," the celebrant gives you "the life of the universe." As parishioners approach the altar to receive the familiar wafers, one woman is singing "The First Time Ever I Saw Your Face" while several folks spin like dervishes, with virtual reality goggles on, discovering for themselves what every three-year-old knows for certain: Spinning in a circle will make you dizzy.

The rave mass didn't cost the participants anything (this time), but most things tantamount to becoming a New New Ager do cost money, and they aren't cheap. Computers, modems, subscriptions to online services — the stuff quickly creates an economic barrier to most, a barrier that severely limits the diversity of the "community" so often sought. Many savvy entrepreneurs are not missing the fact that there is always plenty of money to be made off of gullible people. If it's not the publishers hocking the newest cyberbook, it's the self-proclaimed experts peddling their wisdom to lost souls willing to pay for enlightenment.

It's Halloween, a big night for pagans around the globe. A group of twenty or so, gathered in a San Francisco apartment not far from the Pacific Ocean, is praying to all the dead people it can think of. The leader of this ritual is a thirty-ish woman who calls herself a Shamanic witch. She asks if any of the participants wish to share anything the spirits have said to them. A young man, the perfect picture of youth rebellion in his goatee, sits cross-legged on the carpet and tells the beaming, beatific faces looking at him like puppies awaiting a biscuit: "The spirits said I need to get laid."

The ritual, a reception ceremony for the Dark Goddess of Winter, is actually a class project. Most of the people in attendance tonight are students of witchcraft, hoping to one day attain the Shaman's wisdom. The teacher calls herself Samantha and she is, undoubtedly, a '90s woman: Shamanic witch, psychic counselor, sexual mentor, mother. When not schooling her pupils in the subtleties of Shamanism, she can be found giving private psychic consultations or teaching another group of students the art of Sacred Sexuality.

Looking more like a college pottery instructor than Darren's mischievous spouse, Samantha walks with dangly jewelry and bare feet through her roomful of disciples. She smacks together tiny finger cymbals as she rapidly chants "Duddaduddaduddaduddadudda..." She is calling the Spirits of the Dead from the Four Corners of the Universe. Apparently, her chantings secure adequate results. There are a few visitations by spirits, Samantha tells the apprentices, but the spirits are only the most common, run-of-the-mill variety: a grandmother, a best friend (borrr-ing) and that anonymous, though doubtless sassy, spirit who is advocating sex for our grungy friend. The Dark Goddess doesn't show—Halloween is no doubt a busy night for her—but no one seems to notice.

Samantha has other methods of welcoming winter, most of which have to do with fucking. "There's a darkness inside of everyone," she instructs. "Embrace it. Fuck the Dark Goddess. Let the energy out while you are fucking!" At times, she seems overly preoccupied with fucking. But then again, she is a teacher of Sacred Sexuality, so she must know what she's talking about. And to actually fuck the Dark Goddess ... What could possibly be more sacred than that? All this talk about fucking triggers some lascivious glances, cast-down eyes and nervous smiles. Some of these people are definitely looking to celebrate the darkness with someone else. Samantha's lover, a tall and lanky man strapped tightly into his Birkenstocks, lingers nervously in the corner of the room.

By 9 P.M. her students have become, well, aroused. It is time for the main attraction. A cauldron, looking like a prop from a high school production of *Macbeth*, is brought into the center of the room. It is black and made of cast iron, the size of a large pumpkin. Kerosene is poured liberally into the pot and immediately set ablaze. It is in this cauldron that effigies of summer, the season of the male (surprise!) will be burned.

Samantha gathers the group into a circle around the cauldron and produces an apple. According to her, and, though she would be loathe to admit it, to that paradigm of anti-paganism, the Bible, the apple is a symbol of temptation. She directs the students to toss the apple across the fire to each other like in a game of hot potato, which is (of course! how plainly evident!) a metaphor for fucking. This class exercise takes a few minutes, since everyone has to throw and catch the apple. When the catching game is over, everyone is given an apple to eat. Yum—Red Delicious.

From an altar set in the corner of the room, Samantha and two apprentices grab images of males—postcards, drawings and corn husk dolls—to thrust into the fire. The flames, engorged by this additional fuel, reach to nearly eight feet. She murmurs and chants as the symbolic items are burned. The students radiate awe.

Finally, the spirits must be sent back to the Four Corners. Samantha signals this with the finger cymbals and the "Duddaduddaduddadud-dadudda" chant. She then tells the class, "Let's take all the spirits from the corners of the room and bring them into our circle." Demonstrating the proper technique for this, Samantha stretches her arms above her head and begins a small waving motion with her cupped hands. The class—quick learners all—mimics her actions flawlessly. The spirits, having now been enticed into the center of the circle, can be sent back to their proper domain.

"Gather the energy," Samantha says. "Now, let's bounce. On the count of three let's send them up." The group is now pressing down repeatedly in the center of the circle, as if teaching a slow-learning youngster how to dribble a basketball. The students count and bounce in unison. Upon reaching the number three, the ecstatic group throws its hands into the air, wiggles its fingers and begins shrieking uncontrollably. The spirits are gone, having caught the express train back to Four Corners.

After, the pupils are sitting on the floor socializing, eating chips and M&Ms. It's odd to notice that after this allegedly intense spiritual exercise, a little pickup scene has developed, especially among the women. Two women come up to a tall, attractive blonde, attending her first witch class, and her roommate, a personal trainer. "You are sooooooo pretty," says a stout, raven-tressed femme to the blonde. "I want you to train me," says her companion to the trainer. "What can you do with my ass?" Before leaving through a reception line, phone numbers are exchanged.

You see, all it takes is some free time and an open mind, and you too can achieve oneness, happiness, orgasm. That and the ten bucks you paid at the door. It's inevitable that with any movement there are those who would attempt to cash in on it. When you can identify a market with a good deal of disposable income but lacking something in the way of common sense, you start planning vacations.

Eight bright-eyed young people are assembled in a San Francisco marketing firm's downtown offices. They are each a crisp $50 bill richer than when they arrived. They've been offered wicker baskets filled with deli sandwiches, ridged potato chips and assorted soft drinks. They are drunk with pocket cash, Pringles and Pepsi by the time they are finally marched into a faux-wood-paneled board room, seated around a smooth brown Formica table, and smiled at under the ominous glare of a one-way window's tinted black glass. They are young, smart, ripe; exemplary consumers with a demonstrated predisposed taste for ambient music. They are a New New Age focus group, a New New Age nightmare.

Ambient music: The term was coined by Brian Eno, "the father of ambient music," whose invention of the form in the mid-70s—prehistory by New Age standards—"grew out of his fascination with 'krautrock,' specifically a band called Cluster," explains Brian Long, publicist for the ambient label Astralwerks. Soon the moniker was appropriated by record company publicists and their willing, easily manipulated collaborators in the music press, and before you could say "Air Liquide"—the actual name of an ambient act—"it got somewhat commercially co-opted by the New Age audience, being tranquil and beautiful and passive," Long says.

Like its less accessible contemporary, "techno," ambient is electronic music, created in sterile studios by professional technicians in Los Angeles, New York, London and Berlin. Except that with ambient, all the noisy bits—the low-frequency drum, the metallic crashes—have been stripped away so that only the squishy percussion and ethereal synthesizer remains, slowed down now so that middle-aged parents in their bathrobes can access the newest, most phar-out form of pop music and feel as sexy as a sixteen-year-old on ecstasy.

Record companies with names like Hypnotica, 21st Circuitry, Silent Records, and, best of all, Sm:)e Communications, have sprung up to disseminate this crap upon the masses, and major and not-so-major labels like Island and Mammoth have jumped right in as well. Now it sells as well as any tributary hip hop or independent-label rock release. Though he won't disclose specific figures, Long says that one of his acts, Future Sound of London, has sold "very, very, very well; in the high five figures."

And remember Windham Hill Records? The standard-bearer of old New Age music—George Winston, Michael Hedges, horny dolphins—is not going down without a fight. They have an ambient recording ready for shipping; all they need is a catchy name for a CD filled with chirping birds and bass drum.

So the eight focus groupers sit. They certainly look like members of the ambient CD sampler target market: Five men, three women, all of whom had filled out a survey marking them as frequent ambient music listeners. They wear their clothes casual, their hair long. An attractive and stylish and young woman in a very black suit enters the room. She settles down at the head of the table and smiles. Her voice is soft, soothing, reassuring, like ambient music. She is going to ask some questions. There are no wrong answers. She just wants to know how "we" feel about some ambient music "we" will hear and some visuals "we" will see.

"Do we all like ambient music?"

"Yes," nods the group around the table in monotone unison. "We do like ambient music."

Three minutes of each of the 11 tracks on the CD are played. During each song the group is asked to write down "what comes to mind" on yellow legal pads. The music seeps into the room, and despite looks on the faces of the group which seem to say, "This ambient music is very bad," they listen and they write. Soon the room's little yellow legal pads are brimming with what came to mind. Some have words that sound perfect for bad ambient CDs, warm-fuzzy words like "glow," "aura," "heaven," and "vibrato." Stupid words. Some yellow legal pads even bear little abstract drawings.

Of course, there's always one rotten apple: One young man writes "velvet," "syrup" "echo," "Duraflame" and "marshmallows."

After each selection of ambient music, the woman in the black suit smiles and asks the group to read some of what they've written. The one-way mirror hovers on the wall behind her. It is possible to see one's reflection in its dark glass. When she turns and asks the young man what words he has written, he replies, "wool socks," and watches himself not crack a smile. The woman in black writes it down on her yellow pad, possibly trying to imagine the accompanying cover art.

Later, the group is shown some mock-ups of possible album covers. Each of the boards has one word written at the top with an organized collage of photographs of things like hot-air balloons, pyramids, clouds and smiling multiracial children underneath. A copy tag line stands in bold letters at the bottom. The boards read something like: Passages—A continuous movement or flow; Ascension—The process of rising to higher levels; Spirit—More than a feeling. A way. After displaying each board, our host nods her head almost imperceptibly and coyly smiles in a manner that seems to say "ahhh." Sadly, nobody laughs.

Finally, the group is asked to write down three possible names for the CD, their favorites. One by one they offer their best ideas: "Bridge

Over Ambient Waters," "Heavenly Gardens," "Pathways to Nowhere," and "Echoes of Memories" are the, uh, highlights. Then there are the rotten apple's suggestions: "The Velvet Road," "Velvet Raindrops" and "Velvet Duraflame." Even though it has been made clear that no answers are "wrong," the woman in the black suit shows a visible distaste with the velvet suggestions.

And then, adieu. The eight shuffle out the same door they came in. One waves good-bye to the people behind the black glass. The rotten apple smiles. The other group members smile. The woman in the very black suit smiles. But it is impossible to tell who is getting the joke.

Speaking of whom: Every weekend, in every major coastal city in the country and England, too, teenagers and the younger end of the twentysomething set are blowing $50 on rave tickets and ecstasy, a psychoactive drug that makes you feel like pretty much everyone is cool, nothing could get any better, and you got enough love for the whole planet. Nowhere is the allure of the New New Age so romantically portrayed than in the world of raves. Worse, they're getting bigger.

Days before the "megarave" known as Digitaria begins, Scooter, an artist and set designer associated with Funky Tekno Tribe, the production company behind the event, tries to flesh out the concept a little. "It's supposed to take place on this planet called Digitaria, where everything's dark and evil," he explains. "So it's going to be like a real dark party. The whole thing's just gonna be like 'WOAH!' Y'know?" It's sounding good, sounding different ... a "dark rave." Hmm ... does this mean that there'll be a Gothic flavor perhaps—some Sisters of Mercy? Bauhaus? Clove cigarettes?

Scooter looks blankly. "Naw, man, y'see… the music's not gonna be house, not progressive house, not trance, but deep hard progressive trance."

Digitaria is what is called a megarave by most of the general raving "community" and a "high-profile conceptual event" by others, especially promoters who have noticed, like good young capitalists, that bigger means, if not better, at least more money. Megaraves are quite a bit larger than your average rave—they take up convention centers and airplane hangars and amusement parks and other large gathering places with plenty of space overhead for pot smoke to gather—and they generally involve thousands of people, about a dozen musical acts (most of which are DJs), throngs of booths trying to sell things guaranteed to make you feel more a part of the "community," and more slide projector/video displays than you can blink a transfixed eye at.

At 2 a.m., the horde of revelers at Digitaria's dance floor ground zero seems to be approaching critical mass. Automated cyberlights flash rainbow beams through the cannabis haze, illuminating sweat-soaked and glittery faces arranged into a multiple choice of ecstatic bliss, intense concentration, or outright exhaustion. Heavy, heavy beats are coming down from on high, interrupted intermittently by a series of staccato turntable scratches that send shock waves throughout the crowd. Then the complex matrix of drum and bass abruptly clears away and a deep, sonorous voice rings out across the length and breadth of the Richmond Civic Auditorium: "Repent, for the Kingdom of Heaven is here! It's coming ... a world eclipse ... BLACKOUT!!!" Suddenly it's mass hysteria: Everyone is screaming, strobe lights wash across the room, hands wave in the air, the beat returns with a vengeance. DJ Dan has just begun his set. Rave prime time has arrived, and everybody knows what that means: only five more hours to go, and then it's time for the afterparty.

For those who grow weary of trying to figure out just which sort of beat they're dancing to (Is this deep hard progressive trance or laid-back blunted jungle? Hey?), every rave worth its salt sets aside a chill-out room—a place where one can lay down, relax, and listen to ambient music performed at ear-deafening volume.

It's in the relative calm of the chill-out room that even non-ravers can experience what may be the crux of the rave scene: the uncannily strong sense of good will. It's hard to tell if the phenomenon is driven by the social aspect of the event or the abundance of people on illicit euphorics; it's frighteningly easy to make a number of friends at a rave, even if it's only for that one night.

"I think it's the greatest experience you can ever have, seriously," says Chrissy, 17, a starry-eyed high-school student from Stockton. Digitaria is only the second rave event she's ever attended, and she spends a lot of time blissing on the chill-out floor. "The first one I went to ... for two weeks afterwards I was just so happy, and before I went there, I was down. I've been happy ever since. And this one, I know this one's just going to be that much better!" As Chrissy speaks, her boyfriend Kevin places a reflective happy-face sticker on her cheek. "It's like one big family," says Chrissy. "I feel great, it's just so wonderful."

Over and over again, conversations at Digitaria bring up the words "family" and "togetherness." It seems like everyone at Digitaria is sixteen to eighteen years old, grooving with their rave brothers and sisters, and experiencing a sense of belonging that's in short supply elsewhere in their adolescent suburban lives. In that respect, it's hard to knock them for enjoying the scene.

What can kill the Utopian buzz of the Rave Nation? Certain things: cops, the growing prevalence of "vibe destroying" drugs like alcohol and speed, an ever-threatening "gangsta" presence, and guys who come to raves to scam on X'ed out chicks—all listed by folks at Digitaria as major problems. But it seems like most everyone neglects to list one of the worst "vibe smashers" of all.

The overwhelming commercialization and promotion of the rave scene may ultimately be the thing to do it in completely, or it may be the thing that has driven it from the beginning. When the Funky Tekno Tribe starts calling its megaraves "high-profile conceptual events" and declaring the term "rave" to be passé, you have to know something's up. At Digitaria, it often appears that everyone over the age of twenty has a scam of some sort to pull. If they aren't circulating through the throngs of dancers, passing out invites to other raves or cards promoting graphic design businesses, the twentysomething crowd is seated behind vendors' tables, hawking everything from candy treats and "herbal ecstasy" to oversized T-shirts printed with educational phrases like "AIDS Sucks" and "Chicks Kick Ass."

With their hefty ticket prices of $20 a head ($25 after 11 p.m.), Digitaria's promoters are doing quite nicely. And of course the ecstasy manufacturers, who brew the stuff in basements and sell it for $25 a hit. Ultimately, only those with the bucks are capable of experiencing… well, the Digitaria experience. All other hopeful acolytes are locked out, forced to look elsewhere for whatever sense of "spirituality" and "community" the megarave might have offered them. At that point, where exorbitant price tags are placed on experiences specifically targeted toward gullible people, whatever might be true and real and genuine about it quickly shrivels up and dies.

But the quest continues. People looking for something—solutions, enlightenment, companionship, salvation. Early this century, we heard tell of primitive cultures, on islands in the South Pacific, that developed "cargo cults," quasi-religious movements whose followers attempted to obtain the goods of industrial societies through the use of faith and magic. After being visited by ships from more technologically advanced countries, they would wait at their shores, hopeful that the next wave would bring, from the realm of spirits and gods, gifts from the modern world. The assumption was that the cargo they awaited—full of shiny objects and complex devices, mystery and portent—would bring not only wealth and prosperity, but hope and meaning.

They spent a lot of time waiting. ■

April, 1995

Notes on Contributors

DONNELL ALEXANDER is a staff writer for *ESPN Magazine*, and lives in New York. His work has appeared in *The Source, RapPages, LA Weekly* and the *Village Voice*.

ZEV BOROW was a senior editor at *Might*. He is now a contributing editor to *Spin*, and writes for *Detour, New York, ESPN* and other magazines.

PHILLIP G. CAMPBELL is a staff writer for the *Memphis Flyer*, an alternative newsweekly in Tennessee. He freelances for *Metropolis Magazine*. Since his article appeared, there have been two subsequent Phil Campbell conventions held in Phil Campbell, Alabama.

M. DOUGHTY is the singer for the band Soul Coughing, which has two albums on Slash-Warner Bros. Records. He lives in New York.

DAVID EGGERS was one of the founding editors of *Might*. He is editor at large for *Esquire*, but is hoping to get in on the ground floor of this whole "Web publishing" explosion.

DIMITRI ERLICH's first book, *Inside the Music: Conversations with Contemporary Musicians About Spirituality, Creativity and Consciousness*, was published by Shambhala Books/Random House in late 1997. He is an editor at MTV, and has written about music for the *New York Times, Rolling Stone, The London Observer* and *The New Yorker*. He is a contributing editor at *Interview* and in 1995 came out with an album, *Everything Is Naked*.

MATTHEW GRIMM fronts the New York alternative country band The Hangdogs, and is the editor of *Brandweek* magazine.

CHRIS HARRIS, a former contributing editor of *Might*, is a freelance graphic designer and writer currently living in San Francisco. Besides regular contributions to *ESPN Magazine*, his pieces have also appeared in *Details, Esquire,* and *USA Today*. His travel guide parody *Don't Go Europe!* was published by Contemporary Books in 1994, to very narrow but deep acclaim. His first novel, *Peh!: The Great American Derivative* will appear in early 1999.

TRIPP HARTIGAN teaches creative writing at New Mexico State University in Las Cruces, NM.

MARC HERMAN's work has appeared in *Mother Jones*, *Harper's*, *Civilization* and *Spin*, and has appeared on National Public Radio and MSNBC television. He served as *Might's* political correspondent during the 1996 presidential election, traveling the country in a station wagon, paying for his own gas. He now lives in Alameda, California, and is currently finishing a book about gold mining.

PAULA KAMEN is the author of *Feminist Fatale* (Donald I. Fine). Her work has appeared in the *New York Times*, *Ms.*, *The Washington Post*, and other publications. A visiting research scholar at Northwestern University, she has just completed a book on young women's sexual attitudes. "Paradigm for Sale" first appeared in the *Green*, mentioned below.

DAN KING is a former editor of *The Gargoyle*, a humor magazine published by the University of Washington. He currently teaches American culture to Taiwanese businessmen in Taipei.

KEN KURSON was at one time the bassist for a Chicago indie rock band called Green. Then he founded a financial fanzine called *Green*. Now he writes for and edits a section of *Esquire* magazine called *Green*. His book, *The Green Guide to Personal Finance*, was recently published by Doubleday.

BOB MARGOLIS was recently downsized out of the publishing industry in New York. He has written for *Downbeat* and *Jazz Online*.

MARTHA MCPARTLIN no longer works at Critique Records. She quit shortly after she wrote about her time with David Hasselhoff. A few months later, Critique Records folded. McPartlin now spends her time playing pool.

DAVID MOODIE was a founding editor of *Might*. He is now features editor at *Spin*.

JESS MOWRY is the author of seven books, including *Way Past Cool*, *Six Out Seven*, and the story collection *Rats in the Trees*. He lives in Oakland, California.

GLASGOW PHILIPS was a contributing editor of *Might*, and is the author of *Tuscaloosa*, a novel (William Morrow & Co. 1994, Plume/Penguin 1995), which was translated into three languages and won the Commonwealth Club Silver Medal. He was a Wallace Stegner Fellow at Stanford University, and is a partner in a naming firm, Quiddity.

HEIDI POLLOCK is a regular contributor to *h2so4*, and her work has appeared in the *The Best of Temp Slave*. After years temping for Exxon, she was recently named I.T. Network Administrator, Level II, for the San Francisco Public Utilities Commission.

TED RALL is a syndicated columnist and cartoonist. His cartoons are collected in three books, *Waking Up in America*, *All the Rules Have Changed*, and *Real Americans Admit: The Worst Thing I've Ever Done*. A winner of the Robert Kennedy Journalism Award, his latest book includes cartoons and essays, and is called *Revenge of the Latchkey Kids* (Workman). He was a contributing editor of *Might*.

MARNY REQUA was a senior editor at *Might*. She currently lives in San Francisco, where she is a freelance writer and editor.

R.U. SIRIUS was a founding editor of *Mondo 2000*. He is the author of *How to Mutate and Take Over the World*, and contributes to *Wired*, *Artforum*, and other magazines.

JIM STALLARD grew up in Missouri, went to Stanford, lives in DC, and has written for *Science*.

PAUL TULLIS was a senior editor at *Might*. He is now writing journalism, criticism and screenplays from San Francisco. His work has appeared in *The New Yorker*, *Vibe*, *Columbia Journalism Review* and on NPR.

DAVID FOSTER WALLACE is the author of two novels, *The Broom of the System* and *Infinite Jest*, a collection of short stories, *The Girl with Curious Hair*, and a book of essays called *A Supposedly Fun Thing I'll Never Do Again*. In 1997 he won a MacCarthur genius grant.

ERIC WESTERVELT is a staff reporter for National Public Radio.

JASON ZENGERLE is an assistant editor at the *New Republic*, and has worked for the *American Prospect*.